Find Me, Book One

She believed in the kindness of strangers

H.H. Rune

Cyndie! Thank you for being here. So proud of you! Live Big!

H.H. Rune ♡

HEARTFINDER MEDIA LLC

Dedication and Thanks
Once upon a time, there was a little girl, who was a bit of a dreamer.
The girl was up, down, and all over the place and had a lot to learn in this
world. She was lucky enough to have a Mom who encouraged her to take care
of her dreams. Her mom told her she could do anything, and taught her to
look out for new ways of thinking.
The Mom showed her that there was a lot of life to live out there. As the mother
tried a lot of things herself, the little girl watched. The Mom was always there.
To listen, to encourage and to cheer the little girl on.
And even though she might not have been the perfect mother, she was the
perfect Mom for the little girl.
Thank you for being my perfect Mom,
I Love you very much.
h
Also many thanks to the following for your support
in reading, input & more
S.L, T.N, S.S1, S.S2, K.M, A.N, K.W, S.W, L.B, A.B., W.H. S.P. and M.G
My forever gratitude- H.H.

AUTHOR'S NOTE

T hank you for picking up this book. This book is a realization of an idea that I originally thought of over twenty years ago. It has evolved and changed into many formats. Originally all five books were lumped into one, jumping all over the place with multiple storylines going at the same time. It was massive and needed to be chopped down in order to fit the typical novel word count standards or expanded into a series. That decision alone took over sixteen years to make. It is not perfect, nor has AI been used to write any of it. This book comes from my heart and experiences and is brought forth as imparted wisdom and thoughts about our world.

Please understand that Indie publishing is not an easy thing, and doing everything yourself can be a hard road. I tried going the traditional publishing route for many years, never finding a suitable partner to help me in my pursuit. Querying with the option of sharing five example pages, or ten, cannot convey a multi layered tale such as this.

So, I have done the best I can with what I have. Using the abilities that I was born with and learned over time as a late in life diagnosed ADHD woman, who struggled through school, and finding her place.

This is finally it, and there is more to come.

In gratitude,

HH

Heartfinder Media LLC

Find Me, Book One

She believed in the kindness of strangers, the first in the Extraordinary Life Seeker series by
H.H. Rune

While this work contains shimmers from the autobiographical record of the author, it is
brought forth as a work of fiction. If anyone; by chance, "sees," themselves in the pages of this
work, they may choose to feel honored by the idea that their presence has made enough of a
difference in one person's life to be written about.

No real names have been mentioned for the privacy of all. While some of these events may be
close in time and place to the author's life, none is it is purely truthful, nor is it meant to be.
This series is written from one person's perspective, with her often imperfect memory, and she
intends no harm. Imparted wisdom is shared only to be a "potential," teaching moment that
may help others' in navigating their own lives, however it is not intended to be taken as any sort
of "therapy," or an answer to their own problems as such. The author recommends professional
therapy to everyone, all along their personal journey, as she has found it invaluable herself.
Thank you M.H.

There are some actual places mentioned in this book, they may or may not have been visited
by the author. Mostly it is to introduce random places to readers who may not be big travelers
to invite them to explore more.

Original cover by Scott Poole with additions by Melissa Galland and the author.

Trigger warnings- Death, Depression, Medical emergency, Loss of a loved one, Infertility,
Young trans character, Indigenous injustice, Learning disabilities, Homophobia, Divorce, Infidelity, Drugs, Stroke, Religion, Maiming accident, Talk of suicide, Dyslexia

CHEAT CODE

THIS BOOK USES THREE DIFFERENT TYPE SETS TO SHOW THE VARIED VIEWPOINTS.

The wording in the traveling books themselves, are in bold.

The un-bolded font captures the couriers and travels of the book.

Excerpts in italic excerpts are the author's journal entries, over time.

BOOK ONE

Dear Reader,

     This traveling book is my secret mission to live a more extraordinary life, from within the confines of an ordinary one.

Only five copies of this book exist, and this has made its way to you. You are now and forever a part of this story.

Inside you will find moments captured from one person's life.

Each passage starts with the set of initials of the person with whom I share the connection.

We are all connected on some level. Every person you meet leaves a mark on you, whether good or bad. Often it is the worst people who gift us the best lessons.

It is my hope that this idea spurs you into living in a more extraordinary way. To think bigger, and reach beyond what you currently see.

The memories inside may remind you of a time or a person in your own life. May you think of those people today, for the good or the lessons you learned from them.

Please read this book, then write your name, and location in the back before giving it to someone else. Let's see how many lives it will touch.

If you by chance, recognize yourself in here:
Please bring the book and
Find me....

Wild Idea Me - December 31, 1999

*I*t started the day I decided to no longer wonder about what my life could be, but to do something, anything, to change it for the better. Like a crazy ass Hail Mary chucked long, this literary experiment was my last-ditch effort to finally start living the extraordinary life, I believed I was meant to live. It was the day before the whole world was supposed to explode, lose power, or at least the banking system was supposed to collapse.

New Year's Eve, 1999. I sat at the kitchen table pondering my obligatory list of resolutions while eating breakfast with my husband. My lightly burned piece of toast with a half melted slab of extra thin and fat free Swiss cheese and my can of diet cherry coke was my attempt at a diet breakfast.

Hubby sat across from me, wolfing down his daily bowl of frosted shredded wheat, taking a gulp of coffee every couple of bites, while letting out an obnoxious, "Ah," with every sip.

The girls were watching Little Bear on Nickelodeon, tucked in close together on their favorite Christmas present, an inflatable Queen Amidala chair.

Suddenly, an idea popped into my head out of nowhere, and straight out of my mouth, "I have a great idea!"

He stared open mouthed at me from the fright. "Yeah, what?"

"I want to write up some memories of shared moments in my life, using the other person's initials at the top of each blurb and turn them into little traveling books. Then, I can send them out into the world, to random people, and see if someone would recognize themselves, and me, and they'd bring the book back to me. A social experiment to see just how small this world really is? It will show how connected we all are, what do you think?"

"That could be interesting. To you. Why would anyone do that? A stranger would just throw it in the garbage."

I looked away from him and got up to do the dishes. I turned on the water hoping the sound would soothe me, as I had no fight in me today. Standing at the sink, the hot water steaming up my view, I put both hands on the counter and looked out the blurry window. Why couldn't he just support me in something? Just once?

When he said that it was a stupid idea, I felt adrift in the already turbulent sea of this marriage. Again. Another moment of me feeling ashamed for wanting something bigger for myself or what I could already see for my life.

It had become just another one of our "Dream Crusher," conversations. He, himself had termed them that, as many times, I would come up with what I thought was a fabulous idea, and he would squash it, with his logic, stating the odds of it not working, or hammering in all the potentially problematic aspects. He knew that he did it, and that it was especially hard for me, but somehow, he just couldn't help playing the devil's advocate about everything all the time.

I wish he could see that I am more than just someone to wipe little noses and make Rice a Roni on Thursdays. Someone to make sure there was always beer in the fridge.

While I could spend time trying to convince him that this idea had a shot, I knew it would be a wasted effort.

I washed the pans from the night before, the hot water reddening my hands, but I didn't feel it. 'What if he's right?'

There have been many times that my ideas have fallen away to pragmatism, so many I can hardly keep count. I'd gotten into the habit of just letting my ideas go, and rarely fought for them anymore. But this one, it wouldn't hurt anyone, it would be magical if it happened, what was the harm?

I dried the last dish and walked upstairs to take a shower. It was a habit I had started years ago, in my effort to wash his opinions off of me, a new killing of an idea with a single sentence.

I wet my hair and let the water cascade down my face. Tears ran down in unison.

I need this. I am going to have to just believe in myself on this one. Something to dream about, to hope for, something just for me, for a change. No matter what he said, I will see this one through. I hadn't asked for his help, and the financial part would be almost nil, I can do it. What is the harm in trying? It would feel so good to do something that might turn into something big. I will just go around him. Words I often say, when I am trying to remove his opinion from my mind. I know I will need to do this quickly before I lose my nerve, as my belief in myself to do something bigger than the current me, often waffles.

I feel my energy increase with hope, as I wash the shampoo from my hair. I really believe with my whole heart that people would participate, if asked.

Maybe I'm a dreamer sometimes, but I'm not the only one. Thank you, John Lennon.

Yes, I may be a little naïve to believe that people in general are good. It might be silly to think that we all are connected on some level, but I know we just need to figure out our common threads. I believe that Love and loving each other is the meaning of life itself.

I don't watch the news, or read the hot topic magazines, because they promote and spread the ugliness of what people can be. The press chooses the drama instead of broadcasting the good that happens on street corners, every minute of every day. People helping each other, loving each other. There is so much more good than bad. I MUST believe that. Otherwise, I just wouldn't get out of bed each day.

When I do watch the news, I spend days in tears. I become hopelessly sad after a shooting or an international disaster. Because, I feel everything.

These excerpts would be my way to capture the memories that I have of these people, and I have always loved to tell stories. It is something I always go back to, as often as I set it aside. Maybe, now, at thirty-three, have I finally figured it out? Yes, I will write this.

To get anything published these days, you have to be famous or already have a book on the shelves, but this memory book and its travels seem like a great idea for a story.

My story...

~

A.G.

I had been encouraged by a counselor to cultivate a hobby for myself so as not to lose all of me in my quest to be the perfect mom. An article popped up in the local newspaper for a writer's group, so I pinned it to the refrigerator. Where it sat for I don't know how many months before I finally went.

The meeting took place in the back of an old frame shop, the owner using the space on Wednesday nights to bring the small group of like minded people together; for her, art and writing went hand in hand. I was the youngest one in our circle, but everyone was nice and encouraging as I told them about my genre, children's books.

Sitting around a large white table, many had been coming for years. Old friends, or not friends, I could hear in the tones as I listened. At the first meeting I would be told about the well worn format of the group. One did not share in their first session, but the newby was allowed to listen in and even give feedback if it was constructive. No bashing was allowed and I never felt any of that type of energy in my time there. Each week, the people who wanted to share brought in copies of their selections; the ten to fifteen pages of their current work, and the author would read it aloud. It was the first time I had ever shared like that or read in a group. That alone pulled me out of my comfort zone.

A motley crew if there ever was one, each person, a perfectly packaged and complete character I could and would write about someday. I loved being a part of the group, instantly feeling enveloped with our shared love of the word and need to express it.

Out of everyone in the group I was particularly drawn to you. Your softened red hair mixed with whites, your subdued but strong nature was so similar to my long deceased, paternal grandmother. In my head I knew that you were not actually her, but my heart didn't care, I could pretend. You didn't seem to mind when I mentioned the similarity.

You invited me over to your house. It was unusual given we normally only saw each other on our usual Wednesday nights.

You made me some tea. You'd taken a special interest in me after I shared my awe about your writing, from listening to you read your excerpts each week. You had kept journals forever, it was the reason you had such an astute and detailed recollection of things.

You carefully pulled a copy of your latest book from the stack on your desk.

"I want you to have this," you said with a smile, that tugged at my insides. I wasn't used to receiving gifts from near strangers. Maybe you saw a little bit of yourself in me, a younger writer to urge on.

You were self publishing before it was a thing. Documenting your entire life story, as a gift to future generations. So your children and grandchildren would know where they came from. Your six progeny, and their cousins, all to be recipients of the treasures.

You opened the front cover and inscribed it to me, not knowing how touched I felt. At twenty five I was honored to be gifted one of your volumes. I knew what it was. Years of work, the painstaking process of putting it all together, I could feel the effort in the weight of it. A physical reminder of what storytelling can be. You encouraged me to keep writing, for I had a story to tell too.

Documented inside was your life from the age of six, beginning with your family's move from Arizona to the Pacific Northwest. Penned out in such detail, it was like I was there watching each scene, sixty years prior. Riding in the back of your father's old Buick, the seat was all yours to watch the world go by at a whopping twenty five miles per hour. Even at that, your mother told your father to slow down. Stopping to see the Grand Canyon on the way, you learned from your father about the different geological time periods that sculpted the landscape.

Arriving, finally at your destination, a city where you had other family, you moved into the farmhouse. Your mother started making it into a home. Wallpaper, paint, your relatives there to help with the task. Your grandfather and uncle would come each Fall, setting up a metal roof chute through the bulkhead door of the basement to fill with wood to burn all winter and heat the house. Bathing only a couple times a week, walking through the kitchen where the washing hung to dry in the winter, your drawers hanging outside the rest of the year.

Your traveling salesman father, your stay at home and highly educated mother, meant that were no ordinary country youngster. From what I could tell your lifelong curiosity kept you young and your brain active.

Writing your pages on an early word processor you took the finished work to the local copy store, and they turned them into beautiful books. Your corrections were apologetically stapled to the inside of each because the errors hadn't been caught by press time.

The book's matte, blue cover, had a simple title on the front, hand embossed in gold. Its spiral binding was cost effective and handy making it easy to read and leave off somewhere, without losing one's place. I was the first person outside the family to receive one.

Taking cues from your design, I have made my own memory books, binding them together with a similar style, but a different goal. Mine would be to spark a fire in my life, while chasing my curiosity of how small the world can be. A task to test my whole-hearted belief in humanity.

A literary experiment worthy of my lifelong love of storytelling.

Your gift that day; from one writer to another, a lifeboat.

Its presence, becoming the prompt for one of the greatest adventures of my life.

~

1

ETTA

H. Evans in Leesville, Louisiana was about to get a surprise in the mail. Her house, off the beaten path, had a very run-down mailbox. Her husband Cal, before he died, had agreed to fix it. Now it leans in his memory.

The two of them had a love affair that spanned forty-seven years. Blessed with each other's company and four children, now grown.

Henrietta, or Etta as she was nicknamed, walked out to the mailbox late that summer day. She had spent most of the day baking cookies for the church bake sale. Her chocolate thumbprints and caramel fudge turtle cups were always big sellers.

Expecting to find her large print Reader's Digest magazine inside, or maybe a belated birthday card from her brother, she found instead, a mysterious package. No return address, but a postmark from Oregon. "Hmm, I don't know anyone in Oregone." Etta used the slang pronunciation people not from the Northwest use when talking about the state.

"Feels like a book. Well, I don't see my Reader's digest, so I'll give it a peek."

Etta walked back into the house as the sun sank lower on the horizon. The north star was becoming visible in the sky. It would be wickedly dark soon. Her home in the country had such a beautiful view of the stars, with no city lights to drown out the impact. Often she would sit on the front porch, sipping a cup of chamomile tea while watching for shooting stars while listening to the goodnight sounds of the farm animals. Tonight, a mysterious package would keep her company.

She fetched a knife out of the kitchen and placed the other mail and bills in the bill box by the phone, before sitting down at the kitchen table. Etta was careful as she sliced, trying to make sure not to damage a letter or note that might have accompanied it. There was no letter. Nothing to share any more about who had sent it.

Inside was a small spiral bound book with a blue cover and back. A title of *Find Me*, was hand embossed in gold; it all looked handmade. A simple book with about fifty pages of reading, then lots of lined empty pages in the back.

"Huh," she said, reading the first page inside her head, but finding herself reading the last few lines out loud.

Please read this book, then write your name, and location in the back before giving it to someone else. Let's see how many lives it will touch.

If you by chance, recognize yourself in here:

Please bring the book and

Find me....

Etta felt an urge to tell her husband what a strange thing it was that she received in the mail. Having Calvin gone, she told Francis the cat, instead.

"What do you think of that, Francis? They picked me. I've never even won a dollar in a scratch-it before."

Francis meowed and rubbed up against Etta's leg in response, before climbing up onto her lap and settling in. Etta adjusted her glasses and sat reading the first memory in the book, feeling honored and appreciative of someone sending her something so special.

~

Starting my quest, Me 2000

I sit here, looking into the mirror on the back of the bathroom closet door, putting my makeup on for the day, as always. Sometimes, I have the company of one or two little girls, depending on what day of the week it is, but today I am alone. It reminds me of sitting next to my mother when I was little as she put her makeup on each day. I'd sit with Mom and watch her "put on her face." A base coat of Oil of Olay cream went on before she tipped her glass bottle of foundation onto one finger and blotted it and blended it in. She would carefully line her eyes with a black liner, and I was always amazed she didn't poke herself in the eye. A gray eyeshadow, and some peach-colored blush. She always pursed her lips together as she applied her makeup, I never understood why. She still does.

There were times when she was at work, and I would sit in her spot and put on her makeup and pretend I was readying myself for my own TV show. Sometimes it was a cooking show, with which I had no experience, but often it was just me living my life and talking to the imaginary audience when I would do something funny or smart. It was one of my favorite pastimes as a child, pretending I was somebody and speaking authoritatively about something. Sometimes I would even sing.

Today feels a little different than my typical motherhood day. I have a secret mission to embark on. I look at myself, wishing, hoping, that I have more potential in me than I believe I do.

Often, when I put on my face, it feels like a mask. An outside persona to present in my world. I walk around and do my things and hide a big chunk of me inside, all my little quirks and curiosities about things, not believing I can share them with anyone. I act like I know what I'm doing.

I needed to be excited about something, and the idea came to me. Something that no one would be able to criticize or badger me about or expect updates or for me to write a business plan for. These traveling books are perfect because no one except me will know.

I grab a cotton ball out of my makeup bag and dab the hope filled tears away. Today I will write.

What lies in store for me with this? This potentially lifelong campaign that I am planning, is my way of doing something really big, while staying safely in the same spot and role as expected.

Who am I anyway, to think that my memories would mean anything to anyone? Or that people might connect to the idea enough to help me by passing the book around, and giving a damn?

I won't just sit around and feel sorry for myself today, because of what he said. I will not curse myself to sit back and wonder forever.

His words still nag at me, what if hubby is right? That this is a stupid idea? His belief that no one will help a stranger because he wouldn't.

This idea, like many others, could fall away easily, and become another thing I failed at by not trying. I tear up at the thought. It is as much of a battle within me as it would be with him. Self-doubt is my constant companion.

I might as well try. I already have the stuff and the time away with my girls in school to complete the task today. Yes, I will take this chance. Only I will know if it fails. Maybe I will never know, and the books travel beyond my lifetime, beyond the lifetimes of the people written about inside.

I sit down on the loveseat by the window. It is a loud, red, and white wedding quilted pattern design purchased while fully in my Hunter green everything phase as a stark contrast to all the green. The house was filled with rooster this and rooster that, in those days too. I jumped onto that bandwagon. My house looked like Christmas all year round, or like Christmas and a farm had a baby. Yeah.

Looking out the window, with pen in hand I feel ready to write my passages. To start, I pen all the initials of the people I want to write about on the tops of the empty pages, it will help me stay on task. I can then dive deeper with each person in my mind as their pages come to the front. They are not in chronological order. I leave in the emotions and certain details that would only be known to me and the other person. Moments we shared together. It is evidence of my paying attention to our interactions.

As per usual me, I stop mid-sentence and daydream a bit, looking out the window while the rain falls hard outside. There is a gusty wind, and I see the drops slide down the panes of glass. Chilly. I flip on the gas fireplace. There is a calmness that comes over me, when I am alone, doing creative things I love. A rumble of thunder pulls my attention further into the distance, and I count in my head to see how far away the lightning is.

The phone rings and I let it go to the machine. A telemarketer. I lean back and snuggle deeper into the couch pillows and think of who to write about next.

Remembering back. Trying to think of all of the people who have made an impression on me in my life so far. Ones who have either loved me or wronged me, all taught me a lesson of some kind. Some people I am still in touch with and some I have taken myself away from, for my own good, or theirs.

It is pleasing to think back and realize that I had been lucky in love. Men had loved me, at least a few had said so. All those teenage romances that young girls hope would happen to them, had, for me. Even though I started late, with my interest in boys, not arriving until I was fifteen. I still carry many of those memories with me.

I wrote for hours that day, pouring my words onto plain notebook paper, and the pages had begun to stack up.

The initials were accurate. I had decided to do it that way in order to give the chosen one privacy, yet they could confirm that it was indeed them that I wrote about. I don't know where many of these people are in their own lives, and I do not wish them harm in their current relationships. It's a quest only to see if this is possible, along the same lines as the Six Degrees of Separation Theory, yet personalized.

Maybe the people will feel special? Maybe they never knew what they meant to me? Maybe they would feel more?

I worked to keep the memories short and sweet so that a traveling book reader wouldn't be put out by taking too much time to read it, so they would be more willing to grant my request.

For this to work, the books must be passed on.

I pray that no one publishes the pages on the Internet, which could falsely accelerate the results. I would love it if people could see the parallels in their own lives, or if the book can act as a reminder to tell their own circle of people what they mean to them.

Maybe there are other people like me, who sometimes wonder about the ones who were left behind. People waiting for something big to happen in their lives, then trying to make it so.

My pages complete, I then went to the Internet and picked five random people off the white pages of Yahoo to send the manuscript to. Not entirely random, wink.

I typed up the memories and bound the books with a spiral binding rented from the local office supply store. I packed the back with plenty of extra lined pages for people to write their name, location, and the date they came across the books. The cover and back are a rich navy blue. I picked heavy paper so it would be durable, then carefully applied small, gold lettering of the book's title on the cover and the number of each volume listed inside. Find Me 1 of 5, 2 of 5, etc.

My name is not on them or in them anywhere, but I have included a friendly request page, aimed at each recipient. Adding that to the front of the memory pages, I signed it, Anonymous in my best handwriting.

As I think more about this mission, I feel sly and excited. My life already feels bigger.

Hubby wouldn't suspect anything. This will be a gigantic exercise in self-control for me to keep this secret to myself, as I am usually not that great at keeping things quiet. Especially when I am excited.

Someday, someone I know will find one of these books, and they will come find me. They will recognize their part in my play and will bring one of these traveling books back to me. I know it. I feel it in my bones. Right now, it will have to be my silent personal dream to wonder about amid my busy days.

Sending the books out will have to be enough. It is all I can really do. I am counting on other people to do the rest.

I lay the books on my unmade bed. So hopefully written and bound by hand. Secret children of mine, borne from my very soul.

Find me.

I close my eyes and wish that the people who receive my books will be receptive and open for an adventure. Not someone like hubby, who would just toss it into the paper recycle bin or trash.

Wrapping each in brown paper, I addressed them to the people I had chosen after deciding which state for each and using the white pages website with my own secret way of selecting. I made sure to delete all of the address and memory files, so there would be no evidence left behind in the house, I wouldn't even keep a copy for myself.

I placed the first of the five in a book bag and hid it in the back of the van, placing the rest at the bottom of my pajama drawer, upside down. Each would have their own send off, from a different place as we had some trips coming up. I felt assured that no one would find them as that would mean that someone other than me was putting away laundry. Fat chance.

I cleaned up my paper cutting mess, putting the paper scraps and the extra spirals deep, under some sticky refuse in the garbage can outside. I'd donate the letter embossing set to Goodwill on my way to pick up the girls from school. For not being great at cleaning house, I was awesome at cleaning up the scene of a caper such as this.

Tomorrow, after dropping the girls off at school, I'd mail out the first one. Time is of the essence! Time to fly!

Over this year they will all be out in the world soon, to find their way back to me, someday.

Who knows, this little errand may end up changing my life someday, or at least I had something big to look forward to. Something that was mine alone.

It was an attempt to feel important, significant, and seen. A way for me to potentially make a difference, by showing people that every single one of us has the ability to make an impression on someone, simply by our very existence.

If by lucky chance one of my subjects comes across a book, it would show them what they meant to me. It would also show just how small the world really is.

Please, humanity, don't let me down.

~

1

E tta sat in her easy chair reading the rest of the pages, feeling as though she were watching the events transpire before her eyes. Like short intermission reels, similar to the snippets she watched at the drive in as a teen. She had loved and lost in her life too, most significantly, her beloved Calvin. Friendships had fallen away. Just as in her own life, this book contained both good and bad memories that pulled at her heart.

She admired the person who wrote it for being so honest with a stranger and putting the words to such good use. She felt for the writer.

Thinking back over her own life for a moment, she wished that she had written down memories of the people she had in her life as they were happening. Her memory wasn't all that it used to be, and photographs, often without names on the back of them, didn't tell the story.

This author had really done something, she'd given herself something to wish for; something to wait for; something to dream of.

Etta got to the end of the book and cried. She had come from a long line of sentimentals. It didn't take much for her to shed a tear. A heartfelt commercial, looking into the eyes of a newborn baby, watching her daughter mother her grandchildren. She was a self-proclaimed sap. The tears came, not for the writer and her escapades, but for the memories it brought up in her. The times she had forgotten about until this very moment. Her mind was now filled with many of the people she hadn't thought of in years. Family members she had forgotten to say I love you to, when they were still alive. Ones that she would reach out to now, with this reminder.

She signed her full name in the back of the book and set it down on the handmade doily placed on the dark wooden end table next to the couch. She had made it while pregnant with her first child, Randy.

They had lost Randy in a car accident as an adult. He had fallen asleep while driving and was hit head on by a semi-truck. Sad days followed for many years.

More grandchildren came to fill some of the gap in her heart, and her lap. The kitchen was full of the smells of dinners together, and baking. Always baking.

Randy had been a wonderful son. So loving and giving. His smile and the way he could make anyone feel comfortable. His photo sits in the dining room, so he can always join in at the table. He was always in her heart. And Etta's heart was full.

Etta's stomach growled and she realized she hadn't eaten dinner. There was a lasagna in the freezer; that would do, that would do just fine. She placed the dinner in the microwave and went to set up her TV tray, in front of her favorite chair. She put things in place, that night as usual, except slightly different. Grabbing a single candlestick, she placed it near her water glass, and lit it. She retrieved her best China from the hutch, some of her wedding silverware from the drawer and even a cloth napkin, left ironed for any occasion she deemed worthy.

Tonight, she would have a nostalgia filled dinner with herself and her memories.

She turned on the record player and placed a Perry Como album on the turntable, setting the needle down on one of her favorite songs, *Magic Moments*, to play. She opened the blinds a bit to see the night sky and dimmed the lights inside.

She closed her eyes and imagined Cal walking through the door after a long day working the farm. She remembered her husband's face, dirty with hard work and sweat. It wasn't his face at the end, after his stroke, she saw all the faces of his that she had kept in her mind. All of those looks stored away, going back to their childhood together. The door would slam, and he'd shed his boots and kiss her lightly before going into the washroom to clean up for dinner. He would change his shirt before grabbing her from behind as she stood at the stove.

A lot had changed. A lot had happened. She'd changed too.

These days she would bundle up her hair in a bun most of the time, leaving strands on either side of her face to soften her sharp cheekbones. Some said that she could have been a model in her early years, but without the desire to go make a splash and bring attention to herself coupled with a hearty love of home, she didn't wander out of the town she grew up in.

Cal had been raised here too, luckily enough, right next door. It wasn't any wonder that they'd spend a lot of time together with their mothers being the best of friends. Every weekend during the summers, they would have a shared family BBQ at one or the other's house.

Etta and Cal grew up so close they might have been thought to be brother and sister to a stranger, but there was a hidden curiosity about each other that they kept secret until later in life when they understood what love was, and after their hormones were activated.

It took a couple of years of Cal watching Etta date other boys around town, while being silently jealous, for him to finally ask her out. She had broken at least three hearts that he knew of, but somehow, he still wanted to give it a shot.

Their first date was at the New Moon Drive In theater in Lake Charles. Etta had never been before. They parked up front. Cal bought them some popcorn and a coke with two straws at the concession stand. He handed everything to Etta through the window before climbing into the driver's side. The speaker hung heavily on the window and Cal prayed it wouldn't break it, since he had borrowed the car from his father, he had no time or patience for car problems.

The movie was very popular at the time. H.G. Wells', *War of the Worlds*. Etta hadn't heard too much about what the story was, as she figured they were mostly going to make out, but as the big dramatic and colorful words shone across the screen, she couldn't help but be entranced.

Her parents had mentioned prior to her date that the movie may be a bit scary, as they had listened to the radio version years ago, late at night when Etta was small.

The initial sequence spoke about the planets in the solar system. Beautifully illustrated images of places only seen in someone's imagination. A fireball landed near a town in California, and many townspeople went out to see what and where it was. Etta sat mesmerized, placing one popcorn kernel after another into her mouth without looking. She shook as the fireball started to open, and clung, face first, into Cal's arm in the dark. Maybe he had planned that?

Etta could hardly believe how much could happen in an hour and a half of life. Well, forty-five minutes, then an intermission to walk around, calm down, and talk, or go get more popcorn before sitting back down in the car with Cal, to watch the rest. They did get more popcorn, as they had both scarfed up the first bucket without even noticing.

It seemed to her, at the time, that what happened in the movie could actually happen. Etta hadn't thought much about outer space other than looking at the stars some nights, on the back porch of their family home. This was a whole new way of thinking about the sky.

Cal laughed a little as she clung even harder to him, watching the alien ship attack city after city. People and vehicles were vaporized. Etta hadn't seen anything like it.

Driving back the hour plus to home, Etta was suspiciously quiet. While he wasn't presumptuous enough to expect a kiss on their first date, he wasn't prepared to be punched in the arm and yelled at in her driveway.

"How dare you take me out only to scare me to death like that!? How am I ever going to sleep again?!"

Without their history, Cal might have been devastated, with no hope of a second date. But with Etta, he figured she was just putting on a show.

"But, but, it had a love story in it, right? I thought you would like it," Cal looked up at her, his head tipped towards the ground, him no longer feeling the sting of the punch.

Etta came closer. She gave him another smaller punch to the other arm before piling into his arms for a hug and the long-awaited kiss. She had liked the movie, but she wouldn't tell him right away.

Cal knew she was spicy and fun, but also brave, and he loved it, she wasn't a scaredy cat at all.

This girl had swum in the Sabine River filled with rapids, water snakes, and even alligators swimming around sometimes. She'd jumped, shoes and all, into the pond under a waterfall at the Hodges Gardens, while they were on a field trip, back in middle school, on a bet.

For an extra wager, shouted after she stepped in, the girl dared her to go under the waterfall completely. Etta sauntered right under, pretending to be washing her hair, singing, as two teachers yelled from across the pond for her to get out.

Stepping out, her shoes oozed with pond water, her button-down short sleeve white dress shirt stuck tight to her chest. She covered her lady nips with one arm, pushing her plaid pleated skirt down flat around her with the other. As she walked, her shoes made a sloshy sound, spurting water out of the seams all the way back to the bus.

When the bus driver saw her, he demanded she wait until everyone else got on the bus, before she could get on. She was mandated to sit down on the floor of the bus near the driver, so that the water could drain through the channels of the floorboards on the stairs and out the front door as they went.

It was the longest thirty minutes of Etta's life. Sitting there, trying to hide her actual embarrassment. She wished she hadn't taken the bet after all. Why did she always have to take a bet?

Finally back at school, thankfully it was the end of the day. Etta skipped going back to her locker to get her backpack, and instead she walked sloggily the long half mile home, with a sting in each step from the parallel lines of the bus floor that were imprinted hard on the back of her legs. Thank God Mama wasn't home when she got there.

Cal hadn't been allowed to tell that story to the kids until they were older. She would not have them even considering doing stupid stuff like that, like she had done. To hear him tell it over the Thanksgiving table gave her a rush and a thrill. She hadn't realized he was paying such close attention.

"You are fearless." He would say when he spoke to her, anytime she would get nervous about something.

There was indeed a second date, and a third, and over the summer they began to really fall for each other, not in spite of their history, but because of it. He knew her. She knew him. They felt comfortable together.

The day he proposed, Cal took her back to the Hodges Gardens. They walked the grounds hand in hand for over two hours, wandering through the many "rooms," that spilled from the forest standing sentinel on all sides. Stairs led to new places to see and investigate, large stone steps or decorative concrete ones, each vista had a beautiful view. Everything had grown so much since they were young. Young, and not paying attention at all on their school field trips.

A circular building sat atop the property, modern looking as if a spaceship had landed in the perfect spot to take in another view. It was a reminder of their first date for sure.

There was an organized river that flowed through another part, again, leading to somewhere special.

A massive house sprung from an island in the middle of the lake, which was where the park's owner lived. From a distance they could see the clean lines of the modern house with two or more levels. They had even heard a rumor that the house had an elevator. All surrounded by a stone wall, it was only accessible by boat. The two of them wondered about the inside, and about the people who lived there. What made them build this beautiful place?

He knelt on one knee overlooking the pond she had jumped into those years ago, way back in middle school. Looking up at her, he shared how he had actually fallen in love with her that day, and he had been so glad she didn't go to jail for her crazy trespassing.

She cried at the question, but gave her answer right away, "Yes!"

He hugged her and placed the ring on her finger. Together, they walked the park, gazing at the house on the island, talking, and dreaming together of having a home. He teased that maybe they could get married there.

At the next summer BBQ, they happily announced the news to the families to the loudest cheers she had ever heard. That was forty plus years ago.

Francis jumped up on top of Etta's lap, startling her back to reality. It was late.

She scooped Francis up and headed off for bed. Wrapping her hair in a blue and white paisley kerchief, she put on her favorite daisy printed pajamas, before wandering back to the family room for the book, she'd read it one more time, after all it wasn't hers to keep.

Etta blew a kiss to her husband's photo over the mantle. She missed him. She missed his smell, and mostly the way he laughed. The way he would get tickled when she was riled up about something while being surprisingly supportive of her at the same time. They were a pair for sure. She rarely cried about Cal now, mostly on anniversaries, or the yearly recognition of the day he died. She had her beautiful memories of him to fill her mind and a feeling that he was still with her in some sense.

Her days were mostly the same. The simple routine over and over had kept her sane when he was sick, and when he was on the verge. It was something that needed her, when he was gone. No rest on a working farm.

She'd managed financially, since his passing, as they had always shared in the workings of the farm. Cal had handled the daily work, planting, harvesting and chores, and Etta had taken care of the office stuff. She kept track of all the costs associated with planting and running the sugar cane, and the small menagerie of animals.

About two years before he passed, they had decided to lease out their sugar cane fields to the Poscoe boys down the road. They were younger and trying to add to their own crop. Together they agreed on a monthly stipend with a ten percent bonus cut of all the crop sales for the year. With that agreement, they were able to go on an extended vacation for the first time in their lives. With the land cared for, she just had the house and the animals to take care of.

She hadn't added any animals except a laying hen now and then, as the older ones used up their usefulness. Depending on their nature, they would be able to relax in style til the end, or into the crockpot they went. It had been a while since Etta had offed one of the chicken's herself, seeing and appreciating their personalities. She let most of them be, getting her chicken victims at the local market in town. A trip that also got her out of the house.

At the farm, Etta would go days without talking to anyone, except the chickens. Other than the super early morning visits of the men who came to tend the fields, only her kids would stop by.

She turned off the lights, one by one, on her way down the hallway to bed.

She lay down in the bed she had shared with the man she loved, in the home they had built together. Even after all this time without him, she hadn't moved to the middle of the bed. She always left his side open, as if he was coming home again, and would need a spot when he got there.

The surprise in the mail had led to a wonderful evening filled with memories and thinking of possibilities. Maybe she'd write the cookbook that she always thought about, the idea springing back to life after reading the book. She could go through her recipes in the morning.

What started as a regular kind of day had led to a nice glass of wine, a perfect meal and a feeling that she was very important to someone she would never know. It also teased her that she could look for new things and adventures in her own life.

Etta had a job to do. That little blue book would get a new home, her daughter Caroline was coming for a visit.

Her eyelids drooped and she fell into a restful, contented sleep. She had a lot more living to do.

~

SECRETIVE ME, 2000

I lie next to him with a secret. He couldn't see my smirk in the dark, and he wouldn't know I was beyond tickled with my cunning. Truth is, I can rarely keep a secret and most likely this one wouldn't stay hidden for long either. I am not a good liar, or I suppose, I am not very practiced at it. This will be my challenge. To keep my books' existence all to myself for however long it takes.

He knows about it in the big picture, since I shared the idea with him a few days ago. But would he think I went through with it after he shot me down like he did? Most likely not.

The first of my five little books holding my remembrances of other people, is out in the world now. I couldn't get it back now if I tried. Their mission to journey in search of the people written about inside so they would know what they have meant to me. I pray one of those people will bring one of the books back to me. To hold in my hands again.

It is my own literary experiment to see just how small this world is. While I know the odds of seeing any of my books again is astronomical, it could happen as I dream.

This adventure is something for me to think about on some of my gray and lonesome days. Something for me to hold onto as my daughters grow and leave the nest. Something just for me.

It could happen as I picture it.

I know it will.

Find Me.

~

1

CAROLINE

C aroline arrived at her mother's house around noon. She had already picked up McDonalds for the kids, and they were all enjoying themselves, throwing french-fries at each other in the back of the
car. Caroline ducked, and was lucky to avoid being hit by a flying fry.

"Come on kids," she murmured, "try to save some for eating."

She smiled though, as if to know that the kids would eat enough
anyway and this was much more fun. Pulling into the driveway, she
unlocked and pushed the gate open, then walked back to check her
Mom's mailbox.

Caroline grabbed a Reader's Digest out of the crooked mailbox and
softly closed the bent metal door. This mailbox would need to be ba-
bied now or it would fall down, and mom didn't want it to be fixed.

She looked up into the sky and said, "Hi Pops," before climbing back
into the driver's seat.

Caroline loved coming to visit her mother, and the kids had plenty of
adventures out in the garage. Her Dad "Pops" and the kids had built a
clubhouse in there, when the family was all together one spring weekend. He and the grandkids started nailing together scraps from the old
shed and pieces from the fallen down chicken coop, finally setting up a
nice and rustic, yet sturdy little dwelling up in the rafters of the garage
accessible only by ladder.

The kids would finish their lunch up there, she supposed. Mom
would talk to her about all the gossip she heard at the store that week
and would brag of her latest sugar cane numbers.

"You really know what you are doing, Mom," she would say.

Caroline opened all the doors of her orange suburban, as she had
them set to child safe so they couldn't escape. The kids spilled out
and ran screaming toward the garage. The youngest Timmy tripped

and fell, but amazingly did not spill a single fry. The oldest son Bobby scooped him up, mid run and off they all went to the clubhouse. Caroline came in the back screen door and the hinge creakily announced her arrival. It was another thing Mom didn't want fixed. She put the mail on the kitchen counter.

"Mom?"

"I'm in here." Etta said, starting to get up from her chair. She had been reading the little blue book again.

Caroline grabbed a thumbprint cookie from the plate next to the phone, as she walked in to her mother.

"Yum, Mom. I hope you made extra for us." A crumb fell and she caught it, throwing it back into her mouth.

"Of course, honey, I wouldn't forget about you all. Lots of extras."

"Caroline, the most interesting thing happened. I received this book in the mail yesterday, with no return address, its postmarked from Oregone."

Caroline sat in the chair across from her mother. "What, Mom, you don't know who sent it? You have to be more careful, what about that Anthrax stuff?" She asked, quietly irritated.

"Well, I guess I wasn't thinking about that. Anyway, this book is the most wonderful idea. You must read it."

Caroline had her mouth open to speak when Bobby came running in.

"Mom! Timmy fell off the old truck in the garage, he's hurt!"

Caroline jumped to her feet and raced out to the garage. Etta walked swiftly after her, shoving the blue book into Caroline's purse as she passed the kitchen counter. The boy was crying and shaken; and his arm didn't look right.

"Mom, can you watch the kids? Caroline asked, "I'm taking Timmy to the hospital, I will call you from there."

"Yes, of course. Go."

Caroline ordered Bobby into the house to grab her purse and she sped off down the highway in her orange suburban. A trail of dust flying up behind her.

~

LITTLE SPY ME, JANUARY 2000

I drove to the town I grew up in, only thirty minutes away. I'd send the first from there. Going back is always a mix of emotions for me.

Being one of the less fortunate kids, in a very well-to-do town. I remember the feeling of not having the same as everyone else. I always watched the cool kids around me with all their big stuff. Noticing the brands of clothes that they had that I didn't, how many Swatch Watches and Izod shirts they had. Giant houses, pools, boats. The most fashionable clothes, an actual Sony Walkman instead of my Sanyo. I was jealous sometimes and wished that I could be like them. It wasn't just the stuff though; I just didn't feel like I belonged there. Not really, anyway.

Sometimes, it was nice to see some of the places I remember from my childhood, but often it is bittersweet seeing some business that had folded or been torn down.

New businesses had replaced the ones I remember, and something there is always different. Streets that I had once played on with friend's, are now crammed with mansions. The tree lined lots are gone, as any space became a spot to put another massive house to show people how much money they had.

I drive around seeing a new bunch of people who act like they own the place while their kids, run amok completely oblivious that this is not the real world. A new generation of townspeople. Acting fancy, living rich all the time, this town sits like a timelessly desired microcosm of wealthy indulgence, but it feels like a parasite that will eat you alive once you leave, damned with a legacy of never being enough to live here again. Or maybe it's just me.

Nothing felt the same when I went back, and the ever-changing landscape made me feel sad and unwelcome. An outsider in my own hometown. I didn't belong there now any more than I had back then.

Only the post office was the same, it had not changed. Small, dank with a sign that was almost worn away from the weather. I wonder why this fancy town didn't care at all about that building. Odd. The city spends big bucks fancying up the sidewalks with hanging baskets chock full of greenery and annuals, adding commissioned art pieces suitable for a museum on every corner, yet they leave the town post office as if in a time warp of twenty-five plus years.

I remember my mom driving us there when she took her tax forms there every April 14th. Sometimes pretty late at night. It felt exactly the same.

I pulled into the parking lot, avoiding the long line of cars using the drive through postal box area, and parked in a space out front. I grab my wrapped parcels from my bag on the front seat. This is where the fun began.

Getting out of my minivan, I tipped my hardly worn sunglasses down on my nose and looked around. I imagine myself a well-dressed spy on a mission. The yellow raincoat I wore was the closest thing I had to a trench coat. It fell over my hips, and I swung my large Liz Claiborne purse over my shoulder. I was transporting the evidence for a big case to my contacts. No one could know my identity.

Maybe this wasn't a good idea, I have friends who still live here. I'd have to make this quick. They could blow my cover.

There weren't many people going into the post office today. It might be too easy.

There was a familiar musty smell as I walked in, as if someone had invented an air freshener for, "old".

There was one man behind the counter, and another stealthily avoiding being behind the counter. The second man moved boxes, slowly back and forth, bin to bin, his eyes deliberately dodging all customers.

I settled in for a wait. I had time. It was a good place to people-watch. Another favorite hobby of mine.

The woman in front of me stood bent over with a large stack of boxes. I imagined them being sent all over the world. But what was in those boxes? Probably sweaters, or something else just as lame. Nothing nearly as exciting and full of promise as my parcels.

Standard issue, government, "Muzak," played on in the background. The soft, non-intrusive flutes and strings had a drumbeat that sounded, filling the gaps of the mail shuffling and cash register bells.

The postal worker who had been moving boxes back and forth, finally stepped up to his station and the woman ahead of me jumped forward to unload her arms onto the small counter. The quick-thinking attendant man-

aged to grab one package from going over his side before it fell. I would not be making such a spectacle of myself when it was my turn.

Finally. I handed my package to the man, looking at his face quickly as he was the first real person to have their hands on the books. I wanted to remember him. His eyes were tired and colored a soft gray blue. They spoke to his thirty, maybe forty plus years of working at the post office.

"Priority?" He asked.

"Yes," I answered.

"Is it by chance a book? Because I can give you the book rate."

"Yes, and that would be great."

"You owe me a whopping three dollars and fifty-two cents," he said smiling. I hoped I would remember him for a long time, maybe enough to write about, while thinking back to this moment.

It was the moment where this journey began. I handed him a ten-dollar bill and he returned the change. I took the receipt and left, turning to look back and see the package slide back over the counter and into the jumble of boxes in the big cloth sided bin.

As I walked to the car, all of life seemed to be in slow motion. This was big. My small, cared for deeply, package was off to places unknown. (Not entirely unknown.)

I did it. Across the country, very soon; the chosen one will get a package containing my life. This maybe-crazy dream of mine.

"Who are these people, really, that I picked off the internet? What will they think?"

I pondered all the way home, and told myself stories about the first recipient. Driving almost on autopilot, I pulled my van into the garage an hour or so later, inching forward enough so that the middle of the windshield kissed the tennis ball speared and hung from the rafters. I was home.

With this first launch, I knew my books would adventure for me. God's speed.

~

1

Caroline sat in the waiting area. Timmy was in getting an X-ray and then he would be moved to a room so a doctor could look at him and his results. She knew this was just one of those things that all parents, especially parents of boys were going to have to do, once or twice in a kid's lifetime. She was thankful it was only his arm. Searching her purse for a piece of gum, her hand caught on the spiral of the book her mother had sneakily stuck in her purse.

That book of Mom's that she was trying to tell her about. Oh, well, her Mom probably thought she would need something to read while waiting and worrying.

Caroline checked the book, for powder, for markings, anything. It looked harmless. She opened the front cover and read a short prologue, a friendly note from an unknown author.

Caroline speculated it could be someone playing a joke on her family. Uncle Bill, maybe, he was always pulling a stunt. He might have remembered that Mom gets sad this time of year. She read on. No, something was different. As she read and reread the first passage, it was definitely a stranger who sent this. A woman with unfinished business, maybe desperate to feel something.

She repositioned herself, crossing her left leg, and resting her arms on the padded sides of the chair. Absorbing each word that came to her, it was easy to read, and relate to. It brought up memories of people she had known throughout her own life as well.

She got to the end and felt accomplished. Caroline hadn't read a book for pleasure in months, maybe years. Even though it was a short one, it was complete and that felt good. It wasn't a textbook, or a homework paper handed in by the kids, this one had a pleasant take, and it wasn't for anyone else, but for her, at this moment, in this place.

Grabbing a pen out of her purse, she happily wrote her name, location, and date in the back underneath her mother's name. Just as the book had asked, she decided to quickly pass it along. She and her mother were at the start of this book's ride, and she wished that part of the process would be to hear back from the author when it was found. But she wouldn't be holding her breath.

Instead of giving it to someone that she knew, only to have it turn in circles in this small town, and perhaps be given it back someday; Caroline left it on the side table underneath a stack of magazines in the lobby. She went to the nurse's desk to inquire about Timmy.

The book would sit and be read and sometimes signed but not leave that place for months.

~

D & D

D & D, I am lumping you two together, because you were always together.

I'd moved away from home, it was my first apartment. Not an apartment but an old weird house and the first D had rented it for herself, while going to school at the popular college nearby. The day I moved in the other D was there, supposedly "just visiting." The second D never did leave, but rent somehow was never split into three parts no matter how many times I inquired. Even with that, I was excited to have one and then two new built in friends to explore the new city with. I tried to hang out with you two, but the asking was one sided most of the time.

I remember preparing for my move, spending gobs of money to buy all of the things I needed to set myself up. For some reason the theme I chose for all my stuff was cartoon like, black and white cows. Cows were popular back then, and the inexpensive product catalog that I ordered from would have my room looking stylish with the cows mixed with pink and dusty blue hearts on everything. Wash cloths, towels, kitchen towels, flannel sheets, etc. Everything in my life back then matched. My room was the size of a closet, and the bathroom was downstairs off the kitchen. There was no shower, only a claw foot tub with a spray hose to wash with, it was bizarre, but we all made do.

I was supposed to be attending the community college as my boyfriend was at the University and we wanted to be closer to each other than the hour and half drive time that separated us before. I went to the community college exactly twice. One to sign up for classes, the other time to drop a class I never went to. I actually never went to school there, the idea scaring me to death. I thought

31

I could be like everyone else, get my self somewhere, do the work and become a self sustaining part of society. I found leaving the house difficult, fear consumed me.

What I thought would be shared camaraderie turned into me being the awkward third in what was a long standing friendship. The first D had a boyfriend and he came over a lot and they had sex all the time. She bragged about him and their love life, saying they were meant to be.

The second D wanted to be a fashion model and had taken many courses to do so, but she had fat ankles and those ankles were getting in her way of being successful so she was going to have lyposuction on them just as soon as she saved up enough money. That D had a boyfriend who wanted to marry her and she bragged about how much money he made but she didn't want to get married so young. "I'll probably marry him though," she said.

It was at that house that I found out about what a prolapsed uterus' was and how the first D's mother had that happen to her after having six or seven kids. I cannot remember the actual number. It was the beginning of me hearing about weird medical issues, which I still am fascinated by. Weird, I know.

After the school year ended, you both decided that you didn't want me to live there anymore because it was going to be a double D house.

I once drew a sketch of the second D, which I still have in my art portfolio. I wonder if she made it in her modeling career and if her ankles ever did slim down?

~

I'VE COMPLETED MY MISSION, ME
2000

A *s hubby scooped up spoonful's of the Rice a Roni that he loved so much, I cracked a smile of pure genius. Around the dinner table, my husband and daughters happily told their stories of the worst and best moments of their days, which is our nightly tradition. I kept the very best of my day inside and made up something else to share.*

How long will I be able to keep it a secret? I am terrible with secrets. I need to have the experiment stay true. I couldn't share this with a soul.

After dinner I cleaned up the kitchen and the kids wandered off to watch TV. Hubby and I sat together in the living room, and I watched him blow up monsters in the new video game he got for Christmas. I wasn't into playing these violent games, but when a puzzle came around, I would ignite and try to help.

The hero in the game had a mission and was on a journey to complete it. I was too.

~

1

JUDD

It was five o'clock in the evening and Judd Banks paced the Byrd Regional Hospital lobby waiting for a someone to update him. His wife Cara had started having contractions and was asked to come down and be checked for her progress.

"I am sure she is fine," the doctor had said on the phone, "but I want to check her blood pressure, and make sure the baby hadn't turned since our last appointment, it could be any day now."

The two of them had rushed down to the clinic at the hospital, anyway. It was their first baby, and they were both as nervous as they were excited.

While Cara was the back being assessed; Judd paced the lobby. Posters of people in different stages of illness, with their family members close by, plastered the walls. All of the images of healthcare workers taking care of patients got his mind thinking of what was to come.

Judd winced at the thought of all the things, all the really messy things that were going to be happening to his wife, in the next bunch of hours or days. He was faint at the sight of blood. The first time he had passed out was when he split his lip after the bathroom door opened unexpectedly in front of him at work. He felt the impact before seeing a couple of blood drops falling onto the floor. That was all it took for him to keel over, cold.

He'd recently fainted in their Lamaze class, when they were watching the video of a natural childbirth. Every video after that, Judd had to look away when things got serious. From that moment on, Cara kind of knew she would probably be alone in there for the delivery.

Judd plopped down in a chair, his key belt holder hitting the table beside him. The spiral of the traveling book got caught on one of his keys. He reached down and pulled the book free. He needed to get these gross thoughts out of his head.

Opening to the first page, he started to read some kind of intro, one that was speaking directly to him. He flipped to the back of the book to see the signatures, about thirty, he wondered how long the book had been stuck there.

What a weird thing to pick up in a hospital? Judd looked around to see if he might be on one of those surprise camera TV shows. Everyone around him seemed to be real. One man sat with his foot propped up on another chair, a sour look to his face, as if in significant pain. A mother sat next to her daughter with a large rash splattered across her face. An old man sat leaning over, his head in his hands. These people looked like the real deal.

He turned the page. Reading a set of initials, and the first sentence of the passage, he looked around for a camera again. Seeing nothing, he busied himself with the book. The pages were flying when his wife appeared.

"What are you reading?" she asked.

"Something interesting, I'm not quite done."

"Oh. The doctor said that everything is good, but he thought I would probably be back with the contractions, much closer together. Maybe tomorrow."

She winced in pain, and he knew she was contracting. Dropping the book, he reached for her to steady her. They started for the car, as someone ran after him.

"Hey, you forgot your book."

"Um, thanks," Judd said, taking the book from the young teenage girl. He tossed the book in the back seat of the car, next to the already packed overnight bag and newborn car seat. He might finish it later, while Cara was having the baby. There would be time then, and he was certain he would be of little help.

Judd and Cara drove home, stopping for a vanilla ice cream cone from the McDonalds not far from their house. Judd kept Cara comfortable by sharing the idea of the writer's request in between her contractions. She asked if he would read it to her when they got home, and he did. They laid down on the bed, after having a small meal of a toasted cheese sandwich, with pickles while watching a movie. They snuggled under the blankets and cuddled as close as they could, with Cara being ten months pregnant.

The movie ended and Judd moved to the end of the bed to rub her feet. She had labored the whole time, squeezing his hand or whatever she could get a hold of at the moment; as each contraction got bad for her, letting her grip fall loose when it stopped. Judd kept track by looking at his watch each time, that he could handle.

Cara brushed her teeth, put on a roomie nightgown, and lay down on her left side with an extra pillow between her legs. Judd spooned her and held her hand. Her almost constant hand squeezing told him that she was getting closer, and he lay there, praying she could get a little sleep, before the baby came. There was no sleep for either of them. After an hour, Cara was not only squeezing his hand hard, but whimpering in pain with each contraction, and they were much closer together. About five minutes apart, and regular.

Judd texted his mother-in-law, not expecting her to answer, but she did. She would be saying a prayer for them both, and sending wishes for a happy, healthy baby for them all to love.

At one in the morning, they got dressed, and into the car to head back to the hospital. They were about to be parents. Their son was coming.

It was two o'clock a.m. when they reached the hospital parking lot. Judd helped his wife out of the car, only to have her water break onto the concrete below her nightie. Judd started to waiver and dip.

"Judd, FOCUS!" Cara yelled.

Looking up into early morning midnight-colored sky; Judd held his wife's hand, as they walked slowly into the maternity ward. She was given a room right away. The baby was coming. Very soon.

Baby Ruston arrived at 3:15 A.M.

Amazingly, Judd had managed to stay upright and present throughout the delivery. He was helpful and alert throughout her labor pains and guided her through the breathing exercises. He even cut the umbilical cord.

The nurses took baby Ruston Douglas Banks to clean him up, and placed him down swaddled on Judd's chest, as Cara had already closed her eyes.

Judd held his son and was amazed at this perfect little person he was holding. Such a miracle. Half her, half him. Their son.

As his son slept, he whispered all about the things that they would do together, and how close he promised they'd be. He was so proud.

Judd called Cara's mother, Tessa, as the nurses took Ruston for his post birth tests. It was the middle of the night but Tessa would want to know that everyone was safe and ok. She was exuberant with the news and promised to jump on the next flight to Louisiana.

Judd loved his mother-in-law. He had really lucked out in that department. When his friend's complained about their mother in laws, he had nothing but good things to say about his. Tessa always had funny stories and interesting things to talk about. Judd was looking forward to her delicious cooking.

He knew she was overjoyed about Ruston, and she would be a fun person to hand the little book off to. Really spread it around, maybe she even knew who it was? Either way, the book would be in another town, another state, perhaps closer to finding the author?

Ruston was brought back to Cara, and Judd snuggled into the bed with them. The three of them fell asleep, a perfect little family.

~

GETTING HITCHED ME, 1993

A *fter a swift romance we decided to get married. Too quickly in some people's opinions, but it didn't matter to us.*

I remember when he broached the subject. Only a couple of months of dating and I had moved into his house. We were still gooey for each other. Just another night sitting on the couch watching TV. He looked over at me and said, "I love you so much, I can't even describe it."

"Say it with diamonds," was my funny response, like the radio ad that often played on my way home from work. We laughed and went ring shopping soon after.

Our wedding was small. Held at a quaint Bed and Breakfast in our little city, nestled awkwardly on the main drag. We had to rent out the whole building at the innkeeper's insistence to have the wedding there but the space was nice and her husband was a judge so he could marry us for an extra sixty dollars. Everything came together pretty easily.

The parlor was decorated early for Christmas, and the tree and lights were all set up. We wouldn't have to do a thing. It was a perfect compromise between what our parents wanted and what we were originally thinking.

We had wanted to run off to Hawaii for the wedding, just the two of us. When I mentioned elopement, my mom cried on the spot. Hawaii would be the honeymoon destination.

So we decided to have a small get together, only family and best friends, close by.

Finding a dress was challenging, as we had also decided not to spend too much money. It was his second wedding, and I didn't like to be fussed over and in front of people. It didn't make sense to go blowing thousands of dollars on a dress that eight people, max, were going to see. I headed to the mall, with my maid of honor, and found one in a small bridal shop, it was full length with lacy flutter sleeves. There were beads in certain areas and it cost one hundred and ten dollars. We went to the discount shoe shop and found some white satin kitten heels, as my man was not tall. I'd wear some cute pearl earrings and a necklace from the discount jewelry store. I was set.

Now to figure out what my husband-to-be would wear. He wore casual clothes for work, so he didn't own a suit. I wasn't expecting a tux, but we bit the bullet and went back to the mall and got him a gray suit, with a white dress shirt. We were sure he'd need a suit for something, someday. He could borrow a tie from my dad, and I handpicked it out. Greens and red paisley, to match with the colors of the space and Christmas.

My mother paid for the catered food. Italian from a place we'd never gone to or went to afterwards, as it wasn't that great. It wasn't her fault. We'd picked the place. My father bought the cake. A simple two tier white frosted one, with poppy seed and raspberry jam filling on the bottom which we served to our guests, and some sort of apple flavor on the top tier that we froze and tasted on our first wedding anniversary.

We'd borrowed a cake topper, a cute little Precious Moments bride and a groom, from my friend who had married the summer before.

His mother paid for the flowers, and his father bought us a fridge as ours had died the week before, so we wouldn't have to deal with that in addition to the wedding and all.

Over half of the audience was in the wedding party.

I remember walking with my father to my groom, instantly noticing his tie, full of pinks and teals and a light blue. I didn't say anything, but it was not the one I picked.

My Dad told me later that Hubby had thanked him for the tie when he arrived, to which my Dad replied, "That's not my tie."

Not even married and he was already in trouble.

The ceremony was short. We ate, cut the cake, and wound our arms into a knot to drink champagne, but there was no dancing. When I think back to this time that had passed since our wedding I don't think we have ever danced together at all. That's weird right?

Then everyone left and we went upstairs into our Bridal suite to get it on. We were less than a mile from our house, so it was kind of dumb to stay there. We could have just as easily given the Inn rooms to our mothers' and gone home to our king size waterbed and sloshed around. Might have been more fun.

The room was not to my taste with its flowery wallpaper in purples and greens, and I wondered if it was actually legal to have this much lace. I get it, it's supposed to be fancy, but yuck.

Anyway, we woke up leisurely and went downstairs to have our romantic breakfast and were surprised to see another woman sitting at the table with us, as the Innkeeper brought in the food.

Pretty sure I rented the whole building.

I asked the host, and she said, "No, she was in another part of the building, I'm sure you understand."

Whatever. We went home and readied ourselves for the Christmas holiday. It would be our first Christmas together. Two dogs, two and a half cats, us, and a bright new future together.

~

1

TESSA

Tessa Fordyce resident of Taos, New Mexico called the Santa Fe airport to book her flight. She was going to see her new grandson. If she had timed it right, she might beat them back to the house, and could decorate it a little bit for them. She had arranged that once the baby came, she would come and stay for as long as they needed her.

Her paramour Charles picked her up to drive her to the airport. On the way she placed a sign at her art gallery announcing the auspicious arrival of her precious grandson and that she would be away for an indeterminate period of time but that she had people that could open the shop if need be in her absence. She was thankful to have the flexibility and friends to help her enjoy a special milestone such as this.

Tessa arrived the next day. Driving to the house about an an hour away, she picked up a dozen blue and white balloons and a teddy bear for their arrival home. She let herself into the house with the spare key from on top of the deck railing. She had also stopped at the market and was cooking away, filling the fridge and freezer with meals that could be warmed up easily. All of Cara's favorites and some new ones she'd recently found.

Tessa was so excited to become a grandmother. She was going to be one fun Grammy. She would teach him all about animals and building things. As an artist who split with her husband twenty years before, Tessa had sculpted a life out for herself, and Cara quite literally. Starting with the little sketches at first, she evolved her craft into much larger projects. Now fairly famous for her giant, tile and mirror covered mosaic animal sculptures, she had a nice and comfortable existence in the art community she called home. Many of her pieces had been purchased and placed at some of the finest estates in Beverly Hills as well as for some of the big headliners in Las Vegas.

She kept track of her sculptures, as they felt like her children. If an owner ever went to sell a piece; which wasn't often, she was given the first chance at buying it back in her contract. She never did though. Instead, she called around to other people who admired her work, and they usually found a home.

"You need to give your children wings and let them fly. Not pull them back and keep them." She'd taken the same stance with Cara, never offering an unwanted opinion over where her daughter chose to live. She stood by and let Cara go where the wind and her heart told her to go. As she also had.

Tessa heard a light honk out front and she ran out to greet her daughter. She peered into the back seat at her new grandson, "He's beautiful, Cara," she cried happy tears upon seeing her grandson. "Just perfect."

"Thanks, Mom. I'm so happy to see you."

They hugged and Tessa carried Ruston's car seat into the house. Judd grabbed the duffle and the small diaper bag with the baby start up supplies that were given to them from the hospital. The next few hours were about feedings and diapers and juggling moments to sleep. Cara was napping in the bedroom when Judd came to Tessa with the book.

"Look what I found at the hospital, Mom." He whispered.

"Well, I'd say you found a lot at the hospital," she whispered back, trying to keep their voices low so as not to wake the sleeping baby in the cradle nearby.

He held the traveling book out to her, "I think you might like it."

Tessa took the book. "Thanks, my boy," she squeezed his hand. "Hey you better get some sleep too, I've got the baby."

"Ok, yes, I am pretty tired." He lumbered off to the bedroom.

Tessa looked at the cover of the little blue spiral bound book. "Find Me."

"This is my kind of book," she chuckled softly to herself. She started to read.

The baby stirred and Tessa set the book on the floor, to check on him. She could read anytime. She pulled a chair closer to the cradle to admire her grandson. His hair was dark and lay flat on his head other than the slight curl he had in the front that seemed to have a mind of its own. He was wearing a yellow pajama one piece with happy little elephants on it. It looked beyond cozy. His fingers were so small, and so completely adorable.

She reached her hand in to touch them. Pulling away at the last second so she could warm her own a bit first. She rubbed her hands into her sweater.

It had been a while since Tessa had been around this small of a child. Maybe even since Cara was that little. Now warmed, she put her hand in to touch his little fingers, tearfully comparing the differences. Old and new.

Rough and wrinkled from the New Mexican sun and arid climate, hers were working hands. Worn down by years of working with clay, and grout, cut and scarred from broken tile fragments that broke the skin over and over. Scars from her journey. This life hadn't always been easy. Not to say it was super easy all the time at this point either.

But it was a good life, one filled with creativity and the c'est la vie spirit that might not have come her way, if things had worked out as she had originally thought they would.

Getting married right after high school to the star football player; Thorn Fordyce, seemed like a good idea at the time. He was a fun and cute, and she liked his family for the most part.

In her mid-twenties, she hadn't discovered the artsy side of herself yet, and was content with her part time jobs. Spending the rest of her time traveling along in her husband's eighteen-wheeler, across the United States moving goods for his father's office supply company.

Together they saw many places across the U.S. that Tessa had never seen before. She was especially drawn to the desert states with their warm yet rough scenery. Hot as blazes during the day, then stars that went on forever in the cold crisp of the night. Each place had such different but hearty flora.

She'd first picked up a drawing pad and colored pencils from a local discount store in Birmingham AL. Something to do when Thorn was unloading in the non descript distribution depots.

Animals soon became her favorite subject, and she'd draw on anything when the paper was gone, even sketching on receipts or bills of lading that were strewn around the truck. She kept her drawings in the glovebox and would pull them out sometimes to remember which animal belonged where.

Each place had its own allure. From the flat and one tone plains of the Midwest and South, to the massive evergreen trees that stood over her in California making her feel small. The Pacific Northwest felt like a fairy land, where even the people were sprite like, friendly and accommodating of all types. The island tropical swaying trees of Florida. How could so many beautiful places exist in one country?

Tessa hoped that her grandson would travel. That he would see further than this small town that he had just been born in. He would no doubt be exposed to the beautiful desert when he was big enough to come visit. Tessa had commissioned a beautifully carved toy box at her home for him. She'd been filling it with all sorts of things that he could play with when he came to see her.

Cara hadn't seen many places in her younger years, for as soon as she was born, Tessa gave up traveling with Thorn to instead provide a home base for them all. One where Cara would have a home to learn to walk in, a yard to play outside in and friends her own age. She imagined it was better than the on the go, cooped up life of being in the sleeping quarters of a truck.

Tessa resided in an apartment close to Thorn's family, as they were the only family she had. Her own parents had died in an accident when she was three, and her paternal grandfather raised her. He died when Tessa was in her late teens. All alone, with the help of her grandfather's lawyer, she chose to sell the restaurant he had built and ran for over thirty years. That sale gave her enough money to get an apartment by herself until she turned eighteen and go to nursing school. She didn't get her full RN license until Cara was two.

Thorn kept running the truck across the country, calling every night at around seven in the evening, no matter what time zone he was in. Tessa looked forward to him coming home, and when they were a little family together.

As a nurse, she worked part time with the help of Thorn's mother helping with daycare. This went along seamlessly until Cara was five. After that, the phone calls from Thorn seemed more scattered, if they came in daily at all.

Thorn's once football player body had become softer with the constant sitting and eating junk food on the road; and even when he was home, he wasn't interested in being romantic. After a year of that, Tessa found out the reason. Thorn was away again, heading to Washington state. He would be gone for about two weeks.

A blue envelope arrived in the mailbox, with it addressed simply to "Wife". Tessa opened the envelope, to find a folded letter with a photo of a very pregnant woman tucked inside. She was looking down and cradling her large belly, she was obviously far along in her pregnancy. The woman's eyes were looking down so that her full face was not visible. Tessa turned the photo over to see if there was a name or any way to identify the woman. The words, 'I'm sorry' with a sad face was scribbled on the back in red ink.

Well, Thorn must have found himself a nice stopover, Tessa figured.

She set the photo downside on the couch, and looked over at Cara, playing happily on the floor with her horses. She didn't need any questions from her about the letter, she had plenty of her own at the moment.

"Now what?" she thought to herself.

In the letter, the woman poured out her sorrow; apologizing, saying she hadn't known that Thorn was married. She didn't know he already had a family, but she was carrying his child. In fact, she was pregnant with twins, due very soon. The letter had been postmarked Kansas City, MO. The woman explained that she had only just found out about her, and never dreamed he was married. She had snuck into Thorn's rig in a parking lot one night and was looking for something to write on, to leave him a note. She'd pulled down the visor on the passenger side and a photo of a her and a child fell into her lap. Thorn had a family already. She then searched through the glove box to find his home address.

The woman said she didn't know what would happen now, but that she hadn't meant to break up a family. She didn't sign her name and there was no house number or street address anywhere on the envelope. Tessa felt anger, hurt, but she felt some power in knowing she would decide what to do moving forward.

Ruston fussed, and Tessa reached for him, placing him gently to lie with his head on her shoulder. She rubbed his back in a circular motion and headed over to the rocker set up in the corner. He wasn't quite due for another feeding and Tessa wished that the new parents could sleep a little longer.

A bubble came up and Ruston settled back into a restful sleep with the rhythmic motion of the rocking chair. Tessa rocked him for about a half an hour, thinking more about that time back then, when she had to make a decision to be fine as someone's duty, or give herself something better. So much might have been different if she had stayed with Thorn. She most likely wouldn't be holding this precious baby right now. She was happy she'd made the choice that she did.

Thorn had come home to a note and a copy of the photo and letter of the woman. Tessa had packed up her daughter and left town, leaving him a note. Her note had read, "Thorn, please honor my request for space. You know my temper; this is for the best. Good luck with your new family, hope it turns out more solid than this one. We both deserve to be happy. You are not off the hook as I do expect you to be a father to Cara as well as your twins. Plan on child support, and divorce papers being a part of your life soon."

He did honor her request and waited for her to be in touch with him. By then, he had packed up the rest of the apartment and moved to Missouri to start preparing to be the father of his new family.

On Tessa and Cara's road trip west from Illinois, they stopped in many of the towns along the way to see how each place felt. If it was home or not. Finally, Santa Fe, New Mexico won them over and Tessa found a new full time nursing job.

Still working through the divorce, Tessa arranged to see Thorn on one of his trips westward. She had cooled off, and meeting in a public park while Cara played nearby was a good idea. Cara had been happy to see her dad but was even happier to run off and play with the kids on the slide and swings, while her parents sat on a bench nearby, talking.

Thorn handed her a thick envelope, and a gift bag for Cara. In the envelope were the signed divorce papers, his current address and job information and a stack of her drawings from their time on the road together. He'd kept every one.

Tessa was touched then, as she looked through the stack.

"You are really good, you know." he said. Pointing to one of a Bighorn sheep she had drawnd with wild colors, "I think you should do something with that."

She looked up at him and he realized how that might have sounded.

"I mean, if you want to," he said; suddenly afraid it might feel like he was telling her what to do. He wanted things to stay mellow between them.

"Thanks," she said simply.

Tessa pulled out two small calendars from the inside of her purse. "I've written in these the weeks that would work for me, for you to visit Cara. Basically, it is one week a month that I am willing to commit to thinking about visits. Not that you need to stay all that time, as you have no place here, but these are the best weeks for me. I don't want her sleeping in the back of your truck. If you decide to take her on road trips, at some point, I want you to promise to get a hotel room where she will have her own bed to sleep in. When you have her, I will need to know where you are at all times. Your precise itinerary. Drop off times and dates are to be firm. It might be a few visits before she wants to go anywhere alone with you. You haven't been around all that much."

Thorn agreed to the terms and went to push his daughter on the swing. Tessa sat on the bench, proud of herself for setting some boundaries and taking good care of her new family. Tessa knew what it was like to lose a parent, and she didn't want to remove Cara's father from her life, especially when he was perfectly alive and still able to be a dad.

She hadn't sketched in years but felt like trying again. It was nice to be validated for something other than her nursing work and being a good mother. That conversation led her to a whole new part of herself and life. One that she loved.

Ruston woke up and started to cry. She changed him but he still wasn't happy so Tessa knocked softly on the bedroom door before slowly opening it and lowering him down to Cara for a feeding.

Judd snored softly on the other side of the bed through the whole transfer.

Tessa closed the bedroom door softly and walked back to the couch to retrieve the blue book before going to her own room to get more comfortable.

She kicked off her slippers and lay down on the bed in the guest room. She thought about taking a nap herself, but chose instead to finish reading the mysterious book. When it was done, she pulled a pen out of the nightstand and wrote her name in the back.

She thought she might like it and she had. She could feel the author, and when she closed her eyes, she could imagine her face. Tessa wondered where the author was, and how long the book had been traveling already. She also wondered how much the author was counting on this book making it to her. If she was counting on the resurfacing of the book to make her life feel worthwhile?

Tessa felt lucky. Her go with the flow ways had given her a life with no regrets. She did as she pleased, and people could count on her for her frankness and ability to speak her mind. She was kind though, in her words and deeds and loving to the core.

Tessa had made her own way. While she remained unmarried, her relationship with Charles had lasted ten years already, and held promise of many years still to come. She had creative spirits around her, some living, some passed that she talked to. Angels. She believed, really believed, that everything that is, was meant to be. She closed her eyes and asked the Angels in her life to bless her family and to help the author see one of her little books again. She was meant to play a role in helping the author, she would do her part.

She put the book into her suitcase. She had one person in particular she wanted to share it with. Two gifts on one trip. Her beautiful grandson, and a new view on life to carry on to someone else.

~

LITTLE OL' ME 2000

*H*ome alone. The girls are back in school, and my husband is back to work. I sure wish someone would tell me what I am supposed to be when I grow up. I've always struggled to see any special qualities I have at all, let alone being beautiful, powerful, or smart enough to make a difference in the world.

I was born looking like a little Snow White, my coloring being my mother's dream vision for a daughter she might have one day. In contrast, she was blonde, with light skin and almost clear, light blue eyes. Always squinting in the sun growing up in California, her skin burned often. In adulthood, her blonde hair darkened and she bleached it until I was born. In her mid forties she'd embraced her brown hair, which now had a defining gray streak. The swoosh fell, perfectly framing her face on one side. If I hadn't been caught up in the teasing I was getting from my schoolmates about having such an "old looking" mom, I would have celebrated that she looked like she had just caught a plane back from Paris fashion week.

In my early thirties my hair grew scants of white, that tease me. My hair will not be nearly as striking as my mother's. If I were to ever sprout something as cool as her swoosh, I would try to rock it, like she did. Only now, can I fully appreciate her decision to avoid the upkeep of constantly dying or bleaching her hair, and not taking part in the fruitless battle of trying to stay young.

I anticipate I will have a completely salt and pepper look, someday; like my father, as the years progress. For now though, to entertain myself, as well as to try on different personas to find one I will be happy with, I cover the gray. Bouncing between a rich dark brown, almost black for the winter months, I switch to a fun red shade in the spring to add some spice to my life. The thirty-day boxes allow me to bounce from one color to the next without the lines that occur with permanent dyes. It is my secret weapon for fueling my lack of commitment to a look. I have not tried blonde yet, but I haven't ruled it out, either. Some famous brunette beauties have pulled it off nicely. I have cut my own hair for years. In general I lack the foresight to make regular appointments, only going to get a cut when I can no longer stand my hair.

Instant gratification is where its at. I hate waiting for anything, and if it is scheduled, it's even worse. Plus I have only had one haircut that I absolutely loved in my life, and that was towns ago. I have no hope of finding that stylist again. Every other haircut I've had is subpar. It's often the upkeep and scheduling I struggle with. Making and keeping appointments to go to the hair salon once every eight weeks for a cut, or every four weeks to have my nails done. Nope. Nail polish is not for me either, as I am always busy on a project around the house. Painting a wall, staining something, doing some tile work. Sitting still long enough to have it dry properly is often the problem. And I love gardening, I can't walk past a weed without pulling it, even if it's not mine. If I ever do my nails, they are usually completely ruined in hours, if not minutes.

Not working has allowed me to be able to flit around like I do. As long as I remember to pick up the kids from school, get to the grocery store once a week and have food and beer in the house, my days are mostly my own. It's a good thing and a bad thing. Good because I can volunteer at the girls' school at a moment's notice. Meet up with my husband for lunch, and we don't have to schedule our vacations around both of our work lives, only his. I'm always available if one of the kids is sick and can help my parents if they need something.

Bad in that I often waste my time doing dumb things instead of doing things to better myself or plan for a career. But I do write sometimes.

Massive amounts of time spent watching soap operas.

As a kid, I found soaps alluring during the summers, before I could work or do anything legally constructive with my time. We weren't tasked with chores, and there wasn't much else on TV during the week while Mom and Dad were at work.

My summer days went like this- Wake up. Price is Right with Bob Barker during breakfast. Edge of night, Young and the Restless, lunch, then either General Hospital or Guiding Light depending on which one of those I was into at the time. Days of our Lives if I really wanted to kill the day. I think back. What a waste.

Watching those programs when I was so young and impressionable, has no doubt colored my perceptions about what love was supposed to be. I was drawn into the dramatic, expressive ways people would share and speak their love for each other. It is not even close to real life.

I can't stomach sitting around all day, watching TV any longer, so I eventually took up reading romance novels instead. Reading with whatever time was left over after keeping house, grocery shopping, child rearing and laundry. Plus the errands driving to doctor appointments, taking part in the neighborhood leadership meetings, etc, etc, etc. I'd kept myself busy with miscellaneous things until now. Without much to show for myself, other than healthy, well-adjusted kids and a decently clean house.

Maybe my traveling books will be my greatest adventure of all?

~

1

Tessa stepped off the airport gangplank, back on her beloved, New Mexican soil. What a wonderful couple of weeks she had spent with her daughter, son-in-law, and new grandson.

She was tired, but a good tired. She felt ready for a vacation. Her life often felt like a vacation, with its sunny weather most of the time, mixed with the relaxed atmosphere of Taos. Tessa looked around for her friend Sarah. Seeing her, she waved, and smiled.

Tessa and Sarah hugged. They belonged to the close knit community of creative people with studios in town.

"How are you, how is everybody?" Tessa asked climbing into the car next to her friend.

"Great, but we missed you. Charles has a show this weekend, he was hoping you would come."

"I'll be there with bells on." Bells being something Tessa had no hesitation wearing.

On the ride home, Tessa bragged all about her new grandson. "I will show you pictures as soon as I get them developed, he is such a little doll, and so good. Easy too, it seems and my daughter and son in law are so natural together as parents, it was beautiful to watch."

Sarah smiled. She didn't have any children, so she was happy for her friend, but slightly jealous at the same time, not only for the grandbaby but for some family to see in general.

"Hey, do you want to come by the house, and have a glass of wine and watch the sunset with me? You could stay over?" Sarah asked, hopefully.

"That sounds nice, but I really am beat. I think I want to get home, and just settle in, can I have a rain check?"

"Absolutely." Sarah said, trying not to show the disappointment that she felt. She had been waiting for their interaction all week, and it had been over too quickly.

Sarah pulled her car into Tessa's driveway.

"Oh wait, I have something for you." Tessa pulled the little blue book out of her purse and handed it to Sarah. "A secret mission." She gave her a wink then hugged her goodbye.

"Huh? Oh, ok. Thanks."

Tessa swooped herself out of the car and reached into the back to get her suitcase and carry-on satchel.

Home sweet home. Tessa felt like she could sleep for days.

Sarah held the book in her hand, squinting to read the title in the dusk without fishing around for her glasses. She waved at Tessa and set the book down on the seat.

Find Me. What an interesting title.

Hmm...

~

THINKING BACK TO MY FIRST DOUBT, ME, 1993

*W*e honeymooned in Hawaii, and I grew mildly concerned then, that I might have made a mistake. When one goes to Hawaii, you expect to come home with a tan to show evidence that you had been there. Hubby and I soon found out that we had much different expectations of our trip and having not known each other long enough to discuss such things, we were often at odds.

It poked at me then, an idea that would lay in wait in my self-consciousness nagging at me at every bump, that maybe I had married the wrong man.

For our honeymoon, I had imagined long days on the beach, the sun warming me to the bones, as back home it was a chilly January. We'd relax and sip tropical drinks, and enjoy a luau one evening, and eat fancy food the rest of the time, especially for us plain folk.

In contrast to my expectation, he wanted to stay busy the entire time. There were helicopters to ride, miles of coastline to snorkel, and long drives to the Botanical gardens to do. Not to mention the golf courses on the island. Ordinarily I would have been game for most of that, and excited for the adventure. But hello, I wanted to get a tan...

We managed to compromise some on the trip, limiting our big excursions to once a day and while I got to sit on the beach and get a little color, he busied himself happily snorkeling in the surf, for hours on end.

We went to the open-air market, extracting pearls from oysters, and having our pictures taken with parrots. All the touristy things.

My tan wore off on the plane trip back, and we got down to the business of making babies as soon as we got home.

He was much older than me, and we didn't have time to waste. When I met him, I was in my early twenties, and he was exactly what I felt like I needed and wanted. An older, more experienced man. Seasoned in life and safe. He made me feel important and loved, while tempering my wild unorganized side. He challenged me to reach for my goals instead of flailing around the way I had been for most of my life. It was true though, that when we met, I was just starting to get my shit together.

Painting murals for extra money, nannying for a living, I'd begun planning to move out of my dad's house into a small studio apartment by myself. I was young, and I didn't realize exactly how sheltered I had been. Life would give me more than one tussle soon enough.

He was thirty-four and had set up most of his world already. Being with him meant life would be naturally easier. I didn't pick him specifically for that reason, but it was a bonus. The age thing was a thing that I ignored for the most part, telling myself I loved him enough to perhaps be alone on the elderly end of life because of the difference. It was nice that he wanted to have kids and he wasn't afraid. He was plenty mature enough to handle it. I wanted to have children, more than I'd ever wanted anything in my life.

He had tried to have children with his first wife, even trying IVF treatments to become parents, but the eggs never took.

Near as I can tell from what he told me after the last attempt, she just tweaked, went out and had an affair and left him. He got the house, two dogs and two and a half cats, half, as one never came inside. Even with his total inexperience with children, he wanted to be a dad. I would see once our daughter came; how green he was at handling tiny bodies, but I was a semi expert, and we made our way. For his inexperience, I don't think I ever met a man who was a better dad. He is a total rock star.

When I got pregnant right away, we were ecstatic, but I kept my nanny job in town. During the initial weeks I developed such bad morning sickness I thought I would die. Every day I would get up and throw up. I nibbled saltines in bed before waking, sipped ginger ale out of a straw on the side of our waterbed. (Yes, I do realize that bed might not have been helping, but it was what we had. Seriously funny moments as I tried to get out of it at nine months pregnant. I couldn't leave for the day without him helping me, lest I lay all damn day in that thing.)

Nothing seemed to help with the morning sickness which wasn't really a "morning," sickness as it lasted all day every day, only letting up when I was actually asleep.

After a few months of my whining, my husband's empathy seemed to dry up, and he just said, "You should be used to feeling like that by now." As if feeling like total shit all the time is something you can get used to.

I remember lying on the floor of the bathroom after puking, I had our telephone in the room with me and I called my dad.

"*I just don't think I can do this,*" *I said to him. So tired, so sick, so over this with many more months to go.*

"*Well what choice do you have?*" *he asked.*

I thought about what he said, and the answer was true, yes, I could abort this child because I was sick and annoyed, but any other child that would come after would most likely make me feel this way again, so it wasn't something I could get around, I was going to have to get through it.

After our conversation, it either got better or I was resigned to dealing with it enough to grow the baby and get it out. Around that time I discovered that Dr. Pepper and chicken tenders from Burger King seemed to help with the nausea. I grew that kid on those. (By the way-she turned out fine.)

I knew I wanted to be a mom, I had to have kids. I dreamed of giving my children the childhood I never had, the one I'd always dreamed of. I'd taken notes for parenting watching the massive amounts of TV I had watched, cultivating a parenting style that was a mixture of The Cosby show and Roseanne. The perfect blend of striving, while being a laughable imperfect human too.

My husband was mature, as I said. He had certain ideas about how things should work in life. No debt and no extra spending. The house should be kept up to a certain degree.

For his comfort, he insisted on a couch to have a high back to support his head, and he'd need foot support as well to watch football and PGA golf on the weekends.

The furniture negotiations would continue well into our marriage as I preferred style to utility, and he was all about Lazy boy comfort. He didn't seem to notice his lack of color before me, until I had started bringing some into our home. It was one of the things he was grateful for, he told me later, in passing. It was one of the few compliments that I still carry with me.

I think at first, he didn't mind my idiosyncrasies, and the difficulty I had keeping the kitchen clean while cooking. My lackadaisical reaction to doing laundry, and my near avoidance of all things adult, like paying the bills. I did try to be, Little Suzie homemaker, but found out that my creative side just didn't meld with keeping a spic and span house. Call it a flaw. He did at times, that's for sure.

I got used to feeling like I wasn't doing enough, ever, and that I wasn't measuring up.

His mother also complained about me, (often out loud in front of me), that I wasn't much of a housekeeper. She would visit and stand in the kitchen picking bits off the stove with her fingernail.

Scritch, scratch, "Ew," she would say.

What am I good at, anyway? Would I ever figure it out?

~

A TRULY OVERWHELMING
MOMENT, ME 2001

S *eptember 11, 2001.*

I walked down the stairs as usual to the sounds of CNN on the TV in the living room. About halfway down, I stopped, getting a hit that the sounds and voices were not the numbing rambling of a typical day. Something felt off. Very, very off. I rounded the corner and peeked into the living room; my husband's eyes were glued to the screen.

"Something is wrong," I stated.

"Yes, something is really wrong," he answered back.

It was a school day and a workday, and we tried to go about life as much as we could as usual, with a new raging, hum of fear and uncertainty blaring in our minds in the background.

We didn't want to scare the kids. We didn't actually know what was happening ourselves. Planes were hijacked and flown into buildings, so many dead. Pure shock. How, who, what would happen next?

Were we all going to be attacked now, where we were? Would the bad guys start blowing up bridges and buildings across the United States? What the hell is this?

I'd been there. To the top floor of the World Trade Center. I'd ridden in the giant elevator that weighed us passengers on the way up and again on the way down to show the impact of the acceleration and deceleration on our grouped weight. I'd stood looking out the windows at the top with my forehead leaned up against the glass. Peering out to Lady Liberty as she fought the fog to be seen in the distance. Looking so much smaller from my bird's eye view.

I noticed the flying buttresses atop the sister building next door enough to ask my then architecture student boyfriend what they were called.

Now, the images pouring out of the the news, showed those exact hunks of concrete intact but violently thrown to the ground. Every part of the building and people that used to be in the middle, plunged down into dust and rubble. People, real people, both dead and alive trapped underneath.

We'd been insulated. All wars other than the ones we fought amongst ourselves had taken place on foreign soil. We'd never seen this here. We didn't realize what war was unless we had a firsthand view somehow, somewhere else.

Other countries; ones closer to more action, were accustomed to this terror as a constant reality. But here, we've never really been attacked, we didn't understand it.

Neighbors put up American flags to show solidarity, patriotism, some reserve members were suddenly activated. I was just scared. Was this a safe place to raise our kids now? What was going to happen next?

What I remember most was the absolute quiet of the world outside. Just the birds were singing. A sound that was so often drowned out by the constant thrusting engines of the jets at the airport nearby. Our home was on the flight path, depending on which way the wind blew.

Today was so damn quiet. So much confusion, so much fear.

Would I be shot by a hidden sniper of the enemy for wearing my American flag sweater to pick up my daughters from school? Were there attackers everywhere? Hidden in his random suburbia, that wasn't too far from a decent sized city?

The news was always on that first day, and I would walk in and out of the room depending on how much I could handle.

Over the coming days, we were introduced to a new alert system, one that we would be using from now on, as a national security gauge. Flags flew in front of the majority of homes in the neighborhood, and people rallied around each other. Were we now in a war? Would we be soon?

Heroic stories were told, about regular people tackling the terrorists on the airplanes, crashing their plane into the ground, rather than into another intended target. They'd saved countless lives, but lost their own in the fight.

The firefighters and police and the everyday heroes going back into the towers to save others, the grisly reels of people stuck inside the towers who decided to jump to try to save themselves with no other options. Hearing the voicemails left on loved ones' phones as a last-ditch effort to tell someone that they love them. The absolute heartbreak.

We set up a vigil near the neighborhood duck pond, a decorated soldier gave a speech, and we all stood in solemn silence for the people who were lost. Countless people were still missing, presumed dead.

The definitive feeling that one never knows when our time is up and there are more ways to die than what we usually keep track of. In every state, in every country, there was now a worldwide understanding that we are not safe or promised anything. No one is guaranteed one extra day, one extra minute beyond what has already been planned for us, or what lies in wait from the outside, trying to get us.

With the sorrow came the realization that we only have what we have, in this place, in this time that we occupy.

For me, it was another reminder to get this life right.

~

C.B.

We were together for a few years while we were silly young romantic teens. Growing up together, ease replaced love over time. I remember the night we met. We were under-age drinking at a friend's party when the cops busted it up. Standing next to each other, we scattered to get away from the scene. You stayed with me, knowing I was drunk, and close to my house, we walked back there together in the dark. You were very nice, and I remember how you helped me calm down after the big to-do.

I learned your name, not that day but the next, as other friends of mine knew you. You were from the rival school and were one year younger than me. I didn't think much of the possibility of us, mostly because I was inexperienced and pretty clueless when it came to people who liked me. It wasn't until a friend of mine showed interest in you, that I even paid attention.

"Well, if you don't want him, can I have him?" she had asked.

"Um, no," I said, suddenly remembering how cute and nice you were. Someone said you liked me.

Being with you was easy, and fun, and we learned together about love. What it was, how to be in love, how to be supportive with each other while having separate goals. You were romantic and always remembered our anniversaries. Four plus years together, we thought we would be together forever. And maybe if we'd met when we were older, we would have been. A dynamic duo, you an architect and me in design, we could have built an empire.

We double dated often with your brother and his girlfriend; going on trips, and camping out on the weekends. Jetting into the store each Friday to grab a loaf of white bread and a pack of hot dogs for every meal while away. We'd whittle down a stick to use as our one and only cooking implement with our tiny pocket knives. Ketchups kept from our orders at the Burger King in town.

You had some family stuff that was pretty heavy. Your father was fatally shot, in an altercation between him and your mother's boyfriend. The boyfriend was protecting her, as she had endured years of abuse at the hands of your father. It was self-defense. You and your brother were home at the time. Not a nice thing to grow up with. I would see your real emotion mostly when we talked about that time, you'd cry and say how awful it was. Even with that, guns were still around your house and we would sometimes shoot targets in the woods. That was my first exposure to weapons.

You taught me about architecture and we dreamed of designing and building a house together someday. It was in New York city at the top of the World Trade Center when you explained the flying buttresses that I asked about. I'd watch you make your models for hours on end, knowing you would be successful wherever you went.

We were young, but we were devoted to each other; and even in separation (you went off to college) we stayed close in our letters and phone calls.

I am so thankful to you, as you kept me from making even more mistakes than I could have in my early years.

As we dated, I learned the qualities I would wish for in a husband someday. What I wanted to share with the man I chose to marry, and everything that life and love could be. When we split and you found your perfect one, who became a friend of mine, I happily stood up as a bridesmaid at your wedding, freezing my ass off.

I wish you the very best in this life.

~

1

SARAH

Sarah Mulgate; artist, took the long way home past her old studio space that she kept before the accident. It was actually quite a bit out of her way, but she loved driving by and remembering what her life felt like back then, as a gallery and teaching workshop owner.

Sarah parked out front and turned off the engine, leaving the driving lights on so she could see the façade and details of the building. That place had been her dream since moving to New Mexico thirteen years ago.

It's rustic adobe front with the big, wood, multi paned windows in the front called to her, begged her to take up residence again. The hand carved front door she picked up from Mexico, stood as a sentry protecting the beautiful pieces inside.

Sarah had grown to love welding, and she imagined herself to be in the latest generation of Rosie the Riveters, but with a more modern bent. She had learned herself up into somewhat of an expert in the large-scale metals for most of her career. Over a ten-year period, she became an expert in large scale metal art exhibits.

Her often-massive sculptures were made with recycled metal bits, all welded together into a mish mash of pure awesomeness. She loved the way she could rust the iron a bit, and then clear coat the pieces keeping her one-of-a-kind finish intact. She had countless commissions on her desk, just waiting to be built.

Before the accident, she'd been working on a three-piece series utilizing some large metal steel pipes that were donated by the city after the water lines were replaced. They were offloading the pipes at the back of the building, but Sarah accidentally stood too close. Who knew that pipes weighing that much could bounce? Her big toe of her left foot was crushed.

Sarah was rushed to the hospital, and she nearly lost the digit. She was still grateful it wasn't worse. Her foot was a bloody, wrangled mess. The nail fell off and would most likely never grow back. In the surgery, they stuck a metal pin in to try to act as a new bone. She felt mangled, ugly and was bed ridden for weeks. To keep her toe intact, a metal pin was inserted. The end of the pin stuck out through her skin and would catch on things throughout the day. It was a constant reminder of her maiming.

When she could get out of the house again, she painted the small metal ball, and decorated her sandals with sequins. She had to embrace her new circumstance. The foot was going to look like that for a while.

Even after all these years, with an additional surgery to have the pin trimmed back into the skin of her toe to be less noticeable, Sarah still walked with a limp and depended on her beautifully curved, juniper wood cane to steady herself. Always trying to outdo herself creatively, she tucked some semi-precious stones into the cracks of her cane and painted southwestern animals on the shaft. She was an artist after all, she had to look the part.

The day of the accident had stolen more from Sarah than just her speedy mobility. It was her time and a lot of money, too. She was forced to sell her mother's engagement ring and some other jewelry to pay the hospital bills. At the time, her husband Tobey had "accidentally," dropped her from his health insurance policy, saying that he must have forgotten to fill in all the paperwork that was necessary.

With her inability to build the large price tag pieces she was used to, she was forced to refund her commissions. Once the hospital bills came due, she watched her savings dwindle down to nothing. Still she tried to remain hopeful that something would usurp the inevitable. After nine months of hoping, she let the lease lapse and went about making a new studio at home. She'd have to buckle down to learn a new, more manageable craft. Life could have been so different than it was.

Sarah got out of the car and walked onto the wood clad front porch in front of one of the windows. It creaked underneath her, and she peered inside the dusty pane. She could see the still cozy half-walled office space with her old desk placed near the window. Just as she had left it. A brass tulip shaded lamp shone a luminous circle on the desk, and numerous papers were splayed underneath. The mess felt familiar.

Sarah walked to the front door and reached up to hold the rattlesnake shaped door knocker she had hand-made. Running her hand along the curves she could almost hear the hand cast bells hidden inside the rattle part of the snake, made to alert any occupants. It had a sing song but urgent sound that she missed dearly. She'd left the piece behind at the building owner's request.

When the place was hers, the gallery space had held one or two large installations at any given time. Often Sarah would sashay out onto the front porch during the day and sit on the carved wooden bench to feel a part of the action in the small town. That was the place where she would also draw and plan for her next project. Oddly it still felt like home.

Sarah sat down on the bench and looked down at her hands. The dim light showed the bounty of rings she'd made, some of the first ones she had ever attempted. She hugged herself from the desert chill and remembered back to when she had been forced to switch gears with her art. Her life.

She had played with jewelry prior to her accident, and she could do that work sitting down. To learn more about jewelry making she took some day trips into Santa Fe, and perused the jewelry stores, and Navajo art shops and museums, always paying attention to the stones that were used in the traditional pieces. Red Jasper and turquoise, mixed with Apache's tears, a rounded black obsidian for impact. She purchased some rough stones to put into her rock tumbler and grabbed some raw silver sheets of different gauges to play with. Since she enjoyed using tubes of steel, she tried rolling some of the silver sheets into thin cylinders to bend and see if she could work them into a shank pattern for the sides of a bracelet that she had pictured in her mind.

While her husband was away, she cleared out a storage room off the garage and washed the filthy window with a strong cleaner. Cleats were put up on the wall and she ran three, two by ten wood planks across to make a a new makeshift workbench, which she covered in the center with a large two foot by three foot aluminum sheet, while placing asphalt roof tiles on either side in case of ricocheting sparks. It would also provide a rough surface to catch stones if they tried to roll out of the way. She made a pitch stand to hold the pieces in place as she worked, using chasing and repoussé practices. Everything was trial and error.

She loved the colors of the traditional stones and added in from her own collection of amber if the piece needed it. Sarah borrowed some hand stamp tools from a friend, and purchased a small air torch, and read about everything about the craft. She picked up books at the library and made friends with another jewelry designer in town.

Her first piece was a disaster, but she was able to melt the silver pieces down into little balls that she dropped into cold water to use as accents for other pieces down the road.

Over time she had perfected her own style and was able to start selling to shops in the area and in small boutiques throughout New Mexico. Her arms were covered with bracelets, her fingers adorned with rings. She wore a water bird, a gift from a dear friend on a chain around her neck. The giver explained that it symbolized rebirth, something she must undertake after her accident, and she wore it with pride.

While she admired the traditional styles of the Navajo and Zuni tribes, out of respect and honor of their heritage and place, Sarah made up her own designs using landscape and animals that were more literal than abstract. Her pieces could come from anywhere.

She shivered and decided it was time to go home. Sarah ran her hand across the snake on the door handle once more and shook it just enough to hear the bells. No one was there to answer. Climbing into her car, she felt it again, all of the feelings that she had felt when she lost the space to begin with. It wasn't any easier, even with time.

She felt lost and alone, stuck in this dreamlike desert paradise that she had not chosen. She had tried to make it her own.

~

Spring thoughts, Me 2002

*S*itting in the backyard, the kids play in the sandbox nearby. The sky is so blue today. I suck on a red hot. A jet leaves a white streak in its path. My daughter calls those planes and their contrails, skyscrapers. To me it makes more sense than the usual connotation.

I feel the sun on my back, just listening to the birds and writing this moment. I am just being.

Being still in the moment is hard for many. My husband seems incapable of it. My kids are losing their ability as well. It has been one of our talks lately. I want them to learn to sit still and be, sometimes, to be able to look around in wonder.

I want them to have an imagination like I do, not to be detrimental to their tasks, but enough to entertain themselves without a movie, a game, or having a friend over.

I toss in a couple more red hots and taste the spice in my mouth. My dog barks at an imaginary passerby through the fence. He chases the airplanes that fly over our house too. He hasn't caught any yet.

I should mow the lawn, I should finish the dishes, and I should start dinner, but no. I just want this moment. To watch the girls playing in the sand, to hear their giggles and enjoy them getting along with each other. I want to write about it, so I can remember.

I know there are more sights to see, more sounds to hear and more scents to smell on this sunny, summer afternoon, but at this moment, this is enough.

I feel bad for the people who are unable to stop and smell the roses, who never look down to avoid the bug wandering by to going about its business. So many people can't see what is around them, for their own busyness. They never stop moving.

If they don't learn, they will also miss the rush of the wind blowing through the trees, the bumblebee scooting happily from flower to flower.

I hope my daughters will be able to see the little things that happen beyond and underneath the regular chaos of life.
I am committed to teach them no matter what it takes.

~

1

Sarah pulled her sky-blue metallic Ford Fiesta into the garage at home. She tucked her new book into her macramé purse and swung it over her shoulder. Grabbing her cane from the passenger seat, she opened the car door, pausing for a moment to look down on the floor before stepping out. She had to check for scorpions.

Sarah was home alone again.

Tobias, her husband of twenty-three years, was away on a seemingly never-ending business trip. She pushed the garage door button and walked into the house through the laundry room. Taking a single serve bottle of white zinfandel from the almond-colored fridge in the kitchen, she shoved the door closed with her cane. Her New Mexican sky was calling her. She wished she had someone other than herself to talk to.

If only Tessa would have been up for a visit, and maybe a glass of wine or two? Sarah hadn't known solitude to this level before. Everything out here was so quiet. She was alone most of the time. The phone hardly rang and when it did it was usually a sales call and she would hang up, frustrated that she'd even answered. Thankfully her rock tumbler whirred along, cutting some of the silence.

When she had her studio in town, people would stop in. Even if they didn't buy anything, there'd be a conversation, an exchange of ideas, pleasantries. A connection. As she sketched out on the front porch, trucks would roll by, kicking up dust. There was activity. Sharing her space with other artists meant hearing other voices, collaborating, and brainstorming ideas together.

Making jewelry at home was as quiet and isolating as it sounds. Their home was away from town. Set where the only calls heard were the coyotes, birds, and the crickets; all partying the night away, without her.

The back porch was her favorite spot other than her studio. She had picked up the furniture on one of her out of town trips with her sister and brought it home for the space. The two toffee colored Equipale barrel chairs made with pigskin had made her giddy when she found them in an old barn sale. Always smiling when she saw them, Sarah plopped down in her usual spot, lifting her feet up on the matching stool. The second chair was much less worn than her own, mocking her. Evidence that no one came around.

Ahh. It was especially good to put her bad foot up, as it had been bothering her again. The rigid lower walls were a rustic bleached wood with wormholes. The aluminum framing that held in the screens was pitted with damage from the pounding of sand storms that passed through. Sarah was the only colorful spot in the room. A couple times a year, she would drag the furniture into the house for a few minutes to sweep out the sand that had accumulated from the storms. Sarah looked down at the floor seeing mini pyramids of sand that had built up in the corners, and set a to do item in her head for the next day.

Although the Mulgate's had a beautiful view from the back of their house, the inside was nothing to brag about. Most of the furnishings were from the previous owner, and they only replaced things as they wore out. She and Tobey had talked about decorating the rooms together in their first years here, but style differences and the constant arguing about what to do made them both give up. Chairs were just for sitting in, it didn't matter what they looked like.

It was the art pieces that she created in her studio, that she poured her whole heart into. That passion was what was missing, from the rest of her life.

A great divide had happened in their marriage years ago, and rather than spend time and energy worrying about it, she and Tobey chose to live separate lives, yet keep their tax bracket status. Sarah never dreamed she could live with such loneliness, but by now she was pretty good at it. Or hiding it from others. She hadn't been touched for a long time. Many, many years.

She sipped out of the bottle and set it down on the low table next to her. She pulled a shawl over her legs and traced the moon with her fingers on the horizon.

Sarah thought back to when she first met Tobey. She was just hours out of a relationship, drinking herself stupid at a college production cast party. Tobey held her hand as she cried inconsolably, and he told her that she would find love again someday. The two shared many interests, the arts, their time spent in the small college theater and the many plays in which they both had parts. A sudden trip to Vegas to attend a friends' wedding bundled with a tremendous amount of alcohol, found them dancing out of the Chapel that night, signed up for life. Someone mentioned that they seemed to get along, so why the hell not?

Having grown used to the quiet, things were much weirder when Tobey was home. There were the same few sentences exchanged. He would tell her about the latest at work, mention people she'd never met, and say when he was leaving again. Soon after their exchange she would scurry off to her studio to calm her nerves. She kept his favorite booze stocked in the living room, and more often than not, he'd fall asleep on the couch in there after a few nips. She had thought about getting a cat, or a small dog, but didn't want to risk coyotes dragging off a beloved animal, and she detested the burden of a litter box.

She wished for what her friends Tessa and Charles had: mutual admiration, respect, and a healthy sex life. Overhearing one of their passionate episodes when they all went to Scottsdale together, Sarah wished she hadn't agreed to share the two-bedroom casita. Either the walls were thin, or the two of them were just really loud, Sarah never said anything about it. She tried to hide her jealousy when she was with the two of them. She couldn't remember the last time she and Tobey had touched on purpose, they even prepared meals at different times when he *was* home.

Sarah drank the wine right out of the bottle and dropped the empty into the trash can she kept nearby for that purpose. The bottle broke and made a twinkling sound, a few shards of glass splintering out of the can.

"Score!" she said to no one. She went in to get the broom.

Sweeping she spoke curtly to herself. "What the ever-loving hell am I doing out here anyway? Living like a fucking hermit, cobbling a half-ass life together, every damn day." The tears came. This was a conversation she had with herself pretty regularly.

Stepping back through the slider door, she spied the book from Tessa; half falling out of her purse on the kitchen island. "Oh yeah."

Sarah retrieved the book and grabbed two more mini wines, tucking them into the spacious pockets of her skirt before heading off to bed. She didn't bother locking the house up. 'Hell, a burglar would make life more interesting,' she thought. She stripped bare and let her clothes fall to the floor. No one was home to care whether she kept the house clean or not.

Turning on her lamp, she fluffed the pillows into a nest and climbed in, pulling up the covers to her chest. Red silk sheets, and a woolen Pendleton blanket, both gifts from her wealthy sister Donna, made her feel spoiled and sensual.

Sarah put on her cat-eye-shaped, green jeweled readers, and opened the book. She read the first page. "Not sure I can help, but I'm in."

Sarah read and reread the pages into the night. Precious and fleeting moments in one person's life, made her think of her own long-ago romantic entanglements. How much crap she had already been through. How much more there was to life than what she had. She seemed to be coasting towards death, already, in her late forties? Pathetic.

Tears filled her eyes, as she lay there naked in a puddle of missed opportunities. Days, no, years, of sitting alone when the whole world was filled with people to connect with.

She signed her name with a purple ballpoint and set the book next to her.

Soon she was asleep and dreaming of someone. Someone she hadn't thought about in a long time.

~

MAYBE I HAD WORN HIM OUT, ME, 2002

S ome of our troubles are that I didn't feel supported in the things I wanted to do. To blanket statement say that he had <u>never</u> supported me in my things would be an out and out lie.

Hubby bought me my first sewing machine after I saw a darling little cloth doll at a craft fair and thought I could make that into a business. That was before the frustrating times when the bobbin bound up, and the machine choked and I sputtered many a swear word at it. I decided not too long later that I hated sewing and gave it up.

I'd taken an interior design class at the local college and he was supportive of that, for a time as well as I practiced in our home many times over.

Then there was the business I started when our youngest was one, a child safety product. I developed it from scratch, finding vendors and sourcing materials. I bought all of the items needed to build many completed sets, thinking it was such a good idea that I'd sell out at the giant Christmas bazaar that year. Nope, I was stuck with gobs of inventory and had only a few sales. After that there was a moment where I had to either double down on my efforts, or bag it. I decided it took too much time away from my kids so I closed the business.

When our youngest went to kindergarten, I knew my time at home with no outside responsibilities was nearing a close, so I asked him to give me one year to complete the novel I'd been working on and he said yes.

As it turns out a year wasn't nearly enough time. I couldn't stay focused, each of my aforementioned and failed attempts threw me into more of a depression and saddled me with the feeling I'd never be good at anything so why even try.

My career report card would read: Can't complete anything, won't stick it out when things get hard, doesn't like being told what to do.

He'd push me in the way he knew to, organizing, and setting a deadline, or asking for a plan. But I didn't work that way. I needed to ride the wave that came with being excited about something in order to see it through, and what I needed was some verbal acknowledgment from him or others that I was doing a good job on my path. It was something that didn't come naturally from him, I do not know why.

I'd had businesses of my own ever since I could remember. Starting with my mom making up beautiful business cards for me when I said I wanted to start babysitting, that I hand placed little animal stickers onto to make them more impressive. Little monkeys hanging off my name, a sleeping panda lying atop my phone number.

Then there was the adult sized tricycle that she bought me when I was eleven from an old woman in a mobile home park, so I could sell ice cream out of a cooler off the back of it, that one summer. I'd fetch dry ice from the grocery and ended up eating up all the profits, myself or by handing them out to friends.

Every time I had an idea I was helped along until I gave up on it and moved on to something else. And there was always something else.

My track record of working outside the home other than in a volunteer role was garbage, but I was a good mom, that I could do.

Even without the financial reward, no bonuses or raises, my role at home was one I was proud of whether he said I was good at it or not.

I worried that if I went back to work now, maybe I'd screw up the one thing that I loved the most? My one thing I was good at. I couldn't lose that too.

Maybe if he would have told me he was proud of me; once in awhile, I would have tried harder at different things, but I never heard him say it.

Not ever, for anything. Not even about being a good mom.

If only he would have said he was proud of me, I imagine in my head that it might have made a difference. I may never know.

~

1

Sarah awoke sticky with sweat. Her dreams had turned erotic. Her nocturnal co-star, was Simon from college. He was the greatest love and lover she had ever known.

"Whoa, where did that come from?" She asked aloud, walking to the bathroom for her first pee of the day. Sitting down, she thought, '*I thought that part of me was dead.*'

She pulled a purple chenille robe around her and stepped into her matching slippers. Thoughts rushed around her head, and she wasn't quite sure what to do with them. First, coffee.

Sarah limped into the kitchen and rummaged through the cabinet stacked with mugs, searching for the one she had made in her first term of college. Finding it, she pulled it down and rinsed it under the sink before placing it by the coffee maker that was already percolating along. Thankfully, she'd set it for auto brew the night before.

She'd fallen into a more practical space lately, using whatever cup was in view, then over and over again, never varying them. Her latest, an old paint splattered metal camping beaker had been her go to for at least six months. Sarah retired it into the sink to wash later. First, coffee.

It felt good to feel her old hand made mug in her hand. Made using a coil technique, she'd kept most of the layers exposed to show each loop from the bottom to the top, only smoothing over the areas where her hand would hold on. It still fit her fingers perfectly even though she had added some twenty pounds to her frame. Her digits hadn't changed all that much.

Painted in a rainbow of earthy colors with the glazes she hand picked, she chose to highlight the handle in a rich cobalt crackle. The cup was crooked and cracked, and felt a little like her now. She had glued it back together so many times she hadn't kept count.

Sarah needed to get down some caffeine to open her eyes. She pulled a packet of instant oatmeal out of the cabinet and doused it with hot water from the tap.

Sarah walked out to the porch and sat down with her breakfast to enjoy the morning. A jackrabbit bounced along the horizon, followed by another. Their feet kicked up dust and sometimes a small rock in it's path. She suddenly remembered that she had seen Simon's name in one of those annoying college alumni magazines recently.

"Where is that thing?"

She hadn't read the article when it arrived as Tobey was home at the time. She had planned to get back to it, then forgot. She took a bite of oatmeal and got up to look through one of the stacks of papers in the living room. No. Not there.

She walked around the house spooning in bites of oatmeal as she searched. The papers sitting by the fireplace to burn, maybe Tobey had thrown it in with those? No. Not there either. She suddenly wished she was a better housekeeper.

Sarah knew she was depressed. The all over body aches and pains each day, that were unrelated to her accident. Each day it seemed harder to get out of bed. Sometimes she didn't bother, instead putting on the TV and watching movies all day, rising only to go to the bathroom, or grab a snack she could eat as she lay. It was way past her injury, or anything that would make sense for her forty-eight-year-old body. She rose later and later from bed each day unmotivated. She knew about depression on a general level but hadn't done anything about it. Even with the non-stop Vitamin D in this beautiful region, it was a tall order to expect that sunshine to make her happy.

Most of her days were spent alone, toiling in her workshop, trying to make beauty while stuck in the dark side of her own consciousness. People weren't supposed to be solitary this much.

In between bites of oatmeal and sips of coffee, she found the alumni magazine, having placed it amongst some catalogs on a shelf above the workbench in her studio.

She had put it there for safekeeping, then spaced its very existence from her mind until just this morning. Maybe it was brought on by the memory book from last night, and that dream...

So often, she had tossed the alumni journals in the trash, as she rarely recognized anyone mentioned and she got tired of the organization always asking for money. Luckily, she had glanced through this one enough to see Simon's name.

She poured another cup of coffee and sat down to read the article. She moved quickly through the pages, skipping anything that wasn't about him.

Looking up at the camera, he leaned over a big hole in some desert somewhere with artifacts in the background. A skeleton of bones she couldn't recognize, he was excavating them for a special museum exhibit.

Simon looked just the same. Older, yes. But as cutely, geeky as he used to be. His glasses were the same. Sharp black rims with oval shaped lenses. A dark brown Indiana Jones style hat, and khaki long sleeved shirt with rolled up sleeves. Jeans. She wished she could have seen his butt in the picture too.

Sarah remembered back to the day he broke her heart. Back to their time together. Being with him had been so wonderful, or so she thought. Tears started to fill her eyes and she closed them trying to ride out the sting.

They were seniors about to graduate. She with her fine arts degree with a minor in theatre. He was getting his Anthropology degree. It was Springtime and they walked together, hand in hand to the college square. Simon sat on a bench near a walnut tree and patted the seat next to him for her to sit. She sat, and he grabbed her hands, looking into her eyes.

"You know I love you, right?"

"Yes, I love you too."

"But I can't do this," he said looking away from her eyes.

"What can't you do, what are you talking about?" Sarah's eyes filled with tears.

"Sarah, it's just that I see things with you that I don't want right now. It's just. That I already had a plan for my life, and it didn't include this."

Sarah pulled her hands away, and sat up straight on the bench, looking blurrily across the square. She could barely breathe.

"Is it something I've done? Or not done?"

"Oh God no. You are amazing, I just think being with you right now will stall me from getting to where I need to go."

"I wouldn't hold you back, never. Do you want to write a book, move somewhere? What?"

"I know you wouldn't on purpose, but *I* would make different decisions if we were together. I have to keep with my path, my purpose.

I'm staying in school, so another four years for me, and I have some grant money, and a teacher's assistant job to keep me afloat, but it's not enough for us together. It's going to be tight, and I will be on the move a lot. I can't take you with me."

"I could support us too, I will get a job soon, we can make it work."

"No, I can't have you do that, for us, I'm not going to be in one spot. There won't be a place for us to be together. I will be working alongside an archeologist. We are going to South America this summer, then other places after that too. I'll be learning and, on the go, all the time. I can't do this. I'm sorry."

Sarah melted then, and he pulled her into him, lovingly but not wavering from his position. He whispered, "I'm so sorry," over and over until she couldn't hear his voice anymore.

She didn't have any choice in the matter. She couldn't negotiate, make a case, nothing. Days before, their relationship had seemed so full of possibilities, and promise. Now it was over. Kaput.

She met Tobey that same night. Super vulnerable. So distraught. She'd let anyone close to her at the moment to get any reassurance she could get. Anything or anyone to take the sting out of her forever with Simon, lost. She pushed down all the pain and chose alcohol and companionship in the bed of a stranger that night. And that choice had gotten her here. To this life. To right now.

Sarah read the article. He was speaking at a symposium, not too far away in Mesa, AZ. She tried on the idea of seeing him again. She wondered if he would be happy to see her, or annoyed that she was interrupting his life that he'd made so far?

She looked out the window as a group of Pronghorn bounded past. Fast. Sarah imagined being an animal and never traveling away from the place you were born. Those antelope were born here, will live and roam here within a hundred miles or so and will die here, too. Would she?

Left alone, she knew there was more. The animals didn't know better, but Sarah did. Her marriage to Tobias was a joke, and after that night of dreams, she learned that her passions were still available to her. She wanted to get out of this place, explore more, and maybe get a divorce.

"A divorce." She said it aloud, "Yes, I need a divorce."

Sarah put her coffee cup down on the patio table and went into the bathroom to shower. Not in the habit of bringing up heavy topics to Tobey, she practiced a conversation for her absent husband.

"Tobias, I want a divorce, I want more out of life than this and since you seem willing to live with the status quo, we are not going to make it."

Ooh, maybe she'd leave him a note. He was always leaving *her* notes. This was perfect since she had no idea when he' be back anyway. She was not going be waiting around. But to leave a note, she'd have to be going somewhere.

'Where should I go?'

The water ran off her face, and down the front of her chest. She circled her breasts with her hands feeling alive for the first time in a while. She imagined having someone else share the space with her. Them touching her in all the right places. She wondered if Simon would remember her secret spots.

She washed her rusty red hair with some luxurious shampoo and conditioned it with her curly hair salve. She would let it go natural today. She shaved her legs, and neatened up her womanly area, into a smooth well-kept triangle. It was quite the fuzz.

Shaving her pits last, she often felt uneasy watching, the razor only inches from her eyes. She looked away, and shaved the area, hoping for the best. Finally smooth all over, she imagined lying with Simon, his hands enjoying her soft curves.

He had said not now, way back then. But maybe things had changed?

She drained her hot water tank and reached for her towel, another gift from her sister. Purple with an edge band of satin. Egyptian Cotton. Only the best.

"I'll go see Donna in Las Vegas. I'll call her as soon as I'm leaving, and for sure a quick stop in Mesa, Arizona to congratulate Simon, as old friends often do?" She smiled at the idea and formulated a plan for how she would explain her being there. Seeing Simon and his big discovery.

Sarah wrapped the towel around her body and tucked it in at the top. She grabbed another towel and wrapped her head like a turban, as she started packing for her trip. Throwing all of her clothes on top of the bed, she would organize it more before packing it into her suitcase. She needed to see it all.

Sarah pulled off her towel and stood naked in her bedroom. She grabbed her suitcase and filled it with her eight favorite outfits, a dozen pairs of underwear, her expensive toiletries, and her favorite purple ballpoint pen and journal. Other than what she'd be wearing, she'd leave the rest of the clothes behind.

Sarah pulled together a ninth outfit, her absolute favorite. A white peasant shirt and a purple broom skirt. Adding a belt with a large silver belt buckle featuring red jasper, she added one of her own large turquoise necklaces, completing her ensemble. Tucking half of her hair into a loose bun, she added bobby pins to keep it tidy, and let the rest of her curls dance on her neck. Shell earrings from one of her trips to Mexico was the final touch.

She was light on her makeup but added a little rouge to help blend her freckles into her suntanned face, she packed each item into her travel bag, as she went. She brushed her teeth and downed the rest of the pot of coffee.

Grabbing three large plastic totes already filled with winter clothes out of the garage, she dumped out the contents on the floor of the closet in the guest room, before carting them to her studio. She nimbly unassembled her jewelry set up and packaged each piece carefully with newspaper into two of the totes.

On an ordinary day, she would spread out all of her stones on her desktop to organize them, taking note of each for the color, movement and value. But Sarah was motivated to get out of there. She was cutting her losses. She tossed a few of her favorites in with her rock tumbler. Throwing in some extra metal scraps she had been collecting for a new series she was planning.

She opened the man door into the garage, looking down again, out of habit, for any scorpions that might be waiting for her near the threshold. Clear. This ingrained routine, was more automatic than she realized. All because she had been stung that first week, when they moved in. That damn scorpion, so light in color, so small it might have been a baby.

Man, did that hurt? She would never be able to forget that feeling. First a sharp pain, before settling into a feeling as if her entire leg feeling like she'd hit her funny bone.

With the sting, she screamed, then dragged herself to the couch. Thankfully, she didn't needed medical care, as Tobey applied gauze pads soaked in vinegar and baking soda, on and off for hours from the start. She soaked her foot in ice water for a time too, until it was too cold.

Tobey ended up moving all their stuff inside which hadn't been much since they had purchased the house fully furnished. He set up in the kitchen and made dinner that they ate together on the couch, looking out the large window out back at their first sunset here. Sarah felt useless.

She watched helplessly as every time Tobey walked out to get more boxes, he would glance down at the ground to check for scorpions before each step. The lesson was learned by them both as he never walked anywhere with bare feet either. So afraid too, even though it wasn't him who was stung.

The next day, the sting had dulled to a painful numbness that she couldn't describe exactly if she tried. It felt like her leg had died, she hoped it would eventually come back to life.

That was when the two of them were still a team. Moving out this way for Tobey to be more centrally located for his new job. Sarah was thrilled by the art scene in nearby Taos.

In those days, each sale or project completed was celebrated with a glass of wine and a gourmet home cooked meal together. Those were the days. Even though she hadn't been super attracted to him in the beginning, Sarah grew to love him, and appreciate him, as a friend, a caring companion.

He was nice to have around, when he was happy, and she would celebrate with him, all of his accomplishments too. His promotions and when he got the regional position. But something had happened. She wasn't sure what it was. They hadn't had a good honest talk in years.

Sarah packed another bag of books that she loved, adding the alumni magazine to the bunch.

She penned a quick note to Tobias, drawing a little scorpion under a foot on the bottom of the page, before signing her name, it was one of their little inside jokes. She set the traveling book underneath the note and placed her wedding ring on top.

Sarah put all the luggage and totes in the car and locked up the house, leaving her key in the garage refrigerator egg section, before hopping over the laser to let the garage door close behind her.

She hadn't felt this excited in years. Sitting in the driveway with the car running she texted Tessa, "Great book, I'm coming over."

"OK." Tessa texted back. She backed out of the driveway and headed east into town. Sarah felt exhuberant. More so after a full tank of gas and stopping in to see Tessa one last time.

She pointed her car towards Arizona and was never seen in New Mexico again.

~

REMEMBERING BACK, ME 2002

W e've been through a lot in our years together. With my being so young when we met and married, and then having our daughter soon after. We were parents, still getting to know each other and not surprisingly using very different parenting styles. We'd never thought of it before, never knew it was a topic. He wanted to let our new baby cry for a bit, and I couldn't think of a reason for that at all. It became a disagreement that made me wonder how we would manage, and successfully parent a child or children together. We struggled with the me being domineering in her care and taking over because I had the most experience with children. He wondered how he'd fit in.

It helped my side when the counselor suggested that very young babies are not trying to manipulate their parents with their cries, they are indeed in need of some sort of attention. Hearing that from an expert and with the suggestion from her that he read up on some of the Baby books we had around the house, counseling helped us immensely. Marriage counseling helped us come together again and bridge the gap in our parenting styles and how not only did I want him to build a relationship with our daughter so she'd know she could depend on him, I also needed to have some outside goals that were not attached to her. To keep myself sane. I was told by the counselor to get out of the way on Saturdays to let hubby and baby find that place together. So, I volunteered at a local theater painting sets. Creativity and a deadline to accomplish.

As we were both children of divorce, we were willing to work hard to stay together.

Our first daughter was a smart and easy baby, except for the one day, at a week old, when I binged on M& M's and Hawaiian punch all day. I had felt so happy that I could finally eat what I wanted again now that the morning sickness, was over. I definitely overdid it. Poor babes was screaming her head off and I remember calling the hospital only to have the nurse tell me that it was my diet that day that had blown up my daughter's stomach. I guess I should have read up more about that. She rebounded after some pretty big farts and remained easier than most.

Now in Kindergarten, she is loving school and didn't even look back at me when I dropped her off on the first day. At the time, most of the other children were losing their shit as their moms walked away, while mine happily skipped into the room to see what was up. It was me who was lost that day. Didn't she miss me?

She is confident, self-assured adventure lover. My little soccer player: she loves art, animals and running around with friends. Dance parties to Sesame Street music are also a big hit.

Little sis came along three and a half years later. A more challenging baby, she cried all the time, it was terrible. I couldn't figure out what was bothering her, as I'd long outgrown my fondness for Hawaiian punch and M&M's, at least together.

Thankfully, my friend S.S. next door, advised me to try to stop drinking milk, as maybe when it crossed into my breastmilk, it might be hurting her tummy. That had been the case for her daughter. It worked, and sis grew into a little love bug. Literally holding onto me for hours, or sitting on my lap, she'd follow me wherever I went. I wondered sometimes if she wanted back inside my body. Obsessed with books, and craving two or three binkies in her mouth all at once, she is the house comic.

Together, my husband and I decided that I would stay home with the kids, as being a nanny previously, it only made sense. Was I supposed to leave my children to go and take care of someone else's? So home, I stayed. It was what I always wanted anyway.

We had made a place to call home. The childhood I had always craved for myself was coming true for my children. I was so grateful.

Years passed and things weren't as exciting as they had been in the beginning for us. I was getting so bored with the usual crafts and running errands, that being a homemaker entailed. I had kept myself pretty happy through decorating rooms, sometimes for other people too, but mostly for us. Changing things around the house until it was done. Then I would start over again.

I inspired some of the neighbor wives to start painting and decorating their own homes. Their husbands' started adding the word 'itis,' to the end of my name as if an ailment had taken over their wives compelling them to change their environments.

"Yeah, we are wallpapering the kitchen now. My wife has ____ 'itis." So apparently, I got their wives to spend money. "Oh well," I told them, "You had a good run."

Always wanting something new or a project, I was constantly painting our rooms different colors, finally hub asked me, "When are you going to stop?"

I just shrugged my shoulders.

No clue.

~

1

TOBIAS

Tobias Mulgate came in the front door of the home he shared with his wife Sarah. He couldn't think of the last time he had been there. He leafed through the mail on the entry table before plopping his luggage down on the bed. He had been on the road all day.

He looked around and called for Sarah, who was no doubt, in her studio working on her latest masterpiece.

Nothing.

There was not a sound in the house. It seemed cold too, like the heater wasn't working.

He walked to the thermostat and flipped it on. The fans started up. Good, no problem there.

He went into the bathroom and relieved himself, before hopping in the shower for a quick rinse, to help him relax after his long day driving. He ran his hands through his longer than usual gray curly locks. He hadn't much interest in getting a short haircut these days, preferring to just put his hair back in a close to his nape ponytail for his business dealings. His boss, when he did see him, didn't seem to care.

The style reminded him of the times back in theater school before he had sold out and became a commercial claims adjuster for a nation-wide insurance company almost twenty years ago.

He was rarely in front of customers anymore, managing others for the most part, and the independent contractors across the states meant that they worked for him, not the other way around. They weren't ones to judge him on his appearance, and he worked mostly out of coffee shops along his route.

Tobey traveled to many of the major, weather-related catastrophes around the country, each year, overseeing the regional adjusters and reporting back to corporate, things or policies that would need to change to try to avoid paying such claims in the future.

He didn't like that he was completely under the thumb of the "Man," but what else was there? The inheritance from his well to do east coast, old money family, had long been spent. Mostly on lavish trips, and fancy cars since his parents had passed away over fifteen years ago.

Tobias loved his cars. As a classic Sagittarius, he loved speed. His car of choice bounced between Audi, Mercedes and BMW. Mid-size usually with beefy engines that were able to jump off the start should anyone; anyone at all, rev their engine next to him at a light.

He picked a new car every year, never keeping to a standard lease duration, instead always choosing a new one, swapping them out when the new car smell wore off.

Salesmen at the local dealerships bought him Christmas presents each year, hoping to win his yearly purchase. They took him out to dinner a few times a year too. Their treat.

Breaking leases like that meant one was always in the hole financially. Tobey would pay the new car price, and as soon as he drove off the lot, the value plummeted. Since he drove it for work, his cars always packed on the mileage too, contributing further to a low trade in.

He really didn't care, it was his one and only extravagance. He figured he paid for the cars so he could do as he pleased.

Sarah had given up trying to tell Tobey what to do, in fact they rarely spoke about anything big anymore. Pleasantries, updates on her family side, deaths, births, those types of things. He and Sarah hadn't taken a vacation together in more than ten years.

Tobey wiped the steam from the mirror and looked at himself. He was over fifty now. The gray hair looked good on him, especially with his olive skin. His dark brown eyes looked around the bathroom and he noticed it felt slightly emptier. Wrapping a towel around his waist, he went to the dresser and pulled on a pair of black sweatpants, his chest he left bare. He was still warm from the shower. He let his locks hang loose to dry, drips running down his chest.

Tobey called for Sarah once more. Again, no answer. Since he hadn't come into the house from the garage, he didn't look to see if her car was in there. Maybe she was out? Maybe out with Tessa and Charles? Barf. Those two together were nauseating.

He walked back into the dining room to pour himself a cognac. At least Sarah always kept the bar stocked with the Rémy Martin XO, his favorite. It was also his father's favorite too. One of the only things they ended up having in common.

Tobey opened the new bottle, hearing the pop of the cork, before placing it under his nose to sniff the aroma. He poured heavy in a short glass.

He took a sip. Yes. Hints of vanilla and orange peel tickled his tongue. He took a longer draw and let it pool in his mouth, before swallowing. His stomach gurgled. He hadn't eaten since noon. It was half past nine at night.

From the kitchen doorway, he noticed a note with a book and Sarah's ring left on the kitchen island.

"Oh, a note."

Large, looping purple cursive letters stood out to him.

The note read:

Sorry Tobey, I had to go. I will talk with you soon. Oh, and by the way, I want a divorce. Have a good read. I don't care about the house, just send me half the money when you figure it out. I can't do this anymore. Sarah.

"Whoa," he uttered, reading her words again to make sure his eyes weren't playing tricks. He never expected that she would just go, and leave only a note.

It was quite the shock. It was probably the ballsiest thing she had ever done since he'd known her.

He moved the note to the side and picked up the book. It was blue with gold writing on the front. A spiral in black held the whole thing together. Some kind of divorce handbook?

Shuffling back to the sofa, he placed his glass on the coffee table, before swinging his feet onto the couch. He laid back against the decorative pillows on the suede sofa.

Tobey pulled reading glasses out of the front pocket of his sweatpants and opened the book to the first page.

An invitation out of nowhere. A request. Super weird, no author name, no publisher. Made with a homemade press of some sort. He flipped through the pages to see how long it was, to gauge whether he would need to eat first, or if he could wait until he was done scanning through.

Written in the back, he saw Sarah's scrolling signature, her friend Tessa's name, and some others he didn't recognize, placed onto the lines. Tobey put the book on the couch next to him and set his glasses on top.

"Why not? Nothing else to do, except maybe call a lawyer and a realtor."

He got up again, he was hungry. Given that he never did a daily or even weekly check in with Sarah, and it had been over a month since he had been home, he had no idea when she had left. Anything in the fridge seemed perilously risky. He opened the door out to the garage to check in the large chest freezer, stepping square on a scorpion on the back stoop. Crunch.

"Shit. I hate this place, I'm glad I had my fucking slippers on."

He moved a few boxes off of the top of the freezer and lifted the hatch so it stayed open. A few boxes of hamburger patties; an option, but he was sick of burgers. Tobey continued to dig around for something that might have vegetables in it. A bag of chicken stir fry with included sauce, sat on top of some butcher paper packages of meat.

"Perfect," he thought, pulling it out, and shutting the massive lid, tight. He wondered if anyone would want the freezer full of the contents included in the sale of the house?

Tobey pulled a skillet out from under the island, wiping it first with a paper towel to get the dust off. He set it on the front right burner of the glass stove top that they had purchased last year, when the old coil stove died. It was one of the only updates of any kind they had done to this place, in all their years here. They hated to go shopping for things together, as it always ended up in a fight.

He poured some olive oil in the pan in a circle, and whacked the bag against the counter to loosen up the contents, before slicing it open with a butcher knife. He poured the mixture into the sizzling pan.

Tobey put the lid on to keep the splatter down so he wouldn't have to do as big of a clean for any real estate agent he'd find. It also helps it cook faster. Tobey hadn't cooked for himself in months. Restaurants were his staple.

Ten minutes passed and he kept occupied leaning against the kitchen counter while perusing through the yellow pages for possible lawyers and real estate agents. Ripping out the ads of potential people, he didn't care about keeping it intact. He left the torn pages in a stack by the phone to go through later.

Satisfied that his dinner must be done by now, it smelled ok. Not great. He wondered how long the bag had been in the freezer.

He opened the fridge to grab some soy sauce. It was dumb that Sarah kept it in there, but because of the hot weather, she just did. He pulled it out and shook it over the food that he had placed in a large ceramic bowl. Pulling a bottled water off the back porch, he went back to his spot on the couch to eat. In between bites, he read the pages of the book and at the end, he used his gold-plated fountain pen to sign his name in the back.

"Weird book," he said as he put it down. "Interesting, though."

~

My love of words Me, Always

I love to be read to. I often read to others. Nothing is more loving than sharing a story with someone you care about. It takes one back to being read to by your parent's, those close moments when we didn't have a care in the world and everything was magical. I read to my children all the time and they enjoy the made-up voices and funny sound effects that I add to their books. Maybe it is because I have a hard time reading longer books, my eyes always getting pulled to a different section on the page or while reading along, I start daydreaming and realize I can't remember what I just read.

Reading to a lover feels different. Their is an intention. Lying in bed together, one reading to the other, it gives space to close one's eyes and imagine it all. I become engrossed in the story, I feel a part of the tale. I can see the people, as if they are standing right in front of me. I'm able to envision the events if I read it to myself, but only snippets of the whole because my vision is blurred by having to read and keep track of my place on the page.

When a lover reads to you, you can be in that imaginary place. Walking amongst the scenery, smelling the fragrances described and enjoying the views.

I believe I would have done better in school if I could have been able to hear the stories of Tom Sawyer or Siddhartha rather than hobbling my way through the passages myself. Even Non-fiction is more interesting that way.

My sixth grade teacher solidified my love of listening to stories. Ms. Clarke read to us everyday. Always at the end of the day and only given as a reward if the whole class had cooperated, all day. Tall order for some of those kids, believe me.

As a well behaved, more of a watcher, quiet child for all of my school years, I wished beyond wishes that the other students wouldn't act up and ruin our chances to hear more of the story at the end of each day. Hello! It's James and the Giant Peach, what is going to happen next?

I was always embarrassingly shy, or at least that was what I was termed. I never raised my hand, even if I did know the answer. I played safe and small and was a little mouse most of the time. Looking out the window, listening to the kids around me; I took notes inside my head to learn to be more cool, like them. Hearing them plan play dates or brag about their birthday parties that I wasn't invited to.

Instead of going out to recess with the other kids, to everyday navigate trying to find a new group to play in, I'd spend recess in the library watching film strips of the stories that tickled my brain and imagination. Harold and the Purple crayon was one of my favorites, each one of his adventures bounding from his head, while he was supposed to be doing something else. I loved the ritual of the taking the filmstrip out of the cannisters and placing them into the machine just so. Listening in with the headphones to the audio tapes that matched, always making sure to change the slide when I heard the bell. I was so content in my own little world. I felt powerful being able to set up and run the filmstrip machine, even though I am sure the librarian had to show me numerous times before I got it.

It would be years and years before I would eventually find my voice. My ability to talk to others or feel a part of a group. I usually had one best friend at a time, moving from one to the next, with very little explanation about the transition. No idea why.

When I finally did come out of my shell, my courage came from a bottle. Bartles and Jaymes became my best friend, and in celebration of coming out of my shell, I named my pet mice after those two old men. Jaymes died quickly, but I had Bartles for years and years until he turned into a furry puddle, with his internal organs failing on a massive scale. He had a good life.

~

G.S

When I was younger I used to watch you. I could see your steps just a few years ahead of me. I watched and waited hoping you would notice me. Then finally we were in the same school. I was a freshman, you were a junior and you were so cool. In your wild ways you attracted my attention, being the bad boy in my neighborhood. Alcohol, drugs, partying, but soft on the inside.

In those days if you would have come closer, and showed an interest, I would have chickened out because of your experience. But it was fun to think about being with you. I wanted to pretend we were on the same level. That I could be cool. But somehow I was just like little innocent Sandy from the movie Grease. You were Danny.

Every morning we'd get on at the same stop, I'd pretend I wasn't listening to your weekly wild party escapades as you shared with the other rocker guy B. Just to feel more included in the exchange, I started bringing you two, coffees before school. You liked that; and suddenly you noticed me. I was glad.

I remember you telling a story about one of your behaviors, one that I didn't like and I told you that you had the morals of an ant. Not that ants are especially moral less, but more that they are a small creature, so not really able to hold much. An odd thing to say, I suppose. I can't remember what you did, or what happened afterwards but you always gave me your full respect after that, and we became friends. After high school, we saw each other at a bar and connected again. It was fun to hang out with you and I still had my crush.

I remember when we were in your backyard by the lake, and we went half skinny dipping. Just tops. Well my top, I guess. And that was all there was.

Even later you told me you didn't want to get close to me because I was the marrying kind. A girl who'd want a house and children, and you didn't see that for yourself, but you knew you would try to give it to me, if we got closer. I still think of you and wish you well.

Oh, and I apologize for the coffee, it must have been terrible.

~

1

Since Tobey had found Sarah's note, things were moving fast. His dramatic call to his boss John, feigning a broken heart, had resulted in an extra paid week off to settle things, with more time if he needed it.

"Just let me know what you need, we are here for you." John's voice echoed through his head.

'That was too easy...' he joked as he hung up the call. Those acting classes in college suddenly felt useful for something. He wondered how long he could milk the abandoned husband story. Could he take a month off and just play?

Tobias looked out the back porch plate glass window and smiled. This time back was maybe the only time he had been alone in the house since they bought it.

He had slept hard that night, naked, sprawled all over the bed, and he really, really loved those satin sheets Sarah had left. He was taking those with him for sure.

He'd awakened feeling oddly positive, even with the mountain of items to do. He hadn't shed a single tear. It was all a bit surreal.

He made a pot of coffee and sat down on one of the chairs on the back porch to watch the sun rising in the distance. Maybe this was why she liked it here? Did she like it here? He never asked. Many of Sarah's art pieces had these colors in them. She must have liked seeing this view every day, right?

They had never once watched the sunrise or sunset here together. Even with the many years they'd been married, there was a lot they hadn't done together. Sarah had tried to enrich their marriage for a while, but after a few years, she gave up asking for what she wanted, and settled into just taking what she could get from him. She had her art, and that must have helped her, an outlet to express herself, and be relevant.

Together they really had no chance. Tobey had spent his early teens to mid-twenties being someone others thought he should be, masking his true self, in a decent enough way, as if playing the role of a prince in a stage production. When one does an act for so long, the faked persona starts to become real, and the authentic self gets buried further and further inside.

For so many years he had been hiding his true nature away from her, not quite accepting it himself. He'd come home every week or so, and pretend that things were fine. Pretending that they had a real marriage. He was so damn good at pretending.

It wasn't until a drunken kiss at a company party with a former co-worker ten years ago that Tobey even considered acting on his sexual preferences. Zapped by their sexual electricity; they had an affair for three years, no one was the wiser.

With the note, there was a relief, he could finally be himself and go after what he wanted. No longer in the shadows.

How had he even ended up here? In this place? He hated the dry hot weather. It didn't even matter now. His interest in Sarah had lessened year by year until all the nice fuzzy friend feelings were gone completely, and he had sought other avenues to feel loved. He believed he had hidden it well from her, his almost, animal desire for men. She had never guessed, or at least let on that she considered it at all. To her, he was an asexual being, but inside and on the road, he was aflame.

All kinds of men attracted him. One special one came to mind, a hot slightly younger espresso joint owner, who had a place in the Fisherman's wharf area of San Francisco. Tobey was always going out of his way to see him on his trips there. Tobey could tell he was also gay, the gaydar as people say. The man in California seemed to reciprocate an interest in Tobey, with him always coming from behind the counter to check on him and how his coffee was. He even touched Tobey on the shoulder the last time he was there. The man had only pulled away after seeing the wedding band on Tobey's left ring finger. That was a year ago, and they had seen each other a few times since then. Tobey wondered what the hottie was doing right now.

Tobey shook his head to snap out of what would soon turn into a fantasy sequence and some time spent in other ways. He didn't want to imagine it, he wanted it to happen. But it only after he got done with business.

Tobey walked to the stack of ripped out ads from the yellow pages and started calling. Hanging up if no one answered, he made an appointment with the only guy who did, for later that day.

The agent, an old Vet named Gale, looked in the ad to be somewhere in his seventies. It might have been an old picture. Tobey was surprised when he showed up, he was more in his eighties, but still driving, and he seemed to have his head on straight. Wrinkled and dark from eons in the New Mexico sun, his bolo tie displayed a love for the good ol' days. His whole look and demeanor was that of a gentleman cowboy.

He tipped his hat, and Tobey told him the listing was his.

The realtor was ecstatic, asking if he would need any other help with the move. Storage? Liquidation? A handyman to run through the place to make repairs before people asked for money off the asking price? A reference for a lawyer? His wife handled estate sales in the area too. He was the whole package, and said he had done transactions like this more than a few times.

Tobey said yes to all of it, and after an hour he shuffled the old man out and sat down with the mail again while waiting for the last load of laundry to dry. What was the world record for speediest sale of a house?

Since he wanted to sell the house furnished, and Gale's wife was the expert on that, she would see if there was anything in the home worth selling first, or just leaving everything behind. Nothing was to his taste, anyway.

Tobias sat and went over his list, he could do all the other things over the phone, and he could fly in to sign papers. Sarah would have to, too. He'd call Sarah on her cell when those were ready, and she knew his number as well. This might be easier than he thought. Why hadn't they done this a long time ago?

"Everyone needs an impetus. This was Sarah's." He said as he tapped the book twice with his ringed hand. He thanked her, wherever she was. Her deciding that it was over, would give him a bigger life too.

"It's the only thing of hers that I'm taking with me. Well, and those sheets. Damn."

He set the book on top of his laptop and packed up some more clothes for the trip. He was moving out. He might not have to come back, especially if they could just fax the papers.

Tobey called Sarah's sister's home phone and left her a message.

"Hey Donna, Sarah may be coming your way, she left me a note, asking for a divorce, but no details, I am sorry that she was unhappy. Please tell her I understand, and we will figure everything out. I have already arranged for the real estate agent to list the house, he will handle the sale of that and everything inside." The voicemail cut him off, so he called back.

"Donna, Tobey here, again, I wanted to let you know that I will be taking some time off, so I might not be in range, if Sarah does try to call. I have given her phone number to Gale Price at High Desert Realty, here in Taos. He seemed nice. He's been doing this for a while. So, if he can't reach either of us, any sale will have to wait. I hope Sarah finds her happily ever after. Bye Donna." The voicemail cut off again, as if on cue.

Nobody could say he was being a dick. Sarah had left *him*. Left him to clean up all the mess and just took off. Where was she going anyway? What really drove her into this massive shift with such short notice?

It had been years since Sarah held a regular job, he didn't know how she would manage. Her jewelry seemed hit or miss. But she must have a plan.

Was she leaving Taos for good? He knew that he would be fair with her and split up any proceeds from the sale of the house and furniture. She had kept everything together with him gone all the time, for almost their entire life together.

He probably could have been nicer, or maybe he should have told her years ago, when he figured out that they were not meant to be together. That everything had changed since college, all those years ago, and there was no way to go back.

They did have some good times, and a lot of creativity and celebration came out of their union. She had inadvertently managed to keep him out of trouble for the most part, for a lot of his adult life. Any indiscretions on his part, were kept short, and meaningless. Without her, he would have been playing the field big time, who knows what or who he could have come in contact with?

He waited until the last of his clothes were out of the dryer and put all his luggage in the car. He turned on the outside light, locked the door and slipped the key under the mat for Gale.

He hopped into his BMW and headed out to the highway, throwing an imaginary hat up into the sky.

"Westward HO!"

~

PEACEFUL FOR THE MOMENT ME
2002

I am outside, my day is open. There is a gentle breeze that offers me company. My dog lies by my side. He is an excellent companion. A gift to myself on my thirtieth birthday. My dream dog.

My straw hat covers my face from the harsh sun. The yard is green and lush now but soon the days will pass, and the leaves will fall. I stroke my dog with my naked foot, and he looks at me. It is a perfect sunny afternoon. I am alone at home, in my garden. My sanctuary.

There are no outside expectations of me unless I put some on myself. I have chosen to journal today. Today being the first day I've had to myself in a while. My dog leaves me to bark harmoniously with a neighbor dog. He shuffles back through a flower bed to lay by me again.

This garden I have made is impressive. Most other homes in the neighborhood have a shrub here and a tree there. Mine is a garden filled with garden rooms and privacy.

For years, I'd been studying the ways of Martha Stewart, specifically her garden programs. I devoured everything she threw at me. I signed up for a Master Gardener class to get some real and localized education on how to garden, but never ended up going. Something came up. It became another item to hang in my not completed closet of goals. I'd done rather well, with the design, I thought as I looked around. Without the class, making it up taking into account the sunshine needs and colors that would tie nicely together. Thanks to Martha.

I get up and walk barefooted on the grass to turn on the fountain. The final touch.

The bees busy themselves with the flowers, and I watch with every step to avoid them. Returning to my spot, I pull my journal out from under my chair to write.

My dog pants loudly. He is a breed that can't take the heat, but he stays by my side until he can't take it any longer or I decide for him, whichever comes first. Sometimes I have to throw him in the kiddie pool to cool off. He can tell when I am coming for that, and finds a shady spot for himself.

I look out over my sunglasses at a Bumble bee loving up my California Lilac bush.

I wonder if a bee ever gets a chance to just be, or if it is in its head all the time, planning what flower to fly to next?

I heard a rumor; that according to physics, a bumblebee shouldn't be able to fly at all. Luckily no one told them that.

~

1

Tobias Mulgate pulled into the 7-11 off the I-40 West. He needed more coffee. He had driven all night and had many thoughts along the way. His thoughts went to Sarah. Where was she, was she ok?

What had taken her so long to be done with him?

Yes, they put up with each other in college but that was a long time ago. So many things had changed, but the two of them stayed stuck together, neither one moving off center.

All growing up, Tobey was the life of the party. His family had money, and he felt he owned the world. Travel, fast cars, whatever girl he wanted at the time, he tossed them aside like dollar bills at a strip club until he met Sarah.

She was just so pathetic and vulnerable that night that they met. Forlorn. The only time he ever thought of using that word. Distraught, a mess. He could go on and on. When she clung to him in their shared drunken state, he felt so sorry for her. He couldn't leave her like that to wander the campus, and end up who knows where. How would she deal?

Over the coming months, the once powerless blob of blubbering became a fun-loving confidante who liked many of the same things he did. She didn't squeal too much if he drove fast, and she laughed at all of his jokes. He'd found a best friend, then went for more. Without honesty and growth, marriages rarely stand a chance. When the realization of his sexual preference came and he embraced it, he didn't want to deal with the fallout, so he kept it hidden from her too.

It was easy to keep up the persona of the man she expected him to be. He'd pepper her with the usual questions when he saw her. About work, her foot, what new pieces she was working on. Just like he did as a teen, sitting at the breakfast table with his father, snowing him with the words he'd pulled out of the dictionary to convince him that the private school was worth it so he could stay with his friends and goof off.

But it was done. His thoughts of Sarah ceased. He didn't have to hide anything anymore. With this new freedom, Tobey felt the urge to yell out his truth; finally, from the rooftops. 'I'm gay!'

It was an inopportune moment so he said it to himself quietly stepping over the threshold of the mini mart, the familiar bell announcing his arrival.

"Good morning," said a cheery voice from behind the counter.

"Yes, it is," said Tobias.

He grabbed a coffee; black, and a blueberry muffin for the road. He had miles to go to reach San Francisco. He'd locked in on his first destination, and exactly who he wanted to see.

Now on a mission to claim for himself the life he was meant to live, that little book had set him free.

Tobey sipped the bad, but hot coffee, as he opened the car door, setting his muffin on the roof to put the coffee safely into the drink holder. He shut the door and opened the window to reach up for the muffin. He tore out of the parking lot. No need to waste any more time.

The coffee started to kick in and his eyes opened wider. Tobey sat back in his black leather seat with red stitched detail. Flying down the road, a hard rain started. He felt energized as the drops fell violently against the windshield, until it was too much. He pulled over, underneath an overpass, to wait until the monsoon was over. He wasn't alone. Five other cars had sought shelter. They nodded to each other from their vehicles, one man decided to take a nap and wait.

Tobey's breathing quickened. Jittery with the possibilities. He downed the last drop, placing the cup back into the drink holder. If the rain didn't stop soon, he might need it for something else.

The rain tapered off, and he pulled back onto the highway. Tobey looked out onto the road and down at his hands on the wheel. Nope, he didn't need that anymore. Yanking the wedding ring off of his finger, Tobey tossed it out the window into the wet expanse in between milepost 148 and 149.

Tobey stepped on the gas, he wanted to reach Needles CA, by sunset.

~

REACTIVE ME, 2002

*C*hristmas had been absolute hell this year. So glad it's over. Between the word stabs of my father and brother and the high maintenance-ness of my mother-in-law, I had had it.

With divorce and fragmented families, comes natural holiday turmoil. This year was especially bad as I watched in full view along with everyone else at the table the pissing match between Dad and Bro. It was as if a Lion King had been challenged by a younger male. There was roaring back and forth. They both left. It pretty much messed up the whole day.

Merry F*&^ing Christmas.

I woke early the day after, grabbed a diet Cherry coke from the outside fridge as usual and had removed all the Christmas ornaments already when hubby walked in. I was dragging the tree towards the back slider door when he wandered toward the counter to pour his first cup of coffee.

He knew.

It was bad.

"I'm painting this whole room today. Don't try to stop me, I have to get the ugly family stink outta here before I go crazy thinking about it. So mad! They ruined Christmas!"

"Ok, I will keep the kids busy."

Together we threw the tree out the back slider door and it fell with a thud onto the patio.

"Sick of this," I steamed. He filled his coffee cup and headed off to watch CNN.

He knew that decorating or changing something in the house helped me feel good again. I am allowed full reign to a certain extent, as long as it's not too costly, or he has to be involved in a bigger way than he wants, depending on if football or golf was on.

I did probably take it a little too far when in a premenstrual frenzy, I started pulling the vinyl up off of the kitchen floor without any discussion. He just came home and the floor was a mass of paper colored destruction. I knew we had money to re-do the floors, and I'd spent many hours on my hands and knees trying to get them clean, but I hadn't brought it up with him yet.

He just looked at me, grabbed a beer from the fridge and said, "Well, we can't leave it like that. I guess we will have to call someone."

~

1

Tobias checked out of his room and pulled into the parking lot of the Wagon Wheel restaurant. He was starving. In his rush to pack up, he hadn't thought about snacks and the hotel's vending machines were empty.

He bellied up to the counter and asked for a black coffee while perusing the menu. Vickie turned over his cup and filled it to the top.

"Let me know what you feel like having, love." She flashed a smile and turned quickly so he could get a glimpse of her tush. She looked back his way to see if he was looking.

He wasn't.

So many options.

Vickie came back with a pen and her pad.

"I'll have the Cinnamon French toast with a side of bacon please, it sounds delicious."

'Oh it is honey. It surely is."

Tobey's mother had made the best cinnamon rolls and it had been years since he'd had one. Heck of a nice way to start the morning.

He looked around the place. Part diner and part museum. Full of history, it was the ultimate nod to Route 66. Automobile license plates were everywhere, the aforementioned wagon wheels made up the light fixtures, some benches, and miscellaneous other items were strewn about.

The slightly dated decor didn't bother Tobey, there was a real charm to the place. He'd come back here, that is if the food tasted as good as Vickie said.

He sat enjoying his breakfast and listened to the waitresses banter with the chef. Three cups of coffee in all. Soon it was time to go. Literally.

He walked out of the building through the gift shop, buying a t-shirt on his way. Only another 9 hours or so to go to get to San Fran.

Tobey turned on the radio hoping for a decent station and stopped on a Latino channel. The music was uplifting, wild, and with the flick of the volume knob, loud. All of the things he had suppressed in himself for so long, but not anymore.

Singing his best to the music as he tootled down the road, the hours passed quickly. The breakfast sustained him and he only had to stop twice to get gas and hit the head.

Finally pulling into a parking lot by *Jerry's Java Joint*, he hopped out, bringing the book stowed in his shoulder bag.

He ducked his face down, and hurried into the restroom, to get a good look at himself. A little rough in the face, since he hadn't shaved, but happier than he'd been in years. It showed.

He zipped open a pocket, and took out his travel deodorant, spreading a thick layer onto his pits, before using the toilet. He washed his hands, then splashed a little water through his hair.

Good enough.

The lightness of his skin where he had worn his wedding ring glared at him. Even when he messed around on Sarah, he had kept the ring on, he wasn't quite sure why. Maybe it was so he could feel the freedom now. Now that it was off, for good.

When men don't wear wedding rings, and divorce, their physical body stays exactly the same. He was glad for the physical as well as visual and mental difference. He checked his fly and walked out into the cafe.

In line for a cappuccino, he caught the eye of the guy that he'd been thinking of, the whole time. Great, he was working today, and looking his way.

Jeraldo came closer, excused the barista, and took Tobey's order, himself.

"Hi there, long time no see." Jeraldo said with a smile.

"Yes, but I'm here now."

"Something's different about you,"

"I have news," Tobey said.

Tobey held out a five-dollar bill.

"It's on the house." Jeraldo said, refusing.

"I'm just ending my shift, want to sit down?"

"Sure."

Sitting at the table with two cappuccinos, they talked and laughed. Tobey felt like a moviestar.

"You see, it all started with this book..." Tobey said, pulling it out of his bag for the last time.

"Hey, I have time for a quick lunch, you available?"

"Yep. I got nowhere to be," said Tobey.

They got up together and Jerry went back to the office to get a jacket, as Tobey left the book dangling on the edge of the booth seat by the kitchen.

It was time for the book to move on to someone else.

~

Rainy day me 2003

*T*he rain hit the windows, and I listen. The only sounds are the water droplets, and the scritching of my pen as it dances on the paper. The rain has been coming hard for days now. The sky remains dark. I made a joke yesterday asking people if they had seen an ark.

Today and for the last week, I have given a lot of thought to the rain. Acting like tears from heaven, maybe it is for the goodbyes we say to lost loved ones? Or is it tears from above for the combative state of our world right now? If the latter was true, it would rain all day, every day and never, ever stop.

Rain is needed to cleanse, and give life. Maybe it's also a reminder to slow down a bit, on the road, or in one's homes and in our minds? I know when it rains, I get super contemplative about everything.

I enjoy watching the puddles as they fall, each impact a concentric circle that get bigger and bigger until it eventually hits the edge, then turns inward again. I love the rain. I don't think I could live where rain isn't a common thing.

Last year we hardly had any rain during in the summer, and I got super moody. Everything outside was stale, dusty and hot. When it finally rained, I was happy to stay inside and just listen to the sounds that I had missed. When it stopped, we could go outside and smell the freshness that had finally come again. A good rain can clean and leave the world anew, and a good cry can often do the same when we are gray and stuck.

As the rain hits my window, my pencil captures more, I am thankful for this moment to slow down and think about the world and my future. It's another chance for me to get quiet, and listen. To try to decide what comes next. I am so often looking for answers, just begging them to come. But instead the quiet for me, often brings more questions.

How much of me will people be able to handle if I really show them the real me? If I move beyond my head space and start acting out my ideas. Will I be quickly shut down by those around me? Will they laugh at me if I say I want to be more than I already am?

What if I tried to do something really big, like be a bestselling author? Yes, without a college degree, or as of now, without a tremendous amount of experience to pull from? Just me and my imagination?

Am I powerful enough to fight for the chance this time? Strong enough to set aside the views of others, about how hard it will be, how long it will take? Can I keep up with the commitment of writing each day, to hone my craft, no excuses? I sigh.

As so often my default is to just let it all fall away, especially when things get hard.

~

1

V

Vanessa Langley; or V as she'd asked to be called, came out of the
Java Joint kitchen wiping her hands on her apron while walking
to the bathroom. She had recently moved from her barista position to a
new spot in the kitchen after showing interest in the techniques of the
pastry chef, Knarly.

After using the toilet, she stood at the vanity washing her hands
twice. In the mirror she saw a straggly bang hair over her eyebrow. She
wet her finger and pulled it back into place before grabbing a paper
towel from the dispenser. She was still getting used to the new cut, a
near pixie. It was an attempt to look more masculine, to look a bit more
how she felt on the inside.

Coming home with the new cut, she had told her mom that it was to
keep the hair out of the food she would be preparing, in her new role
at work. But mostly it was just trying out a new look. It was flattering.
Her face seemed more sculpted even without makeup which she had
also given up in the last month too. It was good to stop trying so hard
to be someone she wasn't.

V was happy to have found a safe space to explore her options. The
Java Joint was a destination for misfits, just like her. Kindness and
understanding were somehow built into this place. Some co-workers
were gay, some of the men wore makeup and obvious wigs, but everyone was accepted as they were. V loved that, so much.

V's life was about to get a whole lot more complicated. There would
be a huge conversation to have with her parents. She'd been playing
it over and over in her head for the last few months. With Dad away
on a business trip, V had planned to sit down with her mother to start
talking about the things that had been building up in her head, (his
head), about what might come next.

V came out of the bathroom and looked around the bustling cafe. Yes, it was ten a.m. on a Saturday, but even in the late afternoon, this place was always hopping and filled with great vibes. She grabbed the mini broom and dustpan set from behind the counter and swept the floor a little before grabbing the last batch of dirty dishes from the tables and wiping them down.

V was sixteen when she accidentally mentioned to her parents that she felt more like a boy than a girl sometimes. It was more of a statement to get around one of their questions of the evening. One about whether she was romantically interested in anyone at school. She thought the statement would fall away to 'just dumb things kids say,' but in her own mind, at least, it stuck.

It was supposed to be just another BBQ night at the Langley's and suddenly grew into a conversation V wasn't ready to be in. V hadn't talked about any crushes she'd had, so her parents pegged her as a late bloomer. Figuring that she would be boy crazy any minute, once she found the right one.

She remembered back to her father's reaction to the statement. He hadn't said anything but got squirmy in his seat and looked off into the distance.

"How long have you felt that way?" her mother, Maura asked.

Dad got up for another glass of scotch taking a seat in his easy chair, inside away from the discussion but within earshot.

Vanessa's mother asked a few more questions before getting up to do the dishes.

"For a while, I guess. I just seem to be more attracted to girls than boys, or at least I have more interest in looking at girls. I just don't feel comfortable in my own skin sometimes."

"Do you think you want to talk to someone about it?"

Vanessa didn't feel safe yet to talk about the thoughts that had been percolating through her head. That she was uncomfortable when boys paid attention to her at school, that she wanted baggier clothes to cover up her breasts more. Vanessa had hoped that she was the 'late bloomer,' as her mother said, but when it came to romance she felt absolutely nothing towards men.

"No. I don't know. Maybe, I don't know. Let me think about it."

Maura hugged Vanessa, and whispered, "You let me know."

Vanessa's father vigorously shuffled the pages of the newspaper, so he couldn't hear anymore.

After the slip, the topic hadn't come up again, at least out loud. Vanessa was happy her mom had listened, and been willing to talk about it, the dad card was a big unknown.

Now seventeen and a senior in high school. She was happy in her life and feeling strong enough to take on the big questions. Content working at a place that celebrated the many kinds of people who frequented it, V paid close attention to everyone around her, especially the ones being unapologetically themselves. She was learning to listen to the beat of her own heart, not someone else's. She was a sponge taking in the many aspects of love and self she could see.

As V was tidying, she noticed a book lying on a bench seat, near the kitchen. V walked up behind the front counter and called into the kitchen, "Hey, Knarly, mind if I take my fifteen minute now?"

"Go ahead," he called back.

"Thanks," V said, having walked away, her eyes on the book. She plopped down on the booth seat where she found it.

Reading the introduction, she was hit by the idea.

"From within the confines of an ordinary one," she said aloud but not loud enough for anyone else to hear with the loud ambient noise around her. V read on, she wondered what it was like to have a grandparent that would document their life and share like that. All of hers were gone before she was born.

Funny little reminiscences. Snippets of a life. V wondered if the author had been found yet, or if she was still in the confined place she hinted at. How long had the book been traveling? V turned to the back of the book, skimming over the pages with signatures. Not a lot, but more than a couple. Only two had the same last name.

A man standing near the door sheepishly smiled at her, but she hadn't seen him. The book had been handed off; Tobey's job was done.

~

J.A.

We were best friends in fourth grade. Your parents were both artists. They made jewelry. They also taught at the nearby craftsman school. With your last name so unique, I could find them if I looked.

You were taller than me, with dark brown hair that hung long on both sides, curtaining your face. Beautiful brown eyes. You had a very dramatic quality, much different from mine. I believe your heritage was Peruvian. I was oblivious to the differences in where people come from.

You had a curvy feminine frame much earlier than I did, with wider hips, and a thinner waist. Good for bearing children, some would say.

I would go over to your house, and we would play for hours in your backyard. One time, we found a stray cat back there and I picked it up. I was carrying it down the hill, hoping to take it home with me, when your dog came running at us, barking. The cat leapt from my arms and up onto my shoulders, before settling for what felt like an eternity, perched on my head; it's claws dug into my skull before bounding off and running away. Your dog hot on it's tail. You laughed and said that was the funniest thing you had ever seen. I wiped the blood from the sides of my face and said, "I bet."

Most days I would walk past your house first and we would walk together to school. We weren't in the same classes though, or maybe we were I can't really remember. Since you lived close to me, we spent the summer before fifth grade making a vegetable garden in your front yard. Your Mom had come up with the idea, to keep us busy, I'm sure.

We dug out the weeds, hand tilling the soil with mini shovels and walked together to the corner store, to buy seeds with our own money. We watered it every day, waiting for the plants to sprout. It took a long time. When you went away with your family, I came and watered our garden. It was the pursuit of the garden that was much more important to us, than the actual things we grew. I don't remember eating anything from the garden, because, ew, vegetables.

When summer was ending, your mom asked us what we planned to do with the plot, as the foliage would die off soon, and become a mess, she didn't want that for the front of your house. I'm not sure whose idea it was to destroy it. But once the idea was out there, it became the best idea ever. We grabbed tools from the shed to start chopping it up. We'd make a salad!

You had the hedge clippers and started into the greens, and I am not sure why, but I reached in, at the most unfortunate time, and the blades caught the end of my left ring finger, almost chopping it off. Screams, looking down at a bloody mess, fat sticking out the side of my appendage. I was lucky it wasn't worse. I went home, and mom took me to the Doctor to get stitched up. This was my second bout with stitches. Well, I learned that day that a head wound, and an appendage wound are very different animals. In your head your nerves are further apart, so you don't feel as much up there, but in your fingers, due to the needs and uses of touch, your nerves are super close together. Numbing my finger took five shots, all excruciatingly painful.

The scars from the seven stitches in my finger are still visible to this day. If I hit that finger now, a funny bone feeling shoots through my body. It is hardly noticeable, visually, except that my fingernail has grown back with a line running through it, a forever reminder of a day, where two crazy kids who had made something together, wanted to annihilate it because summer was over.

We wandered apart as so often happens in young friendships. I veered in one direction, and your interests took you in another. I wonder where you are now?

~

1

A voice shouted from the front, "Hey, we are running low on muffins, V can you whip up some fun ones?"

"You got it!" The break was over. V pushed the kitchen door open with her foot and gathered up some large bowls and measuring cups to get started.

Thankful to be learning new things in the kitchen, V was encouraged to create wild flavor combinations for the cafe. She readied her ingredients and stood at the counter remembering how she had found this place, almost eight months ago.

After the Langley's time in Japan, Vanessa had to figure out who she wanted to be. It wasn't just the usual questions of a teenage girl that she was dealing with. What should she do with her interest in the other girls at school, when she was expected to be looking at the guys. She was new and no one knew her story, V could be anyone she wanted to be here in Cali, but who was that?

Vanessa watched how the other girls in school related to the boys and wondered what that would feel like. To like flirting, to tease. She remembered what the girls said to the boys and would try to mimic their body movements and tone of voice in front of her mirror at home. It always seemed to come out wrong. At school, she tried flirting with some of the safer, gooby guys, but she always ended up feeling totally stupid or worse, they'd ask her out. So far, she had said no to their requests. Because God, then what? No.

In her efforts to fit in, she'd made friends with one of the popular girls hoping some of their built in coolness would rub off onto her. Give V a little more cred when it came to making friends. Vanessa helped Layla with geography, and in return she saw how the social circles worked. When Layla invited her over, V had gone not knowing what to expect when hanging out with a well to do, cool California family from "The Hill."

Biking across the Golden Gate bridge from their homes in Sausalito, Layla's parents had stopped at the Java Joint to get a coffee. Vanessa and Layla naively ordered the same thing as Layla's parents did, and both girls added a ton of sugar and cream to their brews, after tasting their first sips. Neither had tried coffee before. Having a coffee drink that she could order anywhere, would give her one less thing to worry about.

The two of them sat down in a booth in the front corner, as the parents walked outside along the wharf in the sunshine. The girls had a full view of the place. Layla started chattering on about something.

Vanessa scanned the café while listening to her friend gab on about this and that, nodding occasionally to show feigned interest. If there would have been a quiz about what she was actually talking about, Vanessa would have flunked for sure. She hadn't taken in a word since Layla had sipped the first sip after doctoring their brews.

"Now, it's yummy."

Studying the crowd V noticed the people sitting with each other. There were two women sitting next to each other at one table instead of across from each other as people often do. They held each other's hands, breaking the grasp occasionally, to take a sip of coffee or wipe their face with a napkin. They snuggled and giggled softly.

A well-dressed older man placed a coffee down on the table in front of a much younger man, who was also dressed in snazzy business attire. Vanessa wondered if they were father and son, stopping in for a drink after a successful business meeting. That is until the "father" sat down next to the "son" and rested his hand on the younger man's leg, giving him a squeeze. Vanessa looked away then, her face flushed. She hoped they hadn't caught her staring.

There were hardly any traditional couples in the place. Each set of people seemed to have another type of relationship going on. Some men were dressed in women's clothing, and some women appeared much more masculine. Vanessa felt like this was a special place.

This funky space was filled with things he had found on the street or in old junk shops. There was a rainbow theme throughout. Large stripes of colors were painted in a curving pattern on the back wall behind the counter, a long stainless-steel counter with reclaimed chunky wood on the front, took center stage, the first thing people saw when they came in. The chairs were also painted in a spectrum of colors, and each chair was different, or at least they seemed to be when Vanessa looked around. The tabletops were a mix of woods seeming to represent the different skin tones of the people who frequented this place. Talk about inclusion, it screamed love.

The music that played in the background always varied. Something for everybody. Reggae some days, Country, and old-time rock on other days. She wondered who was running the radio.

Layla threw a cream tainted mixing stick at Vanessa to get her attention.

"Hey Doofus, let's go find my parents. This place is weird."

Vanessa decided she wanted to come back without Layla and she memorized the cafe's name. Strolling after her friend, she raised her cup to her mouth and threw back the last drops, before tossing the vessel into the trash can outside.

Walking past the Java Joint again on their way back to their bikes, Vanessa glanced over in time to see two Java Joint workers laughing with each other. Might be a fun place to work? At the very least it seemed like a good place to study and people watch. It felt then and it really was; a safe place for Vanessa to explore the things she had been thinking about.

Vanessa went into the cold room and brought out some eggs and milk. She gathered up more ingredients off the storage shelf by the office. She had been wanting to try some different combinations, this was her chance. In the kitchen she went into auto pilot Zen mode, the ingredients almost talking to her, telling her what to do next. She was a natural. She might never have known if things hadn't happened just as they did.

V had struggled to appreciate her time overseas, because of the timing. Developing her hormones and thinking about all the confusion she felt about herself, just happened to coincide with her father taking a job in Japan for three years, when she was thirteen.

Going to a private junior high school in Japan, she was given a typical school uniform to wear. Pleated skirt and a button-down shirt with tall socks and penny loafers, every day. Vanessa could not wear makeup or paint her nails, but that aspect didn't bother her as much as some of her friends. In the three years of wearing a skirt every school day, she grew more irritated from the situation. Wearing bike shorts underneath to strip off the skirt the moment she left school, V would run home and get on larger; roomier clothes. To get rid of the feeling of her skirt rubbing over her legs all day.

She met and became friends with two other kids who felt that they didn't fit in like they should. Ichika was a girl but dressed more masculine after school hours tucking her long hair into a bun each day. She didn't talk about the feeling of being different with her family. Their friend Akio would often wear makeup and nail polish; after school, but if questioned he would just pass it off as practicing for Onnagata, the widely accepted Japanese tradition of men dressing as women for Kabuki theater. He painted his toenails with wild colors, but his glamour was safely hidden away from the school authorities.

The three of them became a close and trusting club of sorts. They would often sit in the park after school. It was with them that Vanessa first shared that she felt like a boy trapped in a girl's body. Akio had confided the same but in reverse to the other two in the group. It was nice to have found people to talk to about these nagging thoughts they all shared. They didn't judge her for it and felt similar themselves.

Vanessa's friends walked the line of doing enough to feel more like their insides, but not doing enough to potentially suffer socially, medically, or financially for it. The two of them had promised to each other to leave Japan and go live somewhere else once they were of an age to do so.

Thinking back to those dreaded skirts, Vanessa felt lucky her high school didn't have any sort of dress code. The only thing they cared about was keeping one's skirts or shorts to a certain length. Basically the girls couldn't show their vagina at school. That was not a problem for V. In America, she knew she had more choices, and a freedom to make them. Still, she rose daily with many unanswered questions. How, what, and when?

Vanessa scooped the muffin batter into the large sized muffin tins. Excited to see how her combinations would be received, one was a raspberry blend with crushed pine nuts, then a blueberry white chocolate one with sugared orange zest on top and a bran muffin with walnuts and dried cranberries for the health nuts. She loved that she could mix things up, and had a great big kitchen to express herself in.

It was almost time to go back to school and she felt like she found the most perfect place for her. She'd work weekends to stay here, nothing could make her leave. Finding the Java Joint and its wide variety of customers and co-workers gave more support to her own exploration and so much more. She'd been given a chance to shine here. To be whoever felt right.

~

RAISING ME, 1970'S-1980'S

*M*y brother and my upbringing had been very relaxed. More emphasis was put on the creative side of who we were, or could become, than in actually getting things done, or being taught what it takes to be a grown up in any way. I had terrible grades, lack of motivation, I was a daydreamer.

When high school came around, many of my friends excelled all around me. They had buckled down and taken school seriously, and were planning their next adventure, college. They were internally driven somehow. Some of their parents paid them to keep their grades up for this last bout, keeping them motivated through their high school years, or so they would qualify for scholarships. I sat in awe of my friends that already knew how they wanted to spend their working lives. A teacher, an architect, a dentist. They knew.

Extra money was scarce at our house, so cash didn't flow my way for grades or anything else. It most likely wouldn't have worked for me anyway. Any motivation to do better in school would have to come from the inside, and I didn't have it. I knew there was no money for college if I did get in, so I didn't really try. Not that I had any clue what I'd study if I did get in.

I set three goals as I neared graduation, six months prior. One, graduate however I could. I stacked up some more counseling office assistant credits, skipping my usual break during the day, or I wasn't going to make it. Two, I wanted to get detention to say to my kids someday that their mother was no good two shoes. I accomplished that by first asking my Art teacher to give it to me, which he obliged in a charitable way, then two I got it for real going off campus one day to McDonalds with a friend, being caught as we returned to campus. So on that count I did better than I needed to. Third, I wanted to letter in something before I left, having not played any sports in all my years there, and not being particularly great at any of them anyway, I signed up to be a scorekeeper for the girl's Varsity softball team, it was pretty easy as I liked to watch and could follow it since my boyfriend at the time was a baseball *player, I was used to keeping track of the game. I managed to achieve all of these with my G.P.A. maxing out a 1.3, pathetic but I graduated.*

My interests wandered so much, between art, writing, decorating and children. I loved spending time with kids. Their childlike wonder was similar to my own that I had managed to keep alive despite my age. Littles are easy, in total awe of a spider building a web or how wonderful it was to find a salamander under a rock. I never stopped crouching down to view a water skipper glide atop the stream, or stopped smelling the different colored roses to learn each scent.

I had bopped from one retail job to another until answering an ad for a nanny position in my hometown. Two kids, a boy and a girl. Instantly hitting it off with the mom after realizing we had both been "Bluebirds," as youngsters, I was hired and spent four years helping raise those kids and watching them grow. All very good practice for being a mom someday.

Being a mom was and is the best job I've ever had, and as it turns out, one of the only things I was good at.

~

1

V's shift ended and the whole team came together for their company meeting. Knarly and V had made up giant handmade pizzas, with all sorts of toppings, cutting them into large squares instead of the usual triangles. All the staff was there, even the people that had the day off.

After they ate, Jerry handed out handmade awards to each of the staff, to show his appreciation for all they did at the Java Joint.

V waited patiently for her name to be called.

"And last but not least, for V, we have this, our hardest worker award." Jerry read the inscription aloud. "A rock because you work hard. A geode because there is so much more to you underneath the surface. We love you V."

Jerry handed V the award, as everyone else looked on and applauded. Some whooped and whistled. V took the award and felt the force of the love and sentiment of the piece.

It was a beautiful purple geode, split in half and mounted onto a stunning but imperfect wood plaque. V was used instead of her full name, and the date of when she started at the Java Joint was also etched onto the plate.

V cried. She hadn't felt such love and acceptance in her whole life. These people, people she hadn't known a year ago, were now so important to her that she couldn't imagine being anywhere else. With the love in the room, she felt brave enough to share something that had been pulling at her. From the moment she woke up in the morning until she fell asleep each night, the voice told her over and over, she could do it, she was safe. Now was the perfect time.

Since this was the place where big things had come into focus for V, it felt right to share the news with all of them first. Things could start happening now.

Through the tears, V smiled and said there was something she wanted to share. Everyone held hands and listened. V explained that she wanted to now be referred to as a he, and that this would be the beginning of the transition to living life as a male.

"While I haven't figured everything out yet, I am so grateful to have you all as friends, uh, family. I am so happy to be in this space and time with you."

V and his co-workers hugged as they started to pack up for the night. It was going to be a very early morning for some, as the cafe opened at five.

V grabbed the trophy and pulled his coat off the hook to leave, remembering the book that was left behind. He glanced down under the counter to see if it was still there. It was. He grabbed it and put it into his satchel to read when he got home or maybe on the way home.

"Do you need a ride?" Knarly asked, holding the door open for V.

"No, I'm ok, there are still a few more trolleys to catch before they shut down."

They walked out together.

V would see just how progressive his parents, Jim, and Maura Langley, claimed to be. With this announcement at work, he would need to finally share with his parents his thoughts, feelings and about how it had all started for him.

Dad was out of town, and V was happy to get to spend some one-on-one time with just Mom. He could try her first, and they could talk about how to help Dad understand. Mom seemed to be more open to the alternate lifestyles, at least she was when V had shared a romantic interest in girls instead of boys.

V remembered her response. "I don't ever want you to question that you are loved. I love you, and I accept you no matter what. Your father may take a little time to come around to different things, as a lot of this is foreign to him. Being born into a strict Catholic family, you know. I will be your quarterback with him. You are on your own journey in figuring all this out, and I imagine so many things are confusing. I am on your team."

He climbed onto the trolley and walked to the back of the car. Most of the seats were empty and there was plenty of room to spread out, so V put his feet up on the seat next to him.

He took the blue book out of his knapsack and read the title.

Find me, Book One.

He read the first entry. An invitation to join in on a mission for the sake of proving that people are all connected somehow, and that we all have the power to change lives. The idea made him warm. He felt that. It was true. The person who took him to the Java Joint had helped him find his extra family, accidentally giving him the courage to venture deeper into who he wanted to be. Layla's presence had made a huge difference in his life, even though she wasn't a permanent fixture anymore.

V read along, looking up every few blocks to see if they were close to his stop. In the book, he saw a few similarities between his and the author's life, but not many. He knew he didn't have any actual connection that might help the author get her book back. It seemed to be written by a woman, who was probably much older than he was. Maybe his mom could help?

With the rumblings of the long day finally taking hold, his vision blurred, and he thought about how he might broach the subject of his new life plan with his parents. One where he may eventually consider having a full sex change operation.

He keyed back into the book two stops before home. Even though the book wasn't a life changer for him, it was at least a good reminder that everyone has their own path, and you never know what direction life can lead you. He could tell that the author was attempting to do a very big thing. Kind of like he was. Different, but still big, nonetheless.

Yes, V would share it with his mom. He read the last page just as the trolley stopped at the Turney St. station. He put the book back in his knapsack and got off, walking the two blocks home under the dimmed streetlights. His Mom opened the door just as he slid in his key.

"Good, great, you're home. Honey, your dad had an accident. I need to fly to Denver; can you stay home by yourself for a few days?" She was shaken.

"Yes, geez, is he ok? Are you ok?"

"Yes, I think, I mean, I hope so, he fell down some stairs at the conference. Luckily it was only a few stairs, close to the bottom, and not a whole flight. But he tumbled hard and hit his head on the banister on the way down. I spoke with the Dr. at the hospital and your dad has a bad concussion. They won't let him fly home by himself, and they want to keep him there for a few days to watch him. I went shopping earlier and there is a ton of food in the house, things you can warm up from the freezer."

"Yeah, Mom, I will be ok. You need to go be with Dad. I can drive you to the airport."

V was bummed that he wouldn't be able to talk to Mom about his decision to start making changes in his life, but Dad needed her right now. He hoped he was ok.

It wasn't the right time, V'd waited this long, what was another few days. He showed his mom his work trophy and she squeezed him tight.

"That is so perfect, and so true," she said after reading the inscription on the front. "I am so happy you have these wonderful friends."

V sat on his mom's bed as she packed. When she wasn't looking, V slipped the traveling book into her suitcase, under some of her blouses. It would give her something to read, in between appointments with Dad. V was worried about him too.

The flight was in three hours, so they had a little bit of time to get to the airport.

Before getting out of the car at the departure gate, Maura leaned over for a hug, and said, "Honey, I was really looking forward to spending some time together, just us. I'm sorry we won't have that time right now. Here are some things to keep you busy, til I'm back."

Maura reached in the backseat and placed a colorful box on V's lap. Inside was a rainbow adorned journal and a few books she'd found to read about being gay and stories of other people who experienced feeling different than their bodies.

"I need you to tell me if you are ever in a place where you are considering hurting yourself. Honey, there is nothing wrong with you. You may just need to work through some extra things that other people don't have to. You can do anything, and I am fully here for you. If there are any thoughts you want to share with me, please do. Also if you want to start working with a counselor at the health center, too, just say so. We will get that scheduled."

"Wow. Thanks Mom."

"I love you, kiddo."

"I love you too, Mom. Safe trip."

Tears filled both of their eyes and they hugged again. V didn't have to worry about things alone anymore. It was nice to hear that mom was on his team. While he hadn't determined all of his next steps, just deciding would mean more conversations with Mom, Dad and a counselor to help plan the way. This was a good start.

This alone time would give him some space to really think about what initial steps he wanted to take, in starting his new life. And thanks to Mom, he had some reading to do.

Dad's health was the priority right this second, and Mom needed to be there for him. As Maura entered the turnstile at the airport, she waved at her child and blew him a kiss.

V waved and honked pulling away from the entrance, feeling lucky to have such a cool and accepting mom.

~

1

MAURA

Maura Langley arrived at the Denver airport and grabbed a cab straight to the hospital at the terminal. It had been about eight hours since she found out about Jim's accident. A taxi dropped her off out front. Pulling her luggage behind her she walked to the information station to find out that her husband was on the fourth floor. In the elevator, a man with a cast on his arm bumped into her, obviously not knowing how far his arm stuck out.

"Excuse me. I'm sorry," he said, before getting out on the third floor.

"Not to worry," she said, right before the doors closed behind him.

Walking directly to the nurse's station, Maura waited for the nurse to be off the phone.

"Hello, Jim Langley, can you tell me where to find him?"

"Yes, he's in getting an MRI right now, but he will be back within a half an hour or so. You can wait in his room if you like. Room 432."

"Thank you."

Maura looked up to see numbers and arrows showing the direction to his room. She found it down the hall to the left, stowed her suitcase in the closet and sat down to wait for Jim. She let V know that she had arrived at the hospital.

Jim was rolled back into the room on a bed, flanked by two nurses. He looked to be asleep. A doctor came in right after and asked to speak with her outside in the hallway.

"Mrs. Langley, we have reason to believe that your husband suffered a minor stroke, and that might have led to him falling down the stairs. Yes, he has a concussion too, but we also saw some bleeding in the brain, in his first scan. We have just done another MRI to see if we can tell if there is more damage or if we need to address anything else. We will know soon."

"Is he asleep?"

"Yes, we sedated him for the procedure to keep him still, and we have him on some blood thinners. We want him to stay here for a few days, to see if things resolve, and to monitor his cognitive skills. He is in good hands here; this is what we do. He picked a perfect city to have a neurological incident in." The doctor smiled then, and Maura smiled back.

"Thank you, Doctor."

Maura sat and watched her husband sleep for a while, texting V with the update, even though she wasn't sure she'd get a response this late.

Surprisingly, V did respond and sent love and hugs to them both.

'It's a little weird to be here without you and Dad, but it's probably what college will feel like,' she texted back.

"Good Lord, how are we to that time in our lives?' Maura asked

'Hey Mom, I put something in your suitcase, when you weren't looking. If Dad is knocked out, you might as well take a look? It's under your button up pink and white striped oxford.'

Maura responded "You sneak!"

They said good night and Maura promised another update when she had more to tell.

Maura pulled her luggage out of the closet and turned it sideways to lay it on the floor. She unzipped it slowly so as not to make a lot of noise. She didn't want to wake her husband. She shuffled the clothes around finding the pink and white top and reaching underneath. She pulled it free. She hadn't a clue it was there. She zipped the case back up quietly and rolled it over by the door, out of the way.

Maura retrieved her reading glasses out of her purse and moved over by the window to an upholstered like hide-a-bed, set up for visitors. On the wall was a switch for a small, focused reading light above her head. She flipped it on. The rest of the room remained dark, and she could just stay over, if she wanted. She wanted to be the first person Jim saw when he woke again. She squinted to read the title, as she needed to upgrade her readers, but had forgotten. Her eyes adjusted as she turned to the first page, and she read at a good pace, for the next hour and a half as Jim slept.

It was a wonder that this book had come into her little family with such tiny odds. Only five copies in all of the United States or world, and here it was in her hands right now. She continued to read, understanding the mission of the author, wishing that she would relate so intently to one of the stories herself to be able to hand deliver it back to the author. Even with the fairly common themes throughout, it was a loving reminder that a moment can mean so much, and we should be grateful for the people in our lives.

Maura signed her name under her daughter's name and put the book back on top of her suitcase to put away later. Pulling a pillow and blanket out of the closet, she lay down on the window seat bed. She closed her eyes. The beeping of the machines nearby lulled her. Even the rhythmical punctuation of the blood pressure cuff going off every fifteen minutes felt restful. Maura was ready for sleep, it had been a long day.

A tear squeezed from her eye. For her husband being in such good hands, for the love of her child at home. She was thankful that both were safe and no matter what was to come, she knew they would tackle it like a family. A few more grateful tears came, and she wiped them onto her sleeve. Even though the plans had changed, and her time with V cut short, Maura knew that out of the three of them, she and V were most ready for the path to come.

The accident might have pressed pause on the process, but maybe it was what was needed. To get Jim closer to understanding. Faced with his own mortality; and gifted with his own second chance, maybe this was exactly the bridge needed to bring him around to a more accepting stance?

Maura turned over to look out the window. Cones from the street lights fell below the tree line, the tall buildings windows reflected the moonlight.

Everyone she loved was taken care of at the moment. Jim, here under supervised care. Vanessa was in good spirits when she left, surrounded by friends. Happy. Purposeful.

Her, or Him.

Maura's daughter may become a son one day. No matter what, Maura wanted her child happy, and living exactly as they wanted. Jim had always wanted a son, maybe he would come around to accepting one a little bit later than usual? This time away would give them all some space to think about what changes were coming, together.

~

CHILDHOOD MEMORIES ME 1978-87

I honestly can't remember the majority of my childhood. I wonder, really, if anyone can, or if we all just patch together a history based on the photos that we see, mixed with the blurbs we hear from the older people who were present in our lives?

Flashes hit me now and again but some events stick out more than others.

My first memory of sitting with my great grandmother on a porch somewhere. An old woman sitting in a rocking chair with a smile. She held a little wooden box outfitted with a trap door close to a slot. When a penny was placed into the slot, a little hand would come out and grab the penny. It was a softer memory, as if I was watching a scene in a movie. It's so weird that I carried that early moment with me, for so long. When I asked my mother about that bank twenty or so years later, she was surprised.

"Yes. Wow, you must have been only about two years old."

I would have loved to have that tricky bank, for my own daughters. When Mom asked her sister if she had seen it in their mother's belongings, alas, it was gone forever from the family. It left enough of an imprint that I wanted to have a physical reminder of it, so once the internet came to be, I went looking for a bank like that. Eventually, I found one, but it was black plastic which wasn't nearly as romantic as the one in my vision, but I bought it anyway, out of pure nostalgia. I pull it out when I have little people in the house, and they are as enchanted as I was.

Then I have a few silly memories of completely random things, like singing, "Tiptoe through the tulips," the Tiny Tim song while doing my best to mimic his voice while dancing atop my tulip patterned sleeping bag at a friend's house for a sleepover. Sleeping over at other people's houses was difficult for me, and often I would go home in the night.

I remember always thinking about things and having to work to fall asleep.

I eventually taught myself this technique. I lie flat on my back in bed. Start-ing at my feet, I imagined my body parts turning into gingerbread shaped appendages, oozing down into a soft curve that melted into the mattress. I continued to imagine the rest of my body parts seeping that way, finally ending with my head. I used this technique into adulthood, and although it only works some of the time, I'm usually closer to snoozing. I also like to rub my feet together when I get into bed, which can be awkward with a lover if they are new. I've always found weird ways to be, and rarely speak my total mind, especially in groups. Unless they know me and love me already.

It was mostly the injuries or the oddities I went through that commanded my full attention enough to remember those early days.

After the divorce, we lived with Mom in an old house with a very ivied over backyard. It was a wonderland for my fantasy world, and I loved it there. One of the drawbacks of such a wooded area was we were always battling flea infestations in the yard as well as the house. We would have to bug bomb the house and leave until the poison cleared. Mom at least made it fun by taking us out for ice cream or something, along with whatever pets we had at the time. I don't remember my friends ever telling me of any 'bombings" at their house, but for us, it was a thrice yearly at least, occurrence.

One day, a flea went to school with me, climbing up from the rim of my socks, up my pant legs and into my shirt, eventually finding its way into one of my sweaty teenage armpits. It made it quite difficult to pay attention in social studies. It bounced around like a ball in a spinning bingo game cage, throughout the entire class, I imagine trying to catch a breath of fresh air. I held my arm down and sweated more, eventually turning bright red and excusing myself to go to the bathroom to get it out.

We never seemed to have clean clothes at home, and my long hair was cut short into a Dorothy Hamill cut at seven. It was fast to take care of, and my mom wouldn't have to listen to me cry when she tried to brush out the tangles. But I hated the cut. I was the only girl in school with short hair and was often teased that I looked like a boy.

Another injury I experienced was when I was at the neighbor's house jumping on their trampoline. (No netting around it, Hello it was the 70's!) I fell headfirst into the springs, slicing a gash in my head. I stood up, blood running down my face. The boy jumping with me was a year or two younger and I remember the fear on his face. Soon after, my next recollection was of me being strapped down to a strait jacket-board at the pediatrician's office when I wouldn't calm down for my stitches. I thought they were going to stick a needle into my brain! Maybe they were talking to me, and telling me I would be ok, but I don't remember any of that, only of being afraid and watching my mom stand by and letting it all happen. Those were not even close to being my only stitches.

Our dog Foxy bit me one day as I walked home from school, probably because she was so excited, but she was gone soon after, I don't know where, Mom would never say.

Being struck by a VW bug, as I ran across the street. It was driven by a new to driving sixteen-year-old neighbor. I remember seeing the car coming down the hill, but I believed I was so fast that I could run across before the car could get to me. Wrong. Luckily, I smashed into the side of the car instead of being under it. Another trip to the Dr. and I came home in a full trunk, body cast, for a broken collar bone and I missed months of school. It was itchy underneath and I'd shove pencils down to reach the itch, often losing them once inside. I did not miss being at school, and I cannot remember anyone coming to see me at home, so I guess no one missed me either. I loved being home, lying on the couch watching cartoons. That is all I remember about aged six to eight years old.

While many of those moments seemed small, and meaningless in the scheme of things, they have stayed with me as some of the only memorable blips.

I think the actual recording of my history started with the announcement of my parents' divorce. It was quite a shock, as I never saw them fight. They sat me down on the couch, and very seriously, told me that they were splitting up. I was nine. None of my friends had divorced parents. I was going to be the freak of my circle.

My brother was only four or five. He didn't really know what was going on at the time, and in fact I can't really remember him even being there for the talk. Maybe he wasn't.

After the talk, I ran dramatically from the house, and jumped on my flower covered, banana-seated, yellow Schwinn. Riding around our circle over and over the streamers on my handlebars yellow streaked along with me. Around and around, I rode until I fell in exhaustion. Tears streaming down my face the whole time.

Then came the years of back and forth, never feeling like I belonged anywhere. Having most of my clothes at one house, always making do at the other.

Weekends with Dad and watching the People's Court with Judge Wapner on Wednesday nights when we went over for dinner. TV trays, Hamburger helper in the flavor of the week. Dinty Moore stew.

Dad made a fun bedroom for my brother and I to share in the apartment but sharing a room with your younger brother wasn't ideal, as I was developing and craved privacy. We had bunk beds, and so many toys and games we could barely walk around the room. No doubt, guilt gifts.

He did the best he could, I'm sure. We were given many things by my dad, maybe it was because, for my father, gifts meant love. His own father had showered him throughout his life with the best of everything from new cars, expensive furniture, really anything he wanted. Money flowed into his household when he was young, as the family had multiple rental properties and a house flipping business. Maybe that is why I wanted to flip houses later in my life too.

Dad filled the walls of his apartment with fancy car posters, Lamborghini's, Ferrari's, you name it. Car magazines were scattered all over the coffee table and hung out in the bathroom. He and my brother spent hours building automobile models, and we'd go to the yearly car shows. If I didn't learn my way around cars, I was never going to have anything to say around there, so I learned about cars. I could name most of them based on looks, or their insignias. I still know my cars.

The separate holidays, our parents dating other people. Sometimes the other person would have kids. From time to time the other kids were cool, most often not.

Over the years the constant split of time started to wear on me. I grew so angry at my dad for leaving us, I stopped going over to his house. He was sad, but didn't know what to do, and he never pushed me.

Finally, Mom sat me down and asked me why I didn't want to see my dad anymore.

In my best grasp of the situation at age twelve, I explained that he had left us, and wrecked our family. He'd torn our lives apart and made everything harder for all of us. I had been silently blaming him for all of it.

I was glad that my mom was honest with me, just then. Choosing to tell me the hard truth. That she had asked him to leave. She couldn't stay married to him anymore.

It was my dad who had been willing to do whatever it took, to keep our family intact. With that I forgave Dad and we have remained close for most of my life.

It was then that I figured out there were at least three sides to a story. Hers, his and the truth that lies somewhere in between.

~

1

Maura woke to a stream of sunlight, warm on her face through the hospital window. She squinted, and turned over to take in her surroundings, remembering where she was. She quietly looked over at Jim. He was still sleeping. He'd been through a lot. She would let him sleep, for at least a little while longer. It promised to be a busy day full of more tests and physical therapy appointments, he would need all the energy he could muster.

Maura hadn't spent the night in a hospital, in almost eighteen years. She'd had many overnights with the many fertility treatments, and then the night after Vanessa was born.

The hospital was both a sad and a happy place for her. Sad for watching her parents each lose their battles with cancer. Watching them become wisps of their former selves. Sad remembering the hopeless days and nights with the many attempts to have a child. Oh so happy when she finally arrived.

Born on a Saturday, in the middle of a rainstorm, Vanessa took center stage as soon as she arrived. So wanted, and fought for. She was the happy result of their many attempts. They had started trying to conceive when they were thirty, thinking they would have plenty of time. Years of tests later, a diagnosis of endometriosis made everything make sense. A specialist suggested to try an endometrial scratching procedure to increase her chances of an embryo implanting in her uterus. Thankfully, it worked the first time, and Maura became pregnant.

After finding out the pregnancy was viable, they didn't waste a minute. There were many joyous months spent getting ready for the baby's arrival. A beautifully decorated nursery tinted in the sweetest pinks and yellows after they'd found out the baby's sex via amniocentesis.

Maura had been so nervous about doing the test, but because she was over thirty five, the doctor's suggested it. They wanted to see if the baby had any issues, not because they would necessarily choose a different outcome, it was more to be able to prepare themselves if need be.

Vanessa came into the world, absolutely perfect. Kicking and screaming, her lungs were strong. The curly blonde hair that grew in around eighteen months, whispered back to Maura's Norwegian heritage. Facial features also grew in akin to Maura's mother who died just shy of Maura's thirtieth birthday. Maura was often sad that neither of her parents had been able to meet their only grandchild.

Bringing her home for the first time, they were touched to find a massive stork wooden figure stuck into their front yard. All the neighbors had gotten together to rent it. Balloons and happy faces were there as they pulled into the driveway. The Langley's settled blissfully into their little family unit.

Maura heard an ahem from across the room and looked over to see Jim watching her. He winked and she winked back, before getting up to sit with him. She had stayed all night.

"Howdy stranger," she planted a kiss on his lips.

"Hi yourself. I hope that bed was reasonably comfortable."

"Not bad, it was ok, yeah, it wasn't the best. But I am glad to be here with you now. You gave us a scare."

"I know, I'm sorry, I'm still not sure what happened. One minute I was talking business with a new potential client, the next, I'm here with people buzzing all around, tubes sticking out of me. Thanks for coming so quickly."

"Of course. Vanessa is using this time to pretend she is away from us at college, we may just come home to a messy party house, who knows?"

Maura climbed up onto the bed and snuggled into Jim's arms.

"Don't you do anything like that again, ok, the three of us is all I have."

"I'll try. How's Vanessa, I know you two were planning on some nice mother, daughter time."

"Yeah, we can talk about that later. I was remembering when she was born. How we waited so long for her to get to us, we'd almost given up."

"Yeah. Life ran us a bit ragged on that one, for sure."

They both closed their eyes and sat in the stillness of the now. There was a knock on the door and a nurse walked in.

"Good morning, Mrs. Langley. I'm Mike, your husband's day nurse. I am going to check his vitals real quick, then help him into the shower. He has an occupational therapy appointment in an hour and he still needs to eat breakfast. You are more than welcome to stay here, or if you want, you could go and get some breakfast downstairs. I'll bring him back once he's through with the occupational and physical therapists. Sometime around lunchtime. I'm here if he needs anything. I think the doctor expects some test results later on this morning."

"Thanks Mike, maybe I will go and check in at the hotel and get cleaned up a bit. I'll be back in a few hours."

Maura leaned over Jim and kissed him on the cheek. "I'll see you in a bit, honey, not long at all. You look good! I'm so happy you are okay and in good hands."

"Thanks for being here, I am feeling better. I have been treated very well here, hopefully today we will figure out a plan. Love you."

"Love you."

~

1

Maura rolled her bag out into the hall and looked around to get her bearings. She pushed the elevator button to go down to the lobby and asked the woman at the info desk to call her a cab. While she waited, she'd grab some breakfast food to keep her going. Maura walked down the long hallway and scurried into the cafeteria line.

Taking a muffin off the counter turnstile, she poured a cup of coffee at the self serve station. She held her tray in one hand and pulled her suitcase with the other delicately balancing things until she could find a spot to sit. She picked a table close to the cream counter, to keep her eye on her bag as she fixed her coffee up, just so.

The coffee didn't taste great, but it was as warm and familiar as she could get. She took a bite of the chocolate muffin, crunching the large sugar crystals on top. She never ate this way, but calories were good. She hadn't eaten for a good fifteen hours.

She sat daydreaming about how their little family had evolved over the last seventeen years.

With Jim finding success with his seminar circuit, Maura and Vanessa were often on their own. Working part time at the arts center, she was allowed to bring her young daughter most days. Little Vanessa grew up playing. Learning to walk in the aisles of art shows, dancing backstage to the many performances, they were surrounded by all sorts of people, hell bent to celebrate their talents and creativity.

From an early age, Vanessa picked out her own clothes. She'd mix colors and have wild hairstyles too. Sometimes she just lucked into the style after a nap, other times she would ask for the foam curlers her mom kept around for special occasions.

In middle school, Vanessa auditioned to play a street urchin in Oliver Twist, eventually being handed the lead role. She stole the show with her performance of the young boy who wanted, "More."

At thirteen, Jim was offered a contract position to take over a leadership team of a company based just outside of Tokyo, Japan. It was an incredible opportunity, and while the company wined and dined them in Tokyo, Vanessa stayed back with a friend of the family, sharing a room with all of their kids. It was as close to having siblings as Vanessa would ever get.

The couple decided that the opportunity was too good to pass up, and they packed up their home, putting everything in storage, and flew across the world. Saitama, Japan welcomed them in, they were all excited to live and explore their new home together.

Maura swiftly got to know the train system. She was quick to teach Vanessa how to navigate back home in case they ever got separated by accident stepping on or off the train.

Arriving there at the end of July was perfect to get situated and give Vanessa some time to acclimate to the culture before school started up in early September.

Mother and daughter spent their first few weeks exploring Saitama's Museum of Modern art, the ancient buildings in the Edo warehouse district, and seeking out the many botanical gardens in the area to give their eyes a break from the concentrated gray, city blocks.

A favorite became the Kyū-Furukawa Gardens with its western styled stone manor overlooking a formal English royalty rose garden that spilled quickly down the hill to the beginnings of a traditional, Japanese garden. Sitting by the beautiful pond surrounded by stones, and low-lying plants, they enjoyed the sculpted shapes of the Mugu pine trees that had been pruned into perfection over many years.

She and Vanessa would spend hours walking the pathways there, weaving in and out of the garden rooms, stumbling into new little pockets of heaven. It was as if The Seven lucky Gods of Shinto had hand placed each stone or plant just so, to make it perfect, yet keeping it imperfectly natural as well.

On their outings Maura and Vanessa would often sit down on the little benches at the numerous viewpoints taking in each carefully chosen scene from that part of the garden. The cityscape; always, in the background. Moments of calm in the busy city. It was such a beautiful place to explore with her daughter.

For Vanessa's fourteenth birthday, Maura took her to participate in a tea house ceremony in the Chashitsu hut. They bowed as they entered, not only for custom but also for the low height. The doorways; small to encourage humility and calm. They sat on simple grass woven mats and drank matcha. A powerful aromatic green tea served in handmade ceramic bowls. Little sweeties made into flowers were a beautiful accent, and delicious.

Those three amazing years in Japan had flown by, and suddenly they were all back in the states again, and Jim was in the hospital.

Maura's name was called over the intercom system, and she put the coffee cup and muffin wrapper into the garbage before heading back to the hospital entrance to catch her cab.

On the ride to the hotel, she texted Vanessa, to let her know that they had done some more tests on Dad, and they should have more info, sometime today.

V texted back, 'Ok mom, I am going into work, I will text you when I get home, maybe we can do a phone call later. Love you. Tell Dad I love him too.'

Maura put the key card in the door lock of her room and put her luggage on the bed. She crossed the room and put her purse on the desk. She needed a shower.

She went into the bathroom to see if there was a fan to turn on, but she couldn't find one. Hopefully it was automatic. She pulled the spigot out, tuning it to a hot warm temperature, before pulling up the plunger to activate the shower head. She had been burned too many times trusting someone else's adjustment.

She pulled off her shirt and jeans and tossed them to the ground in the corner before stepping inside. She stood and wedged the curtain into the corners so the fabric sheath wouldn't chase her body around the whole time. Maura hadn't had a shower curtain for years, she preferred glass shower doors to the insanely clingy curtains, any day.

She wet her hair under the paltry water pressure and squeezed some shampoo from the little bottle into her hands. No suds. Nuts, conditioner. She applied the other one. Closing her eyes, she felt the bubbles doing their job and wished that someone in the hotel industry would just put decent sized writing on these micro bottles they offer, or better yet; just a big S for shampoo with a big C for conditioner. Who really cared about the brand? Just make it easy. Geez.

Her hair did not typically respond well to softened water and she could tell it was going to be that kind of day.

Maura rarely felt clean when she traveled, strange beds, questionable cleaning practices. How often did they really change the bed skirts or shampoo the carpets? It was anyone's guess. Even the chairs were suspicious.

Washing her body with the hotel bar soap, she wished she had remembered to bring a razor, and some of those other niceties from home. Packing so quickly, a few items were skipped. Away from home, she would often end up with frizzy hair, no matter what products she tried. She always packed some hair accessories to cover up the problem.

She closed her eyes, letting the water rinse out the conditioner, while wondering how long she would be here, in Denver.

The doctor seemed positive last night, and Maura tried to keep herself from thinking the worst about Jim's condition. He seemed pretty much himself this morning when they were talking in the room.

Twenty six years. It was hard to believe it had been that long.

She turned off the water and grabbed a towel off the bar, wrapping it part way around her. Hotel towels were so small. Maura always kept everyone in bath sheets at home. She had her preferences, only compromised on while traveling. Each inconvenience, the softened water, the smaller towels, the gigantic bulbous pillows that were on every hotel bed she had ever slept in, wore on her and she sighed. She missed being home.

She wrapped her hair in another towel and went to pull an outfit out of her suitcase. A few articles of clothing and the family album she'd brought with her, fell to the floor causing her to flinch, which invited the larger towel to fall to the floor with them. She didn't bother trying to catch the towel or tuck it back in to stay on.

"Screw it." she muttered. She picked up the album and placed it on the bed to look at, before going back to Jim.

Maura settled on a pair of blue jeans with the pink and white oxford shirt, that Vanessa had placed the hidden book under. An oversized dark gray wool cardigan would help keep her warm from the Denver morning nip in the air.

Back in the bathroom, she wiped a towel across the steamed-up mirror.

"No fan."

Using the blow dryer to make a circle for her to see herself, she dried her bangs brushing them down so they wouldn't naturally twirl. She bundled up the rest of her hair into a banana clip and applied a little makeup. Softer hues to be casual.

"As good as it's going to get," she said, taking one last look at herself. She opened the closet and removed a bag holding a blanket, that the hotel kept for their chillier residents, she threw it over one of the chairs and sat down to look through the album.

It was the album she'd made for Vanessa. The one she had hoped to give her for her eighteenth birthday. The story of where she came from.

Pictures of her and Jim's parents, and of the two of them while away at college together in Ontario. The photos were a bit grainy but she could still see Jim's *cute as a button dimples* in all the pictures. She was struck with the casual hairstyle she had back in the day.

They had met in an art appreciation class. It was required for him and he had never been interested in art. She was happy to share her knowledge, especially about her favorites, Cezanne and Gauguin.

She was working towards her university diploma in Art History, and he was almost finished with his BBA. A typical business student. Driven. Focused. A real promoter.

For her planned trip to the Royal Ontario Museum for a class project, she asked him to go along. She could tell he was out of his element, walking the halls. He'd never seen anything like the many pieces of art from all over the world. The fact that he seemed to enjoy himself, told her that he was more cultured than most of the business students she had met.

In their senior year, after spending almost most of their sophomore and junior year attached, they took road trips to meet each other's parents. Things were getting serious. The photos in this section were some of Jim and some of her, but rarely any of them together. They hadn't stopped long enough to ask a stranger.

After they met each sets of parents, they moved in together for the latter part of their senior year, off campus in a little apartment. They didn't tell their families about shacking up until much later, and frugally picked up furniture around town. Garage sales, estate sales, each weekend was an adventure. Some of the pieces were pretty much junk, and some others, they still had. All ones they had fixed up together, stripping, re-staining or painting to suit their combined style.

It was fun to play house and they considered themselves compatible. Compatible in a comfortable and respectful way, while at the same time, they shared a nice spicy rapport in the bedroom as well.

They just fit. She smiled at the thought.

After graduation they took off for a trip to explore Europe together, with monies given to them by their families. They toured France seeing all of the beautiful cathedrals and the Louvre, taking the boat to spend some time in Greece along the water before coming home to start their working careers.

It was in Greece that Jim popped the question. He had picked up a ring in one of those junk shops back home over a year ago, paying close attention to when Maura said she had liked it. As Maura walked off to look at something else, he had the counter person put it on hold for him, until he could come pick it up without her.

"Maura, I love you, will you be my wife? I know the ring is not much, and I do hope to buy you a really expensive ring someday, but for now, could this be a placeholder?"

It never was replaced. That ring and the one she gave him from the very same store were still on their fingers today. There were a few photos of their wedding, and a few more with her pregnant. Finally the page where Vanessa arrived.

Sweet photos of Vanessa running into her father's arms when they'd meet him at the airport. The two of them sitting on the couch reading a story. So many happy memories.

She knew her husband was a loving and supportive man. She'd seen him so sullen and vulnerable when his parent's perished in a plane crash, and when her parent's had been sick. The soft caring hold he had on her, every time the pregnancy stick showed no baby. They knew they only had a little while longer with Vanessa, then their pack of three would be two again, it would be another opportunity for them to discover the new people they'd become.

The album didn't seem to fit as a gift any longer. They would keep it for them. Maybe a better gift would be two supportive and caring parents, who accepted their child as is? That would be the best gift of all.

She knew Jim was stressed about the talk of Vanessa becoming a man. He just didn't understand it.

"It's just such a big decision," he'd shared later on, "What if she's wrong?"

Maura imagined a world where her child would be free of the judgement of others for the decisions and actions of taking care and living fully as the person inside. Maybe someday, that wish will come true. That one day, everyone will be free to walk the planet just as they are.

Maura called to the front desk to get a cab to come and pick her up. She had about a half an hour until it would come. She grabbed her purse and the album and walked down the corridor to the cab that was waiting for her.

~

1

Maura arrived back to the hospital and stood by Jim as the doctor spoke to them about Jim's condition and their next steps.

"When Jim arrived here, he had a noticeable slag to his face on the left side which made me concerned about stroke in addition to the fall he had taken. That has resolved but I wanted to run additional tests. He said he remembered feeling a little dizzy and out of it before the fall, so I believe Jim had what is called a transient ischemic attack. It is commonly called a mini stroke. These events are sometimes a precursor to a more serious stroke, so it is good to look at where we can improve things such as diet, exercise, and keeping his blood pressure under control. Often heredity can play a part."

Maura spoke, "Transient, does that mean it moved on, that he might not have lasting effects?"

"Basically, that's a good way to describe it. We did see where there was some inflammation, which shows there was a blockage, but it passed, the TIA made his balance poor while he was on the stairs, and that's most likely what led to his fall. We have him on some blood thinners and some anti-inflammatory drugs right now, we would like him to continue those until you get back to your doctor back home. They will then put him on a protocol and a plan for helping avoid any more episodes."

Jim held his wife's hand and looked into her eyes. "This is very good news." Maura smiled.

Their eyes welled with tears.

"I was so afraid I wouldn't be able to get back to you and Vanessa. I am so happy to have this as a warning sign to get back on a healthier track. I cannot imagine life not being fully there with you two. You are my whole world."

Maura blinked away relief filled tears. "Now what?" she asked the doctor. "What do we do from here?"

"I'd like Jim to stay one more night, so we can make sure his medicine is dialed in before he leaves the hospital. To make sure he is on his way to a full recovery from the concussion. I really don't think he is going to see any permanent damage from this. But be aware that you might still see some emotional changes, along with some memory loss. They should be short lived. Mention anything and everything to your doctor back home. Nothing is too unimportant to mention."

He handed them some pamphlets on TIA to read over.

The doctor paused on his way out of the room, "Oh, I don't want him flying right now. Ideally, we like people to wait at least two weeks after an episode, to avoid the pressurization changes. Any chance you two would consider a road trip to get home?"

Maura squeezed Jim's shoulder, "A road trip. Yes, it's been ages. Literally forever, since I've had you all to myself, and even longer since we have taken a road trip together. I can rent a car. Let's do it!"

The doctor smiled and left the room, they spent the rest of the afternoon thinking of places they could see on their way back to San Francisco.

They could ink out the drive and Maura would reserve a car. They brainstormed. Moab, Zion, Las Vegas, then driving up the California coast. It would be a great trip, and they'd have plenty of time to talk about Jim working on his health, and about how to come together and support their child.

Maura knew that Jim loved and wanted Vanessa to be happy, he just didn't understand. She would be the mouse in his ear reminding him of that goal each time he was having a hard time with the transition that was coming.

Maura climbed up into the hospital bed and lay next to Jim. They watched tv until they both fell asleep and when Mike brought dinner in for Jim, that evening, Maura took a cab to the airport to rent a car, also picking up a few maps for their travels to look at back at the hotel.

Sitting on the bed with the maps all around her, she felt so fortunate that Jim was all right, as things could have been so much worse. They were given a chance to be together, and time to get him healthy.

She picked up the book again, and thought a moment about its future before setting it back on the nightstand. 'Who would she give it to now?'

She checked in with Vanessa to see if she wanted it back, otherwise she would give it to the very nice day nurse Mike, who'd taken care of Jim at the hospital.

Maura liked Mike from the moment she met him. He was warm, upbeat, and caring. She could tell that he had a big heart and would be a good steward of the crazy adventure in book form. She was thankful Jim had spent some time with someone who might positively affect his rather strict perspective of people who lived alternative lifestyles. Perhaps her husband would now see that everyone deserves the ability to be happy, no matter who they love or how they want to live?

Mike was the perfect person to pass the book along to, hopefully one step closer to the owner.

She punched the massive pillow a few times before removing it from the pillowcase and throwing it onto the floor. She folded the rest of the towels that were clean in the bathroom into a rectangle and tucked the bunch into the pillowcase. Finally, she had a flatter pillow to sleep on. She set her alarm for seven, and lay down, feeling comfortable after mapping out the first leg of their trip.

She woke up to the buzz of her alarm. They had a big day ahead.

~

NOT GOOD ENOUGH, ME 1979-1998

*I*f I start to think back on the times in my life where I started to believe I wasn't good enough, a few imprints are attached to my father. Albeit completely unintentional by him, I'm sure.

When my parents divorced and my father started dating, it was back when some local newspaper rags offered a personals section. People would write about who they were and what they were looking for in someone to date, and it was printed in the paper. Once it was distributed, women, men, anyone, could read the blurbs and write to the people hoping to get to know them. My Dad wrote one, looking for a great love.

I remember the day when he showed me all the letters that he had received. He laid out a bunch of envelopes on the coffee table, and said, "This is how many women want to meet me." A huge stroke to his ego, I imagine it must have been.

Like in the Pina Colada song, his ad was a covert attempt to find someone, without having to put himself out there the old-fashioned way. It was a real thrill for him. He kept some of the letters for years. Pulling them out to look back at them, imagining the women pining for him.

In my view, he tossed the letters that came with no photo, as if they were non-existent, and got down to looking at the others. Each note, handwritten with effort, had actual photos enclosed, instead of copies, as computers were not yet widely used at home. He showed the photos to me, but not the letters as many potentially had inappropriate things in them, I was guessing. As I looked through the photos, making sure to keep them with their respective envelopes a pattern appeared in the women my father preferred.

All of the women that he would contact were blonde, blue eyed, tall, but not too tall, and slender. He told me as much in that action, that those women were the only type he was after and has confirmed that preference over and over throughout my life.

The brunettes and redheads were culled out without reading the message or considering who that person might be on the inside. It didn't matter if they shared interests, for this go round, he was going to get the Barbie doll he sought.

There is no way this view would have escaped any child, put in this position.

I was ten.

Dad preferred blondes. So, to me, blondes <u>must</u> be the most beautiful women. And I wasn't that. Not even close. I was short, brunette with hazel eyes. I was never going to be tall, and I was not, most likely going to be stick thin either.

And what did I do with that information as a ten year old child trying to figure out the world, and herself in it, you may ask?

Well, I internalized it right then, that if I was not a beauty, I must be the <u>anti-beauty</u>.

I spent many years and tons of energy avoiding being around blonde girls and women that were my father's type. All so I wouldn't be faced with feeling like a troll when I was around them.

It became a forced division of sorts between myself, and nearly half of the people I had access to be friends with. I kept to my own kind.

My people were the imperfects. Some were heavy or had a little extra. Crooked teeth, or oily hair. All had some visual flaw that helped me feel ok about myself.

And what's weird is, I couldn't see any flaws in the blonde, tall, blue eyed women, at all. Most likely because I wasn't close to them, to hear their complaints or insecurities but I just knew that they must have it all together, right? I put them all up on the pedestal of perfection and looked up at them as if they were the be-all-end-all based on looks alone.

This thinking stayed with me for YEARS!

It wasn't until I was an adult, and we moved in next door to a woman who I wouldn't have picked to be friends with, (based on my previous bias) and our kids loved each other, and our dogs loved each other, that I had to face this stupid fear of bringing these people into my life and learn to get over it.

That, and then I birthed one.

Our second daughter came, and I was so surprised at her looks. She was blonde with blue eyes that stayed blue. I couldn't avoid this type of person any longer. I mean, my parents were blonde when they were younger, but a blonde/blue was not what I was thinking my husband and I would get, with me a dark brunette and him a redhead.

She was and is amazing, and I have such a love for her, that it forced me to heal that part of myself that said I couldn't be friends with or around blonde women.

And my little daughter G has flaws, and feels, the same uncertainties and insecurities as we all do. No one gets away unscathed through life.

To some people, the idea of censoring out potential friends based on looks alone is stupid. To carry around a prejudice like that, is completely ridiculous in the first place. But I think my palpable age, mixed with not being sure of myself in general yet, helped brand an X on my psyche that became hard to shake, or even quantify until later in life.

No one is perfect and trying to be perfect or trying to look for some perfect person that you believe you will find, especially based on their looks is a very limiting take on humanity in general. His commitment to seek his perfect woman has kept my father quite alone in his post divorce life.

My father ignores his own flaws, believing that he should still have perfection in another despite his own imperfections. His benchmark of an appropriate age in a woman; also, does not move. He believes he should have someone close to my age or younger. In this, he continues to hold possible mates away, because they are not his ideal, while never acknowledging that he himself is a work in progress too.

And what's weird is, he totally owns being that shallow. Living with his choices. Dreaming of the ones that got away...

Sometimes he will jump back on a dating site to see who's out there, and he seems forced to tell me about it, like I am his little dating buddy. There to hear all about the ones who want him, or the ones who pop into his profile and wander about. Then he talks himself out of getting out there and doesn't respond to the women because to put himself out there, would mean that he must face and show his own vulnerability. He can't have the ones that are young and beautiful because that time has passed for him. So instead, he will have no one.

So alone he has been. And I have listened to him the whole time. He affirms his excuses for not trying or not giving someone less than his ideal a chance.

I have tried to tell him that no one is perfect, and the point of a relationship is to find someone who is imperfectly perfect for you. A person who can lift you up when you are down in the dumps, or someone that you can spend your time with. As the years go on, just having a wonderful companion to sit in the car with or go have a meal together could be the goal. There are so many ways to relate to someone, attraction and looks should be only one of the ways. Not all of it.

Inasmuch as I know as an adult, my father never intended for me to feel this way about myself, and he would be sad and sorry to know the friendships I've skipped and the lack of confidence I have carried because of it, it did happen.

It took a lot of unpacking and resolving that none of those feelings were about me at all. It was just some hang up or dream he had in his head, that ultimately was unrealistic and super isolating.

I wish he could see that it didn't have to be that way.

~

S.D.

We met in paradise. We were both nine years old. My parents had taken my brother and I on a once in a lifetime trip to Hawaii, apparently as a last ditch effort to be a family.

An entire month in the tropics. It was summer and the weather was incredible. My younger brother, my grandparents, my parents and I, all staying in a small house at the back of an ocean front property.

I don't remember the inside of the house per se, but we ate a lot of Top Ramen, and played cards when we weren't body surfing in the ocean just out front. As the weeks progressed, my skin baked to a fine cocoa color, while my brother, poor kid, burned over and over again.

There was a larger house on the property, closer to the water that another family had rented. It was yours. I cannot remember how long you were there.

I couldn't believe we were the same age, and how lucky it was that we could play together! I think you had a sibling too. But again, I wasn't paying attention to that.

We'd eat breakfast at our respective houses in the morning, meeting out at the beach soon after. We had boogie boards, and spent endless hours swimming out and coasting in on the waves. I found sand in areas of my body I hadn't even discovered yet.

Who knew that belly buttons could fill up with sand too?

We ate lunch together on your veranda sometimes and were fast friends. We said we would be friends forever. Pen pals. I think we both wrote maybe three letters before it stopped.

I have a few pictures of us together, in our twin swimsuits, a one piece with a drape and split front. We were so tan. It didn't show anything and gave us a little coverage for our rounded butts that had just appeared. At least mine was new to me. Before I paid attention and became ashamed of it.

I remember when your family was leaving, we were sad.

I could never forget your name, and could probably find you someday, if I tried, if you ever left a reference of your maiden name on anything.

But, I am not sure if you would remember me.

Your eyes were a ice light blue, and your longish hair a blonde cast over a darker golden underneath, you seemed at ease by the sea. Maybe your family came all the time?

Maybe your family stayed together, for your whole life, instead of like me, having it blow up and scatter?

Do you remember the time we were in the surf, and one of us turned around to see a tiny baby jellyfish swimming close to us. Talk about walking on water! We got out of there quick!

Our time together reminds me how easy it is for a child to make a friend. When we are small, vulnerable, and willing to say hi, and ask to play?

And that we tend to lose that quality as we get older. Sticking to the ones who are already close for another reason or wander in the same circles.

I wonder if your eyes shine as bright as they did back then. Breathtaking.

~

1

Maura walked out onto the hospital's fourth floor for the last time to pick up her husband. Jim had his breakfast, showered by himself, and was dressed and ready to go. They would need to go by his hotel on their way out of town, to pick up his luggage and laptop that had been left in the room from the accident. The kind people at the hotel had stored it for them, after hearing what happened. Jim was more than ready to go, and was already sitting in the wheelchair, holding his discharge papers when Maura arrived. Mike stood at the helm.

"I really hope you two have a great trip home," Mike said. "Sounds like a killer adventure."

"Me too," said Maura. "It's time we had some time together. Anything I need to know?"

"He has the paperwork that calls out the medicine and at what intervals. We already filled the prescriptions to have enough for about three weeks in case you take more time than you thought. I'm really happy you both get this happy ending, so many times I have seen people have a stroke and they are affected for months, years or for the rest of their life."

"We are lucky to have this second chance," said Jim, waving at all the other nurses, in the hall, as Mike wheeled him into the elevator.

"I'll miss you around here, we had some pretty good talks. I'm happy to have met you." said Mike.

"Yes, I feel lucky to have met you too, Mike. Good talks."

Maura went to fetch the car from the lot and pull around the front to get Jim. "I'll be back in a minute."

Mike and Jim stood waiting.

"So you think I should just try to listen to what my kid is going through. That I should imagine being in that position myself?"

"If you can. Your child is trying to stay in touch. You have been invited into a very confusing time for them. If they didn't love you and care about what you thought, they could easily keep you on the outside, and just go it alone. Many people do, they have to. Does it really matter to you what they look like on the outside, or who they love, if you can see the light of happiness and contentment coming from them? Could you just love them?"

"Vanessa is still trying to share with us. It's a gift, I know. She is my child. I have a lot of work to do. Talking with Maura will help me get around my thinking on the subject. The long held remnants of a religion, I no longer ascribe to, for other reasons, should not matter. Flawed thinking, judgements. This accident taught me that we are not promised anything in this life, and I want to be around. For her, or him, whoever they need to be."

Mike took out his wallet and showed Jim a photo of him and Jeffrey. It was the first time he had shown any part of his personal life to a patient. "Here is my someone special. I feel so fortunate to have found him. Love comes in all shapes and forms."

"Thanks Mike. I'll remember everything we talked about. I have some mending to do, on the other side. I mean, not many have a chance to have a daughter and a son in one lifetime with their only child? Could be fun having a son."

"That's a good way to look at it," Mike smiled.

Maura pulled out front and went to open the car door for Jim.

"Oh hey, Mike, I have something for you. It was something Vanessa gave me before I left home, and it needs a new home. Do you think you could help me?"

"Um, sure." said Mike, taking the book and tucking it under his arm to shake hands with them both.

"I'm always looking for something to read, thanks! You two take care of yourselves and each other, and that beautiful person back home that you made together. I have a good feeling about you all."

The Langley's drove off, waving out the window in their wake.

Mike was left with a smile, a deep satisfaction for a job well done, and a new book to read.

~

ME, WONDERING WHERE I FIT, 73-99

I *was told, as a child, that I was brilliant. I excelled in the Montessori*
preschool that fed my wonder. One day, close to Christmas, I came home,
pulled some red and white bendy straws out of the kitchen drawer, and bent
them into faux candy canes for our tree. My mother told me that I walked on
my toes like a ballerina most of the time and loved learning about new things,
especially animals.

Once in traditional public school; however, things changed. My inability
to sit still or focus on the one person standing at the front of the classroom
became difficult. There was no moving around the room, like before, or choos-
ing lessons I was interested in. As the years progressed, my having to keep
track of my homework while learning about stuff that didn't matter to me
became fairly impossible. I was in my head a lot and dreadfully quiet. Hardly
talking at all, hoping always that the teacher wouldn't call on me because
most likely I wasn't going to know the answer, and I might not have even
heard the question. Still, I managed to skate through.

In high school, I failed pre-algebra twice before finally making it through
to Algebra. Then I failed algebra twice, and finally as a senior, my ability
to graduate was in jeopardy. My father went to the school to talk to my
counselor, and I was sent back to general math, not because I couldn't take
either of the Algebra class again, but because my dad said his kid needed a
win.

I aced that class, and thankfully graduated, but just barely.

My parents had first row, season tickets to my patched together mess of a
school career. But they kept trying. If "You're smart, you just need to apply
yourself," wasn't the battle cry for my entire childhood, I don't know what
was.

My parents advocated for ways to help me learn better. Mom asked my
language arts teacher in middle school to sit with me and have me spell the

words out loud to her instead of writing them down. She reasoned that there must be a way to pull the smarts out of me in some way, as she knew they were totally in there.

But I liked to watch people, and I liked to tell stories. "She's a daydreamer," was written on most of my report cards. "She's just not here, when she's here."

I was labeled so early, and the daydreamer one seemed to stick. It still applies. I did not like to sit and be told what to do, or what to think. And good God, don't ask me to read a book. A whole book? I couldn't.

I'd fudge my book reports by reading the back blurb, and sometimes buying Cliff notes if they were available to help me get by. Reading a whole book by myself was downright impossible, unless it was rainy outside and I was really into the story.

If you believe and others tell you, and they use your past results to prove it; that you are not worth spending time or money on, you can't help but believe it too.

I was so glad to finish high school. The day after graduation, I slept in, knowing I would never again have to go back to school a day in my life, if I didn't want to. I wouldn't have to suffer the daily failures or be graded on anything again. Or at least that was what I believed.

Each job brought more doubt about myself to light. The 'not good enough monster' would visit me, often at night, chasing me, and torturing me in my dreams. It showed its ugly head during the day too, especially when I needed extra time to know what I was doing.

Maybe I was drawn to spending time with children because with them, I had the upper hand mentally. I automatically knew more than they did, simply because of I'd lived longer. I could tell them stories or lies if I wanted, and they would believe me because I was a grown up.

"I've been to the moon." I said once and was gifted by a super surprised little face looking up at me with deep admiration. I did correct myself and said instead that I was born the year the U.S. Astronauts went to the moon. The littles didn't care if I had a college degree, they only cared if I made yummy lunches or snacks and played games with them. I let them win until they were old enough to handle losing. Which seemed to be aged seven, at least that was what I heard on an Oprah Winfrey parenting topic program.

I could do my art with them, and they would tell me how good I was. I could still teach them things that they didn't know how to do, and they were happy. I still carried in me that same childlike wonder, that others lose, over time. Easily sitting and watching ladybugs with the small ones or picking up a caterpillar and letting it crawl all over my hand with its little, tiny feet, tickling as it went. Running through the gigantic summer sprinklers at the school in our clothes and walking home soaking wet. Dressing up and having parties with a theme. Planning my daughter's birthday parties was the most fun, and I always went over the top with it. Finally, I was good at something.

I got my first glimpse of the mom life I wanted when I was a nanny in a well to do neighborhood in my early twenties. I watched and saw what really-together, suburban Moms were like, as I watched their kids. Most of them stayed at home, at least while the children were really little, hiring me to go off and do social things together or having a day to run errands.

They drove minivans or Suburban's if they were too cool for a van. They had beautiful houses and hired a decorator to help them make everything match. Their kids were dressed in the cutest clothes, and they all took family vacations. Sometimes together with other families, two or three families all piling into a big house together. That life seemed like the dream.

I wanted to someday have what they had. That strong bond of family. A mom and a dad with kids, all living in the same house. Moving about together in the world knowing they were a unit. It was something I never felt I had.

I had a non-traditional childhood, but when my parents were still together, my father stayed home with us for a time, which I can't remember a single day of. Mom went to work, and again, I don't remember a single day of that existence either.

I do remember years later, watching my mom sit at her drafting table, designing a building while taking architecture classes at the University in town. She made a model for an egg to survive a drop from a two story building using only rubber bands, some glue and toothpicks. Hand painting wallpaper samples from England for her clients, to give them a one of kind dining room in their old Craftsman home.

I also remember her leaving my brother and I with a bag of snacks, and some books in the small airport lobby somewhere, while she went out for her flying lessons. I never went up in the airplane with her, and I don't know if she ever got her license. She didn't become an architect either, as my father wasn't supportive, and we would have had to move to another city for her to continue her studies. She decided on a path to do as much as she could towards her dream, while staying static where she was.

It was just another time in my life that I saw my mom step away from her dreams, for the "good," of someone else or the family. I imagine that is partly how I came to excel at it myself. It seemed to be some kind of badge of motherhood or a sacrifice to show that one was a good mother or wife. That it is our jobs to support others' in the dreams that they had, instead of pursuing our own.

In my stay at home motherhood, I had taken on a supporting role in my own life. Everyone else's needs or wants were always above mine. Or maybe that was just how it felt. For a time anyway?

As my girls got older though; their school math became so hard that they didn't come to me for help anymore, thankfully going to their engineer father instead. Possibly at my suggestion, as I didn't want to have to figure it out myself. A new place to fail.

I would need to hang out with an even younger crowd to be seen as successful or smart, or maybe it was just math that I would forever stink at.

Many of my friends were doing well. They had careers and were "stable." They made their own money and bought their own houses. I, in contrast, had been carried by the work of others to this place in my life. As a child of a divorce, I knew that families can easily fall apart, at any time.

I had grown up in a house plagued with feelings of lack, believing that everything was supposed to be hard, and that life often sucked. That most things don't work out as you planned.

I sat often in my two story home worrying that people would find out I was a sham, or that I wasn't as smart as they thought I was. That my lack of a degree would keep me or my children from being invited to be a part of big things anymore.

I hadn't believed in myself, or felt worthy of spending any time, energy, or money on myself to make myself into something bigger. I'd have to do it from out of sight. Away from the critics, the ones who would tell me I wasn't good enough.

But I know there is something inside me. I see glimmers of potential sometimes. I feel that I have something inside me that can make a difference in the world somehow, but how, where, and when?

I know I need to build myself up into someone I can be proud of. I need action. Which path do I take? The road less traveled using my own inherent talents, or the road already packed with traffic, going to work for someone else?

At least I did something big and brave by sending out my traveling books. I imagine the fanciful journey they are having.

I will see them again.

That, I am sure.

~

MIKE

M ike Billows strolled into the hospital cafeteria and ordered a coffee. Waiting in line for his beverage he noticed several attractive men looking at him. He was flattered but happy to be off the market now.

Jeffrey and he had been dating for over five months now, and it seemed to be getting serious. It was rare that they weren't together after work. Mike had grown used to sharing his bed again, after a long pause from serious relationships.

They'd been talking about moving in together and exchanging rings. Toe rings to start.

Mike smiled at the thought of having a barefoot ceremony where they would place rings on one another's toes. Mike wished they could marry legally, but that would have to wait. He had waited a long time to be in love again. He so hoped that Jeffrey was his perfect one.

His cell phone rang, and he put the book down on the counter to answer it. He tucked the phone under his chin, and picked up the book also grabbing his coffee from the barista. It was his brother Henry, his fraternal twin. He sighed a big sigh before speaking.

"Hey. Melanie didn't come home last night."

"I'm so sorry, have you talked to her today?"

"No, but when I called her office, they said she was in a meeting, so I guess she's alive."

"I was thinking about coming over later, want to talk then? I feel like she needs an intervention or something, this isn't her."

"Mike, I'm so afraid I'm going to lose her."

"Listen Henry, I just know it's going to work out. I know it."

"Thanks, that's my other line, Mike, I gotta get this. Thanks for coming over tonight, we can order a pizza or something."

"Sounds good. Hang in there." His last statement was interrupted by a dial tone.

The cafeteria was packed, but there was a small table by the kitchen. A quiet spot to decompress for a few minutes. To think about how to help his brother. He could feel the pain his brother was dealing with. Identical or fraternal, the two of them had always had a powerful connection.

Henry and Melanie. Those two. Ever since middle school Mike knew they were meant to be together. The feeling had always been mutual, until earlier this year.

Melanie had started a new job and was impressed by her boss and his ability to handle tough situations. After many long hours, and late-night dinners staying to work on one proposal or another, the boss suddenly became more than a mentor.

Henry told Mike that he knew they were having an affair, he could tell by how short their phone calls were when he called her at work. How she worked longer hours and how short she'd be with him, when she *was* home. Mike was beyond sad about how their love story was changing right in front of his eyes.

Mike had twenty minutes of break before he had to get back to his shift. He could sit for a couple minutes and read. He opened the odd blue cover of his new book to see if there was a description of the story. Nothing on the back, only a gold plated plea on the front.

What is this? he said to himself. Before he knew it, he had finished the book, and noticed that his coffee was cold.

Shit, how long had he been sitting here? Mike glanced at his watch, *a half hour? I got to get back upstairs.*

Mike slipped the book under his arm and ran to the elevator leaving his cold, half full cup of coffee on the table. Only a few more hours until he could be with Henry. Mike got to his desk, and texted Jeffrey. '*Hey, I'm going to my brother's tonight, he needs me.*'

'*Yes, go, I understand. Good luck, love you.*'

Mike was grateful to have found a partner he was excited about spending his life with. Jeffrey had been so worth the wait.

~

A BIG REMINDER NOT TO WASTE TIME, ME 2001

A gathering in front of her gravesite, this beautiful person, gone. The minister kept saying her name wrong, I winced every time.

He was sharing the words that I had written about her, as a favor for her daughter. She was beyond grief stricken, I was more than honored to help.

The pastor confessed that he hadn't known her, as we all did, but the stories that we would now share would help him understand what she meant to us.

We all stood in a long silence, until someone stepped forward to relay a memory. A moment I also witnessed.

I looked around at the many faces. Somber at best. Her grandson, only four years of age, sat quietly on his father's lap, not understanding what was happening. Her two daughters, one born to her, one gifted to her by chance, cried together and I wanted to wrap them both in a monstrous hug and make it better somehow. But nothing could be done.

It is final. No do overs. No take backs. This was it.

It was easy to put my words to paper from my safe space at home, but saying my feelings out loud in front of a group, where I knew so few people? I wasn't equipped.

What if the words came out wrong, or I didn't say it right? I begged my brain to remember something that I could convey. Nothing, not good enough to share like that.

I felt it though and wanted to scream the only words that came; into the wind, "she mattered to me!"

I bowed my head, paralyzed inside, and whispered the other unorganized words that I wanted to share with her, hoping somehow she'd hear and understand.

I told her how everyone that was there, was reliving a time with her, but many were not used to speaking out in public and they were either too grief stricken or embarrassed; like I was, to share. That I hoped she understood. I believe she could hear what our hearts were saying. I wished I could be brave, to remember an eloquent moment worthy of her last celebration. I hadn't prepared for this, no one sent an agenda.

She was the first person who I had been close to that went through the process of dying within view. Diagnosis, treatment, failure of treatment, then gone.

Gardening was her passion, roses her most favorite bloom. She taught me how to trim the rose stem to encourage new growth. She did not have an easy life, but she made do and everything that she did, she did with love. She had shared that she collected plants and roses with similar names to those of the people she loved, so no matter where she was, she'd always have them around her. I started to do the same.

In conversation she would sporadically wink at me as she talked, it always made me feel special. It was a wink of I see you, I see you paying attention to what I am saying. She was a bright spot in the often rough surroundings of regular life. A smile on her face always, despite the shitty life circumstances of a cheating husband, she lovingly raised his love child after he was out of the picture. The cancer came aggressively and took her fast. Those who stood there that day were forever changed by her in some way.

The gathering moved closer together so that everyone could hear the remembrances being spoken. A laugh would erupt now and then. Strangers; most of us to each other, were now forever joined together in love and appreciation of this one soul. Bonded with a loving understanding of the sadness that we all shared by her leaving this world.

"Where is she now?" I wondered to myself as the pastor took back over the proceedings.

I like to believe that she is puttering around in the garden of the afterlife, trimming the roses back so new life can spring forward. I believe that we will meet again, either in her next new life down here, or in my transition to the after world.

Most people I am around do not believe the way I do. That we get more than one chance at this. Life, that is.

The fact that I can walk amongst these people without judgment is refreshing to me. Not that I proclaim my beliefs to anyone. This is neither the time, nor the place for a discussion of that sort. Those conversations rarely come at all. Maybe with too much wine and a loose lipped chat over Bunco.

The time for comments passed, and we moved onto prayers. The well known prayers that were known by all, seemingly, except me. I listen to the words carefully and close my eyes and bow my head to play along. This quiet mo-

ment is all we have left to say goodbye. We'll be leaving her here. But also taking her with us.

She was my first real experience with losing someone as an adult.

My first exposure to death was as a teenager. A fellow student took his own life, and I went to his funeral with a friend who knew him well. She needed support. I hadn't known him but I sat with her, fully feeling the grief of the room. The overwhelming loss and regret. The wishing that everything was different.

Sitting in a pew, I knew I didn't belong there. The sobs and sadness around me were surreal. Set in a big church, a dwelling I hadn't spent much time in either, the place was full. I looked around at the many faces, all torn apart in some way. They seemed soothed with the words that were spoken over the casket, and the congregation, they heartily agreed on the idea that he was in a better place.

People were just all in with this. The ritual, the cast of characters. The word. I envied them for the comfort they felt on this dark, dark day.

My spiritual upbringing was much more loose, definitely more on the woo woo side, instead of the organized religion side. My parents went to mediums and talked to dead people about their problems. I was taken to life-enriching seminars that lasted for hours or days and had to either sit still and be quiet, or take part in the class. Once my brother and I were placed in a closet-like room, with coloring books and things to do, where the only thing to eat was Wint-O-Green life savers. We ate boxes of them, it's probably the reason I cannot stand them to this day.

Being in this church, surrounded by these people and these beliefs was as confusing as it was beautiful. This boy was loved, but he either didn't know how much or something else took hold of him and wouldn't let go.

When my grandparents died, they lived far away, so their complete disappearance was more of an abstract concept for me, only noticing or remembering that they were not alive anymore when I thought of them or didn't receive a card on my birthday.

But my rose loving friend was close by, this was serious and impacting. When I heard she was sick, I knew I had a choice to make. Sneak away, to help keep myself from hurting more about her passing or stay engaged and love her all the way through. I'm an adult, after all. It's a part of life. None of us escapes this eventual reality, for ourselves, but we get to decide how much we want to be involved in the journey when it comes to others.

As a child, when someone falls ill, the child is usually kept away from seeing them in the hospital, all hooked up to machines. We are held away from seeing the life drain from their face, their faint smile often turning into a painful grimace as they melt away from their bodies, in search of peace.

As an adult, the act of dying becomes more real. More solidified. Our own lens of mortality becomes crystal clear.

We only have the time we have. No more, and no less. So, what we do with the time we are given, is especially important.

Animals are given a benediction in this way, as they do not comprehend or understand that they will die. At least this is what we believe. They wake each day; live their best life. Their tasks of feeding themselves, sleeping when they are tired, and making offspring. Then they either keel over after a certain time period or are killed in some sort of accident or to be used as a meal for another.

I have wondered if birds just fall from the sky? Dead. That one minute they are just flying around as they do, minding their own business, then croak, they halt flapping and smash to the ground?

Each time we see or hear about someone dying, we all go inside ourselves and start asking the big questions of our souls again.

Are we living our life to our fullest? Have I told the people that I love that I love them? Can I forgive myself or that person for something that was said or done? Is this all there is? Am I fulfilling my purpose? What am I here for?

I will take those questions and my memories of her, home with me. Her life and death beseeching me to try to claim what I ultimately want in this life. Even if I believe I get more chances to live and get it right, it's no use wasting this one I have now.

The pastor spoke his final words to us. It is the quote I had chosen for her and this occasion.

And.. If the essence of my being has caused a smile upon your face or a touch
of joy within your heart, then in living, I have made my mark.
Thomas L. Odem Jr.

~

1

HENRY

M ike Billows pulled into his twin brother Henry's driveway. He was met with a beer as he shut the door of his Volvo.

"She's still not home."

Mike twisted off the cap and took a swig.

"Wait, I forgot something." Mike walked around and opened the passenger side door to grab Find Me, Book One. He pushed the door shut with his foot and looked over at his brother.

Henry was a ghost of his usual self. Never had he dreamt that the super couple of Henry and Melanie would have trouble. They'd been together since middle school.

One time Mike came home after basketball to a big mess in the house. Henry and Mel had made instant mashed potatoes for a snack and started an epic food fight in the house. What a sight! The three of them busily cleaned up the mess, laughing their asses off while scraping the walls and ceiling before the Billows' boys parent's got home.

Those two were inseparable, first friends, then more. The *more* came in high school when Melanie was approached by a football player, and Henry finally told her that he loved her so she wouldn't go out with him. It was almost nauseating to see how gooey they were for each other. They even made mixtapes for each other. They had only been with each other. Both believed it would be enough.

The last few years were different. Life was harder. Melanie couldn't conceive a baby that they both wanted so badly. They had been to specialists and there wasn't anything wrong that the doctors could find, with either one of them.

Two years went by with them loving and supporting each other while trying. Hope and then disappointment. By year three the stress had gotten to both of them.

Melanie announced that she didn't want to talk about having a baby anymore, and any attempt to console her was met with anger. Anger at Henry, anger at God and mostly anger at herself. She'd taken the responsibility for their situation, with no real evidence.

She started using the spare bedroom, the one that was supposed to house a child as the household dumping ground. Boxes of photos, old clothes, remnants from high school. Christmas wrapping and decorations. Her art supplies gathered dust.

That was the hardest for Henry. To see his amazing wife torn to shreds the way she was. By year four they'd stopped having sex. Not even for fun.

"Sex is unproductive, so what's the point?" she would say.

Henry in the meantime had been confiding in his brother. Good ol' Mike was there to listen to them both, even without any first hand experience of being in a heterosexual relationship. Mike had known he was gay by the time they all heard the word on the playground the first time.

Melanie would talk to Mike sometimes too, but the last time she'd reached out, was months ago. The great disconnect between the couple, had hit their longtime friendship as well.

Henry and Mike sat on the front porch and drank their beer. Henry had brought out a bag of chips.

"Dinner." He said, throwing the already opened bag to his brother.

The sky darkened with night and clouds showed in the distance. Not happy white clouds but apprehensive, secretive billows that held who knows what. They sat in silence, just being there together until Mike spoke.

"Hey Henry, I was given this book today, it's like no other book I've read."

"I've read them all, they either say be a man and drag her back home, leave her, or ignore it and the affair will fizzle out on its own."

"It's not that kind of book. It isn't a self-help book. It's a book holding the memories of someone's life, their dream really, and they need our help."

"In case you haven't noticed Bro, I've got my own problems, why would I want to read about someone else's?" Henry shrugged and Mike reached inside the front door to flip on the porch light to be able to read the first passage to his brother.

Giving up on fighting, Henry took the last swig of his beer, closed his eyes, and listened.

Dear Reader,

This traveling book is my secret mission to live a more extraordinary life, from within the confines of an ordinary one.

Only five copies of this book exist, and this has made its way to you. You are now and forever part of this story.

Inside you will find moments captured from one person's life.

Each passage starts with the set of initials of the person with whom I share the connection.

We are all connected on some level. Every person you meet leaves a mark on you, whether good or bad. Often it is the worst people who gift us the best lessons.

It is my hope that this idea spurs you into living in a more extraordinary way. To think bigger, and reach beyond what you currently see.

The memories inside may remind you of a time or a person in your own life. May you think of those people today, for the good or the lessons you learned from them.

Please read this book, then write your name, and location in the back before giving it to someone else. Let's see how many lives it will touch.

If you by chance, recognize yourself in here:

Please bring the book and

Find me....

"Dang. This calls for another." Henry reached into the cooler for another beer and asked Mike if he wanted one too.

"No, I'm good." Mike said. He wanted to be able to drive home tonight.

Opening the beer with his key chain bottle opener, Henry nodded at his brother.

"Well, I don't need another thing hanging over me, do I? Read it to me, I'm too wasted to see the words." Henry sat back and closed his eyes, letting the words wash over him.

There was a calm peacefulness in Mike's voice that kept Henry quiet and engaged. It had been years since anyone had read aloud to him. Maybe since he was a little kid. It might have been his brother Mike back then, too.

As the experiences in the book painted pictures in his head, Henry softened. He marveled at the many experiences the author had shared about her romantic loves. The bouts of friendship, family, and adventure, shared so vividly in her words.

He was more than a little sad when it ended.

Many of the things he had also experienced, but with one startling difference. All were with Mel. How many people can say that? He wondered. Look at how much the two of them had been through already?

They ordered a pizza. Supreme with lots of meat on it. It arrived half an hour later.

As the two brothers sat in the red Adirondack chairs that Henry had built for Mel for their first wedding anniversary, the pizza delivery driver pulled up to the house. He was a young kid, but married, they noted by the ring. He was rushed and flustered. They gave him a twenty-dollar tip and the driver hugged them both in response before he left.

"Can I have that book?" Henry finally asked.

"I brought it for you, maybe Mel will read it too. A little mission for you two to do together. Pick someone else to give it to anyway."

"I hope so. God, I really love her. We have to work this out. We've been everything to each other, and we can get that back, I know it." Henry managed a smile. It was small, but a smile, nonetheless.

Mike put his hand on his brother's shoulder and gave it a pat.

"She'll be back. I have a feeling."

They fought off bugs until 11:30 p.m. when Mel's Subaru station wagon pulled into the drive. She was finally home.

Mike walked to his sister-in-law and hugged her, she reciprocated and kissed his cheek. Mike waved goodbye to his brother and put the key into the ignition of his car. He watched as his brother and Melanie walked into the house together.

He pulled out onto Jamestown Street. As he neared the highway, the sky opened up, dousing his car to the gills. He switched on the wipers and cranked the radio volume to high.

"Looks like we made it," by Barry Manilow played on his favorite station.

~

PICKING ONE THING? ME 2003

W*here do I belong? I never had the feeling that I totally belonged or knew what my "thing," was; that is, until motherhood. But motherhood does not pay cash money.*

I have many interests, but starting an actual career means you have to pick something. For real.

Over the years, I have been creative in our home. Designing and painting the rooms whatever color I chose. Decorating some rooms, repeatedly. So much so, that my husband teased me that the walls are thicker at our house, because of the many layers of paint.

Hubby had been pretty good natured about my design adventures, and my mishaps too. The time I wanted to expand our pantry closet by knocking a hole through to the little used coat closet, only to find out our water softener system was in the way. In my quest to remove the appliance with no knowledge whatsoever, I had a neighbor come help me shut it off, accidentally shutting off water to the whole house. Luckily hubby got it fixed.

"Why didn't you just wait for me?" he asked when he got home that night. "I don't know, I just couldn't."

He was one of the lucky people. Practically born knowing he would be an engineer one day. Always curious, always looking to see how things worked. His parents had let him take apart the toaster and other things, knowing that it must be his path somehow. Building an A-frame fort in the back yard of his house, with little supervision. He is always anchored in reality; and what he could see, and prove, I am however the dreamer of the household. The creative one that makes things pretty, but who can't seem to settle on just one thing. This seems to be one of our key differences.

Maybe it is why we were drawn to each other in the first place? Him with his routines, and the way he did things, and me flitting around, being spontaneous and playful. Whatever the reason, it's made our life harder too. He was always so sure of everything. I am just plain all over the place.

I could go back to being a nanny or work in a daycare, I suppose. Having spent over ten years of my life rocking the Barney life, can I even hang with the grown-ups?

I dabbled some in neighborhood government, so maybe there was something there? I waited for the answer to come. I looked at interior design school and pulled together the information and costs. When I mentioned it to him, he said, "Ok, well, that is a lot of money, so you are really going to have to commit to finishing." Those words cut deep, and I lost interest. I couldn't make myself complete anything, really, and school still scared me to death.

The previous year, I had asked him for some capital to start buying houses to flip them. I had a decorative knack, after all, and that is what my grandfather had done for his livelihood down in California. I'd been an avid watcher of all the shows on HGTV. It could work. My hubby was mad-handy, and I could do the design selections. It would be easy. Something fun we could do together, or so I had thought.

"Let's see your business plan then," he stated, and I was instantly crushed.

I didn't know how to do a business plan. How else could I convince him to do this with me? I mean wasn't it good enough that I was his wife, I actually had to put forth all that businessy organizational effort for him too?

Another idea to set aside, not believing in myself enough to try. I wait for my epiphany. My artistic expression continues to tease me, to paint, to write, or to design something.

Everyone knows that artists and writers don't make any money, I'd heard it said over and over. It's not a real job. They said.

I continue to search my brain and my heart for a passion that could reach beyond my years of tending to my littles.

What will fire me up?

~

1

MELANIE

H enry had been begging his wife Melanie to go to counseling for almost a year, and she finally agreed that night just to be able to go to sleep.

Henry left the traveling book on the kitchen table before leaving for work the next day. Melanie found herself staying home from work to read it. The memories pointed her back to all the challenges that she and Henry had shared in their long history together. How Henry had helped her through the sudden death of her father that left her feeling lost and abandoned.

Henry had helped bridge the gap between her and her mother so they could grieve together, instead of them both suffering on alone. He had walked with her through all of the messy stuff she had been through in life. Her time without a job, and her feeling of being uncertain as to her purpose. He encouraged her to take more art classes as she came home smiling each time, so excited to tell him about what she'd made. Each test that came, they had handled it together.

Until the crest of the infertility.

Melanie had always had a good man in Henry, but she had allowed herself to forget that. This book was a good reminder as it showed how important having the right people in your life was, as well as how critical it was to get rid of the ones that weren't good for us.

Did she really want to be with someone else? A new man with whom she would have to start all over with? It could be years before they'd understand how she liked the towels folded in the bathroom, let alone how strong she liked her coffee each morning.

Maybe she could move beyond the self-inflicted pain and punishment of her infidelity and try again with Henry? Especially if he was still willing, even after all she'd put him through?

Melanie spent the day in her sweats, mascara sunken around her eyes. Her hair was tangled and oily from the tossing and turning lying next to Henry all night. She didn't bother sprucing up. She was going to sit in the garbage filled choices she'd made, wanting the outside of herself to reflect how she felt on the inside. Ice cream for breakfast with a piece of chocolate cake and a grilled cheese sandwich for lunch, she ate crap to punish herself for what she had done.

The affair was foolish and luckily so far, an unsuccessful attempt to end her marriage. She'd been trying to free Henry from his commitment to her, but he was too stubborn. Man was he stubborn.

Numbly, she walked the hallway looking into each of the spare rooms, catching a glimpse of each photo of the two of them that hung throughout their home. She begged her brain to break down the wall she had built around herself to deal with the pain and sadness of their childlessness. She hadn't cried in so long.

She pulled out a notepad and wrote, *I just wanted to have a baby with my husband, that's all. Why, God? Why couldn't you help us?*

She scribbled madly over the words, using up the available pencil lead, breaking the tip with its force. The tears started then, coming so hard and strong, she couldn't stop them. It was as if the dam had finally broken inside of her heart, and she was paddling like a madman through the rapids of her total despair.

Doubling down on the shame she pulled out all of their old scrapbooks to remember their perfect life together. Each high school dance, graduating from college, every trip they had taken together. Their wedding. Tears fell on the plastic covered pages and she wiped them away with her fingers, her wedding ring in view. The day Henry carried her over the threshold of their first house after saving together for the down payment for eight years. Melanie sat tossed like a lump of laundry on the couch covered with photos of the two of them splayed all over her.

Now professional at stuffing her feelings, the torment she felt for the child who hadn't come was all consuming. Pent up, she hadn't let herself cry in more than a year, maybe longer. Instead, she'd hardened, ignoring her husband's requests to talk about it, or even his attempts at a loving hug. She would look away quickly when she caught his heartbroken face. She hadn't allowed any of those feelings to show. For any reason.

All she had wanted was to make Henry happy, and she couldn't because they couldn't have a child. She felt a failure.

The two of them never thought that they would have trouble conceiving. They were both healthy and came from families where each sibling had a few kids each. No fertility problems amongst their cousins either. They wanted so much to express their love for each other in the form of a child. It was to be the ultimate gift. Alternatively, she had turned away from him, hurting him even more.

In the beginning, it had been *try* this, and *do* that. She'd go to the Doctor and get some more information, write down her cycles and keep track of her temperature every day. So much effort and thinking about when and how they should do it, the tracking became a full-time job.

Abstractly, they thought about options such as IVF, and surrogacy, but they hadn't researched it as they kept believing it would happen. She wished they had.

Melanie pulled herself up from the couch and walked into the kitchen to make a cup of peppermint tea. The vapor pierced through her now slit eyes and made them water again. She placed the steaming teacup on the desk in the office. It was the room that was supposed to have been a nursery by now. She opened her computer and drafted her resignation from the company where she worked and met the man with whom she had the affair. She didn't want to see him again. Didn't want to think of him again. He was nothing. She'd used him as much as he'd used her, knowing she was married, he came on strong anyway. She called one of the office managers to say that she would be out indefinitely, her letter of explanation was on its way.

It was a start.

Melanie knew they would be ok financially for a little while, and if saving their marriage meant maxing out the credit cards, so be it.

Taking the yellow pages out of the kitchen drawer, she leafed through to the marriage counselors. She circled a few to show Henry when he got home from work. Mark Hansen, Yolanda Peters, Wayne Huff. She would let Henry choose, but she knew which counselor it would be. Wayne Huff, as John Wayne was one of his favorite actors.

It was a messy, emotional day of facing all of the shit she had been hiding from. Deciding to finally accept her misdeeds and clean up the mess that she had made, made her feel as powerful as it did vulnerable. What if Henry said no?

Henry got home to a swollen eyed, disheveled, mess of a now open wife, they ate leftover pizza and watched the movie, *This is Us,* on the couch touching toes. Through the mutual bawling, they held onto each other at the end, and decided to hit the hard stuff with their new counselor, Wayne Huff as soon as they could get in for an appointment. It was a turning point. Henry held his wife and pretended that everything was fine again. Believing it still could be.

~

L.P.

Your purpose in my life must have been to spark my risky side. Daring me to join the dating service, to sink my last three hundred dollars into a future or possible future partner. You were doing it too.

We were friends and you were a little older than me but we worked in the same profession. I looked up to you as someone who was able to have that job pretty successfully. You had a house, and drove a nice car. You also traveled often. I'm not sure how you managed. I helped you redecorate your house with the bright tropical colors you loved from your trips to random islands in the Pacific.

Wishing for a child of your own, despite your lack of a partner, you pursued it another way and eventually got pregnant. I was happy for you and helped you decorate your nursery.

I became pregnant too, our kids could have grown up as friends. And they most likely would have, until you said something that broke the bond. You told me that you would be a much better mother than I could ever think of being. That was enough for me. It was time to part ways.

There was just no way of coming back from that.

I hope that you have had a wonderful, enriched and purposeful life. Thank you for being my friend when you were.

I thank you for the two beautiful children I have and the husband I never would have met if it weren't for you.

~

STUPIDLY ROMANTIC, ME 2003

*I*t seems like everyone around me is so needy. Things or people are always interrupting any writing time that I seem to be able to carve out for myself. Maybe I am just being selfish. While these occurrences are perfectly natural and expected, they chip away at my progress. They also tell me that I have people around me, and that I'm not alone in this world. At times there is nothing I love more than being a mother, a wife, a giver.

Sometimes, I just want someone around me who sees the other me. Someone who appreciates my brain. My curious nature, my words, my writing, someone to like me for me. I imagine that someone, someday, will tell me that I am beautiful, attractive, smart, exciting, and enchanting.

Men smile at me in the grocery store, and I look away, not sure what to do. When I get attention it's like my body knows and wants to evade that attention, because I tend to put on an extra ten pounds as a coping mechanism.

We have been to the counselor again and he asked us to start dating again to get to know each other all over. This was not our first attempt at counseling, as over the years we have gone many, many times. Multiple times with multiple therapists. I am thankful he will go, as many men, flat out won't.

We are past our seventh year of marriage, that critical year everyone fears but it does not mean we are smooth sailing by any means. We fight over the same things. I want more for us, and he is happy with what is.

In this round to keep our marriage together, we are taking turns picking dates for each other. I know hubby loves live theater, so I bought tickets to a small town play for the evening. He is impressed with my choice and appreciates my effort. How I wished there was a magic pill that I could swallow to bring all of the love I have had for him back to life. We are trying, and both of us remain hopeful in our future.

When we got to the theater, I am taken in by the quaintness of the building, the smallness of scale, and the colorful and interesting people that run this place. It's a perfect venue for a story. I allowed my mind to wander as we waited for the show to start.

While there, I imagined a rendeavous with a stranger. It's not exactly something you are supposed to do or think about when you are working on your marriage, but I couldn't really help myself. I decided to write about it here.

My eyes locked on him the moment I stepped in the door. A man decked out in black jeans, and a black leather jacket. He screamed actor.

The chandelier lit up the open foyer, and we gauged where to pick up our tickets. The man in black, followed me with his eyes as I walked before handing me a program. Staring, he added a smile. Up close he was handsome. Tall, with a head full of dark, almost black, curly hair. Unruly. Animal. Passionate. The few grays in his hair spoke to his experience in life and most likely in love. I wondered how successful he had been at the latter.

The small-time playhouse, was showing a production of "Same time, Next year." Taking me back, I remembered the movie fondly, with Alan Alda.

The play about star crossed lovers who become significant to each other over the years; despite their own tethers, unfolded before us. Their once-a-year affair that became a need. I wonder if I could get away with something so devious. To meet up with someone every year throughout my life? A love affair that may fill the gap of the passion I felt was missing.

It wouldn't take much effort to make sure I met the man in black. I could offer my services to paint scenery. I can paint nearly anything. Surely they would have need for the next production? A theater set, or two, we would most likely share a moment.

He looked at me a few more times as I sat in the audience, next to my significant other. My black, low-cut collared sweater, we'd look good together. I wondered if he was really watching me too, or perhaps he would turn to look, perceiving my gaze?

Not now, I tell myself. I can't risk an encounter. I sit flushed and fascinated.

I wondered what the man in black enjoyed, and how he had found himself a home in this tiny theater. I wondered who he was. What was his name. What did he like for breakfast?

I have so much life in me, so much curiosity. A hunger for more.

The show ambled on. The false couples on stage, both coupled already, had settled for the comfortable love in their marriages, similar to mine.

He loved me, I knew. I prayed he wouldn't ask me the same. Not this minute. My heart dances away from myself, to frolic, to play, as we watch.

Changes in our dynamic are not an option, but I willed a way to light my insides again and help them glow. And burn for my husband. Weighted with the only love that I have, I am wasting away.

It's just a show, just entertainment, but the idea could work. Couldn't it?

Intermission came and I stayed in my seat. Not wanting to be anywhere close to leather jacket. To tease myself with desire.

Surely, I would smile too big, or shake hands too long, if we met. Aloof is not in my repertoire, so I feigned tiredness, saying it was the wine that we had shared earlier as my reason to stay put. Significant other left me then, to get a drink and stretch his legs. I sat alone with my mind buzzing with ludicrosities.

I could leave a note for the man in black. Paint him a written picture of what I could see, a proposal of what could be, and leave it behind, anonymously?

Dear Leather Jacket... I mused.

How would he react? Was he himself attached, and would his woman understand such an obvious, attention starved attempt from a lonesome stranger?

That evening, the smile he gave me was enough, because it was in his smile that I heard the words, "I see you."

Snapping back to reality. I am reading WAY TOO MANY ROMANCE NOVELS.

My marriage is in trouble. Again. We are not a team. Something must change, and I need to stop expecting magical romantic moments to happen to me. Silly girl, get over yourself. This is real life.

I would love to feel those romantic gestures from him again. To hear him say again, the things he used to say and to have him do the things like that he used to do when we were first together. Years ago, he told me how much I added to his life, and I felt it. It's been years since I've heard anything in the same vein. I want so much to be talked to, touched, loved, and seen again. Sometimes this life is enough for me. But other times I want to scream. It's all just a memory. One day becomes another and another.

I do love it when we laugh together. It is then that I feel the closest to him. When we have a funny moment shared, or laugh at an inside joke. In our early days together, we did puzzles and played mystery type video games that teased our brains and made us work on each mission together. Now, though, we mostly just watch sitcoms; other people in love or not, in the evening when the kids are in bed.

I try to be seen by him. To be pretty if only he'd notice. I shower, clean the house, put on a nice outfit, and greet him at times with an open beer.

Lately though, he sees me, my makeup tired from the day, wearing a sweat-shirt with a sometimes matching scrunchie in my hair. And it doesn't seem to make a difference.

Sometimes I just feel like a warm body next to him.

Why can't I have a magical storybook love? Is this really it? As good as it gets? If the bills are paid, and the kids are settled, and you have a home? Is it enough?

I know reading romance novels is not helping me with my satisfaction of our marriage. It's likely harmful, as no real love story could ever compare to the fanciful imaginations in those books. They are so popular though, most likely because a lot of women also feel unsatisfied.

Love starts out so intense in the beginning, until real life circumstances take over. Schedules, bills, a mortgage, doing dishes and laundry, it becomes so uneventful.

I wish he could think back sometimes, and remember what he loved about me back then. To appreciate the me that I am now. But we change. When I ask, he calls our love, a mature love.

Stupidly or hopefully; I believe that somewhere, someone is thinking of me in a love hungry way. He is waiting for me to come find him. He will appreciate the creative writer, imaginative me. He will see that my ideas have value, and that my dreams are worth fighting for. He will celebrate this woman who is filled with ideas and a deep desire to travel. We will see; together, how big and breathtaking the rest of the world is.

I want big conversations. I want more of all of it. A great love is possible. Right?

I know what a comfortable love is. Is this is all there is?

Almost a passenger in my life instead of the driver, I watch and wait for something to happen.

~

1

The Billows' had been through so much already. In their first session with the counselor, Melanie broke down, confessing that the affair was the only way she could think to push Henry away so he would leave and go find someone who could give him a child.

It was her emotionally warped way of saying that she loved him so much; she wanted him to have what he wanted, even if it wasn't with her.

Sadness overtook Henry's eyes, as he heard and then fully understood what had brought her to that place. It beat him that she hadn't felt like she could talk to him about it. Her extreme and sacrificial attempt to take care of his wants, over her own, had endangered their future together.

"I'm so sorry, I'm so sorry," she said over and over.

"I don't care about a baby; I just want you. I want us, and whatever comes with being together." Henry reached for her, and they wept together, pulling tissues from the box placed in front of them for the purpose by therapist Wayne Huff.

It wasn't about the guy, and what the guy could give her instead of him. It didn't have anything to do with their relationship at all. She figured it was the only way that he might leave her, and even that hadn't been enough.

The affair hadn't made Henry doubt their love. He believed that they had a once in a lifetime kind of love. If they had kids, or didn't have kids, it wouldn't change the way he felt about her. Nothing she did, ever could.

She had been his best friend, his lover, his wife. His meant to be.

Together they could climb out of this hole and crawl back into the sunshine together, where they could both grow, to become a couple again.

Dr. Huff gave them assignments to do at home. Some that would help build back trust and understanding. They had to brainstorm, envisioning together what their lives looked like, *if* they had kids as well as without. They wrote up a plan. Their plan.

One side of the paper contained a world pursuing other ways to have children. Adoption, either locally or overseas. Fostering, finding a surrogate or continuing to try. The other side was to accept what was and love on their friend's kids and nieces and nephews instead. They could volunteer with less fortunate children, and travel to areas that needed help.

Travel would be something they wanted to explore more together. That topic was on both sides of the paper.

Melanie wanted to get back to her art too. She imagined a series of paintings trying to capture the intense feelings of infertility, the suffering and rebounding. One perspective, the woman's. Another, the man's. Pieces bundled together to show a shared story. A project to work on and work through together. She could paint her guts out, and incorporate Henry's heart on the subject, when she needed to express the masculine side. She would use the room that they had set aside for the baby, giving it a new purpose. A life of its own.

She conceived of a whole collage series symbolizing letting go of one idea to make space for another. Tips on avoiding detrimental behavior in the midst. Navigating the choices and how they handle the many disappointments. The tide of hope and losing it again to find acceptance despite how things were supposed to be. Recommendations for counseling, talking to friends. Listening. Together.

She too had been touched by the little book that had come into their lives two plus months prior. She had read it multiple times, racking her brain, wishing she knew who the author was. How she could connect the book back to her. She knew that it had come to Mike from someone from the West coast, or at least that is what Mike thought. Did they know anyone out that way, that they could send it to? It's a big place. No one really. Most of their friends out there were busy corporate climbers. As she had tried to be, to forget their childlessness.

How odd that it came to them. With billions of people in the world, why had the traveling book been plunked into their laps?

Stories of love and loss *are* universal; she suggested to their Dr. Wayne Huff that bright Monday afternoon.

"Everyone has their own hardships, but if we connect and share, many of our stories are the same, and we can learn from each other." She squeezed Henry's hand.

It was their tenth session in as many weeks and the boyfriend boss had become a distant memory. With Melanie quitting her job when they started counseling, she hadn't started looking for something else, as they had both decided Melanie needed a break, to heal, to build back. To discover the new person she wanted to be.

She started taking better care of herself. Walking every day and eating healthy food. She rested and started meditating. She tinkered around the house, getting to all the little things that she had always meant to, and being in her now studio for hours at a time. She listened to music as she painted. In recent days, her paintings were becoming more filled with color, versus the early days of the tonal hazy grays and browns. The sadder paintings.

Henry was happy to see the color coming back into her, and into their lives. They painted their bedroom a fresh lovely Mediterranean blue, that mimicked the sea where they had spent their honeymoon in Greece. They were holding hands more and cuddling on the couch again.

Melanie cooked most of the time, but Mike's renewed spark for Japanese cuisine again, had them trying new recipes once or twice a week. He remembered his time as a foreign exchange student there, way back in high school. That was the only time they had been away from each other, and now they were back to basics. Remembering what lit them up when they were kids. Sharing and growing outwards towards each other.

Henry and she had started being sexual again only a month ago, and found that the bedroom gymnastics were better than ever. Fresh, but still familiar. They wanted to wait to hear each other out completely and take the time necessary to forgive.

"How are you two feeling? About everything?" Dr. Huff asked.

"We are doing amazing," said Melanie.

"Just awesome," said Henry.

"Awesome." parroted Melanie.

"Is there anything else you wish to discuss today, or should we tie you two up with a bow and send you on your way? I say that to mean that I will always be here if you ever feel like you need a tune up. We've come a long way. You've both come a long way."

Henry and Melanie looked at each other. Henry spoke.

"We decided we are all good, Doc. And we brought a going away present for you."

Melanie reached into the canvas bag that she had silk-screened in her third year of college. She was using all of the things she loved rather than what was considered, *fashionable.*

Melanie presented the book; now adorned with a single strand of raffia, to Wayne Huff –their therapist.

"What is it?"

"It's kind of a handbook, for life."

"Someone's life." added Henry.

"Well, ok, then. Thank you."

Dr. Huff walked the couple to the door, and shook hands with Mike. He was reaching to shake Melanie's when she pulled him into a hug. He was happy to see them go. Such a nice couple, they just lost their way for awhile.

"Feel free to reach out again, should you ever need to chat." Dr. Huff said as he closed the door to get ready for the next client.

~

MAYBE NOT REAL ESTATE, ME 2003

*R*eal estate school. While I imagine I would be decent at finding people homes that would fit their lifestyle because I am a good listener and love helping people, I do wonder about my ability to handle the paperwork and numbers. I shudder at the math that would come with a class and a career like that, a massive hill to climb.

Not that I am unable to do it, it's just that it is not where my heart beats. I know when I am not following my heart, my mind and efforts wander.

I sat alone in the room, waiting for the first tape to begin.

"So this is how they do it now," I said aloud to no one. No classroom necessary, no teacher or fellow students to learn and ask questions with, just hours and hours of audiotape lessons, with no filmstrips to accompany them. Shame.

Having diagnosed myself with functional ADHD, I am able to manage life most of the time by writing reminders on the tops of my hands.

I wonder exactly how long this class would hold my attention. Sitting alone in a blank, off white room with no windows while trying to concentrate on the monotone voice droning on in my head, I closed my eyes and tried harder. Two minutes in, I opened my eyes again and start thinking about all the changes I would make to this room if given the opportunity. A nicer color on the walls, maybe some furniture that wasn't from the nineteen seventies? This place was as inspirational as an insane asylum.

I have no chance.

Five minutes in, and I need a mental break. I remove the headphones, glancing at the little analog counter meter on top so I could go back to my place when I was ready. The sound of the tape turning was bliss.

Definitely in need of some motivation, not to mention some drive to complete this.

Where does that come from? How does anyone do anything, especially when it's boring or hard? How do people find their spot?

Many things inspire me for the short term but to have long lasting appeal, for me there has to be a creative bent. Making something out of nothing, inventing something that solves a problem, or just being playful with art supplies is where its at. Especially if I can do any of those things with children. My usual pulls of interest are not thought of as actual money makers. People tend to give their opinion; as such, sometimes more than once.

Writing, No.

Art, No.

Design, maybe if I had a degree? But that would mean school. Ugh. Going to school could send me back to my quiet shy self, where I never talked or took up any space at all, hiding away; begging not to be noticed, unless, that is, the teacher would let me get drunk first to have more bravery about everything? But ah, that may be frowned upon too. Maybe that is how people do it?

The scritching of the tape pulls me back to reality. Will I be able to track the real estate contracts and negotiations? The calculations that will be required to help get my clients the best deal; sitting in on inspections, or offering the opinion that they walk away from a property. Real estate is losing its appeal by the second.

"What am I doing here? Even though I'm afraid to try things or step outside my current box in the search for a new job, I'm not willing to settle yet, on something that isn't me. Sigh. When will I grow up?

People work all day, everyday, at jobs they hate, or don't interest them anymore; but in my family we were encouraged to do what we loved, even if it didn't pay very well. Mom had her own business, and sometimes we had very little but she seemed satisfied, even happy. Her more, lucrative career had lost it's zeal and she quit, so money isn't everything, clearly.

I'm spoiled at the moment, I know. Sheltered, even. Somehow I believe I have time to find my thing. Having married well enough, we have plenty even without any income from me, and I do volunteer a lot of my time helping others. With all that we have, I often feel guilty for what my married family has that wasn't there in my origin family. I had to finally let go and understand I couldn't save everyone. Everyone has their own role to play.

If saving the world is a hidden desire of mine, what on earth am I doing in real estate???

Realizing I was having a major ADD moment, I punched stop on the tape player and rose, walking out of the building with my hand to my head feigning a migraine. Feeling more alive just walking down the hall, than in that cold room in the real estate office. Finally, windows to look out of. The internal smile from my leaving and knowing I would never have to sit in that sterile room again, I felt such a sense of relief.

Outside, I squinted from the sunshine, and hopped in the car to put the top down. The canopy inched tighter, creaking into place right before I hit the gas. My hair, whipped over my face whacking me in the eye, over and over. I nudged my knee into the steering wheel to stay straight and pulled the rubber band I kept around the gear shift, free to bundle up the attackers. Slamming in the clutch, I grabbed the shifter again, over and up into fifth gear to race further away from that place.

Noticing a hawk atop a phone pole in the distance, it spied it's next meal, and lunged downward into the brush, disappearing. Maybe that's what I needed. To have to worry about where my next meal was coming from to get me going. Surely it would. My safety net life was easy, but there was still something missing, if only I knew what. Will I ever find my purpose?

Will my little books find their wayback to me? While I wait, will I lose my mind in life's daily drumming that is my current destiny?

I cranked the radio to an old love song channel and Stevie Wonder sang, "You are the sunshine of my life".

Honking twice at the farmer who waved, I smiled and went tooling down the road. I really like to do so many things. Maybe its the idea of picking just one, that scares the hell out of me. I imagine myself stuck in a job, for years, doing the same tasks day in and day out, and I'd rather die.

If I listen to my heart, I would write.

Novels, or maybe all kinds of books. I could resubmit my children's stories again to a publisher, and keep looking for an agent, but God, how many rejections can someone possibly get? One of them has got to take.

What am I saying?

I have written a book, and somewhere, someone could be reading it right now...

~

1

WAYNE

T herapist Wayne Huff finished his long day. In his line of work, he must have heard it all. The morning had been spent helping a young man cope with the molestation he suffered as a young child at the hands of a pastor. After lunch he spoke with a woman dealing with extreme sexual addiction, mixed with random pill use to cope with her urges.

Only after the Billows' session had his day improved. They had been coming for a few months now and were finally ready to be on their own. He had seen them find each other again, and he was so pleased to be a part of their reconciliation.

The foundation that they had built together was strong. It had been damaged a bit by life and certain circumstances. They were talking about adoption, but whatever they chose, they would figure it out together. If they figured it out, they would make very good parents. The two had so much love together to share with a child.

Another couple had come after them, and in their session, were happily shocked to hear that neither of them wanted to have children, but they had been too afraid to tell each other. They *and* the Billow's graduated from therapy that day.

Wayne wasn't the typical therapist. He encouraged his patients to progress and move on with their lives faster than some. He didn't kick them out if they still needed help, but the idea of being a lifetime listener to people, who weren't willing to do the work to change or make a different choice, was not something he could get behind.

His practice was small, and he didn't advertise. His clients found him mostly by word of mouth, and he liked it that way.

His office was decorated sparsely with a few photos of sunsets and sunrises on the walls. He liked to travel and would get out and hike when time allowed. His bright red hair had started to soften tonally with the additions of the white hairs that were coming with his age. Forty nine on his next birthday. He didn't look it.

Wayne had added a secondary specialty in Neuro Linguistic programming to what he had to offer clients and had been quite successful with it with some. The practice of taking a person back safely in their minds to times of trauma or imprinting and helping them to change their responses to certain situations from their past. To desensitize them somewhat.

One client, a middle aged woman, was able to be taken back to a time when she was abused by an old man when she was only eight years old. Wayne talked softly to her, as she lay slightly reclined in an easy chair with a blanket over her. Warm. Safe. She closed her eyes, and he took her back to the moment of the abuse, over thirty years prior.

"You are standing to the side of your timeline right now, watching your life. Now, I want you to imagine standing on the line instead. You are currently facing backwards toward your past. I want you to remember that time where he hurt you. How do you feel? What is happening?"

"A man is touching me, he's older. Old. He has his hands around me pulling me into him, close. His hand is cupping my breast. My non-existent breast."

"Are you scared?"

"Yes."

"You are safe here, you are not there, you are here with me. That man is no longer real. Focus on you. Can you see yourself?"

"Yes, I am young. So young." She had started to cry.

"You are your older self, as you are today. You are safe, here with me. But you can now comfort your younger self. What would you say to her? Was it her fault?" he asked her.

"No, she was a victim, she didn't know what to do or what to say, to make it stop," said the woman.

"What would you tell her?"

"I would tell her that it wasn't her fault, and that the man was bad. And that she would be ok. And to tell someone. Her mom."

"What else?"

"I would hug her tight." Tears leaked from her eyes as she spoke. "I will protect you now."

"Good, now I want you to take her back with you to the timeline. I need you both to turn around and look into your future together. She will always be with you. But you are no longer the victim of this man. His hold on you is over."

In front of her was the future for her, she stood safely in the now, and behind her was the past.

That completed exercise had left a very good impression on Wayne, in his journey of becoming a psychologist. Even though many people who are not fully educated in therapy attempt this, he found that the approach had been helpful on more than one occasion for Regressive therapy techniques.

Wayne believed there were many ways to help people. He wasn't going to be picky or snobby about the options.

Wayne felt good about what he did, he liked a good puzzle and that is what he felt therapy was, unlocking the past to lead to the future. He liked the difference he made in other people's lives.

Now his own life? That he had not figured out yet.

Thankfully, or not, his life was so busy he hadn't really noticed.

~

W.K.

A nice repartee we had over the internet as I looked into something new. You held the knowledge of a sport I had always wanted to try and now was the time. The meeting with you went well as you described what I could expect and what I needed to do to partake. I soon noticed a difference between us that would make our communication difficult.

I have a theory that there are maybe about fifteen personality types worldwide. Each person falls into these categories, and we see them over and over in different packages throughout our lives, gravitating towards some, avoiding others. When I meet someone, I often think, 'That person is a Dave, because they reminded me of Dave. That person is a Marie, etc.' The names inserted stemmed from the original person I met, thereby becoming the monikers of that type of personality in my head. Not that I share that with them.

Sometimes you find someone that you are instantly comfortable with, because they are similar to another friend or family member.. They are not exactly the same, but have enough attributes, either physically or in their mannerisms, and interests, that we can lump them both together. We are more similar to each other than we think.

On to you. You were a little different in that I hadn't experienced your specific personality type in male form yet, and my exposure to the female version had moved on, so I felt out of practice. In my head, you were definitely a Marie. Super analytical, and needing to dig out every bit of what I meant in whatever I said, every time I opened my mouth. No matter how I worded anything, there was a chasm between my speech and your understanding, it felt like it took days to get on the same page. The process always makes me feel like an idiot, even if I had more knowledge of the topic to start with. You were that type, the one that just didn't get me, no matter how hard I tried.

I am liked by most people I come in contact with, my humor warming them to my presence early on before we build whatever we do. The Marie type frustrated me, but with years together and a common goal we were able to build what I thought was a nice friendship. I am not so arrogant to believe that everyone should like me, but I try hard to see people and meet them where they are, hoping they will do the same.

With you, I tried a few times, in my usual way, to bridge the gap. Cracking a joke or offering a compliment or something, but there was no emotional response. Only a blank stare that told me there is nothing in common here, no matter how hard I try. In frustration, I got quiet. This is how I was with you. Let you run the show, pick all topics of conversation. A surface friendship is all we would have because I do not feel safe to be myself around you. I walk cautiously around the questions and supply monosyllabic answers. Any attempt of humor is wasted. I guess it was a growth filled challenge to be around you. As I am in a small community leadership role, it is imperative that I am able to relate to many different types of people. You were great practice anyway.

I know in this life I will run across many more people like you, ones who don't immediately get me, or perhaps they never will. I need to learn that I can't take it personally, it is just another thing to note about humanity at large. We have people that we instantly connect with, and those we don't. Walking in different circles, sometimes they are neighbors, parents of our children or work colleagues. We can only do what we can do.

If we were granted one magical meal where we suddenly and naturally understood each other, I imagine we might have had an interesting chat. Alas, it was not to be.

~

1

Wayne turned and locked the office door before coasting down the corridor after a fruitful, but very long day. The walls were a sterile off-white with no artwork, other than the bland, washed-out thrift shop prints of old beach landscapes here and there, that hung crookedly most of the time.

Like his job at times, this building held no beauty. His profession was witnessing and helping to process the very gray days in people's lives. No one came to see him because they were so damn happy.

Driving through town, he noticed the restaurants filled with people. Through the windows they sat paired up and laughing. Twosomes were all around him, and he was alone. He often encouraged his clients to get out of their own way and take a chance on something to make their life more rich. Relationships, and getting out into the dating game. Chasing a long held dream of singing or creating something they saw in their head, to show the world.

Wayne would putter around his own head every six months or so, like his own internal check in that he did with his patients. If he'd actually stopped to document his own history as he did with his patients, he'd most likely been able to put the pieces together of why he was the lone wolf on his journey with few intimate relationships.

As a child, they moved a lot, so he didn't have time to connect with the other kids. Also being the only child with a controlling mother, she disguised her fear as love. When his parents died, Wayne's initial reck-lessness led to a broken ankle and three months sitting on the couch thinking about all he wanted to do but couldn't. The time wasted after he'd wanted to feel some absolute autonomy over his life at last. After that, he was always on the move, trying some new sport or adventure to scare himself into feeling something, anything. He'd shut off many of his emotions early on.

As the only child of a serviceman, he had come to expect the same perfection from himself and the people he chose to spend his time with, as his father had expected of him.

Wayne contemplated doing the work on himself for himself, to get into therapy and finally tackle his own baggage, but he found that he kept postponing each appointment. His life was always ripe for a deep dive, but he needed to commit to it. Something always seemed to pop up in front of the personal work when it came to priorities. His work, a new hobby, a seminar in some far away land.

Wayne missed the closeness that came with being in a relationship, and Lord knows he missed the regular sex. From time to time, he had a woman or two who he could call in the middle of the night, out of their mutual physical need. They seemed ok with the arrangement for a little while, wanting little attachment themselves. As time went on, they would find someone else who gave more or wanted to be exclusive and they would sever the liaison and move on.

Wayne was on his own again, single and unattached for the last two years. He wished at times that he could find someone who didn't care about the day to day relationship stuff as much as he didn't. Someone so busy with her own life, she didn't set expectations on him. A female version perfectly matched to his relational vagabond self. There just didn't seem to be any out there.

He helped many couples through their difficulties, but when it came to relationships with women himself, he was challenged. His "type" was a bit wild, the ones who were a bit of a mess. He would find one, start thinking she might be the one, but over their time together, he would end up analyzing her, and subsequently try to "fix" her. He couldn't seem to get it through his head, that when these women talked to him, they just wanted someone to listen, not point out what they could do to fix their problem, or have him all up in their business about what to do. Typical of the male and female dynamic, really. He hoped to learn to be able to set aside his role of psychologist when it came to his love interests. To give other people grace and let them be their authentic selves.

As he grew older, the women who wanted children fell away, and that was better for him as he didn't want kids. He'd have been tied down then, and many of his activities were dangerous. Rock climbing, canyoneering, and white-water kayaking were some. One kayaking trip became the scariest, with him tackling multiple waterfalls in a contest with a bunch of twenty year old's before an injury and near drowning, caused him to retire from the sport permanently.

He had hiked many miles of the Colorado Trail, taking weeks away from his job and responsibilities. Many of his friends couldn't understand his need for the solitude, the quiet that came with being on the trail for weeks on end, talking to no one. But for Wayne, it was extreme opposite of his every day. Out there, there was no listening to the problems of others. The only sounds were of his own crunchy footsteps, walking away from societal expectations and pressure. The birds singing and the strong, gusty wind were his only companions on the trail.

His in-town quiet came in the form of home at the end of each day. Unlike the office his house was filled with color. Art procured from all over the world, as well as some from his parent's home, he appreciated each piece and their story. A wine connoisseur, he hand picked each bottle for his wine cellar. Going deeper than the pretty pictures on the label, he read every note and tease the bottle bragged about. Everyone around him knew he liked a nice glass of wine, now and again. Tonight would be such a night.

Wayne picked up Thai food from his favorite place, and grabbed a pint of Ben and Jerry's, Cherry Garcia ice cream from the mini mart next door.

Once home, he would pop the cork on his Domaine Ampeau Meursault La Piece Sous Le Bois- vintage 1995. It would be in celebration of "helping save," his one-hundredth couple.

He also had that new mysterious, homemade book from the Billows' to crack open. It enticed him, even though he hadn't looked at it yet, and he wasn't sure why.

Wayne slid the key into the lock of his brick 1890 Georgian style home and stepped inside. Per habit, he locked the door behind him, and set the keys on the side table before heading to the kitchen to set up his meal and put the ice cream in the freezer.

Wayne had recently completed a remodel of his kitchen, even though he rarely cooked himself. He was proud to have used all sustainable and recycled materials. He had paid much more for them; he knew, but he was pleased with how well the space turned out and felt good about doing his part to help the planet. He ran his hands over the wine colored countertops made with FSC Certified paper and resin, it was warm to his touch. The kitchen was more or less a backdrop for the

"Wine Adventure Nights," he would host once a month with the same small group of friends. The built in theme was faraway places, and each month he would focus his effort on a certain region or country. Purchasing a box of researched wine from the chosen area, he had dinner catered in with a similar food that matched. His caterer liked his new kitchen too, she loved his adventurous food gambols as much as he did. Once, he hired a musician with a sitar to come and entertain his friends.

He set the Thai food on the counter and pulled a plate from the cabinet. He uncorked the longed for bottle of wine, to let it breathe. Placing the food items on his plate so that none of them touched he put the plate in the microwave for a minute and a half, on high. The buzzer sounded after he had set his place at the island bar. He turned on some slow jazz to let the day roll off of him.

Pouring himself a glass of wine he set it next to his placemat. He placed the book the Billow's had given him on the counter in front of him.

The microwave buzzed again. He retrieved his plate and sat down. He undid the raffia which until then had hidden the title. Find Me, Book One. No Author listed, no publisher, no copyright, no Library of Congress info on the inside cover. Nothing.

"Huh." His brow furrowed.

He opened to the first page and read the plea as he took a bite of salad roll with peanut sauce.

It was an invitation to participate in an experiment. An incredibly fascinating plot, he read the bolded paragraphs, relating to some himself, while many others through his clients, over the years.

He wondered who the author was. Maybe a client? That would be nuts. Where was she, what she was doing right now? Is she still waiting on the other ones? Would this book ever be returned to its rightful owner?

The huge question fell on him. He soon finished the pages and realized he had hardly touched his food.

Grabbing a pen from the hall side table, he signed his name and location in the back of the book before going to warm his dinner again. Retrieving his thrice heated food from the microwave, he walked past the kitchen island and settled into his rugged brown leather chair in the lounge instead.

Through the window he could see the full moon peeking out behind the branches of the old oak tree. It was the same moon the author might be looking at right now, thinking about her books, and where they might be. No dates were given in the books, Wayne could only guess it's travel time based on the signatures in the back, about twenty.

Tipping his wine glass to his lips, he drank a sip, and swirled the liquid around with his tongue, but not swallowing. Letting the wine sit in his mouth, he tasted each note, before opening his lips and taking a deep breath in to punctuate the flavor even more. This was a very good wine. Dinner was great as usual, and he had a good book that was making him think. He finished his food, put the plate in the sink, and turned on the TV.

The News. Mostly bad, as usual, but the final piece was a spotlight story of a local woman who had just turned one hundred years old. She spoke of how grateful she was to have been alive at this time in history. She had seen so much happen in her many years of life. Sharing her thoughts on some of the monumental changes that had happened in the world, during her lifetime. Vehicles, women's rights, photography, progress of some sort on virtually everything. Some of the places she had seen in her hundred spins around the sun. At the very end of the piece, she shared her secret to a long life.

"I did what I wanted, even if it scared me. I tried everything I thought I might love." She smiled big. "And I never stopped falling in love with something new."

Brave woman. Wayne thought. The night had been filled with so much spiritual nutrition.

Wayne wondered if the author of the book, one of five would have to live to be a hundred years old before she would see one of her books again. Whatever happened he hoped that she would make it, that it would happen for her.

He also hoped that someday, she might share it, and be on the news so he could see it. Knowing that he was a part of her story. Now *that* would be good news. He sat and felt special. He was now a member of a very exclusive club.

All day, every day, he listened to other people's problems. Offering solutions sometimes or just listening as they resolved, themselves, whatever topic they were working on. He rarely thought of himself. What about his feelings, his problems, his dreams? His dreams. It had been so long since he had dreamed of something.

"I'm always telling people how to change their life for the better, to strive for their very best self. Shouldn't I do that for me too?"

Wayne closed his eyes and listened to the music playing on the tv in the background, it was one of the old woman's favorite songs, as they closed the show.

Frank Sinatra's, *Come fly with me,* soared out of the speakers to him.

It had been years since he had heard that song. His father used to play it back when he was a teenager. As the piece reached a crescendo, he rose from his chair. He unlocked and opened the front door, looking out into the brisk night toward the moon sailing high in the sky.

The lights of an airliner soared overhead, blinking green and red, off and on. He could hear the sound of the jet engine heighten as it climbed to a higher altitude, feeling the thrust in his bones, he remembered back to his childhood and watching the jets take off at the airfield.

"That's it. I'm doing it." He turned and ran into the den, slamming the front door.

Grabbing the telephone book from the desk, he flipped it open to A for Aircraft. Aircraft schools. He had always wanted to be a pilot. Even toying with the idea before college, but his mother had begged him to stay safely on the ground. She couldn't stop him now.

"I'm going to do it!" he yelled, not caring if his neighbors heard him.

"I have plenty of money. I'll take a month off and immerse myself in the study and practice of flying. I bet Jane can see my patients. Heck, she can have them all, and as an extra bonus I will give her that book. This book that helped me reach back into my soul for a long-lost dream."

Wayne got up and poured another glass of wine, sitting again in his easy chair, he lifted his glass to his father's portrait.

"Time to fly, Dad," a tear fell from his eye.

~

WORKING TO BETTER MYSELF, 2004

I had worked to discover the best of myself this year. Working out, finding a group of friends, to spend time with. Some of us had started playing indoor soccer, on a whim, and none of us had ever played the game before. We'd only dropped off our kids at practice in their tiny little cleats and shin guards. The first game teased us that we could do anything we set our mind to.

I had shared my idea of living an extraordinary life within an ordinary one with these women. It was the reason I said yes. The idea of just doing one thing out of the typical norm to get us started. I try to do at least one extraordinary thing every day, even if it is just trying a new food or drink.

Our little group branched out and together, we did a fun run, a 5k, and the ideas kept coming. I never would have dreamed that at 187 pounds after the birth of my second baby I would start playing goalie on a women's indoor soccer team. A winning team no less. The opportunities are endless.

At first, our husbands were supportive. Yes, they were reaping the benefits. Their wives were in better spirits, we were less stressed at home. There was more sexual activity. Wink, wink. So why would they complain? It was still a shock that on the whole they were ok with us spending time and a little money on ourselves, away from the family.

Then we started inviting the men to participate with us.

I had thought that being a wife and mom meant you had to give up everything for your family and spouse, destined to become a robot doing chores and other tasks that are expected, to keep everything running smooth.

How refreshing it was to know that the husbands, who we married all those years ago wanted to be helpful and supportive to us in reaching for our new goals. They had become willing allies for our adventures.

Kinda made us appreciate them even more. It did for me anyway. I watched how he would take the kids and even talk about doing some things with his *guy friends. He must have craved the same feelings of independence that I was feeling. The feeling that sometimes a person can have it all. That we are more than what we do everyday. Our usual role does not define us.*

My life is mostly made up of the events that shape a textbook suburban housewife's life. House, car, trying to get back into the workplace, after years of watching Barney. Watching the kids go off to school. Feeling like your purpose has left when they skip off to class. Watching them grow into actual people. Individuals.

I'm trying to build myself up so I have something left when they go. It's a process for sure.

~

1

Wayne called the pilot school the next day and asked when their next session of flight school was.

"First Friday of every month," was his answer. "Right around the corner."

He had time to wrap up some things, before jumping full throttle into his new goal.

Wayne hadn't spent much time with Jane, the therapist who worked down the hall. She was about ten years younger and had left her practice in Nebraska to come to Denver to be closer to the family, she had said once in passing. He didn't think she was in a relationship or had any kids. At least she didn't have any personal photos of any kind in her office. She seemed to work a lot of long hours like Wayne did. She might have mentioned a cat. An animal that Wayne had no opinion on.

The old mid century building had about ten counselors renting offices there. She and he were the only generalists, others were faith based, or specialized in grief counseling, drug abuse, or marriage counseling exclusively. A few others had specialized in children, and ADHD/Autism spectrum therapy.

Wayne didn't like the idea of turning away people in need. Especially people looking for a counselor. It shouldn't be hard to find someone to talk to when life is hard enough at the moment. He wasn't sure why, but people rarely came in until they were at their wits end about something. Well, maybe he was in the same boat.

Wayne had gone to school at the University of Denver and graduated with his PhD in Clinical psychology. He grew up in rural Aurora outside Denver, when his father was serving at Buckley Air Force base. He'd watched the planes take off from the airfield and imagined what those giant Golf balls were used for, the massive globe buildings that lined the edge of the campus. Sometimes his dad would drive him around in one of the jeeps, and show him some of the planes up close. Wayne was always fascinated.

When Wayne was old enough to perhaps join the armed forces, though, he didn't feel the desire to go and be bossed around at boot camp, and then sent who knows where and be told when to go and do something. He enjoyed aspects of the life, such as the travel promised, but could not handle the lack of control over his whereabouts, and that was a big part of the job.

Instead, he stayed close to home, helping his mother as his father fell ill to Alzheimer's early in his seventies, finally dying in his early eighties of a heart attack.

His mother had managed to keep her husband home for three years, before moving him into a care facility close by. His mom developed cancer about the same time that Dad started having heart problems. She would visit as often as she could.

The cancer and treatments wore his mother down to the bone. Wayne was by her side when she died only three years ago. Wayne's mother had begged him to calm his adventurous pastimes, relaying that she was constantly petrified about his way of life and all that kept him in jeopardy. In her life she had endlessly worried about losing her husband, and now had a son, with daredevil tendencies as well. She lived in the land of worry. Wayne's deathbed promise to her to be more careful, made him back off of his pursuits, for a month or so, but he couldn't live the rest of his life in fear, as that wouldn't honor anyone.

He called and told his patients for the day that he'd be moving them to someone else for a while. His most delicate clients had been seen earlier in the week, and he was sure he could continue to juggle them and his new school routine too.

At the end of the day, he passed by Jane's door with the Clinical profiles for his easier patients, and the blue book he needed to pass along. He knocked on her door, but she was in a session. Putting the patient notes into her locked mailbox outside the door, he wrote her a note, and stuffed it into the front cover of the book.

She would see it soon enough.

The note read...

"Don't believe what your eyes are already telling you. All they show is limitation. Look with your understanding, find out what you already know, and you'll see the way to fly." ~Richard Bach.

Jane- Please take my clients for a bit, the clinicals are here. I gotta fly. I will be in touch soon. Wayne

~

DISCONTENTED ME, 2004

*I*t's weird. Yesterday I saw so many options. Today, none.

I spent my birthday at the coast, with my mom and two daughters. My husband stayed behind so he could work on a project that could possibly save his job.

Layoffs in the company were planned and his job has been in jeopardy before. He shared the possibility with me, and I was almost excited that for once I could see a different life for us. We could sell the big house in the city and move to a small beach town only a few hours away. Buy two houses. Live in one, while fixing up the other one to sell, and on and on. Our profits becoming the income source for our family. Something we could do together. We could work together and play together. As a team. We have both always wanted that feeling but so far, have been unable to get there.

I shared my idea with him, and a single sentence from him that morning dashed all of my hopes of that life, before I had even gone to the bathroom for my morning pee.

He said, "I've done small towns."

I asked him where. He named the town where we had started our life together.

"That's not so small."

"Too small for me now."

And the conversation was suddenly over. No budging, no discussion, just a no.

Today I feel as if he isn't open to building anything together anymore. To me the idea was a way for us to find our way back to each other. Build something. A new adventure. I saw it clearly. Our family, so connected. Sharing a mission with the ocean as our backdrop, we could have ourselves a wonderful life managing the ebbs and flows. No longer reliant on a corporation to keep us afloat.

He has made so many of those limiting statements through the years.

"I'll never own a truck."

"I don't even have to go into that restaurant again."

"I won't ever have a cat again."

Unmovable statements. If I lump them all together, there could be a handbook filled with the no's in this house.

I imagine his statements manifesting as an immovable railroad spike through one of his feet. Tethered, he can only pivot around himself, never actually moving forward or in any other direction. Stuck in his stuckage, keeps me stuck as well.

Even the little things that could spice things up around here, he denies me those as well. No blue jeans or colored underwear, preferring his khaki dockers and tighty whities that he comes to bed in, each night. Oh, so sexy. Not.

Seems like I will always be living in a subdivision with strict CCR's and just sit waiting until retirement, when we sell the big house and go live on a golf course somewhere, where the most exciting thing that happens is an wayward ball in the yard.

And I know for a lot of people, that would be the best idea ever, but for me...not so much.

I have this one and only life, and this one chance to live it, and I need to crack this baby open.

But, I have married a roadblock.

~

1

JANE

Miss Jane Monroe walked to the door. Spying the flag up on her inbox, she said goodbye to the court-imposed client, Jose Morales, and he grunted in return.

'Tough kid.' she said to herself, opening the door with her key and taking the package back inside with her.

Jose was her last client of the day, and she was glad. He always took the wind out of her, energy wise. There didn't seem to be any improvement or hope of any growth with him. They spent their hour jockeying for a position of power, so far he was winning.

It was always, "Why do you want to know that? I can't remember. Who cares?"

He was exhausting.

Here she was, still fairly new at this still, and already overwhelmed with one person, a younger one at that.

How was she going to reach this kid? A man really, she was as scared of his future, as she was in his presence. If he knew that she would be in big trouble. She plopped the envelopes on her desk and walked back to lock the door. A diet Mr. Pibb called to her from the small fridge behind her desk. A bag of microwave-buttered popcorn spoke to her as well. Worried that she was now having auditory hallucinations, she popped the corn and pulled the tab on the soda can. Taking a sip, she let out an ahh, and leaned back in her chair.

The chair had been her uncle's, he gave it to her once he found out that she would be following in his footsteps into Psychiatry. The leather was old on the seat and the back, the oak wood arms felt strong yet worn. This chair was built to last.

She had been mostly happy with the profession, and the pay was good. The hours could be long, and some days it was depressing carrying around other people's pain.

The microwave buzzed and she opened the bag on the side, using it as a bowl.

"Lunch."

She looked at the book that accompanied the files. What is this? Some kind of new psychiatry test? She found Wayne's note tucked inside and the quote made her stop and think. And then she read, "Take my clients..."

"Crap, he left me his clients and took off? Shit." She counted the cases. "1,2,3,4,5,6. Six more clients...people I don't even know." she let out a big huff.

Wayne must have cracked wide open to do this. She wondered if she would be next. He always seemed so together to her, totally under control, almost stiff. If Wayne could tweak after more than 10 years, she would freak, any minute. She took another swig of her soda and shoved a handful of popcorn into her mouth.

"He is going to owe me, BIG." And payment would be sweet. Maybe dinner, maybe even dancing. She would make him pay up. He was pretty cute in that Indiana Jones kind of way.

She sighed. Yes, she could take care of this, but she wondered if he was ok.

She leafed through her rolodex and found his cell number.

"Hi, Jane." Wayne answered, sounding almost cheerful.

"Wayne, what are you doing?" she said in a calm voice. "Are you ok?"

"I'm great, I'm driving home from my tour of the flight school. Sorry to leave you with my caseload, but I did leave a parting gift. Have you read the book yet?"

"No, I was too worried about you. What happened?"

Wayne felt warm with her concern and spoke softly.

"Read the book Jane, I will be out of the office mostly until August, but then I will be back."

"You owe me," she relayed trying to sound stern.

"Anything you want," he chirped, enjoying the banter as it had been a while.

Somewhat shocked at his response, she gulped quietly. "Uh, ok."

"Hey, no one in the files is especially troublesome. Mostly they just need to talk, and maybe you could share a different point of view that may help them more than I've been able to. And read the book, Jane, I will be in touch soon, Bye."

"Bye."

She slowly placed the phone back onto the cradle.

Apparently, she had a book to read. She packed up her new client files and the new book and headed home. She had known Wayne for six years now, and nothing so far had ever made her feel like he even noticed her at all. But he must have. She had certainly noticed him.

She tossed another handful of popcorn into her mouth as she climbed into her car. She looked in the rear-view mirror and smiled at herself with this new chain of events, and the tingles she felt.

She found herself stupidly smiling most of the way home, too.

~

Thinking about my Books me
2004

L *ately I have been thinking so much about my little traveling books. Was it just a stupid idea, like my husband said?*

I mean, it really is ridiculous. The astronomical odds, the massive ask of the world? Does anyone actually care enough about a total stranger to try to help them? Does it even matter how nice I asked?

There is a tornado in my head. Spinning about the things I am considering. A new career, possibly ending my marriage? What am I going to do?

Will these feelings of unhappiness just stop on their own? Is this a mood, or a lull, or like he says, "that time of the month?"

Or is this what real marriage ends up being? Forever?

If I jump, what if I'm wrong? What if I wreck everything and this is what all marriages are like? That this is as good as it gets, and I didn't know and walked away?

Maybe everyone feels like this?

Lonely sometimes, while sitting in the company of someone else? Someone you promised to love til death do us part.

The excerpts in the books might seem like love letters to some, while opposite to others. What if those written about inside don't see the absolute flattery of being penned about, either good or bad, enough to help this hapless dreamer? What if someone decides to wreck its already miniscule chances?

I pray that the books fall into the hands of people who can relate to hidden dreams of their own, someone like me who wonders what else there is to life while you are doing and being what you are supposed to be.

No matter what, I am glad I sent them. I did it, rather than just wishing I had, and wondering about it forever. Even if none actually reach me, sending them will have to satisfy for now. I took a damn chance.

Life is too short to wonder what might have been, or what could be. Still, even with more time passing, depending on strangers, and the distance the books will have to cover to come home again, I believe in my heart, they will find their way.

It's a little something for me to look forward to. I need to believe that my little life can count for something. C'mon books, get moving. Keep moving. Please.

I need something big to happen in my life. Something I can call my own. Pronto.

~

1

Back at her apartment, Jane Monroe glanced at the new book on her coffee table. So haphazardly thrown into her life, she wondered what it could be about.

The book was interesting on a psychological level as well as a personal level. The volume made her colleague chuck a month's worth of patients and income. Something snapped in him when he received it, deciding to take time away from all of his patient's problems, their regrets, and complaints and focus on something for himself.

Jane thought about her nightmare client, Jose. If he even made it to thirty, he'd be back in therapy with a laundry list of regrets. His temper matched with a massive amount of "not giving a shit about anything," had him behind bars for most of his young life. At seventeen, he better make some changes if he wanted to become a contributing member of society. *If.* It was a big if.

Their three months of forced therapy had produced little, sans the sexual innuendos that had started last week. Another attempt at him screaming into the wind that he didn't care, and that he knew he wasn't worth the time to save.

Jane reached over her cat Scruffy and picked up the book to read. If it made her crack too, well, she could use some time off, she supposed. At least enough time to occupy herself with her recently ignited interest in the oh so curious, Dr. Wayne Huff.

So what if he lost his mind for a moment. Maybe she could help him through this midlife crisis? What if all he really needed was a good therapist? She smiled at her own joke and let her stroking hand come to rest on Scruffy's back. She nestled the book into her bent legs, her feet resting on the edge of the coffee table.

Opening the first page she was pulled into the pleadingly vulnerable intro. A traveling book. One of five. Five.

It had been so long since she read anything for fun. This blue book was light on pages but beckoned for her to keep reading. She hadn't had an invitation like it. She sighed when she reached the end, closing the back, leaving her hand there in thought.

Moments in someone's life. Small interactions with people that helped mold the author into who she was. Sculpting her like art. We are all formed by our experiences, and the people we surround ourselves with. Even the toxic ones. Often, they have the most impact, the most potential to change us.

A first love, even one that does not endure, can carry with it, all of the emotions. It is a training ground, for all that come after. Lessons learned. A friendship that ends somehow, a trust broken, or different viewpoints that count. A teacher that cultivated a kid who was struggling to find his place. A parent or relative that showed a child something new or magical or burdened them unintentionally with their own fears and anxiety to walk the planet with. Each a powerful legacy.

She set the book back down on the table and crossed the room to fetch a pen to write her name in the back, picking up her guitar instead. Covered in dust, she wiped some hair off the strings and shook it to hear that the pick had fallen through the sound hole. Instead of fussing to retrieve it, she fingered a few strings and started strumming. Her digits stung with lack of practice, and it felt as if she was learning for the first time all over again.

The guitar was a little out of tune, but not bad. The notes danced from the instrument and hung in the air. Jane was transported back to her teen years. Back when she gave openly of her thoughts without the professional tone of voice she now often felt herself using. Therapist speak even in most social situations. As a teen, she embraced the world as it was, and it, her.

Now, she was somewhat cynical, still with an underlying hope for humanity, she had chosen her profession to heal people. She had helped a lot of healing happen. Jane could be proud.

Again, Jose, her biggest challenge to date, popped into her head. She so desperately wanted to make a difference in his life. Not for any reward but to give him a chance to be all he could be. Maybe this book could help her do it if she gave it to him.

Help her, help him.

She strummed lightly on the acoustic, and the rhythms agreed with her. The sound catapulted into the air and bounced off the walls. She closed her eyes.

This little book did have some sort of a magic touch. One that inspires, possibly great things. Simply falling into someone's life, makes the recipient think of the times in their lives that they had forgotten about, or buried with the ins and outs of daily living.

It was a reminder to pay attention. That every moment shared between two people has the opportunity to change someone. Hurt someone. Heal someone.

Wayne Huff hadn't cracked. He had gotten it. Just as she did now.

He was becoming more intriguing by the minute, and suddenly she felt intriguing too. And talented and intelligent, and more alive than she had felt in years.

Her nights popping popcorn in the microwave and watching reruns on the history channel were over. At least for a while. She set the guitar down on the couch and picked up the pen she had been after moments ago.

Writing her name in the back of the book, under Wayne's, she imagined her last name changing to his.

One never knows. After all, she did have a little debt to collect.

~

V. S.

My aunt. I only saw you maybe two times in my life. The first time I was a little kid and you rolled in with your husband at the time in the biggest R.V. I had seen in my life. Flipping your long blonde locks as you exited the side door, you had long, long eyelashes and looked like a movie star. I thought you were. A blonde Cher.

Your fingernails were painted perfectly, and you had a shapely figure, basically you were a magical beautiful princess coming to our house to stay and visit. You painted my nails and put makeup on my face. I felt glamorous even though I was still rocking the Dorothy Hamill haircut that my mom insisted I get after she didn't want to brush out my tangles anymore. The haircut that made me feel like a boy. Another story.

The second time I saw you, we were visiting you, my dad and brother and me. You had two cocker spaniels that humped each other all the time, but no one said anything about it. My eyes were pulled to the activity, and I wondered why you never stopped them. You were married to a different husband this time, and I can't quite remember what he looked like at all. But you looked the same, still so fancy.

I remember reaching out to you when I was getting married, a last-ditch effort to show I had more family than the few members I usually had access to. I wanted you to be there, and you said you would come. But you never came. Our flakey family was on point. I didn't think of you or reach out again. We were all estranged on that side.

Dad told us how you were adopted into the family as a baby. You were very wanted, as my grandmother couldn't have any more children. Her first child died, then Dad came, and to try for any more children could have been deadly for her or the baby.

Dad remembered riding in the car very late at night, to AZ, and arriving at a small shack. There was an exchange. A thick envelope of cash, and a baby was placed in my grandmother's arms for the ride all the way back to CA. Dad was young and the details weren't much more clear than that.

When I asked him if he thought you had been adopted legally, he was sure that you had been. Your mutual father was above reproach.

But I can't help but wonder; late night drives into the desert, her Native American heritage, was it on the up and up?

We were never close enough for me to ask if you ever sought out your birth parents. I wasn't around to build the trust, and neither were you. Maybe you just felt rejected by the whole thing and never thought to ask. It was a thing back then.

An easy, win-win exchange of a child, one family solving the problem of not being able to provide, the other receiving a blessing for another's empty womb.

I wonder about it all sometimes, but it is not my place to ask these questions. AZ has closed adoptions, so the records won't open until the child's ninety-ninth birthday if the person lasts that long. Seems like someone could find some answers, somehow.

You had five, six or seven husbands over your lifetime, I couldn't keep track.

I imagined you never felt settled and safe in your spot. Always wanting to fit in, but never being able to get there.

If you hadn't felt close with the family that you went to, maybe you would have been better off with the other one?

We will never know.

~

1

J ane Monroe planned to spend most of the weekend in her head, sitting on the floor of her closet. That traveling book had brought up some memories for her, and she suddenly found herself wanting to reminisce and mentally visit some of her life.

She pulled her college memory box off the top shelf of her closet. It was filled with class papers, some photos and a thick old notebook diary she had written in, pretty regularly in her first four years of college.

Jane received her undergraduate Psychiatry degree from University of Nebraska in Lincoln. Moving on to her Masters and Doctorate at the University of Nebraska, Omaha. Omaha was a much bigger city than Lincoln was, and Lincoln was much bigger than the town she grew up in, a cozy little place called Ravenna.

Her father worked for Burlington Northern, and her mom worked at the town library after all of her brothers and sisters had gotten established in school. She had four brothers and a sister and they all grew up energetically wired on the farm that was shared with her grandparents. As the youngest, Jane saw all the kids leave town, going to the big cities, just as soon as they could.

They were a happy family when they were together, but tended to stay more distant most of the time. Jane didn't know why. Maybe so much togetherness growing up, or they were all working on their own plans and goals.

Jane had only been with Noah in high school, and had one other lover on an especially drunk night, one of her first days of college. He was her one and only one night stand. He hadn't left much of an impression as she couldn't remember his name anymore.

In her sophomore year in college she met Nate. She hadn't really been paying attention to him, as he was so serious and acted all business in their study sessions. He was tall, strong, and had beautiful black hair and rich brown eyes. He was quiet, but wicked smart, and his opinion showed sometimes if he fell into a topic he was interested in. Jane and he would get into intense verbal discussions so passionate and long that the rest of the group would leave the library without them noticing.

Jane was drawn to him for a reason. His slow to answer cadence in groups commanded attention but not in a 'look at me,' kind of way. He sat by, and never interrupted anyone. He was adept at listening and engaged with everyone fully with the same commitment to hearing what it was they had to say.

She had asked him one day, as they walked back to their cars, "Hey, what is your deal, for a guy you are really good listener."

"I've been studying some of the Indigenous tribes, and after learning more about them and how they speak to each other, I have been forever changed with how I communicate. In both talking and listening. They believe that words have power, and one must be careful with each word they bring forth. They are intentional, and speak each word slowly so the person hearing them will have the ability to take it all in. It is a gesture of respect and humility, that they are not speaking to be over someone, they are speaking to have the other understand while giving them the time and space to do so."

"Gosh, that is so different from the way we usually talk, all fast and trying to get to the point."

"Words can hurt, attack or mend, choosing and using them thoughtfully gives you the best chance at togetherness no matter the topic."

"I want to hear more, can we talk about that over dinner?"

"Sure." A small smile appeared on his face then his eyes fell away from her.

"I'll meet you at the pizza place, my treat."

Nate nodded.

They sat in the back of the restaurant, thirty minutes before closing, and told each other all about how they grew up.

Nate from downtown Omaha, and Jane coming from rural Ravenna. It was funny how both of them had been excited to go to Lincoln, Nebraska for school. For Jane it was a much bigger town than she was used to, and for Nate a smaller one.

She thought back to how fired up and sad Nate had been at that time. He would tell her things that shocked her about how the local Ponca tribe had been treated in the past up to then.

"So much has been lost and taken from them. In 1966, they were "terminated" by the United States government. Can you imagine that? 'Terminating them' meant taking away all of their rights and their land as a group; officially disenfranchising them as an entity. Over and over in this country's history, these people have been dismissed, killed, stolen from and abused almost to the point of their actual and total cultural extinction. We have introduced disease, alcohol, and other substances that have annihilated thousands. God. I would work for no money, if I could. I would do anything to try to make a difference in just one of those people's lives. We have so many reparations to make, as I see it. I want to help with that. Whatever I can do to help with anything."

Jane had put her hand on his, as they sat in the booth, she cried alongside him. Him pouring out even more transgressions that were made against the indigenous people of their area.

She felt more than ever that her sheltered upbringing should not sway her from learning all she could alongside Nate about the original people.

Growing up in Nebraska, Jane knew that the Native Americans were here way before the Europeans, and that the government came in and stole their land from them. But she knew this on more of an abstract level, not the details. When she studied further, she read about the many tribes who were unsettled from their lands; moved and dismissed as a people by the United States government. Their travels were dictated by the government and they couldn't move off of the reservations without being potentially brought up on charges, and tried as a criminal in the U.S. courts. The history of Standing Bear and his trial bothered her every time she thought of it. She wrote a paper on it, in her junior year in humanities. It was so messed up.

Nate had grown up in Omaha, but wanted to try out a smaller town for his undergrad work, and to attend a college with a lower price tag and smaller class sizes to be able to see if working with the tribal community was what he wanted to do.

He rented a room from a spinster in town, and stayed off campus. Jane found out later the spinster was actually his auntie, but he was shy about sharing that. Appearances and pride were super important to him, and he didn't want anyone thinking he was getting a handout.

His place was out in the garage and had its own door. He could do as he pleased. There was a sink in the main part of the garage with a small fridge. He had turned the old workbench into a kitchen of sorts, and made most if not all of his meals there on an old Coleman camp stove. The small bathroom, literally a metal stock tank with a shower curtain around it and a toilet, sat anciently in the back corner of the garage. Pipes exposed and all. The concrete felt cold and Jane rarely took off her shoes. Except to climb into his bed.

She started going to his place only after one particularly romantic late night tryst in her car. Her small Toyota Celica was not exactly easy to be passionate in, since Nate was so tall. Jane had roommates, so they often went to his place, and she remembered that first day, when he had neatened up as she was walking in. Tossing clothes into a hamper from atop the couch right before she sat down on them. He hadn't been expecting company. This was just the start of their romantic interludes.

For as brainy and shy as Nate was, he was a very tender and attentive lover. It was almost as if he had taken a class on what turned women on. Maybe he had.

She closed her eyes for a minute and flushed just thinking about him. His hands on her. How safe she felt, while with him. She shook her head, bringing her back into the now, and got back to her box of memories.

Jane dug through the pages and pages of exams, papers and sports paraphernalia from school. She had been a cheerleader in those early years, rallying for the Cornhuskers, before becoming overwhelmed with study, and turning into a bookworm to stay afloat. She rifled through more papers and came across one of the few photos of the two of them, taken in a photobooth at one of the small county fairs. His serious smile, no teeth, and the way he had his arm around her, squeezing into that booth had been fun. The last shot was a kiss shared for the camera.

Jane sat back against the wall of her closet, and closed her eyes. She could almost feel his touch again. The soft way he would move the hair out of her face to really look at her, deep into her eyes. He was such a soulful person. Penetrating.

That was ten years ago. Jane hadn't thought she and Nate would stop talking after she left to get her Masters degree in Omaha. Jane pursued her doctorate as well, but Nate stayed in Lincoln after starting to work as a counselor for a Ponca tribe based health center not far from the college. They had lost track of each other. Jane remembered being happy for him in his pursuit, one that he hoped would become his lifelong calling.

Jane loved him, although she hadn't said it out loud, only whispering it once as he slept next to her. She didn't know if he secretly heard. Nate had never uttered the words to her either. If he did love her, he kept it hidden pretty well. But Jane felt loved by him, when they sat together and shared a meal or when he held her after their lovemaking.

Jane pulled out her handwritten journals she had kept from her time with Nathan, and got up off the floor. She plopped onto the couch. Scruffy meowed next to her, wanting a stroke.

She read the pages taking her back to the days when they were snowed in, studying for their final exams, and sustaining themselves for days on canned chili, barely warmed, with some tortilla chips. The passages she wrote while waiting for him to come back with a Runza sandwich to share, a treat for special occasions, such as an aced test. She found the days she wrote about when she thought she might be pregnant, but didn't tell him. Only to have her period arrive three days later, along with her mixed emotions.

Those reminders of moments passed, brought into her mind again by the little book that Wayne had given her. It had been an active Saturday morning of totally living in the past. She put the journals down on the couch cushion next to her and went into the kitchen.

Where was Nathan now? What would she say to a client who was revisiting the past like she was today?

Grabbing a bag of carrots and some ranch dressing out of the fridge, she opened a can of diet Cherry coke. After a few crunchy bites, she grew tired of carrots, and laid the bag and dressing on the coffee table. She washed down the last bits of carrot from her mouth with the soda and pulled her guitar from its hanger, pushing the journals to the floor with her foot.

Strumming, she tried to play the only song she had ever really taught herself. "*Here comes the sun*," by the Beatles. Over and over she played until it flowed easily, and she closed her eyes, remembering that she had often played that song for Nathan on her beat up guitar while trying to get it right.

After the fifth time through, playing to her satisfaction, she put down the guitar and went into the bathroom to put her hair up into a bun. She grabbed the little blue book and threw it into a book bag and set it down by the front door. Pulling on the sweatshirt she wore yesterday and some wrinkled jeans from her closet floor, she tugged on her favorite sneakers.

She needed to know where Nate was. Give herself some closure, or maybe she would reach out to him, to say hi. Maybe she would share with him that him teaching her about how the tribal people spoke with each other had helped her in her practice. She was a great listener and spoke carefully when she did.

She headed out the door to the public library. Research. Arriving late morning, she walked past the video section where she often loaded up on DVD's for the weekend; heading instead to the reference section. She climbed the stairs of the beautiful lobby, as she had so many times before. It was filled with encyclopedias, atlases, and phone directories of many of the cities in America. She grabbed a couple phone books from Nebraska. Lincoln, and Omaha areas, just in case Nathan might still be in the area and laid them out on a big table near a bank of computers.

There in the Yellow pages of Lincoln, Nebraska for 1998, on a page for tribal counseling was Nathan Fye. He's still there. At the same place he had started over ten years ago.

Jane moved over to one of the few computers in the section. She looked up his name on the internet.

An article in the local paper highlighted his celebrated role as Director for the health center, and another one linked to a naming ceremony for him. It said that "Nathan Fye, having discovered his own Indigenous heritage, has been given his own Ponca name in celebration of his commitment and care of the Ponca people."

The front page photo showed Nate, standing next to a beautiful woman; his wife, as Jane determined from the caption below. They were both dressed in traditional regalia. Jane straightened up in her chair and went on to read the article.

"Nathan 'Found His Way,' Fye, while searching for his natural birth parents, has found that his ancestry is Ponca, the very tribe he has dedicated the last twelve years of his life supporting and advocating for. He has finally found his people.

After being given his adoption records by his parents for his twenty-fifth birthday, Nathan recognized a familiar Ponca name, and spoke to his friend, the tribe Elder, Walking Strength, about his wish to be recognized officially as a member of the Ponca tribe. With his resolve and care for the Ponca people, the Elder was happy to reunite him with his tribe and give him his Ponca name in a private celebration.

"It's like he knew all along." said Charlie 'Good Rain' Nobel, a co-worker of Nathan's for the last five years. "His spirit was always Ponca."

Jane felt a tear of acceptance and joy form in the corner of her eye. She had the answer she needed. Nate had made the difference that he had always wanted to. He had reached the level of trust and commitment in the beautiful community he pledged to serve, and stood tall with a pride. She wished she could feel that for herself. Everything made so much sense now. His devotion to their betterment, the way he felt every discretion as if his own. He must have somehow known that these were his people all along. She knew he was adopted, but he never let on that he might be of Native American bloodlines.

Nate must have been overjoyed at the findings, his energy was placed properly. The people he loved so much were his own. More tears fell as she realized the true magnitude of what Nate must have felt. His own internal compass had brought him home.

She closed the tab on the computer, and put the phone books back on the shelf. Nate was happy, settled and also very taken.

She crossed to the history section and looked for a book about Standing Bear and his trial. The one she saw on the shelves the same one that Nathan had recommended all those years ago. *Standing Bear and the Ponca Chiefs,* by Thomas Henry Tibbles. It was time to read it again. Jane would also be looking for other ways she might support the tribes around her.

The excursion had produced a lot. What she had missed in the years since Nate, all holed up in her apartment watching movies waiting for something to happen to her. If she wanted to have any sort of an active social life, she would need to get out more.

Turning to leave, she removed the little blue book from her bag, and walked down the stairs and to exit the building. She had thought of giving the book to her troubled client Jose, but somehow she wasn't sure he would get it. She considered leaving it in the check out bin, but at the last second, she left it on a bench just outside the main entrance.

This whole thing had made her wonder whether she was spending her spare time wisely. Maybe she hadn't let herself get close to anyone since Nate because he felt so right for her? That she was waiting for him to figure it out, and standing by. But now she had the evidence that he had totally moved on, and was also fulfilling his life's work.

She hadn't tried very hard to connect with anyone, or gone to places where she could meet new people. Here she was in this great town, full of creative, interesting, and vibrant people, and she had a fog over her eyes, incapable of seeing any of it.

Jane walked across the street, looking back, in time, to see a younger man pick up the book, look around, and put it under his arm, before continuing on his way down the street.

She noticed a paper sign on a telephone pole announcing an open mic night, for this evening, at a local bar, not too far from her house. She decided she'd go, after grabbing a quick bite to eat somewhere close and going back home to shower and spruce up.

Jane peeked again towards the man and wished the traveling book, "Godspeed."

~

DEPRESSION KICKED FOR NOW, I THINK? ME 2004

*M*onths have gone by since I lifted the blanket of depression from my eyes with a healthy balance of diet and exercise. The meds might have helped out too.

I have spent the last few months on a quest. A quest to better myself on my journey towards my claim of living an extraordinary life.

I wonder what my little books are up to? Have they reached someone who might know me?

I lay next to him, awake. I often think of my little books. Tonight I lay listening to his incessant cough that would be calmed with a simple dose of medicine, if only he'd take some, I wonder more. He finally gets up and leaves. Down to the couch to watch TV til some magic visual potion puts him to sleep.

I am too excited to sleep. I think of how far I've come. How many suddenly look to me for encouragement and answers. It's fascinating how many people we can touch on a daily basis. My children, my children's friends', my spouse, my friends, my parents, the other board members of a mini-government I helped start. It's really incredible.

Do other people wonder and feel how entwined we all are? How interwoven and dependent we are on each other or to each other each day?

I think of these things in the moments between the moments.

My friend's nephew. Dying from the injuries he sustained in Iraq. Tragic. A twenty one year old Marine attacked and now gone. Missing from the fabric of humanity, I feel the hole that he has left. The closing doors, the lost loves and the very vacuum that his disappearance has made.

If I feel I touch so many lives everyday, what of the lives he would have touched, in the days, weeks and months that were robbed of him.

Live your life, people.

Actively <u>live it</u>.

Don't just drive to work everyday like a zombie watching your bank account go up and down like a heartbeat. Look down at your hands once in a while and watch them grow older.

Older with life experience. Older with the touch, love and hard work of a living human being. Live with intention. Live more. This is my vow. My current circumstances keep me grounded. Grounded in knowing that right now, this is where my place is. With my husband and girls. Without the wherewithal to travel extensively and abroad, and without the freedom of being alone in the world, I make different choices.

I walk instead with the intention of living an extraordinary life from within the confines of an ordinary one. Little things can and do make a difference. Even a thought outside my comfort zone gives me a thrill.

I look around and say, "Why not? Why not me?" I am lucky to have found some friends who embrace the idea that we can be different today than we were yesterday. Inside at least, where it counts.

We play soccer, not for a college scholarship or cash or Olympic greatness. We play because it feels good and we have claimed Monday nights for us.

All of us, in our mid-thirties and forties, we aren't kids, yet we feel young and vibrant with each kick of the ball. Each game won.

Two years ago I would have never said yes to soccer, now I can't say no. Two years ago I wouldn't have run in the race I am excited about running in, next month.

It all started with a request of myself to live an extraordinary life. To not sit back and ask myself, to lie there on my deathbed and have very little to look over.

My life will be rich, not maybe of actual riches, but of the bounty that life has to offer.

We need to remember the people that die before us, and we need to stack their dreams on top of our shoulders and carry them with us.

Do more. For them, for us all. Reach out. Go beyond what we think we can do at this moment. Thrive. I will continue to try to wring out every bit of life with my aging hands.

~

1

DUNCAN

The new owner of the little blue book, waited at the crosswalk for the light to turn. He couldn't believe his luck after leaving his own book at home. Safely tucked under his arm, he reached into his back pocket to pull out a flier he'd picked up.

He was looking for a certain restaurant. As a food critic for the Denver Star, he loved trying out new places he would hear about. The light turned and he stepped out into the crosswalk, accidentally dropping the book onto the wet ground.

A quick grab, and he kept on his way. Only about three blocks from the new taco place that was highly recommended.

Duncan Shots arrived at the restaurant, and said hello to the hostess. She led him to a table by the front window. It was 11:30, so the lunch rush hadn't happened yet, he had timed it just so.

It was a good time to have the full attention of the kitchen to get his order correct, and to wait around and see how the restaurant filled out with customers. See what types of people were attracted to this place, how the wait staff handled the crowd, he would be able to catch the overall vibe.

When he sat, Duncan would often ask the people at other tables what they thought of the food they ordered, to give himself a bonus sampling of what others enjoyed without having to taste everything on the menu.

Tacos were pretty simple. Unless the meat was totally spiced wrong, you couldn't really screw it up. It was all about the toppings, the meat and the sauces.

Duncan was a bit of a purist, picking one taco with carnitas, cilantro, cabbage, guac, and tomato, and another, a cajun fish taco with a white sour cream/lime sauce, radishes and farm lettuce blend. He added some chips and their homemade salsa to his order, and waited for the food to arrive.

It was odd to find a random book outside the library, as most books lived inside. He had glanced around a little, before grabbing it, but it didn't seem to belong to anyone.

The slouchy lady in the sweatshirt he'd seen didn't look attached to it, since she was so far away. She was also seemingly on a mission.

Duncan squinted at the cover, and pulled his glasses from inside his dress shirt pocket to see what it said. He wasn't really dressed up, just a plaid shirt with leather ribbon pocket detail, in a mix of lime greens. Blue jeans, and a baseball hat, black with a White Sox logo, finished his ensemble.

Duncan Shots, named to be a great basketball player one day, his eventual height and complete lack of interest in the game rendered it not to be.

He had moved from Chicago, to Denver about four years ago, after his particularly hard break up with Chenise. He really thought they would be together forever. He had asked Chenise to marry him, and she kept saying, she wasn't ready. Years went by, with him asking every six months or so, hoping for a different answer. Each time, it was the same. Not yet. It broke his heart and he couldn't understand. Didn't she love him? Finally, after asking the last time, with the answer being the same, Duncan sublet his apartment, packed a bag and moved West. She didn't follow, and their strained communication had all but ended recently.

Duncan's mother came out to visit once a year, and his sister and he just talked on the phone since she was afraid to fly. Duncan hadn't had either the money or desire to go home. To drive by all the places he and Chenise would go together, or potentially see her out with someone else.

Duncan's chips and salsa arrived first and they were warm from the fryer. A plus, but no salt, a minus. He doused the batch with salt, and dipped one chip into the salsa. There was a tang of pineapple which was surprising at first, then settled into a nice flavor in his mouth. Corn pieces brightly punctuated the red chunky condiment with slivers of cilantro thrown in.

He was picking his adjectives and writing the article in his head, with each bite.

The tacos came to the table, and he watched as a few more people streamed into the restaurant. They looked like a bunch of college kids,

coming in for a good, low priced lunch. He would touch on the afford-
ability of this place, as well as the food and decor.

Bright stucco yellow walls, with dark wood trim molding. Sombreros
and fake tropical plants were scattered around. The booths had orange
striped plastic cloth seats with a dark wood back, carved with dancing
people. The people who owned this place were not afraid of color, that's
for sure. Low volume mariachi music played on in the background.

The kitchen was loud, with pots and pans clanging, and a few people
yelling orders as they came in, no doubt from the endless ringing of the
house telephone which sounded over the music. Someone called back
to the kitchen to see if a big to-go order was ready.

As the place filled, Duncan noticed a new waitress struggling to keep
up, as her trainer had left her in the dust to help more customers. He
watched the crowd. Everyone seemed to be eating and enjoying the
food, they left little behind and bussed their own tables when they were
done. Whoever owned this place had taught his patrons well.

Duncan placed the spiral book onto the table, and moved the chips
to the outer edge of the table away from him. He might take those
home, and make some nachos later. He needed to focus on the tacos
that arrived at the table.

First the carnitas taco, yum, the sauce escaped his mouth and he
dabbed it with his napkin. Another bite, yes, it was good, almost to die
for.

He opened the book, and read the intro, and had just turned the
page, before plunking the last bite of his carnitas taco into his mouth.
A couple of chews in, his tongue caught on something sharp as he
swallowed. A bone?

Duncan tried to cough a bit, to dislodge the hard object, only to have
it plunge further and catch in a bad spot of his throat. He couldn't
cough, breathe. Nothing. His eyes started bulging in fear.

A fellow customer noticed him flailing his arms, and got up to ask if
he was ok. Duncan shook his head, sideways, and no sound came out
of him. He felt his eyes start to water, and desperation filled him.

The table emptied as all of the students next to him gathered around
to help.

"Call an ambulance!" shouted one, to the hostess up front. Another
tried giving him the Heimlich maneuver.

The hostess talked on the phone, as everyone stared wide eyed into
the gathered group.

"Is there a Doctor here!? Anyone?!" One young man shouted.

Jane Monroe who'd been eating a taco salad and reading her new library book in the back corner of the cafe, stepped forward, "I have medical training."

They sat Duncan on the ground, and the masses got out of the way.

"The ambulance is coming!" yelled the hostess.

She looked at her watch as she assessed the situation. Reaching her finger into his mouth to see if it was something she could grab or pull into a different position, she pulled back not wanting to push it even further into his windpipe.

'Shit,' she thought. "This man was going to die if he didn't get some oxygen now. Who knew how long the ambulance would be?'

A full minute passed, as she and the other young man tried other things. Hanging him upside down, with the help of the students and whacking him on the back. This was a stubborn obstruction.

Finally Jane shouted, "Get me a tall glass of tequila, a straw and a clean knife from the kitchen!" She had exhausted all other options.

The list was echoed all the way back to the kitchen, and the items arrived to her, within seconds.

"Stand back." Jane said to the majority of the students. "Except you, stay here." She grabbed him by the front of his shirt. "I need you to hold his hand, and keep him still. Can you handle this?" She looked him dead in the eyes.

"Yes, I am a physiology student. I got you."

She spoke to the man filled with terror.

"Sir, I am going to open your airway, when the ambulance comes they will take you to the hospital, but if I don't do this now, you are not going to make it."

He nodded, before losing consciousness. They laid him flat on the ground.

She poured some of the booze over her hands, wiping some gently on his neck, before dipping the paring knife into the rest of the glass to cover the blade. She swirled it, pulling it out, to shake off the excess, before closing her eyes and using her left hand to find the spot she had felt on the cadaver in her comprehensive first aid training years ago. She opened her eyes to make sure she was right.

Just under the Adam's apple, she sliced an inch long cut horizontally, deep enough to enter his trachea.

Jane was happy he wasn't overweight, so she could assess the area properly. She hadn't done this before. Not many people probably had.

She dipped the straw into the tequila before inserting it into the hole she had made. It acted as a new tunnel for the air, and a dam for the blood and tissue that wanted to fall back into the wound, but mustn't. This would get him *some* oxygen until the ambulance came and they could get him in for the emergency surgery.

The student pulled Duncan back into himself and held him in a slightly inclined position, so he was more upright. The blood could then drip externally, rather than have it fall back into the wound and perhaps cause another aspiration. Jane checked his vitals. He was breathing again, his heart rate still high but stabilizing.

Duncan opened his eyes and looked around. He had been out for about five minutes. The same students were standing around him, and they cheered when he made eye contact.

This guy was going to be ok.

The ambulance arrived and two paramedics came in with a gurney.

Jane spoke to them, "I sanitized the knife and inserted the straw at," she stuttered as she hadn't documented the time to be able to tell them.

The helpful young man said, "It was 12:35, by my watch."

Jane looked over at him and nodded.

"He did lose consciousness for a few minutes but I am not sure if that was from lack of oxygen or the fact that a stranger was coming at his throat with a knife. He is alert now, but will need some help making his neck look good again."

They moved him slightly to retrieve his wallet, so that they would know his name to ask him. Make sure he hadn't struggled with oxygen hypoxia.

"Sir, is your name Duncan?" the dark haired one asked the man.

He nodded slightly, and looked over at Jane. He held out his hand to her, as if it was nice to meet her. She reached back, her hand still bloodied from the procedure. Taking her hand in his, she didn't hold it in a business like fashion, but one of care and concern like an old friend.

"Duncan," she said and he smiled weakly.

The paramedics took his vitals, and put him up onto the gurney. One of them took Jane and the student's name and phone numbers.

"We are going to take him to James Medical center, do you want to ride with? He will go right into emergency surgery to remove the blockage."

"I will call the hospital and go see him after he is through surgery, tomorrow, unless for some reason they need me for something tonight."

The paramedics nodded and Duncan smiled at her before being wheeled out of the restaurant.

The crowd cheered with gratitude as Duncan was wheeled out of the restaurant, now with a standard trach tube sticking out of his neck, instead of the bendy straw that had been there before. Duncan also felt relief.

Jane hugged the student who had helped, and asked his name.

"Jeremiah Flannery. Maam, thank you for helping that man, I saw he was in trouble, but I didn't know what to do."

"Well, I am glad we were both here today, you were a huge help. If you need a letter of recommendation for your medical career, you just give me a call."

Jane handed him one of her cards, and noticed her old friend, the little blue book on the floor a few feet away. It must have been kicked clear in the commotion. That same book she had left on the bench had found its way back to her.

It must have been Duncan who picked it up. Jeremiah spoke again, after seeing Jane spy the book. "Oh yeah, he was reading that when I noticed he was choking, maybe you can give it back to him, since you are going to the hospital."

"I will." Jane crossed in front of a few people, and bent down to pick it up. There was a round of applause.

"I guess we were in the right spot at the right time," she said. "At least for him."

The owner stepped out of the restaurant with her as she left, "You get tacos once a week for life. So will he, if he wants to come back."

Jane wasn't sure that would be something Duncan would want to do, but she thanked him, and walked the six blocks back to her car.

She placed the familiar blue book on the passenger seat and drove over to the hospital to meet her new best friend.

~

1

JANE, AGAIN...

W hat a day. Her initial reconnaissance mission, to learn about Nate. That coupled with her decision to get out more, she was grateful she had chosen to see another part of the city, instead of just heading back home after her disappointing finding about Nathan, at the library.

Jane knew it wasn't healthy to live in the past. She always encouraged her clients to move on from that space, why had she accidentally fallen into the habit herself?

All the way home, Jane reasoned with herself that she hadn't put it together until now. She hadn't realized she was pining. Going to her work and home and back again had become a rut she wasn't paying any attention to. Nate had moved on, and so should she. This book had come into Wayne's life, and its presence spurred him into action. It had come into her life, too. Twice now. Surely, that should be the message to her too.

The small stop to try a new restaurant hadn't been exactly what she had in mind, but she was proud of herself for stepping forward when she was needed. By all counts as a psychologist, she could have sat back and said she wasn't a medical Doctor, or sat back as a spectator, and ignored the whole scene. She could have offered treatment to the ones who witnessed the traumatic event of seeing someone die. But her additional medical training had helped save this man today. She was thankful she took those classes. Happy that she had added that level of detail and training to her quest to help the "whole person," in her career. What else was she missing?

Later, at the hospital, Jane read the rest of the little book to Duncan. He motioned for her to take it back, when she asked if he wanted it. He answered back on the little white board that the staff had given to him.

Yeah, I don't really want to see it again, ever. But you can come see me whenever, friends for life!

The following day, Jane went to visit Duncan again. He was sitting up and working on his food review for the paper. He pointed to the bottom of his piece, *Thank you to Jane Monroe and Jeremiah Flannery for saving my life at Taco-Rama this last Friday. I am forever in your debt.*

She squeezed his hand and said goodbye for now. "I'll check on you tomorrow. Let me know if you need a ride home from the hospital or anything. If you ever want to talk about what happened, let me know. I'm a good listener."

Again, he wrote on the board, "Thanks, I may. First, I have to get out of here, and I want to go home to Chicago to see my family." He erased the board and wrote again, "There's this girl. It's time." He wrote a big smiley face underneath the words and reached out for a hug.

Jane would have to find someone else to give the book to. As she walked down the hall, a male nurse looked her way with a nod and a big smile. Was he flirting? As she passed him, she read his nametag. Mike Billows, R.N. He pointed to the book and smiled again. She turned away confused, crinkling her face.

Odd.

Maybe Jose would get another shot at getting the book from her, after all?

~

Struggling Me 2005

T *oday, I took a big risk. I finally told my husband that I wasn't sure I loved him anymore. I was tired of holding it in. The secret I was keeping made me feel even more alone than I may feel without him.*

I told him up at the mountain when we were skiing as a family. The girls were in their lessons. I figured it was safer there as I wanted to make sure he couldn't just leave, because I knew that wasn't what I wanted. Frustrated and hurt, he left me to go ski alone.

We spent the next few hours avoiding each other. I decided to give him his space, to let him think. I wanted to be honest to see if now the healing could start.

Finding a path back to each other. I have loved a lot of our life, I love our kids, I love the future we could have if we could get through this right now.

I've spent so much time needing him for everything I forgot how to want him.

He asked why I wanted to be married to him, and I couldn't answer.

It would be easy to let go now. It wouldn't be difficult to get him to leave.

That isn't what I want. I don't think.

I don't know what I want. I guess I want to feel excited when he comes home from work. I want him to think of me as his equal and his love. I want to feel the same way about him. I want so much to get out of the quagmire that exists when I think of us.

He says that a mature love doesn't have all the bells and whistles and that our kind of love floats below the surface. It's more of an understanding. It doesn't need to be said.

I spent most of the next day backtracking on my initial statement.

True, I was scared and hurt when he left me alone on the slopes. I felt jealous as he skied off with another woman for his lesson. Things are very confusing. I told him today that I think I need to love myself before I can love anyone else.

I have spent most of my life believing that I am incapable of doing anything. Even taking care of myself. I went from my father's house to his house. I have never been independent.

This time in my thirties is where most women find themselves. I'm already supposed to have all the answers and all that I need.

I am not supposed to wonder. I am supposed to know. I'm supposed to feel as though I am an adult.

I wish I had it all figured out. I told him I wanted him to say that he loved me enough for both of us right now and that we could work it out together.

He said that was "insane, childish and immature. Teenage thinking or something out of a romance novel. Relationships don't work like that."

I am thankful he is still here, and so thankful he is willing to try to work through this with me. He didn't have to but he is and I am so grateful.

There seems to be an understanding that we will do what we need to do, to find our way back to each other.

He really is a good man. Why can't that be enough?

~

1

Wayne called Jane at home that Sunday evening, to see how she was doing. He had seen her on the five o'clock news that night, describing what had happened the day before. She answered after the second ring.

"Hi Wayne, how are you doing?"

"I'm good, how are *you*? I just saw you on the news." His face was clenched as he walked past a mirror in his hallway, before running his hands through his hair.

"Yeah, that was wild, yes. I was suddenly back in college, in the cadaver lab, working on someone. Thankfully my instinct kicked in and I remembered what I needed to. He was in really bad shape. I'm so glad I added those extra classes to my schedule."

"Jane, it's incredible. I'm amazed. That guy was so lucky you were there to save him."

"Thanks, me too. I think I have made a new friend in Duncan. He will be awesome to help me find some new places to check out in the city. I want to get out more."

"Yeah? Me too. What are you doing tonight? Want to grab a late dinner?"

Jane walked past the mirror in the hall, as she spoke on the phone. Sweats again, with a bun, no makeup. "Um. Sure? but I will need about a half an hour. Is that too late?"

"No, that works, I am just getting back from the flight school right now. I'm so excited for the stuff I am learning, and I bet you are still running on some good adrenaline yourself. Want to meet someplace or should I pick you up?"

Jane thought for a second. She wanted this to be a date, if only to tell herself that she had been on one recently. It had been at least a year since she had gone out with anyone.

"Why don't you come get me, then I will have more time to get ready."

"Great, I know a little Italian place we can go to. No tacos." He laughed. "They are open late, and the lasagna is to die for."

"Um, can you not say die? Sounds great though, I'm famished."

Jane texted Wayne her address, before jumping into the shower, for a quick cleanse. She towel dried her hair, adding in some leave-in conditioner, before scrunching it up. Naturally curly, she didn't have to do much to get some lift. She picked a pretty bra, one that she didn't wear often and some lacy underwear, to feel more sassy under her clothes.

She pulled the light chain in her closet and perused the racks for what might be attractive and clean. Grabbing a pink cable knit sweater off the shelf, she pulled it over her head, before sliding into a denim mini skirt. She was thankful she had remembered to shave her legs yesterday.

Jane didn't want him to think she was trying too hard, so she kept her makeup simple. Just enough to show off her blue eyes. A dash of mascara and some pinkish blush was all she needed. She fluffed her hair and made it to the door just in time to slip on some black flats and grab her woven tan purse before hearing a knock.

She took in a deep breath and let it out slowly.

"Hi," she said, opening the door, her lightly damp hair framing her face, fresh with a smile.

"Hello to you." Wayne said.

Wayne peeked over her and into her apartment for a second, until she asked, "Are you ready to go?"

Scruffy came to the door to investigate the stranger, right before Jane closed it. She reached down with a pat, and said," I'll be home later, Scruff."

"That's nice you have a cat, that would be one pet I might be able to handle. Lower maintenance, you can take off for a while and they don't care. Not as much work as a dog."

"Yeah, he's great. He's ten years old now."

"Is that old for a cat? I have no idea, we didn't have any pets growing up. Dad was in the military and we moved a lot when I was younger. He finished out his career at Buckley Air Force base."

Jane learned more about Wayne in the last few minutes of talking in the elevator, than she had known of him in the six years of sharing a workplace. Outside of the office, he seemed more animated, friendly. Maybe the time off helped?

He opened the car door, and she climbed inside and buckled up.

"We are going to Antonio's, they kind of know me there, and they have incredible food. A nice wine selection, and the personalities of these people are one of a kind. You will soon pick up on all of the family dynamics. Movie worthy Italian family. They talk really loud, almost yelling, but there is a whole lot of love in the place."

"Sounds perfect. So is this my payback for you dumping a bunch of clients on me?" she asked with a smirk.

"Well, I guess so, but also, I want to hear about what you went through, and also what you thought of that book. Crazy right? The insane odds of it landing in our lives, in the scheme of things?"

"Yeah, I hadn't thought of that. The woman doesn't have much of a chance of seeing her books again. When you take into account America's current population, our best guess of the years she has left in her lifetime, I think it's safe to assume that she is an adult already, in conjunction with her belief and her total dependence on other people caring? Dang."

"Exactly. I calculated it out to one in almost fifty seven million, with its odds improving the more it is passed along. But, geez." Wayne said.

They pulled into the parking lot, and stepped into the front lobby. It had stucco walls painted a soft gold, Italian tunes piped loudly into the area, adding to the ambiance. There was a low podium up front, and a large woman in dramatic makeup came from behind it, towards them. She grabbed Wayne in a warm hug, while looking Jane up and down, then she smiled.

"Jane, this is Isabella or Izzy as I call her. Izzy, this is Jane."

Before she could put her hand out to shake Izzy's, Jane was enveloped in the warmest, most motherly hug of her life. Man, she could feel the love coming from this lady.

"You hungry, kids?" Izzy asked.

She grabbed two menus from the stand, and motioned for them to follow her as she talked about the night's special.

"Mattie has made his famous Bolognese sauce to go over my fresh Orecchiette, made just this morning. One of our family favorites. We send it through the salamander with a topping of shredded provolone until it is melty and a little crispy on top. It comes with a big salad, peppered with fresh salami and mozzarella and our homemade dressing.

And of course our complimentary fresh sourdough bread, for dipping in olive oil and garlic."

Jane had to keep herself from drooling. "Um, I'm having that, please."

"Make it two. Oh, and can we get a bottle of Classico Chianti from Lamole for the table?" Wayne added.

"Nice choice," Mama Izzy said.

"How long have you been coming here?" Jane asked when they were alone again.

"I came here with my parents, so probably twenty years, or so. Isabella and her husband Mattias, have owned it for thirty, and their kids are now taking over, but they can't help but come in and work. It's such a part of them. Mattias does a lot of the cooking and bread making, and Isabella does the sauces, and makes homemade pasta a lot of the time."

"Can't wait to try it. So how is your new passion? Getting anywhere?"

"I have a lot of ground school to do, so I'm not getting up into the air yet, but that will come. I am on a bit of a crash course, but not literally, hopefully." he smirked. "I hope to start my actual flying lessons this coming week."

"Very exciting, have you always wanted to fly?"

"Yeah. Growing up near airplanes, I dreamed of flying, but I never wanted to go into the Air force like my Dad. I knew I needed more freedom. I wasn't going to be able to handle people telling me where to go, and what to do. I told my folks early on, that I wanted to fly, but my mother begged me not to. She was always afraid that something would happen to my Dad when he was on active duty. She was so happy when he became grounded for health reasons, and started with the logistic support. I guess she put her fear on me for all that time. Or I let her? I stayed on the ground. Mom is gone now, it's time to get on with my life."

"That's funny you said that. Hey, want to hear a funny story, kinda odd?"

"Always."

"So you gave me the book and I read it. It made me wonder about some of the people I've known in my past. One in particular, really. An old beau. I went to the library to see if I could find out what he was up to. I had the Find Me book with me. Then on the way out, I left it on the bench outside the door and a man picked it up. I thought I was done with my part. But, no, come to find out, the man who picked it up, who I'd only seen out of the corner of my eye, ended up being the same guy, I ended up saving in the taco place. Isn't that crazy!? Anyway, he had just started reading the book at his table, when the choking started, and it was tossed out of the way in the commotion."

"Then, what happened?"

"Well the incident as you know, and then..." Jane pulled the book out of her purse, and placed it smack on the table. "He gave it back to me, so I'm still not done with it."

Wayne's eyes grew big and he shook his head. "Seriously, that is nuts."

Jane shrugged her shoulders as two large rimmed bowls of steaming orecchiette were placed in front of each of them. Divine.

Wayne reached his fork out to Jane, and they cheered their forks together before diving into their pasta. "That is a hell of a story. So what about the guy?"

"He's in the hospital, he's ok, but they had to do a clean up surgery to remove the obstruction. I had just bought him some time with my hack job. They figured out it was a hunk of smoked meat, the kind that gets real crisp on the ends. It happened to be the perfect size to block his airway."

"No, I mean, the guy. The one you wanted to find out about. You know, at the library."

Jane had a mouthful of food, but was tickled inside that he asked. She held up a finger in a wait, sort of way, trying to savor the yumminess in her mouth.

"Well, I found him. He's married, looked pretty damn happy in the newspaper article I found."

"I'm sorry. Or not. Depending on what you wanted out of your search."

"I mean, I guess I still kind of wondered if our connection could mean something again? That book made me wonder. I haven't had a lot of relationships since college, mostly because I work a lot, but that guy made the biggest impression on me, I guess."

"He must have. Do you ever find that you analyze people that you go out with? I struggle with that one. A lot. I tend to be attracted at first to the crazier ones, as they are fun and entertaining, but I find myself running away after a while."

Again, Jane had a mouth full of food, so she nodded. It was so delicious, maybe even the best thing she ever ate, and she was enjoying it as well as the company.

She swallowed. "Um, maybe? But I can't think of a time recently. Do you think you pick women to date who are going to end up making you run? Maybe you have some reason inside to want to be alone? Maybe your ingrained selection process for women makes it so that you, and only you, stay in control of your life and whereabouts at all times?"

Wayne hadn't been on a date with someone who was so capable and schooled in psychoanalysis. This was proving to be really interesting. He sat back and looked at her, crossing his arms.

"Are you analyzing me?" He couldn't help but smile at the pure lark of it.

She also sat back, and grinned back at him. "I thought we were talking?"

"Touché"

They laughed.

Reaching for a hunk of bread at the same time, they accidentally touched in their hungry efforts.

This Jane was fun, how had he never noticed it before? Maybe instead of looking for the crazy-sexy, he should try smart-sexy? A woman that could not only put him in his place about his stuff, but who he could enjoy a good verbal volley with too? Wayne mused.

Jane snatched the piece of bread for herself and dipped it into the olive oil, making sure to run it through the balsamic smear on the side. She popped it into her mouth.

This Wayne was an interesting character. The backstory on his parents and growing up in a military family jived with some of his relationship avoidance. While she hadn't had a military upbringing, her farm family meant chores, organization, and an overall obligatory busyness. She got that.

"So what else do you like to do, Jane, when you aren't analyzing your fellow colleagues or saving people's lives?"

Jane chuckled, "Well, I think I haven't spent enough time looking around to see what I could enjoy in the city. Back home, I liked being outside, doing some river floats or kayaking. I like museums. There are so many geologically fascinating places to enjoy in Nebraska, where I grew up. Chimney Rock, Indian Cave state park and Toadstool Geologic are pretty awesome. And I love animals, so the Henry Doorly Zoo and Aquarium will always make me happy."

"Have you been to any museums around here?"

"Oddly, no, I'm dying to go to the Denver Botanical gardens. Maybe when it warms up again."

"Maybe so."

Izzy came by the table to check if they had room for dessert. Jane had stuffed herself silly, and Wayne groaned, rubbing his belly as he was also very full. They apologetically declined.

In typical Mama Izzy style, she packed up two desserts for them anyway. To go. Her treat. Homemade Tiramisu with a small container of espresso sauce on the side. Jane held the box, dreamingly admiring the layers of deliciousness and the final flourish of whipped mascarpone topped with a chocolate covered espresso bean. The desserts teased them from their see through containers all the way back to Jane's.

Everything had been so nice. The evening, the food, the riveting conversation.

As Wayne dropped Jane off at her door that evening, they shared a hug. "Well, I have to get up early, I have some new clients to tend to in the morning." Jane cracked at him.

Wayne felt the burn. He had dumped his clients on her, to go chase this dream of his. He would definitely feel more guilty about that on his way home, because now he knew how great she was.

"Thank you for doing that, I promise to help you with something that you want to do, sometime. Maybe, I can scale back on my flight schedule, and come back before I was planning?"

They walked the hallway to Jane's place. She turned to him.

"Hey, chase the dream, Wayne, it's ok. Your clients seem pretty tame, it will all work out. Hey let's do this again sometime?"

They heard a scratch coming from the other side of the door. Scruffy wasn't used to being excluded, and he could hear them. He wanted to say hi.

"I better go in." Jane said a little embarrassed to have invited Wayne out already.

"Thanks again, I had such a great time, it was nice to get to know you more. I didn't even mind you getting in my head a little bit back there. It might be time to consider some of that stuff?"

"Anytime." Jane said.

Jane unlocked the door, and Scruffy popped his head out into the hallway, before persuading her to come back into the apartment. She closed the door behind them.

Jane picked up Scruffy and plopped onto the couch, to digest, and rewind and relive the evening.

The cat snuggled into her, and settled in on her chest, lightly kneading her sweater.

A text hit her phone.

"Get out of my head." It was Wayne.

Jane smiled, and wrote back. "No."

"I had fun, Scruff. He's really interesting. And I do like a little friendly banter mixed with razor sharp wit."

Jane fell asleep on the couch, and woke to her alarm going off at eight a.m. in the bedroom.

"Crap!" she swapped out her sweater, rubbed the mascara off from below her eyes, and tousled her hair. She ran out the door, without refilling Scruffy's food bowl for the day.

It had been a really full, life changing, and mind blowing weekend.

~

ME, ESCAPING 2005

I have been to the sea today. A day out with my closest, dearest friend. It was a day I needed desperately. After feeding the children breakfast, I kissed them both and told them I would be back, and to have fun with their Dad.

Inside I thought, "If I don't come back, it isn't because I didn't want to, it would be because Mommy didn't have a choice."

You never know when you are going to die. I wanted them to know I love them and that I wouldn't leave them on purpose. I couldn't say it that way, anyway. To do so would put the idea of me being gone forever in their minds, a worry, with no evidence. Part of me wanted to stay at the coast. All of me knew I wouldn't leave them.

I had a weird premonition that I wouldn't make it back home, as promised. Or maybe it was just a piece of me that wasn't coming back. I needed to leave it there. My sorrows, my disappointments, my expectations thrown into the ocean to be washed away.

I really have so much. I need to focus on what I do have, rather than what I don't have.

My friend and I shopped at the outlet mall then drove with the top down to a nearby beach town.

I could smell the sea air. I wanted to go to the ocean then, right away, but my friend kept seeing cute shops to venture into.

Finally I said "I want to see the ocean. I need to sit in front of it for ten minutes and just be there."

I parked and we finally made it down the steps to the beach itself. My friend kept her shoes on, because she didn't want to get dirty. I shed mine two steps from the bottom of the stairs.

I needed my toes in the sand now. Right now. This ancient sand, once rocks that had worn down over thousands, maybe millions of years. The grains filled in between my toes, the first layer was warm although it wasn't *a particularly hot day. Each step drove my feet deeper into the sand, and that layer below was cold. It didn't matter. It held me. The full strength of the worn down rocks, reminded me how strong one can be, even in the unraveling. Even in the erosion of form itself.*

I walked, listening to the crashing waves, smelling the crisp wet air and hearing the gulls fly by and talk to each other. To me. I love the ocean, the sea, every morsel of my being draws me here. When I am lost. I feel complete by the sea.

I stroll closer to a sandbar, and look back to see my friend standing in the same place where I took off my shoes. She isn't walking on the beach today. She looks annoyed.

I go it alone.

I walk to where I can't feel her judgments anymore, and sit on my shed shoes watching the children ride their beach bikes, a dog chasing a ball.

Mostly I watch the sea. In and out, the gulls fly up and settle down near the breakers only to be disturbed again by the next wave. I pull back my sunglasses to see it really the way it is. The horizon, so far in the distance.

A sunny day, hardly expected on a Sunday in November. By all rights there should be a storm, or at least a windy socked in day. But not today.

Today is beautiful. It is as if God woke up that day and smiled on that beach, saying good morning or good day to all the people there. A gift for all the lucky ones who were there to experience it.

The sun was starting to set as I sat, playing with the sand. Letting it run through my fingers as I watched and waited, still, for the calm that comes over me when I am here.

Funny how philosophical one gets while standing or better yet sitting in front of such a force of nature and its many friends.

My friend comes up from behind me. She tells me how she would come to the beach with some friends and then need to get away by herself too.

She would look over at the massive rocks and think, "Look at that rock. It's there, and it's been there and will continue to be there, through the ages. How silly and insignificant are we?"

She walked off, probably feeling philosophical herself.

She is right, these earthly monuments and the ocean's motion make everything else pale in comparison. What is reality? That rock is reality. The ocean is reality, and beauty. The beauty that is within each one of us and in everything.

Don't we all, each one of us have our own dream, our own perception of what life should be like? Shouldn't we want that for each other?

I have made an effort towards my dream. Out there, somewhere I have little fingerlings of my soul present. I am exposed.

Things are happening, and while it is my little secret, I love to wonder where my books might be by now.

I awaken every day to my hope that someday, as I walk the planet, living my life, I am one day closer to seeing one of my traveling books, and the person who will deliver it.

Who will it be? Will it be someone I have loved, or a friend that knew me back when these events were happening? Maybe it will be a family member I have written about, who remembers the shared moment.

I have been blessed with many friends. I have been open to them. They have seen my many faces and my many, many moods. I have been fully present throughout my life.

Thankfully I never saw a reason to let drugs live my life for me. Not even a cigarette.

I could never figure out why someone would want to roll leaves up into a paper and then smoke it. Aren't we always trying to get away from the smoke at a campfire? I remember camping with one of my initials.

As teenagers, we went camping almost every weekend. Once we had brought a raft and we all took turns tumbling over a small waterfall in it. No life vests. 100% stupid, yes.

I remember almost dying that day.

They said I wasn't under for very long, but I remember seeing my life flash before my eyes. Just as they say. Pictures and faces filled my head as I scrambled to reach the surface. My boyfriend said he was just about to jump in for me, when I came up.

This week will be our second appointment with the new marriage counselor. I am quite lucky that my husband will go. I know he loves me, and he is a good man. A great Dad, friend and a provider.

Even in my safety I sometimes feel like I did underwater all those years ago. The visions of events and faces play on in my head, but I am stuck underneath, scrambling to get to the surface.

I have always said that I want to lead an extraordinary life.

Maybe through my books that will happen. At least I know my books will have an extraordinary life. And that might have to be enough.

~

M.S.

My first pubescent crush. You didn't have to do much for me to fall for you. I was taking the bus on my first day of high school. You were in the seat behind me. I didn't know you, and you didn't know me.

I didn't notice you really, until you caught my eye and said. "You're cute."

I am sure my face turned bright red, as I remember it becoming really hot in that moment. I had always hoped that I was cute, enough to get by anyway, but you put it out right there, right then, on the most vulnerable day of my life.

I thank you. It was fun feeling special; it was fun to ride the bus. It was fun to be me, that day. I had a fan. Later we found that we had common interests.

You were older, and you teased me. I was younger and took it. We had many great walks, always talking about big topics.

Remember that injured robin I took home on one of our walks home from school?

Or was it a blue jay? It died.

That was sad, I have always had a soft spot for animals, people too.

I had a soft spot for you for a long time.

~

Requests and revelations, Me 2005

O ddly it was probably the dumbest stuff that may have led me to throw my hands up into the air when it came to our marriage. The things that came when I felt like I could do no more.

I knew how he was, that change was hard. He preferred his days to be mostly the same, watching his CNN in the morning with coffee, then breakfast of a choice of three cereals depending on his needs at the time. Raisin Bran for most days, switching to Cheerios if he was minding his cholesterol levels and Frosted mini wheats on weekends for fun.

His outfits were made up of the same pieces in shirts and pants, but in different colors and sometimes patterns. Colored golf shirt on top, Docker's extra roomy legged pants on the bottom with the annual change to Docker's shorts during the summer.

I begged him to just put on some jeans, once in a while, even if it was just for the weekends. So I could see his butt. I asked him for years. He refused.

I remember watching an episode of Dr. Phil one afternoon, when I was in my brain about our marriage. Still wishing things were different with us.

Dr. Phil was speaking to a couple or maybe it was just one person, I can't remember which. What I do remember is him saying that when you end a marriage, a person needs to feel that they had done everything they could possibly have done to try to make it work. Then and only then will they have earned their way out of the marriage.

By this time, I felt I had done that. All of it.

We'd been through years of counseling off and on together. Multiple counselors, in multiple cities. We had tried both female and male practitioners, so we knew that the sex of the therapist hadn't affected our care. We'd always do the homework that was assigned, but so often the work or the plan was not sustainable and we'd fall back into our old natural and often hurtful patterns.

We'd read The Five Love Languages book aloud to each other, fully understanding each other's love language enough to be able to supply it to the other person, even though we had different results. Because of our shared knowledge of the love languages, we both knew that choosing not to speak that way or offer acts to each other in their preferred love language was actually a choice we were both making. That decision was us turning away from each other.

Knowing "how," to speak to each other but purposefully denying the other that gift felt like a stab to the heart. An action we both knew was detrimental to our marriage.

He is an "Acts of Service," type. Meaning, he feels most loved when I am doing chores or tasks for him, but if I was tired or hadn't done something that he had expected me to, even if he hadn't mentioned how important it was to him, he felt unloved. Unloved and disrespected somehow without any such intent by me.

My Love language was "Words of Affirmation," meaning that I needed to hear loving comments, or to be told that I am okay or loved. I dreamed of being told I was beautiful, loved and needed. His conscious choice not to supply me with those types of declarations, made me fall out of love over time.

So much of me knew that love shouldn't be this hard all the time. That togetherness in a lifetime love relationship should be easier.

I longed for someone who was just automatically on my team. Someone that had my back, as I had his. I wanted to wholly feel the internal calm inside that comes with my partner cheering for me in whatever goal I had going at the moment. I would happily do the same for him. Whatever it was that the other one chose, the partner should back them simply because. Within reason, I suppose. Like, don't sell the house to move to Argentina without having a discussion about it. Duh.

I didn't like to be questioned so hard all the time about my goals. Having to beg for his approval to pursue my ideas and paths. To have to supply all of the data beforehand with no ability to learn and grow as I went along.

Together should have meant shared goals and dreams and supporting each other in them. That was what I wanted, needed, when I dreamed about my life partner.

I cannot say that our marriage was all hard or all bad, as it totally wasn't. There were many really great times that we shared. So many fun times, and happy escapes together.

Starting our family together. Our daughters' first steps, days skiing as a family, and our crazy road trips. Watching Seinfeld together in a lump on the couch. Having Seinfeld practically be our family's religion. Not that there's anything wrong with that. We would always know each other in those ways, and nothing could take that away.

We both loved the girls, and would do anything for them, however I knew that by example, I wanted our daughters to see two healthy, happy, and whole people living and loving each other. Two loving parents who were really into each other instead of two people just living in the same house.

My parents used to say that it was better to be alone than with the wrong person. When you are a kid and you hear that statement you aren't quite sure what to do with it, as when you have parents that are split, life is harder, so you often wonder how different things could be if they had stayed together. I get it now.

But is it a cop out, to leave even when things aren't abusive, or without cheating or mistrust? To just want out because there must be more.

The whole enchilada?

~

1

J ane unlocked the door to her office that morning, with two minutes
to spare before her first client was to arrive. She grabbed a diet
cherry coke out of her mini fridge for a jolt of caffeine, and chugged
most of it at once, right out of the can. She belched loudly, right before
there was a knock at the door. She prayed that the door was sound
proof, but suddenly wasn't sure. She opened the door to find one of Dr.
Huff's client's standing very close on the other side. Had he heard her?

"Um, hello. I hope I am in the right place. Are you Dr. Monroe?"

"I am indeed, you must be Roman Sharp. Is it ok if I call you Roman?"

"Yes, sure. That is fine."

"Well, Roman, I hope that we are able to help you in Dr. Huff's absence. Would you like a beverage? I have sodas, water, or I can heat up
some water for tea in the microwave?"

"No, thank you. I'm ok. Just ate."

"Great. Dr. Huff gave me your file, and I understand you are working
on developing confidence. Is there something specific you are wanting
to achieve that I should know about?"

Roman sat down on the couch, as Jane filled her usual spot.

"Well, I have been at my job for about ten years now, kinda stuck in
the same position. I've taken some classes to help improve my chances
to move up in the company, but I am not getting anywhere. No one
seems to want to give me a chance."

"Are you looking to move into a leadership role? What is it that you
do, currently?"

"Right now, I work for a shipping company, putting routes together,
and sending new pickup instructions to drivers. It's decent money, and
I know what I am doing every day, but I am bored. I know all the guys,
the truckers. I'm just stuck."

Well, what would you be doing, if you moved into the area that you want to be in?"

"Probably more like sales, I guess? I want to help find the companies that need our services and get them signed up. The other guy I see doing that, has an awesome car, a pretty wife, and a family. I want all of that."

"And you think that the job you have will not get you that?"

"I mean, I guess I could have a wife and a family, with my job, but not as nice of a house, or car probably."

"How important is that to you?"

"I think a woman appreciates all that stuff, that's all. I haven't really been dating much, probably because I don't feel like I have that much to offer. Also, many women in my age range have kids already. I kinda want to start a family with someone together."

"There's a lot to unpack in there. First, what classes have you taken, as you said, to improve your chances of pursuing a promotion?"

"I took some public speaking classes at the community college, some general accounting, and negotiation ones."

"How confident are you speaking in front of a group? Even a small one? Do you mind being the center of attention?"

Roman thought for a moment. "I actually really hate it."

"Alright, how would you start with a new prospect? Would you want to stand up in front of a group, and present something, or would you prefer to take a single decision maker to lunch somewhere, to seal the deal?"

Roman thought again, Dr. Huff hadn't asked him anything like these questions. These ones were pointed and hard.

"I'll rephrase. Pretend, I am a potential client. Someone who may or may not want to find a new shipping company. Give me your spiel."

Roman sat up straight. "Ms. Monroe, I'd like to talk to you about the company I work for, as I think we could possibly help you be more logistically successful in your business. Do you have a few minutes to talk with me?" Roman waited for an answer.

Jane played along. "Well, Mr. Sharp, great name by the way. I am pretty busy. Do you have a cliff notes version?"

"You bet. Thank you. Harkinson trucking is a family owned company based out of Denver, Colorado. We have been in business for seventy one years, and have a nationwide reach. Our drivers are contract drivers with the option to consolidate with us, and share in employee type benefits, or they can work independently whenever they want. Because of that flexibility we have one of the happiest teams around. Our drivers have all kinds of trucks, from the Double rig to the refrigerated, as well as the flatbed. The one thing I am most proud of with our company, is that our logistics team only assigns jobs, and sets timelines, based on safe and realistic time constraints. We do not want to endanger our drivers by having them push themselves to exhaustion."

"Wow, Roman, that was awesome. Have you ever walked into your boss, and said that?"

"Well, no."

"How do you suppose he would know that you think like that?"

"I'm pretty quiet at work. So no, I haven't shared that with anyone."

"Do you believe that it's true?"

"Yes. One hundred percent." Roman gave a double thumbs up.

"It sounds like you have a really good feeling about the company you work for, and given that you are one of the people setting schedules and deliveries, you are a big part of why it is such a good company to work for."

"Yes, I agree." Roman puffed out his chest a little, but not on purpose.

Jane noticed. "Tell me more, what else do you like about the company?"

"They treat their office people really well, too. We have good benefits, good pay, and a nice, safe place to work. Once a year, they organize a group event at a big picnic area, so we all can get to know each other better. We even meet the trucker's families at the events. Unlike other trucking companies that run their team ragged, our guys are pretty well balanced. If they are gone overnight on a run, or for a few days, we make sure they have days in between to be with their families."

"Sounds like a great company. Do you think they have room for another salesman?"

"I don't know. I mean we are small enough to care about people, but large enough to get the job done."

Jane sat back and crossed her arms. A large grin lit up her face, as she looked at him.

"Roman, that is the best, but most heartfelt slogan I have ever heard in my life. Have you ever thought of doing some marketing for the company? Or being some kind of an ambassador?"

"I never have. Is that a thing?"

"It sure is, it's a really big thing. And there are a lot of classes that teach about Marketing and Advertising too."

Jane switched gears. "Let's go back to something else you said, about thinking that women appreciate a man who has a good job, and that you felt like you didn't have a good enough job to be able to be with a woman. Where does that come from? How long have you felt like that?"

Roman slunk down on the couch a little bit. "Well, my Dad is a lawyer, and my brother is an accountant, with his own firm. My other brother is a car salesman. I mean he's a manager at a car dealership. They all make good money. More than I make."

"What if I told you the median salary for someone in our local area is about forty thousand a year?"

"Well, I make more than that. So that's good. Hmm."

"So if we take away the idea that you need to earn a certain amount of money to be able to date someone, what else is stopping you?"

Roman took a deep breath. "Huh. I'll have to think about that."

"So, Roman, I want you to think about that for our next session, and I'd like you to share all that great stuff, the points that you think about the company, that you shared with me, with your boss. Even if nothing happens with that, it will probably make his day too."

"Yes, I can do that," said Roman. He got up, and Jane also rose.

"Thanks. That was really good. I really do love the company I work for. It's a good feeling, and not a lot of people have it."

"So true." Jane opened the door, and Roman stepped out over the threshold.

They waved. "See you next week." she said.

~

ME, SECOND GUESSING MY MARRIAGE, BIG TIME 2005

*I*t's bad again. Marriage is so hard. I am not feeling premenstrual, I am feeling really empty. The criticisms I feel sometimes for not being just like him or thinking like he does are weighing on me. I just want to scream. Doesn't he know that all I need is for him to tell me that I am special and needed by him sometimes? Even once in a while?

I guess my life isn't very exciting, and maybe if I had a job I would have more things to talk about, but all the ideas I can come up with don't jive, or wouldn't make what he wants me to make to have it be worth it, or they don't excite me at all, and I would hate it and be miserable, would that be better?

Why does he make me guess where I stand? I need to be talked to. I told him, I shine elsewhere. When I stand at the front of a classroom teaching the girl's classmates about art, I am making a difference, but to him there is not value there, unless I make it into a business with an income. When he's not there, I have people tell me how creative I am. But not him. Never him. Nothing I ever do is good enough.

The one who is supposed to love me beyond anything cannot say one good thing about me, to my face?! What is wrong with this picture?

I am tired. It gets bad and I just stay quiet until I can't take it anymore and scream.

He sees my struggle to keep up with everything, and I ask for help and he gets mad and tells me all of the things I'm not doing for him and that's why he doesn't do the things for me. Like that will help.

I'm not sure what I can do anymore, to have him see me. He is annoyed with every house project, every creative endeavor that I embark on. Everything about me seems to irritate him.

I imagine in my mind's eye, I am alone on the beach, with my toes in the sand. The waves are nipping at me a few feet away. I look out and see the bright sun over the horizon. The blue of the ocean and the blue of the sky blur until one shade of blue is all you see.

My footprints lay behind me like the moments, both good and bad in my life. The surf comes up and fills them all in, erasing them. That is the nature of life. Each person feels something or experiences something, then over time, the urgency or memory disappears. Replaced by the ones and the events that come after. I walk on.

I am calming just thinking about the sea. I need to go, more often, to put things in perspective.

Yes, it still bothers me that he refuses to give me the support I need, that I ask for.

That he can't see any value in who I am and what I can do, if given the chance.

Something has got to change, and quick.

~

E.R.

We were sisters. Not really but almost. Your dad dated my Mom for years. We went on trips together. We grew up together.

You and your family expanded my very small world. You were younger than me by a year but somehow you were much braver. While visiting Disneyland, we were allowed to go off on our own, armed with our tickets and some pocket change for lunch, we got separated. The difference of how we handled that experience would tell volumes of how you lived, versus me.

You-Not feeling bothered much with the situation, you started hitting all the rides, and enjoyed yourself, not worrying at all where I was, or if you would ever see me again.

I, however cried and walked up to the nearest adult in a costume I could find, ending up in the lost and found room at the massive park, surrounded by tons of other lost children, much younger than I was.

You strolled in hours later, having spent all the money and ridden out your tickets. "Where were you?" you asked, "that was great!"

"Um, hello... I am totally a kid, lost at Disneyland, how did you not cower in fear and run to the closest Mickey Mouse club member like I did?"

That time we pretended we were from a different country on the bus and spoke a pretend language to each other as the people around us looked on. I didn't want to do it, but you said, "Hey, we are never going to see these people again, in our entire lives, why do you care what they think?"

Years of camping adventures in the desert? You driving the motorcycle while I rode on the back, you falling, and getting your leg burned on the exhaust. Playing Joust at Newberry's.

Such good times. I'm really sorry I barfed watermelon on your head that one time when I was carsick. I have to admit, you took it pretty well. Our parents split years ago but we managed to stay in touch as adults.

You are the best. I love you E.

~

Showering for comfort, Me
2005

S *howers have become my respite from all my hopeless and raging*
thoughts.

There were many days when I would take more than one. One in the
morning to ready myself for the day, another at night to wash off what the
day had left on me. Or to escape my thoughts, imagining them flowing down
the drain.

Sometimes, in the shower, I wept. The sound of the water, dutifully cam-
ouflaging my sobs.

I imagined the water washing away the uncertainty of how I felt in my
marriage, and the empty feelings of not being good enough. The constant
doubt of my capabilities, the never believing I would become something.

The things I am good at aren't especially appreciated around my house.
Designing the rooms, painting murals or putting up wallpaper were just
things that would need to be done, or projects that cost money, and he didn't
really seem to care what the house looked like, anyway. As long as the house
was kept up, and he had underwear in his drawer, and a beer in the fridge, I
was good.

If I tried to be fancy with dinner, and try a new recipe, that wasn't really
appreciated either. And good God, don't add any capers or cilantro to any-
thing. More no's to keep track of.

It was just another evening of discontent, and I excused myself to take a
shower, saying I needed to warm up my bones. Not sure if I would cry that
day or not, I sat on the shower floor, and noticing something I had left from
another shower sitting episode. I have often slunk down to the shower floor
on particularly rough emotional days.

Words of encouragement, or a question. Odd he never noticed but I guess he
preferred the downstairs bathroom for his business and it wasn't really visible
while standing up in the shower.

Over the next few months I would have countless moments of sitting on the floor of the shower, wishing, pleading for something different than what I had.

If I was making the right decision, in remaining where I was and settling for myself remaining so small, living with myself and my choices.

I didn't feel any power over my life, or my experience. Maybe it was what came with depending on another person while keeping your children at home? I felt stuck, invisible, unimportant whether it was true or not.

They don't give out awards or bonuses for motherhood. There are no yearly reviews, or paychecks. It's one of the only jobs in the world, where you can get lost in the work of it. I love being a mother, and the gratitude I feel for being able to stay home and be with my kids every day is immeasurable, I just want an Atta Girl sometimes, that's all. Because it's not always easy.

~

1

Jane went back into her office, closed the door and looked in her desk for some snacks. She must have something.

Ah, a year old, plus, granola bar. Perfect.

Grabbing another soda from the fridge, she chowed on the coconut chocolate something, while sitting in the chair with the rest of the client briefs left by Wayne.

She had only managed to scan the first one, and she had another one of his clients coming in under an hour.

She opened the folder for the next client. A paragraph filled the front page, with only a few pages behind. She started reading it aloud in between bites.

"Debra Stern. Middle aged woman. Married. Jewish ancestry. Three kids, all grown. Struggling with her husband. He wants to stay living here in town, and she wants to move to Hawaii. Three sessions so far, she mostly complains about how large and empty her house feels, that she wants a new adventure, and she feels fat. Huh, Wayne has a funny way of describing people in his records. Pretty short, and direct. It does give me a good snapshot though."

She finished her bar, and took one last sip from the soda before getting up to use the restroom before Mrs. Stern's appointment.

She put all the files in the drawer, closed it and locked her office door behind her as she made her way down the hall.

This hallway was so boring. Jane hadn't really registered just how pathetic and plain it was. Two washed out pictures hung crooked side by side. She straightened them on her way. She wondered why the owner of the building would even have beach pictures anyway? We live in the mountains. Dumb. With the outdoor surroundings exploding with such beauty, absolutely none of it was captured in this place whatsoever.

The bathroom was just as bad. A cream on white striped wallpaper, and more seascape images, washed out, in outdated, chipped gold frames. The toilet partitions were painted a baby blue. Yuck.

Jane walked back to her office, and sat down at her desk to make a quick call. She wanted to check on Duncan before she met with Mrs. Stern. Hear how his decannulation went. Check to see when he might be back on his feet again.

She called the nurses station.

"Hello, this is Jane Monroe, I am calling about Duncan Shots. I understand that he had his trach tube removed today, is he doing ok?"

"Hello, Ms. Monroe, please hold a moment."

Jane waited on the other end, pacing around her office. She was hoping he hadn't had a hard time, and that his wound was healing ok. Her lifesaving efforts had been expedient and not necessarily cosmetically minded.

"Yes, Ms. Monroe, we see you on the approved list to speak to about his condition. He is doing well. Right now, he is learning about the care he will need to do, for the wound, and we are testing for leakage. If all goes well today, he might be able to leave tomorrow, our assumption is that the wound will heal on its own. It wasn't as large of an incision as some we've seen."

"That's great, will he be up for visitors, you think?"

"Most likely. Maybe try to come after dinner, that way no interruptions, in case we need to do any suctioning or make any adjustments during his meal."

"Great, thanks."

Jane hung up the phone.

Awesome. He is going to be ok.

~

MEDIOCRE LIFE OR NOT, ME 2005

I look down at the story of my life, as it is currently written. My daily exchanges with my life partner are deflating. How can two people, who are so different from each other really stick it out long term?

I said to a friend, on one of our walks. "He just doesn't get me."

I wonder how many people feel that way? That try as they may, they are always misunderstood by their partners in their daily lives? Is that what marriage is?

It's amazing to me that I have picked someone who continually questions my viewpoint.

I look around me. I have everything, materialistically, that I could have wished for. The beautiful, intact family I dreamed of having when I was young. Everything I felt I didn't have growing up.

A seemingly stable marriage, even though it feels boring at times, we have a shared companionship and enough money in the household to keep the heat on. Something I hadn't always had when I was a kid. I remember the stress she was under, and how Mom had to buy firewood at the grocery store every couple of days when our furnace broke in the middle of winter and she didn't have the money to fix it.

Why is it, that now, when I seem to have everything I ever wanted, that I am searching even harder for something to hold onto?

Maybe my mother found her marriage as empty as I do sometimes. Maybe she searched so hard, she searched her way out of that life and the perceived stability that there was?

Am I doing the same thing?

Life gets more complicated when you have little souls to take care of. They are such a part of me, I tell myself not to do anything to jeopardize their future, to not be stupid.

But am I, in my life example, showing my daughters that there are times in your life which you should settle for less than what you can have?

There is no question in my mind that I was absolutely and hopelessly in love with my husband when we got married. We used to make love in the backyard under the stars, and sometimes we would write love notes in toothpaste to each other on the bathroom mirror.

Back then, he would tell me how much he loved me, I felt seen.

There were common interests, and we held a shared vision of what our life would be. That was before the practicality of everyday life and pent up resentment from uncommunicated wishes fell in.

Oddly enough, both of our parents divorced when we were both nine.

For me, my parent's marriage or lack of marriage was the only example I had to learn from, about what family togetherness was supposed to look like.

Our former neighbors, my former best friend's parents across the street were who I looked up to, mostly, for that marital imprint. I craved the love and togetherness that I saw with them. They even looked alike. Our time living there was short lived, as we moved away when I was eight.

My grandparents lived far away. I had no aunts or uncles, nearby either, to experience what having an extended family felt like.

As a family we were already an island, just as we were. Just the four of us. And when the fracture came, my brother and I became debris of the whole, floating in the ocean, trying to find something solid to hold on to.

When I fantasize about what a perfect marriage is, it would be two people who are committed to continue to grow together, always. From a healthy and loving place, where each person was supported and celebrated by the other, for being exactly who they are.

That is what I want.

~

1

Mrs. Stern stood waiting in the hallway, as she had knocked so softly, Jane barely heard her the first time.

Jane opened the door to find a beautiful middle aged, redhead. A little overweight, maybe, but not even close to obese, and she was impeccably dressed.

"Hi, I'm Debra. Dr. Huff said I should come see you, while he is away. Seems odd to start with someone new, but if this is how it works, I guess it will be ok."

"Hi Debra, I'm Jane Monroe, but you can call me Jane if you like. It isn't super common to have clients switch therapists like that, but sometimes it is necessary. Maybe our time together will give you another view of the things you were discussing with Dr. Huff?"

"Sounds good." She came into the office, looked around and sat in Jane's typical spot.

"Ok," Jane said under her breath.

Jane moved over to the sofa on the other side. This was a first.

"So, what would you like to start with, maybe I can hear a little backstory?"

Mrs. Stern reached into her purse, and pulled out a stack of index cards. She handed them to Jane.

"What's this?"

"That is my life story. Everything I could think to tell you about who I am, and the times I have struggled with in my life. The hard stuff. The basics. You know, so you can know me faster and save time."

Jane started leafing through the stack. Where she was born. Only child. Her parents were dead. Three grown children, one boy and two girls. She graduated from college with a business degree, she's owned three businesses, all were sold to others. Some cards had words in different colors.

"What do the colors mean?"

"Green is the good times, when I was happy about something. Yellow is when it started out bad, but there was a lesson in it, so it was ok, after all. Red is all bad. Purple is my husband. All the things we have gone through together, and what we have built together."

"And the black and purple mix?"

"Oh, yeah, those are the reasons I want to kill him, sometimes."

"Are you speaking facetiously? Or literally? I do need to tell you that I am bound to our confidentiality, until and unless I have reason to believe you will harm someone or yourself."

"No, totally kidding. I love my husband, I just want him to do what I want."

"And what is it that you want him to do?"

"I want to sell our house, and move to Hawaii, or someplace tropical, and warm. This place has its own beauty, but I want to feel like I'm on vacation all the time."

"That sounds nice, so what's the hang up?"

"My husband wants to stay here. Live here forever, I guess. He doesn't want to move, he's afraid of clearing out the house, and starting over. He's so used to things the way they are."

"Have you directly asked him? Told him that you want to move to Hawaii and why?"

"Well, no. I show him pictures in the magazine's of Hawaii that I've subscribed to. He should be able to figure it out, don't you think?"

"I have not really met any true mind readers in all of my years doing this. What does he do for a living?"

"He's an engineer. Electrical engineer."

"Debra, can I be frank?"

"Sure."

"I can't speak to all engineers, but most I have come across are thinkers. They require evidence or a plan before they will put much effort into an action. Have you done any of the planning research for a big move like this? Are you thinking he will still work, or are you both in a place where he can retire, if he wants to?"

"I mean, yes my husband is like that. No, I haven't done any research. Not like he would, anyway. I've gotten out of that habit, as in our life together, he tends to take over in that way for the big things. He has to flush out all of the options to his satisfaction, I haven't chipped in on any of that for years."

"Have you told him directly that you would like to move?"

"No, I should probably do that." she mumbled, spinning her wedding ring.

"Ok, let's think about this for a minute." She handed Debra back most of her cards, and gave her a pen.

"I want you to turn them over, and let's think of all the potential arguments that he might have against the idea, and you can write them down. So you can think of alternate arguments, or statements. To better make your case. If you give him all the evidence, along with a why, he may just jump on board? Especially if you frame it with the goal as you wrote on this purple lettered card, *"I want to have an adventure, and fall in love with my husband, all over again."* Jane held it up for her to see.

"Ok. Let's do it. Um, the cost of the move, well maybe we can sell everything and start from scratch over there. Quitting his job. Honestly, he is so grumpy every day when he gets home, I can't believe he would fight me hard on this one. We are in good financial shape, my husband and I have multiple apartment complexes, so money is a non issue. And the property management company pretty much handles that for us now. Ok, Leaving the kids. Do they ever even call? Hardly, they are all out building their own lives, which is much healthier than them living with us forever. And, um, the kids would come and see us, because we would live in paradise! This is easy!"

"Sounds like you have some really good points in there, is there anything else you can think of, objections he might have?"

"Well, maybe his Mom. She's in a nursing home here, she's comfortable, and stable, and very accustomed to her space. I don't know if he would consider moving her with us."

"Is she healthy and rational enough to have an opinion about something like that?"

"Oh yeah, she was just tired of doing her own laundry and cleaning. She's fit as a fiddle."

"Maybe you would have an ally?" Jane said with a wink.

"Maybe so..." Debra smirked back.

"Looks like our time together is coming to a close, is there anything else you want to share before we wrap it up?"

"Only thanks. This is a good start. I like your office here, it's much more colorful than Dr. Huff's office and the ghastly hallways and bathroom of this complex are so depressing."

Jane laughed, "Thanks. I like to have mementos and fun stuff around me."

Jane closed the door behind Mrs. Stern.

Another good session. She wondered why Wayne had all the fun clients, and she was stuck with the tough ones?

Jose was coming in tomorrow. It was his last court mandated session.

Jane would have to give her recommended follow up to the Judge next week.

Jose had worn her out. Mostly because after every session she felt so hopeless. How could she reach this kid? She pulled his file and put it on her desk to take home to look over again tonight. Maybe she can find some answers before it's too late?

Her efforts to move the book along had resulted in saving a man's life, and gaining a new friend. Maybe giving it to Jose *was* the right thing to do, after all?

It was up to him how he would use it.

Surely he would feel something, right?

~

SLEUTHING ME, 2005

*W*ith the inception of the internet, a new door opened into the past...
A gateway that could mess with my life.

I remember attending the seminar with Mr. Stability where we learned about it for the first time. He was beyond excited about this great new thing that was coming, and as a technology geek he had to find out about it.

It was held at the college nearby, and we got a babysitter for our young daughter, and turned it into a date.

We sat listening intently as the instructor said that there was a new nationwide network built; over the phone lines, connecting colleges to be able to share information, on a small scale at first. A person would log into the network via their computer, and could see college papers, dissertations and other info via the education based portal.

On the pull down screen they showed chosen examples of what one could find in a search on the "Internet." They showed graphs and statements about something having to do with gorillas, and a college paper written about Thomas Jefferson. They showed countless white pages of script, and many people in the room were all excited.

Talk about dull.

I remember saying to my husband as we left to go back to the car, "That will never take off."

It would become just one of the inside jokes we shared. And we would laugh, over our years, about it, as the internet grew and changed into something that would become such an integral part of our society.

My husband signed up for internet service as soon as it was offered in our area, and we would have the annoying connection sound beaconing through the house for hours. With the verbal chime of, "You've got mail," bellowing out every once in a while, too.

At the time the internet came in through your phone line, so we could only use one or the other until we added the extra phone line. So strange to think back on what it had started to be, and what it had turned into.

A powerful way to connect to other people, not always for the best reasons.

~

M.H.

E ven though she is no longer with us, I include her in this journal because she impacted me in ways I had to share.

I remember her yummy Zucchini bread that she baked into the small sized Yuban coffee tins and sent to us every Christmas.

She was smart and giving and a gem. Her glacier-colored hair was curly and teased of her long life. Her smile, her laugh, and the way she used to say in her twangy southern accent, "Well, hi there..." when we would arrive to visit from up north.

Grandma grew up having the best of everything and as a teen, she'd go with her mother and sister to New York City. "Just the girls," she said. They spent days away exploring and shopping, to lavishly outfit them all, in the very latest fashions of the 1920's. Part of the perk of being the daughter of a wealthy golf pro back then.

That was before meeting my grandfather and falling in love with the shorter man with a maimed leg and limp due to polio. Grand-dad had big dreams, a kind heart, and a brain full of ideas of how to make it big.

She was promised to another, a well to do man before she met my Grandfather, but in the end, she chose love. Together, they lived a more meager life than the one she had grown up in, but she adapted and was grateful for what they had. She held her head up high and dressed well for every occasion. She loved shoes.

As she aged her fingers bent into her palms, a hereditary illness she'd seen her mother suffer from, but it never stopped her from doing things. Golf, knitting, pulling hot dishes out of the oven using oven pads instead of mitts because mitts wouldn't go over her fingers. When I asked her about her hands, she told me that they could be fixed, surgically, but she didn't want to risk losing even more mobility, so she made do. Her mother had been afflicted as well. It became a badge for her to wear, straight from the family tree.

Even from afar, my grandmother grew to become my moral compass. Teaching me the importance of writing thank you notes and never giving a purse or a wallet as a gift without putting a little something inside. A penny, a dollar, whatever one could spare.

I will never forget how I let her down once. Mom had asked me to clean up my room, then left Grandma and Granddad in charge of us for the day. I had a friend over and wanted to goof off, so I avoided picking up my room. Coming downstairs for a snack, she asked me if I was done. I didn't think she would climb the stairs to check so I lied and said yes. She was old after all. I was wrong. She marched upstairs and discovered my room a total mess.

"I'm very disappointed in you," she said, and I was crushed. It was worse than a paddle to the behind. I never wanted her to feel that way about me again.

When I was an adult, and Granddad had passed, my mom and I went to visit her. She was living in an assisted living home. It was a nice place and the people around her seemed friendly.

I remember taking a walk with her, all decked out in her wide brimmed hat, and white gloves, necessary accessories from her multiple skin cancer episodes. She pointed out the Four o'clock flowers and explained that they were named that because they opened each day around four p.m. She loved the joyous shape of them as well as the vibrant color, such a sharp contrast to the earthy tones of the desert. Having lived all over the country, she found or planted color wherever she went.

On Thursdays she'd have her hair set, and the nice ladies would usually trim her nails for her. The week we were visiting, she missed her appointment, and her nails were too long. She asked me if I would trim them. It was strange to be taking care of her rather than the other way around. I remember holding her hand in mine. How soft her skin was, like a baby's. By then her hands were even more frail, her fingers even more crumpled in, almost to closed up entirely. Her long nails poking into her palms.

She trusted me. I was honored to help. Accidentally pulling some of the skin of her finger into the snipper section, I was about to pinch it closed when she winced, and yelped, "Wait!"

I stopped just in time, and felt terrible, wishing I had been more careful. More patient. It was another reminder that I often need to slow down when doing something.

Before Mom and I left for home, I sat with her, just the two of us. I was in my early thirties; she was just past ninety. She broke down. "I just don't know why I'm living this long."

The tears falling from her light blue eyes, punctuated every soulful word. She had already outlived her husband and one of her four children. There was a pretty good chance she was going to lose another one of her children soon, as my aunt was very ill with a mysterious and untreatable liver illness.

"A parent should never outlive a child," she said crying harder, pulling a tissue out from under her watch band, to dab her eyes. We cried together, her from the rawness of a longer-than-wanted life, and me with the helplessness I felt to help her. Life was not even close to fair.

Her accident soon after seemed serendipitous. A broken hip. Not usually life threatening. The doctor said that she would need an operation to fix it, and they scheduled it for the following day. She was pretty healthy all in all with her daily walks.

She died in her sleep, the night before the surgery. Just shy of her 92nd birthday. I imagine she must have had a talk with the big guy upstairs, about her being ready to go, and somehow, she and he had made an agreement together.

We lost my aunt pretty quickly, only a month after, and my uncle, her oldest child, that same year too. Three of her four children, were gone. She must have known.

I will miss her forever, but I feel calm and grateful, knowing she was ready to go. She lived and died on her terms.

I wish the same for all of us.

~

WHAT AM I DOING, ME, 2005

W *ho knew that so much chaos, and upheaval could come from a single act, one born out of what I thought was an innocent curiosity? It all started with my high school reunion that was coming up. A website whose purpose was to bring people together enough to compile a database for such events, but it became an excellent tool to find people and get back in touch.*

I am sure I wasn't the only one to look up an old crush, to see where they lived and what they were up to, it was just for fun.

The little "Hi," I sent on the website; for me, suddenly became much more. His animated response, a shared excitement to be in touch again, and some confessions about how we had felt about each other back then. Over a month it became sharing confidences, and sharing things about our spouses that we found lacking. The conversations became a second secret life I was having, and it was thrilling. With every message came more talk of all of the things we two had in common, things that would obviously make us good together.

He told me I was beautiful, a compliment I so rarely got, I didn't know how to respond.

Thinking back, I am not sure who sought out who on the site, but the messages sent back and forth were life-giving to get. I'd run home to the computer, it was exciting to be thought of by someone, so conveniently and safely located on the other side of the country. It felt nice to be remembered fondly.

It felt like a new world. My life was very settled, no excitement was in store. I had everything most people could want, when looking at us from the outside. But I had sat wanting so much more.

I'd fantasize about what a life and love could be with my new internet pal in my own head. Could we have more? Months went on like this. Us delicately dancing around owning the emotional affair we were having. Not acknowledging the fact that we were both being unfaithful to our spouses, just by talking to each other in the way we were. Cheating, even though physically we were far apart, and hadn't seen each other in decades.

My days were lively again. I'd run home from the store to see if there was a new message, always hoping that there was. It was my own little fantasy world, and he was plenty far away to keep me from actually doing anything bad...

Then a message came in that could change everything.

My online admirer was coming to town, and wanted to see me.

Could I, should I, steal away for an afternoon walk with a friend? For old times sake?

~

1

Jane ran home at lunch time that day to feed Scruffy. She had left in such a hurry that morning, she had forgotten. Scruff was plenty vocal about the misstep when she arrived.

"I'm sorry Scruff, really sorry," she said as she filled his bowl and made a quick turkey sandwich for herself to scarf down on her way back to work. She also grabbed the enticing Tiramisu out of the fridge to help her overcome her usual two o'clock energy slump in the day.

Arriving back at work, Jane opened the door to the large lobby of her workplace. She was becoming more and more agitated by how everything looked and felt. She popped her head into a few open doors to introduce herself and asked the other occupants if the building bothered them too. After five doors and five affirmingly negative responses about the decor and professional appearance of this place, she decided to draft up a flier to get everyone together to talk.

This was a building full of qualified specialists. People who were very important and key to the health and wellbeing of many people in the Denver metropolis.

What they had here, if they organized a little bit, was a mental wellness center. One that could become a hub of health. With just a little bit of work.

Jane contemplated all of what it could be. Something that she could be a part of, something she could build to help others. Her passion for helping people could be extended into helping others with their quest to do the same.

She imagined Art therapy sessions in the main lobby area, bringing people together, and helping them at the same time. The high skylight above, albeit filthy at the moment, filled the space with light.

The ceiling was a mix of old, worn out, brown stained, paneling, with a rustic stone fountain in the middle that hadn't worked a day in the time she had been here. The bones were good, this place *could* be something great.

Spontaneously, she sent an email to the landlord to see if he would consider selling the building.

He responded within seconds, with a hearty "Yes."

"Shit." she said to herself, "Now, I might actually have to do something?"

She'd have to think about it some more, put some real numbers and a plan together.

She wrote back to him. *Thank you Mr. Jessup. I am contemplating, please give me two weeks to decide.*

Jane would need to get a loan to buy the building, and put in extra to get it fixed up. Her brothers were business owners, they might have some tips on how to do it. She typed up her flier to leave for her colleagues asking to meet as a group the following Friday night, after regular hours. She would bring snacks, or maybe get food from the taco place where she had met Duncan.

Javier's business had taken a slight hit since the incident and she wanted to help him out too. It had been an accident. It was just a matter of cutting up the crispy chunks a little smaller, it shouldn't be a death sentence for the business.

Jane stuck flyers under each of the doors, whether the people were in session or not.

She was hopeful that it might come together.

If she did it right, with a lot of hard work on the front end, owning a wellness center and collecting rent from all of her colleagues could be a way for her to have more free time to explore her other interests. Maybe some more charity work?

Jane loved the idea of getting out more, and having more people around. Gathering others to build something bigger was better than sitting back, everyday and waiting for something big to happen.

It had been another long day for Jane. Crammed with both Wayne's and her own clients. Five sessions so far, she only had one the next day. It was her last session with Jose.

She had tried so hard in their time together to get through to him. Trying to gain his trust, but his wall was too high.

He wouldn't talk about his family, and from his records, his father was in jail. His mother was a drug addict before she died, so she wasn't around either.

His grandmother, who raised him, had died five years ago, and Jose and his sister were put into foster care, and separated. Since then, he had basically taken to the streets.

A tragic story, yes. One that claims many kids in today's society. Yet there are many who rise above their circumstances, and move on to live big happy lives. Often contributing to others because they had been there.

Even in her irritation, Jane wanted Jose to ascend his current status and become something he would be proud of. There were no school records in his file. It looked as if had stopped going when his grandmother passed, and never went back.

In their next session Jane hoped to ask him about that, and see what his plans were for his future. Maybe she could help steer him in a direction.

She was sure going to try.

~

Just me for once, 2005

I decided to go for that walk with the man from my past. He and I spent one magical afternoon just walking around town, together. I had arranged that my daughters would be playing with friends after school, and told my husband I might be too late to make dinner. He knew of the meeting, and that he was an old friend, I had told him that much.

Hubby said he trusted me.

We met at a local mall that we both were familiar with, not far from the city we grew up in. When I saw him, it was as if no time had passed. It was as if he was walking towards me in our old neighborhood. He had that same mischievous grin on his face, that I remembered. His gait. Everything about him was the same. How could that be?

He told me later, that the moment he saw me, he wanted to run away. Part of me wished he had.

He was one of the many men who had caught my romantic attention in my younger years. Twenty years had gone by since I had seen him last.

Over the years, I had wondered about him many times. We had flirted back in the day, but never acted upon our mutual admiration. For me it was fun but frustrating. He teased me, and we soon settled into a friendship that impressed upon us both. Enough to see each other now.

I didn't realize he would hang on to the memories as I had. Carrying a suitcase of moments shared together in each of our minds.

How easily we fell in step with each other, walking the mall then out onto the streets in town. That was all that we did. An innocent stroll.

We talked about many things together that day. Our spouses, our children, his job.

It wasn't until later on in the day that I told him about my traveling books.

It was supposed to be a secret. But I felt I could trust him. He would be one of the only people on the planet to ever know.

I don't know why I wanted to share it with him, I just somehow felt it was safe for me to share. Maybe it was because it felt like the biggest thing about me? My most exciting part. As a stay at home mother, and wife I didn't exactly have the most glamorous life, no job to brag about, no big project I was working on to talk about.

Our conversation that day deepened all the way into our souls. We talked about God, life, and what we each hoped to bring to the world. I expressed to him my yearning to live a bigger life. To travel, and to have a partner who would be open to the possibilities more. Someone who understood me.

All very dangerous things to share with someone, when you are supposed to be faithful to your spouse. It was wrong, but I couldn't help myself.

I wanted him to know how much he had meant to that young girl I was long ago. His compliments back then had lifted my being, at a time of great self doubt. He ruined me though, as it taught me to expect compliments every once in a while.

Our time together was waning and I needed to go.

Back to my life.

I asked him coyly if he would meet up with me in another ten to twenty years or so.

He said he didn't want to wait that long.

"How about tomorrow? I will still be in town."

~

1

J ane got home that evening with Jose's file for homework. She just had to figure out how to help Jose. This was her last chance. She put a turkey pot pie in the microwave and sat down with the file and the traveling book on the couch.

Jane would read it again, and look for any ideas that might help her. The microwave buzzed. If she was going to give it to Jose tomorrow, she wanted to make sure she had gotten the most out of her time with it. She plopped the pie out of the tin upside down in a bowl before taking the steaming pile into the living room to get comfortable.

She summed up what she knew.

Ok, it was written by a woman who wanted to write about the people in her life. People who had made an imprint on her. Big enough impressions to write about, and to remember and share in this way.

She opened the cover to read the author's plea again.

Dear Reader,

This traveling book is my secret mission to live a more extraordinary life, from within the confines of an ordinary one.

Only five copies of this book exist, and this has made its way to you. You are now and forever part of this story.

Inside you will find moments captured from one person's life.

Each passage starts with the set of initials of the person with whom I share the connection.

We are all connected on some level. Every person you meet leaves a mark on you, whether good or bad. Often it is the worst people who gift us the best lessons.

It is my hope that this idea spurs you into living in a more extraordinary way. To think bigger, and reach beyond what you currently see.

The memories inside may remind you of a time or a person in your own life. May you think of those people today, for the good or the lessons you learned from them.

Please read this book, then write your name, and location in the back before giving it to someone else. Let's see how many lives it will touch.

If you by chance, recognize yourself in here:

Please bring the book and

Find me....

She closed the book again. Closing her eyes, she poked her finger into the pages to randomly pick a passage inside, calmly begging for a clue. She flipped the page open.

M.H. It was about the author's grandmother. She read the words aloud.

I will never forget how I let her down once. Mom had asked me to clean up my room, then left Grandma and Granddad in charge of us for the day. I had a friend over and wanted to goof off, so I avoided picking up my room. Coming downstairs for a snack, she asked me if I was done. I didn't think she would climb the stairs to check so I lied and said yes. She was old after all. I was wrong. She marched upstairs and discovered my room a total mess.

"I'm very disappointed in you," she said, and I was crushed. That was worse than a paddle to the behind. I never wanted her to feel that way about me again.

"Yes! That's it!" Jane hurled herself towards Jose's file, spooking Scruffy. She put her bowl down next to her and Scruff sniffed at it longingly.

Jose's grandmother had raised him after his parents went to jail. There must be something in the file about her. Maybe the memory of Jose's grandmother would help her, help him?

This crazy book had brought so many things together lately, it had actually made a difference not only her life but others as well.

It was what her got out of the house to seek closure on the Nathan thing, and had caused her to start looking at the world around her and what she could do to make it better. She had even gotten a date out of it. Hell, she had saved a man's life because she was out of the house that day, running around. Duncan might have died, if she hadn't been there.

And now, suddenly she was contemplating buying a building and starting a wellness clinic where people of all sorts could come for help and treatment for God's sake. Surely it could help Jose.

~

Wanting to escape, Me 2005

*A*gain the lonely feelings, the wishing that I could just get away.

The vivid dream I had last night. I awoke this morning, not knowing what was real.

Hubby had left me, we were to be divorced. Now I needed to tell the children.

In my dream, I had asked him if he would plant a tree with me. A tree that would have represented our family. A new life to grow with, together.

I said I was tired of planting all the trees, and needed some effort from him.

Still in the dream, I left to go out with a friend. I received a message on my cell phone to go out and find a job tomorrow because he had left, and my security was over.

I started to think, "What am I going to do? How will I tell the kids? How will I explain to them that he left because I decided that my being happy in this life was more important than their family?

To tell them that I wasn't feeling that love anymore with their father. How will we get through this?

At breakfast, I tried to tell him of my dream, not all of it, but some. He just said hmm, then asked if my feelings were bruised from our fight the night before? (He never physically abused me, ever.)

I simply said that I was reeling from my dream, as I always put more credence on dreams than he did.

I believe that dreams are truth-telling episodes that your mind is showing you to try to get you to understand something or to get used to an idea. He believes, if they are anything at all, that they are flukes of nature, probably related to whatever food was ingested the night before.

I had some time to think that day as I watched our children rise and ready themselves for school, them participating with their friends and living their innocent lives. They have a carefree life.

I could ruin all of it in a heartbeat. The trauma of divorce could lead to probable obesity, emotional problems, an eating disorder or two... I worried how my daughter's would react.

Their lives were in our hands. We had the power. My own mother had chosen herself, and we suffered. I would not do it.

I would sleep next to a man who I wasn't in love with anymore.

My apathy grows and grows.

Finally, I am numb. And one hell of a great actress.

~

1

JOSE

Jose Morales held up his pants with one thumb as he sauntered into Dr. Monroe's office.

"Hey Doc, happy to see me? I know you are going to miss me, when I stop coming round."

"Hello Jose, how are you today?"

"I'm smokin', just got a BJ from my buddy's little sister, while he was sleeping, talk about hot."

"B.J.?"

"Yeah, I'm sure you know a thing about them..." He winked at her, his open eye twinkling.

Jane broke the glance, and looked down at her notepad. Her hope of a good session was wrecked again.

Why, today? Why, when she was so energized about what was possible, did she have to deal with this? Again. Was he totally a lost cause.

He had done his best to use up all of her interest, hope, and empathy she had for him, but she still had hope.

Much to her horror, Jane had picked up some of his lingo, in her attempts to bond with him somehow and was surprised when she used certain terms of his, in her everyday conversations. He had made an impression on her, but so far not a good one. Jane didn't like that, and she just didn't like him, but maybe he could change.

She didn't like that she hadn't been able to get through to him in their sessions so far. His very presence felt like a big failure to her, sitting smugly across the room on her couch.

But today, Jane had a secret weapon. Jose's grandmother would be in session with them today, sprinkled smartly into the conversation to see if he too didn't want to be a disappointment to her.

"Jose, since this is our last required session, I want to go over some things to hopefully help you in your near future. Have you thought about how you will take care of yourself? Like a job? Do you have any interests that could turn into work?"

Jose was used to this question, as he was often hit with it when he was with his parole officer. It stumped him every time. He tried to remember liking anything.

Jane saw his delay and asked some additional questions. "Do you feel like you are kind of good at something? Cooking, cars? Did you help your Grandmother around the house?"

Instantly charged at the mention of his Abuela Jose looked down at his belt and played with the chain that was attached. Now he would be thinking of her all day. How dare she talk about her, she never knew her? His Abuela was the one person he cared about. Who had cared about him. Even his sister had left him in the dust, after going straight from foster care into an administrative associate training program at seventeen. She was now working for a hot shot finance company, and didn't even call him anymore. Not that he always had a phone that worked, or the same phone number.

"Nah, I'm not good at anything. Unless selling drugs or going to jail are jobs."

"Well, funny enough, there are people that "sell," drugs, they are called Pharmaceutical sales reps, and they go around with the medicines they represent to doctors and hospitals. It can be a very lucrative profession."

"All those drugs have weird names, it would be hard to keep track of that weirdness. I've heard some of them on TV. How about a job going to jail?"

"There are many professions within the criminal, social work, arena. Parole officers, counselors, guards in the prison system. Many of these positions may not hire you since you have that felony on your record. Let's look at some other options."

Jane pulled out a notepad from her desk drawer to start taking notes.

"There is a book put out by the U.S. Department of Labor and Industries that is filled with all of the current occupations that are in our society today. Every single job is listed, and it categorizes them into different parts of our country. Each job shows the typical beginning wage, as well as what the person could expect to get paid at different levels in their career. What I really like is that it also mentions some personality attributes that people tend to have that could help them be successful in each career. For instance, a web designer may like computers, and working by themselves. Things like that. It's basically like a giant catalog of possibilities. Here, I wrote down the name of it, you can ask the librarian to bring it out to you, I'm not sure they check it out. Spend some time looking at some options. It is massive, but just look at the table of contents, to find certain areas you might be interested in."

Jose took the note from Jane, and put it into his front pocket. He'd drop it on the floor, "accidentally," someplace.

"Jose, do you think you would like to continue your education? Maybe get your GED?"

"Nah, probably not."

"Why not?"

"Cause school is dumb. You sit there all day and the teacher just talks at you. I never learned anything at school. I learned everything I know on the streets, hanging with my people."

This was the most Jose had ever said in one of their sessions. Jane felt she might have touched a nerve, but hopefully one that was open and potentially fixable.

"Did you learn anything from your grandmother?"

Grr, again. Jose didn't want to think about his grandmother and how disappointed she would be with how he was living his life right now. Selling drugs, even though it was mostly weed but the hard stuff too, if he could get it. He just didn't have a good supplier right now. Abuela would pinch the top of his ear so hard, and swat him, if she knew. Especially since Mom and Dad had been losers with that stuff too.

"Yeah, she taught me stuff. I did all the yard work at her house, and I fixed stuff that broke if I could. She taught me how to cook too."

"Oh really, what can you make?"

"Abuela said my mole' sauce was even better than hers, I also make good enchiladas and tamales."

"That sounds amazing, would you consider going to work in a kitchen of a restaurant?"

"Nah. Well, maybe?"

"Jose, I need to step out for a second. I will be right back."

"Uh, ok, doc." He scrunched lower into the cushions and rested his hand on his crotch.

His mind pulled to sitting in the kitchen with his grandmother and moved his hand away.

He could smell the kitchen and the sauces and meat she made. Her tacos, the family dinners, and how she would let him spread the sauce sometimes, and then when he was older, he could fry the tortillas a little before dipping them into the sauce for the flat pan enchiladas.

He was hungry, and irritated. Abuela was dead. She couldn't see him, help him or hug him anymore.

His anger grew, she was the one person who cared about him in the whole world. Even Therapist Jane didn't give a shit, he knew. She was just doing her job, she didn't really care, nobody seemed to anymore. He was a lost cause.

He slumped down even further and put his hand back on his crotch. Fuck it.

~

WALKING ON A BARBED WIRE
FENCE ME, 2005

*I*n total I spent two wonderful afternoons with the man from my past.

With him, I am me. I am not a wife and a mother. I am an intelligent woman, with something to offer in a conversation. A beautiful creative woman with thoughts, opinions, and great big dreams. For the first time in a long time, I felt seen and heard.

We sat together on a shady park bench for hours as pigeons cooed around us hoping for a nibble. We had nothing to give them or really, each other.

I will never forget how he treated me those days. We shared, we laughed and we gave all we could to the experience that was us on those two afternoons. Time passed with ease and comfort. I didn't want to think about leaving.

I had my responsibilities at home and was scared of the reaction I might get from my husband for being away again, most of the day.

We were just two old friends catching up, I told myself. I challenged my guilt with the statement that I so rarely do anything completely selfish. Most if not all of my actions are in doing for others. I shouldn't feel guilty or pained for these two walks with my past. I didn't break my vows. Sleep with him, or abandon my family.

Moments before we had hugged each other goodbye, we knew that this was it. This time, these moments was all we would ever have together.

Desperately, or stupidly, I thought about running away with him and living a new life together. We could venture out together and explore the Universe seeking answers to all of life's questions. In our small time together we had shared a lifetime of dreams with each other.

He had to leave so he came close, and leaned in for a kiss. My whole body stiffened at the thought of his lips on mine. There would be no turning back then. Love could only follow, the total apocalypse of my life coming with it.

He saw my fright and covered it up by saying "Of course, on the cheek."
I let him. His hands on my shoulders, his lips soft on my face.
He pulled away slowly and I could feel his scent go with him like a whisper.
He nodded and turned, and I watched him walk away. My chest hurt. A physical pain that felt like a piece of my soul was being pulled from me, leaving a gap.

It hardly seemed possible that so much connection could come from only eight hours of time together. Eight hours and twenty plus years. The fact that we had held each other in our minds for all of these years, spoke to the fact that we did have a bond.

My feelings had started with the messages. I was not innocent in this. It was wrong.

Faced with the reality that I will likely not see him for years to come, if ever at all, I am left wanting more and in a struggle. I would spend the next few days making amends for the inconvenience I have caused my husband, and the lack of me I have given my children these past two afternoons.

But I am where I am supposed to be, where I am needed and loved. He will be back where he belongs too.

Back home, I hold my youngest in my lap, her arms and legs draped all over me, it becomes apparent that all at once, I am blessed. I've been able to stay home with my children as they've grown. It's been the most amazing gift. My life is here, with my wonderful family.

I tell myself to remember that...please.

Leave it alone, I say over and over inside my head. Leave him alone. It's done.

Forget him. Live your life and be grateful. Try even harder than you ever have before. Do whatever it takes.

Seek what you already have. Be satisfied. Please...God help me, please.

All the sayings I've heard over the years slog over me. Marriage is work, you must stay together, you promised, you made a vow, til death do you part. You said it!

My brain begs my heart to listen, to think back to the feelings that made me love my husband in the first place. To remember all of our good times. To celebrate how far we have come together, and how amazing our kids are. Our family, the kids that WE made, who we both completely adore. Whom I adore.

I bargain with myself and with anyone who might be listening upstairs or even below, to make me believe that I am already in the right place.

I sit in my head, trying to convince myself that at least I haven't done anything I can't live with myself about.

Right?

I'm not so sure.

We saw each other, now I can leave the whole idea of him alone now, right?

I can just stop, get back into the groove of my life and be satisfied, maybe even happy?

Right?

~

1

Jane stood in the hallway a few doors down from her office, dialing a number on her cell phone, trying to be quiet. She reached Javier at Taco-rama on the first ring.

"Jane, what can I do for you? How is Duncan? Is he ok?"

"Yes, last I heard. I haven't spoken to him in a few days now. I have a favor, would you maybe try out a kid that I know at your restaurant? He has a passion for cooking, apparently he makes a mean mole' sauce. Could you use somebody over there?"

"Yes, I could, my line cook quit this morning. He said he wanted to work the ski resorts. I could use someone right away."

"He's only seventeen. I don't think he has much of an education, and he has a little bit of a record."

"Yes, Jane, that's ok, I've been working with some vulnerable youth at the center. I believe everyone deserves a second chance. I am happy to try and help him out."

"Awesome, I will send him your way, and keep me posted if it works out, thanks."

"Thank *you*." said Javier.

Jane went back into the office, and found Jose rifling through the papers on her desk. When he saw her, he dove back into his spot.

She ignored his intrusion. "Jose, I want you to go and talk to my friend Javier. He has a Mexican restaurant and he needs another cook. I told him about you. I am also going to report this opportunity back to Judge Simpleton as a necessary meeting for you, to report back to your parole officer. If you want to stay out of detention or jail. However you want to play it."

Jane handed him another piece of paper. It has Javier's name, phone number and address of the restaurant. He put it into his pocket with the other slip.

"And one more piece of homework for you to take on your journey."

"Man, lady, you have given me a ton of stuff today. What do I get, if I do it?" he challenged back while looking her up and down.

"I hope you will get a lot from it. It's just a little reading, then you just sign your name at the end and give it to someone else. That's it."

Jose didn't like to do something for nothing, and reading was especially dumb.

He hated it because the letters jumped around on him, and he imagined them laughing at him. He had cheated in grade school to get by, and in middle school things got even tougher. He just couldn't read right. Course he wouldn't tell anyone that. His friends would think he was an idiot, and he was too cool for that.

Jose grabbed the book and headed for the door. 'What was with this chick? Why did she even bother? Didn't she realize he wasn't worth it? His future was probably ending up dead on a street somewhere.'

This lady had gotten him a job interview at a place he would never find because he couldn't read the damn piece of paper it was written on. On top of that he was also supposed to go ask some librarian for a giant book about jobs, which he would also never be able to read, *and* she gave him a book that he had to read and then give to someone else? Like who? Who was he supposed to give it to?

Jose was glad he was going to meet his crew after this dumb appointment.

Jose tucked the book under his arm feigning the appearance of a good student as Jane watched him drift down the hallway and out the front door. When he reached the sidewalk, he opened the front cover of the book.

The sunlight hit the pages and the letters mocked him immediately. Jumping from one place to another, he couldn't recognize any words. He slammed the book down on the ground and was tempted to throw it into a nearby garbage can. Picking it up, he stopped himself at the last second.

"No way, I can do something better with this piece of crap homework from *Dr. Monroe*," he sneered, spitting on the ground before lighting up a cigarette and walking away with the book tucked under his arm again.

He reached into his front pocket and pulled it right side out enough so that the other notes from her fell out onto the ground. He was lightening his load, for good. He didn't need her or her ideas.

Jose was doing just fine, he erased her image from his mind. She was worthless but her stupid book would provide the day's entertainment, so that was cool.

~

No turning back, Me 2005

*L*ike a child looking out painted shut windows at a parade going by, I felt like life was passing by in front of me. I turned, peering back into my safe little bubble, then looked out again at the party going on outside.

Could I stay here forever? Be content knowing that there was more beyond this, but not taking my chance to see it?

I never thought I could become a homewrecker, especially one of my own home. Of being someone that was capable of cheating on a spouse. It just wasn't me or was it? Every single thing that I believed was missing from my life when I was a kid; the intact family, enough of everything not to have to worry or struggle with money all the time, it still wasn't enough.

Once you have been exposed to the idea of "more," whether it be from interpreting the lives of your friends, or watching a television show or reading those dumb romance novels that I had picked up years ago; the tease of finding one's great romantic love is something a person must fight for.

It becomes nearly impossible to sit back and just accept and embrace the life of sameness.

Living on the outskirts of one's potential soon becomes a death sentence of the spirit. A feeling that cannot be ignored or set aside as okay.

The voice will continue to nag at you, poke you in the heart and say "Hello, are you sure?" until you either pay attention and make a change or commit to fully numbing yourself to its voice.

Everything about this life was about to get really messy, but I couldn't think about all of that right now, or maybe at this point, I had given up trying.

Feeling something was better than feeling nothing, any day of the week, I told myself. I tried. I really did with my husband.

I couldn't change him without him, and I couldn't go back to who I used to be.

So, I opened the door and stepped out of my life to join the parade, not knowing exactly where everyone was heading.

And with that step, I was now on a track, one that would blow up this life as I knew it.

Kaboom.

~

1

Jose didn't mention all of the things to his friends that the Doc had thrown at him. He didn't show up to meet Javier at the Taco place either. He knew that some of his homies could read, and maybe they would have helped him get there, but he was too embarrassed or proud to ask.

The small group pulled their truck into the parking lot behind the closed movie theater. The building had been burned out in an arson fire, and was never fixed. It was now a great place to score drugs or get it on with the honeys.

It seemed like a good place to let him do something with the book, worthy of the total rage he had inside.

He set a broken hubcap in one of the vacant handicapped spots, and tossed the little blue book in its jagged bowl.

Having scored a few M-80 firecrackers from a buddy last summer, Jose was happy he had kept them for this occasion.

This was the perfect way to get rid of this stupid book.

He placed one M80 underneath the book, the wick sticking out from the side.

A fellow homie went to light it with his lighter.

"No, let me do it," he said forcefully as he slapped the lighter away.

Jose reached down, and touched his cigarette lightly to the wick of the red firecracker. It caught immediately.

They all jumped back.

"Bam!"

The hubcap flew up into the air and the book fell down in semi tatters.

He grabbed the hubcap again, and put the remains of the book back on top to light another M-80.

This time, Find me, Book One was blasted, and left aflame, it's mangled spiral having been caught in the spokes of the hubcap with the blast. The grease on the hubcap encouraged the joined carnage to burn, and a dark, chalky smoke spiraled up into the air. Hoots and cheers erupted from the small demented crowd.

The abused pile continued to burn for a few minutes, until the victims lay ashen, the book's spiral binding left as its only reminder.

Jose kicked the spring into the air with his boot. It landed in the already charred, dead bushes nearby.

Find Me, One of Five, is Lost.

~

READER'S GUIDE TO FIND ME, BOOK ONE

O ver the course of this book we see the struggles within the author as she tries to find herself.

1. What issues do you think she might be dealing with to bring her to this point?

2. Have you ever wanted to do something big, but didn't end up following through? Why?

3. How many dreams have you set aside to live your life up until now?

4. Who was your favorite courier of the book?

5. What did you like about that character?

6. Did you meet any characters you hated?

7. Were there any initials you related to, and why?

8. Have you told the people in your life what they have meant to you?

9. If you were going to write about your life, what would the title be?

10. Do you think the author will stay in her marriage or do you think she will run away with the other man? Why?

11. Do you feel the author is a terrible person?

12. Will she learn her lesson the hard way in Book Two?

13. Were there any scenes that made you cry?

14. Do you know people like the characters in this book?

Resources and places listed in this book, to dive deeper
~Hodges Gardens, Florien Louisiana-
https://www.hodgesgardens.net/
~Wagon Wheel Restaurant- Needles CA
~Transgender studies
~Neuro Linguistic Programming
~Buckley Air Force Base/now Buckley Space Force Base-
https://www.buckley.spaceforce.mil/
~Ponca Tribe-https://poncatribe-ne.org/
~Chief Standing Bear-https://chiefstandingbear.org/
~Hand ailment of author's grandmother-Dupuytren's contracture
~Dyslexia-https://dyslexiaida.org/dyslexia-basics/

When we search out the experiences of others and try on their point of view, we become closer to calming the waters in the turbulent sea of our world. With Love, H.H. Rune

ABOUT THE AUTHOR

H.H Rune is a freshly diagnosed, middle aged neuro-divergent writer, watcher, and extraordinary life seeker. She has been telling stories since she was a child. Ever the dreamer she believed that a life of sharing her characters and ideas was possible, even after giving up over and over again. She had to learn to do everything a different way as traditional schooling did not work for her. She believes that an extraordinary life is possible for all, one just has to say yes a little bit more.

In this series of five she will tackle many of the issues women face today. While many of the themes mimic her own life, this is brought forth as a work of fiction. I am thankful that even though this road has been long, I am still on my path to realize the real me while hoping to inspire others in this great big crazy world we live in.

Book Two- tease

Heart finder, Me 2005

***Stay tuned for the next book in the Extraordinary Life Seeker series,
Find Me, Book Two, currently slated for Fall 2023.
Check out hhrune.com for updates and news***
I know, I miss them too. If you want to hear more bits about the char-
acters in this book who left too soon,
sign up for my newsletters to hear more about them and other ponder-
ing thoughts.
It's been a pleasure, Sincerely H. H. Rune